Crimson
Shores

Crimson Shores

The Crimson Series
Book 6

Georgiana Fields

ISBN: 978-1-736 4600-0-9

Cover Design:	Gina Dyer
Photography:	Gina Dyer
	Depositphotos
Editor:	Mary Marvella

Dedication

For my readers and everyone who has supported me on this journey.

Chapter One

Karma stared at her computer screen while Creedence Clearwater Revival played on the radio. She set the mason jar of Pinot Noir on the end table. Tonight was a time for celebration. After four months and too many boxes of wine, the embezzled moola would be returned to its rightful owner. Who said accountants and geeks couldn't be superheroes?

When her BFF, Danielle Rossi, called, asking if Karma wanted to make big money, she couldn't say no. Well, she could…but face it. Who in their right mind would turn down a gig like this? She'd be getting paid four times her usual amount to audit a fortune 500 company's files. Talk about a dream come true! To add the cherry to the top, the CFO had given her carte blanche. Dang, the man had a sexy-dream-voice. Maybe someday she'd meet Morgan face to face. The final perk was her BFF's husband, Magnus, had hooked her up with one of the world's best hackers. The man was a living legend.

"Now, for some fun. Bah-hah-ha."

"Dang, girlfriend. That laugh of yours sounded so diabolical." Dani chuckled in Karma's ear.

"Thank you. So, where's Morgan tonight? Hot date?" Not that Karma really wanted to know, but yeah, curious, seeing she'd expected him to be on the phone with them.

"Ooo, do I hear jealousy?" Danie sing-songed.

"Hardly. I've never seen the man. Heck, for all I know, he's short, fat, and bald. He's just a voice to me." A sexy as hell voice that made her come by saying hello.

"You've hit the nail on the head." Dani laughed. "Morgan's dealing with a family problem. However, in a month or so when this blows over, Karma, I want to introduce you two. It's been ages since you've dated."

"Yeah-yeah, don't rub it in. Besides, I've been busy with the move and all." Karma continued to key in the code to shut those butt wipes down.

"Morgan tends to be a player, but who knows, maybe you'll be the one to tame his wild ways."

"Like you did for Magnus?"

"So," Dani droned. "any idea as to who these bastards are?"

"Not really." Karma and Percy had finally traced the IP address, but they still didn't know the perpetrator's identity. They did, but they didn't.

She recognized a pattern in the code used by a hacker she'd crossed paths several times in the last five years. The individual calling himself Copperhead666 had started out catfishing seniors. Now it seemed he'd upped his game. "Percy said he'd deal with the problem."

"You can be assured I will. Bloody bastard."

Something about a British accent cursing made Karma laugh. "I know you will, Percy. When I told you who it was, you let loose a whole lot of hate-fire."

"Hate-fire?" Dani chimed in. "Dang, girlfriend, you sound southern."

"Because I am. Nerdy, curvy, and southern fried." Karma had her split-screen up. One side showed Percy Westmorland, hacker extraordinaire. The other displayed files they'd discovered through a portal buried deep within DuMond Enterprises' payroll site. "What I don't understand is how Copperhead got hold of Wolfmoon's intercompany email." She had to hand it to her nemesis. Over the years, he'd honed his skills. Copperhead was good, but he wasn't infallible.

"I have a hypothesis. I believe Copperhead is working with a disgruntled associate."

"I see something hinky! Crap's that's a load of dough. I ain't talking scones, either. Holy cannoli! When Magnus said it was substantial, he did not say it could pay off the federal debt. Are you seeing what I'm seeing, Mr. P?"

"Affirmative, love." God, she loved Percy's accent. "I believe he wanted us to think we were dealing with corporate espionage."

"I agree, but one thing is bothering me. This pattern doesn't look like what I've seen from him in the past." She didn't like what she saw. Copperhead had also gone after employee information. Opportunity, maybe? Still, he hadn't done this with past businesses he'd hit.

"I agree. What is your opinion on why he's targeted these employees? It doesn't make sense. Most of them are newly hired, and not a one is high ranking in the company."

Was Percy testing her? "Easy marks. I think the money was his real goal, but he went after these employees' information to sell on the dark web. By the way, I like the gray with purple tips. What is your natural hair color? We've worked together for four months. Well, ...not together, but you know what I mean. You change your color weekly. If I colored my hair as much as you, I'd be bald."

He laughed. "But a pretty bald."

Viktor, Percy's husband, came into frame. "He's a platinum blond, love."

"Damn straight, I'm platinum," Percy teased. "Bloody hell!"

"I see it." Karma quickly attacked. Her fingers flew over the keyboard, blocking Copperhead's attempt to hack her.

"Brilliant, love. Good show."

"Thank you. Thank you very much." She took a small bow or as much of one as she could sitting. "Oh, lookie here."

"I see it." Percy made a face, causing Karma to choke on her wine.

"What—what—what? Tell me," Dani whined. She must be taking lessons from her kiddos.

"Hate to tell you, Dani, but it looks like Magnus is the one funneling the money to an offshore account."

"And he didn't give me access? Well, bless his heart. Sex slave," Dani shouted. "Are you funneling money to any offshore accounts?"

Karma cringed, yanking the phone from her ear. "I take it the twins aren't home, and hey, eardrums. Don't yell." She switched the phone to speaker to save her hearing.

Percy laughed. "As long as you've known Dani, you didn't realize she only knows one volume."

"The boys are at Lacrosse practice, and Megan and Maggie are at my mom's. Sexy says it ain't him," Dani rattled on.

"Uh-oh!" Percy threw up a wall blocking the hackers.

"Uh-oh, what-oh?" Dani asked. "What's wrong?"

"The hackers are trying to hack us. Again," Percy droned. "I say Lady K, do the honors."

"With pleasure, Mr. P. So, here a click, there a click, and I just bit your ass. Booyah!"

"You go, girl! Dani, you may inform Magnus the money has been routed back to Wolfmoon Corporation." Percy leaned back, lifting a brandy sniffer. "A toast."

"Well, hold on, let me refill my glass." Karma gasped the blue screen of death appeared. You're Dead, flashed on her screen in white chiller font.

Someone slammed against her door so hard the drywall around the door frame cracked.

"What was that!" Dani shouted in her ear.

"Someone slammed against my door." Karma stared in disbelief.

"Get out of there now!"

"Don't have to tell me twice."

They slammed against her door again.

Grabbing her phone, Karma ran to the window, flinging it open. She'd barely climbed out onto the fire escape when her door gave away. Not bothering with the stairs, Karma slid down the railing of the escape as she had when she was a kid. Her feet slammed on the asphalt street.

"Get to the goldfish," Dani shouted in her ear.

The goldfish was a sign for a Chinese restaurant nearly two blocks away. Karma and Dani kept saying they'd eat there but never got around when Dani visited.

"Who are those people?" Karma gasped out, running down the sidewalk. Running was not her thing. *Please, God, don't let the friction from my thighs start a fire.*

"I...I don't know."

That was a load of bull, but Karma couldn't argue at the moment. Hell, she could hardly breathe. She pushed herself harder, slamming her feet to the pavement. Her legs burned, her thighs burned.

Salvation! Up ahead, the glorious red and yellow neon sign glowed in the night. "Almost there."

"Magnus says to ditch your phone."

Well...she was planning on getting a new one. Karma dropped her phone into a storm drain, then hurried past the alley.

Someone jumped from the shadows. "Where do you think you're going?" A man dressed in black grabbed her arm.

Karma kicked and screamed, trying to fight him off. Her glasses flew from her face as the creep covered her mouth. Another man jabbed a needle in her neck. Her blurry vision faded, and she couldn't move.

"We got her."

Three words, then everything went black.

~ ~ ~

Usually, the morning was his favorite time of the day. Not today. Morgan headed for the Corporate office of Wolfmoon Corporation. His gut had been in a knot ever since Magnus called. How had the hackers found Karma? Morgan couldn't buy Percy's excuse of someone in the company opening a viral email, giving the hackers a backdoor. Yeah, companies all over the world had suffered ransomware attacks. Heck, it'd even happened to several city governments across the country. So, it was possible Percy was right, but Morgan had his suspicions. He refused to believe the breach in security happened because an employee opened an email. No way, no how.

His other question, why go after Karma instead of him or Magnus? They'd taken every precaution to protect her, routing her computer IP address through the company's. Granted, Morgan wasn't as computer savvy as Karma or Percy, but there shouldn't have been a way for them to have pinged Karma's location. Someone in the Council had to be behind this and was sending him a message. Which would explain how they got through the corporation's firewalls. Well, if they thought this wolf would comply, then the entire Council could kiss his furry ass. Morgan wished Royce would go ahead and kill the lot of them. *If that doesn't make me sound like the murdering assholes, I don't know what would.*

He was supposed to have been here the other night, overseeing the takedown of the ones who hacked into the corporate accounts. Even if he had, he couldn't have stopped what happened. He would have been in his office and Karma in her apartment. None of this was supposed to have occurred. Everything they'd planned went to Hell in a handbasket, and she'd been kidnapped. What ate at Morgan the most was the kidnappers hadn't once tried to contact them, demanding a ransom. The good news, they hadn't sent a body part as proof of life.

Morgan's wolf paced in the back of his mind. The loco beast was nearly rabid.

If they'd harmed one hair on her head, the assholes were dead. Royce could have the new liaison, whoever the hell it was, cover up the execution. His wolf agreed.

Okay, so Morgan's plans to ask Karma out were derailed for now. He'd get her back, then buy her new flowers, 'cause the ones he'd purchased for her were wilted. Instead of a night on the town, he'd take the curvy, feisty woman someplace special...like Paris.

We have to get her back first, his wolf growled.

They would. Heck, he'd hoped they hit it off when they finally met. Karma was funny as hell. He loved her sassy mouth. He'd only seen a photograph of her taken over five years ago. She was pretty, with curves in all the right places. Maybe he was crazy, but he borrowed the photo from Magnus's desk then made a copy of it. Morgan kept the picture in his desk drawer. If anyone ever found out what he did, they'd rag his ass about it. Morgan didn't care. He wanted to meet her and spend time with her.

There was something about Karma's witty personality that drew him to her and her eyes... Damn, she had gorgeous chocolate brown eyes. But someone had to throw a monkey wrench into his plans, and he'd wager his savings it was the Council. Had to be, especially with the timing of everything. Karma's kidnapping and the Council deciding to come after Simone, his brother's mate, all at the same time, couldn't be a coincidence.

Morgan steadied the chopper as he brought it in for a landing on top of the Wolfmoon Corporation building, setting it down smoothly. He rushed through shut down and was heading toward the door in record time.

He barely had his code punched in when the door jerked opened. Magnus DuMond's usual carefree smile had been replaced with a bleak, tight-lipped one. "My office, we'll talk there."

"Excuse me, Mr. DuMond, Mr. Wolfe. May I have a word?" Blythe strolled toward them. Morgan groaned inwardly. He didn't have time for Blythe's trivia questions. The woman was as useful as tits on a frog. He should've given the job to Avery.

"Not now, Blythe."

"It's about the charity event in Whaler Bay."

"I said, not now." Morgan strode down the service hall.

"How bad?" Morgan glanced at Magnus, trying to gauge the situation. The man had erected an impermeable wall around his thoughts.

"Percy's waiting online, and Dani's wearing a trench in the floor."

Morgan exhaled. "I don't feel like dealing with a hysterical woman."

"Dani?" Magnus chuckled. "Oh, she's not hysterical. I'd say more homicidal."

"Not much better." Morgan strode into the office, finding Dani pacing in front of the windows. He gave her a tight-lipped smile as he continued toward the desk.

"Oh, hell to the no." She stormed toward him, grabbing his arm. "Magnus called you two nights ago. Where the hell were you? They've had Karma for two friggin' days!"

He could give Dani a sarcastic answer, but. "I was over Missouri when I received the message. I had to land, make arrangements for the girls to drive on before I could get back in the air. Then, I had wiring issues with the plane. I phoned your mate and was in contact with Percy." Something else that ate at him. He'd checked the plane. There was no way the wires could have come loose in the manner they had.

"So, you landed the jet on the rooftop?"

He didn't have time for her Q and A. He had to find Karma. "No, I landed at the airport and took the helo." Morgan jerked free of her grip, striding forward.

"You're furry." With a grim expression, Magnus handed him a glass of whiskey. "Drink this first. You'll need it."

Morgan took a swig as he stared at the wedding photo on Magnus's desk. Morgan's eyes focused on Karma's image standing to Dani's left as cold ran through his veins. *She's not dead?* He sent his thoughts to Magnus, unable to voice them.

"No. I thought it best to tell you this in person."

Morgan slammed the glass down. "Tell me what?"

"There was an incident at one of our hotels." Magnus's eased down into his seat. "Apparently, the girls disobeyed everyone's orders and stopped at one. Hunters tracked them."

"How?" Morgan scrubbed his hand over his face. "Are they alright? Miranda didn't ring me."

"They're all fine. Apparently, someone lied. Simone's trackers were never removed from her."

"Does Quaid know? What about Mavis? She's the Healer in charge while my brother is pulling his head out of his butt."

"Your brother knows, and Mavis is en route to ensure the other women's trackers were indeed removed. Royce has also been informed."

Morgan shot back what was left in the whiskey glass. The burn of the alcohol didn't numb the fear eating at him. "What about damage control?"

"We sent in a cleaning crew. While they were there, the second team struck." Magnus held up his hand, stalling Morgan's questions. "Don't worry, we didn't suffer any fatalities or injuries. The girls are at Declan's. Quaid's there now. However, with Mavis and your brother both unavailable, I sent Cade to rendezvous with Ryder and his team." Magnus turned his computer screen so Morgan could see it better.

The face on the screen wasn't the one he'd expected. "Fiona? Where's Percy?"

"Yes, well, we know my sweet brother is the fava, but seeing he's busy with another emergency, you have me, gents. Besides, you took your bloody time getting here."

Crap, the last thing he wanted was to piss-off Percy or his sister. The man was extremely protective of Fiona. But Karma's life was on the line. "Fiona, I—"

"Stow it, wolf-boy. We're on the clock. So, bringing you up to date, the guys tapped into the local CCTV and, through a sheer miracle, located the van in the warehouse district. As Viktor said they would, they did retrieve her phone but haven't turned it on yet. As soon as they do, we'll have her precise location. If they don't turn on her phone, it's fine. The team is using thermal to find which warehouse she's being held. Declan's second is on the line, standing by."

Magnus handed him the phone. "It's your call, Morgan."

His call. An excellent way to say if Karma died, it was on him. "Give me the deets."

"We've located her and are in position. Once we get her out, we'll take her to West Grove."

"No. Ryder, once you have Karma, bring Cade and rendezvous with me at Crimson Shores."

"That's not the plan, Morgan."

Killing Ryder was out of the question only because the kid was Vaughn's nephew. Morgan's wolf howled at Ryder's insubordination. But now wasn't the time to argue. Every second could mean Karma's life. "She's…special, Ryder, and considering recent developments, I feel my place will be safer for her. If need be, use gold."

"I understand."

"Good. I'm flying out now. I'll be there before you arrive." Morgan hung up then pulled out his cell.

Mavis answered on the first ring. "I've already spoken with Quaid. As soon as I'm finished, I'll head back to West Grove and wait for their arrival."

"No, she goes to my place. I've instructed Ryder to use units of gold. She doesn't die."

A long heavy sigh came over the connection. "Gold? Does she know about us?"

Morgan glanced at Dani, and she shook her head. "No. Don't worry about it. I'll handle it."

"Royce won't like this."

Probably not, but thinking about all the crap Morgan's family had suffered in the last few years, he didn't give a damn about the consequences. "I said, I'll deal with it. I'm flying out now."

"Not to West Grove?"

"Do you really need to ask, Mavis? Especially with what happened with Simone?"

"A cabin in the woods is not the same thing as a medical facility, particularly when we're talking human. If she were Dhampir, it wouldn't matter if I took her to the city dump. But hey, I'm just a Healer. What do I know?"

He disconnected. Depending on how this went down, Karma might not be the only one to lose her life.

"Gold?" Dani glanced at her mate. "What's he talking about? What's gold?"

Morgan pocketed his phone. "Gold is a mixture of blood from the most powerful Dhampirs. I hope it's enough."

"Enough?" Dani narrowed her eyes. "To do what?"

"To keep her alive." He headed toward the door. He paused and turned back. "Where did you store Karma's things?"

"Why?" Dani huffed. "By the way, Morgan, you're furry."

Magnus looped his arm around his mate's waist, pulling her against him. "Which is why we don't antagonize, love. It's in the warehouse here, Morgan. Taking Karma to your cabin may work out for the best, seeing the charity event is being held at the resort nearby. Killing two birds with one stone?"

"I need a bag for Karma and quick."

Dani's face lit. "If you're going after her, I'm going. too."

Fur pushed from Morgan's skin. "I don't have time. Get me a bag and meet me on the roof."

"But—"

Magnus covered her mouth. "I know, Karma is your bestie in the whole wide world, love, but Morgan's got this. Trust me, love." He kissed Dani's temple. "He'll take care of her. Now. go pack a bag for Karma and be quick." As Dani ran down the hall, Magnus narrowed his eyes. "You've never met Karma, have you?"

"No. I've only seen her photo and spoken to her on the phone. Why?"

"Just wondering. You know you owe me for pulling the reins back on Dani."

"As if. The woman's your mate."

"Yes, Dani is my mate, and I will do anything for her. You have to realize she and Karma are sisters of the heart, meaning the bond is stronger because it's been forged by love. Anything that hurts Karma hurts Dani, pissing me off."

Morgan rolled his eyes and headed out the door. If he were ever blessed with a mate, he would never hand over his man card. Never.

His wolf laughed.

Chapter Two

With every breath she took, pain tore through Karma's body. Her left eye was swollen shut, and blood blurred the vision of her right. Her lip was swollen, split, and bleeding. She couldn't feel her hands as the jerks had the zip ties so tight they'd cut off her circulation.

Karma didn't have a pain tolerance. It was nil, negative even, but she wouldn't cry. She didn't do tears. Fainting she could do. She'd pass out when they punched her face. If that wasn't bad enough, the drugs they injected her with made her nauseous. She'd puked on herself, twice. Apparently, her captors didn't like the odor any more than she did. They hosed her down, leaving her drenched and cold. The one thing positive about her situation, she hadn't been raped…yet.

Sun shone down through the skylights on her, and the smell of seawater was strong. She had to be held in the warehouse district on the wharf. How long though? They could've had her days or hours. If she could only escape. Because yeah, no one would rescue her, and she sure as heck didn't have a fairy godmother.

Oh, God, she had to get out of here, and when she did, every one of the assholes would pay. All of them. Psycho Asshole would be the first she'd make pay, followed by Evil Prick. Then she'd go after the others who lingered out of sight but laughed each time Psycho punched her.

But the first thing Karma would do was kill Dani because this was all her fault. Even if it wasn't, it was. But if Karma killed Dani, the twins would hate their Auntie K. Yeah, it would be bad, seeing David and Danny were as vindictive as Karma. Megan and Maggie would probably order a hit on her. Blasted little kids. So, killing Dani was out. No prob, Karma would just maim her a little.

The drug was making her crazy. She had to think, had to escape.

Her fitness tracker was smashed by Psycho Asshole and of no use. Evil Prick had run a scanner over her. Guess the ass feared she had another tracker shoved up her butt.

God, if they'd just leave her alone long enough for her to get free, she could escape and find help. Maybe if she kept her eyes closed, they'd think she was still unconscious and wouldn't hurt her, at least for a little while, until she could regain her strength and escape.

Someone fisted her hair, yanking her head back. "I know you're awake, bitch."

Oh, goodie, it was Psycho Asshole. Karma pried open her eyes as much as possible and peered into the crazed face of her tormentor. His dark blond hair was immaculate, but the glazed look in his brown eyes told her he was drugged out of his ever-loving mind. No surprise there. Nothing was worse than a mean drunk or addict. You couldn't reason with them, no matter what.

"You thought we wouldn't find your phone, didn't you?" He shoved her phone at her face. "Why isn't it unlocking?"

"Because you punched the shit out of her. I told you not to hit her in the face." Evil Prick cupped her chin, digging his finger into her aching cheeks. "You wear glasses." He smiled, and his pale blue eyes shimmered, not in a nice way. His smile sent chills through her. "I can tell because you have the divots on the side of your nose. So, you have to have a backup method to unlock your phone when you wear them."

"Nothing is on my phone, but fingerprint." She shifted her attention to her swollen hand. If they turned on her phone, it might increase her chance of escaping.

"Well, that's not working." He dug his fingers deeper into her cheek. "I'm going to ask you one more time, then I'm going to start breaking bones. "Password."

"Don Knotts is hot. All one word, capital D and K, but there is nothing on my phone."

"I'll be the judge of that," Psycho said, typing in her password.

Evil leaned down and licked the side of her face, sending sickening chills racing through her body. "While my associate searches your phone, where did you wire the money?"

"Again. I didn't. I don't know. It was handled by Wolfmoon."

He punched her gut, and she nearly puked. "Where did you wire the money?"

"I didn't. I was hired to do an audit, found the discrepancies, and followed the trail. People at Wolfmoon then took over."

He slapped her, jerking her head to the side. "They own the best hacker in the world. Probably the universe. Why hire you?"

Just because you can hack a computer doesn't mean you can balance a checkbook. "I'm a forensic accountant. When companies hire me, I go through the books, looking for any discrepancies, no matter how small or, in this case, how big." It was the truth, plus she and Dani were BFFs. Karma was also a pretty good hacker. Not as good as Percy…yet.

"It was compensation owed us." A cold evil grin spread across his face.

"I'm not finding anything on her phone. Not even a call log." Psycho swung his fist, striking the left side of her face, and hitting her already blackened eye.

Karma screamed with the pain.

He drew back his fist again. This time Evil Prick stopped Psycho from hitting her.

"Can't interrogate the dead. Now, who in the company hired you?"

As mad as she was at Dani, there was no way she'd throw her or Magnus under the bus. They meant too much to Karma. Morgan, on the other hand, was a voice on the other end of the connection, even if she'd had some pretty naughty thoughts about him.

"Shouldn't take much thought." Evil sneered.

"Morgan. Morgan Wolf," Karma pushed the name past her lips and the pain.

"Liar," Psycho screamed. The crazed look in his eyes terrified her more than anything. "I'm Morgan Wolf!"

Liar. Dani and Magnus knew Morgan Wolf. They wouldn't have lied when they'd introduced him over the phone. Granted, Karma never met the man, but he didn't have a high-pitched, whiny, little voice.

Evil glanced over his shoulder at Psycho. "She knows you're lying. If Morgan hired her, then I can guarantee they also had Westmorland in on it." Evil stared at her, and a look she could almost call pity flickered across his face. "The money's gone. This was a waste of energy."

"What about ransoming her?" Psycho glared. "She has to be worth something to them."

"Nope. She's pissed somebody off. The woman isn't anything but cannon fodder to them, or they'd already have been here. Let's go. We'll find another way."

"I. Want. My. Money!" Psycho curled his fingers around her phone then punched the side of her face, jerking her head. Her neck popped, and her cheekbones cracked.

"Technically, we stole it, then they stole it back." Evil glanced at someone behind her. "Take care of it, but wait until we're off the premises. We need to set up alibis."

Through her blurred vision, Karma watched as the two strode away. *Take care of it.* Were they going to kill her, torture her more, or worse, sell her for her computer skills? Life was too precious to throw away, but right now, she wished this was like the movies where she'd have a cyanide capsule hidden in a tooth. The thought of being tortured for the rest of her life wasn't appealing. The echo of the metal door closing at the far end of the warehouse sent fear through her. A tear snaked down her cheek. *Please, God.*

"It's been long enough." One of Karma's abductors strolled toward her. "If they hadn't turned her face into hamburger, I'd say we fuck her before we kill her." He yanked her head back. "Or we could eat her."

"Have at it," another said, "I'm trying to watch my cholesterol." The warehouse erupted in laughter.
Assholes.

Lord have mercy! Whatever they'd injected her with had her hallucinating. Men dressed in black with their faces covered materialized out of thin air. One of the masked men swung a blade, cleaving off the asshole's head in front of her. His head fell, turning to dust when it smacked into the ground.

Karma screamed, then screamed louder when the body crumbled before her.

Shouts and gunfire filled the warehouse as more men dropped from the ceiling and rushed through the walls. Through. The. Walls!

"Karma, you're okay," one of the men reassured her. "We're getting you out of here."

Oh, hell, she was dead. Figments of her imagination were rescuing her.

"Watch out," she shouted.

Her rescuer ducked, barely missing having his head cut off by a machete-wielding creep. Her rescuer's body grew, morphed, and the thin fabric covering his face tore as he changed into a werecat. A frigging werecat with whiskers! He twisted and shoved his hand into the other man's chest, tearing out his heart. It was worse than she thought. She was suffering from a drug overdose.

Another man in black fatigues dropped to his knee before Karma. "We're going to get these zips cut from you."

The werecat stood protectively over them. "She reeks of Whitehall."

"I thought the scent was familiar. Royce will want to know this, as will Morgan."

Her heart shuddered at the mention of his name, and she lifted her head. "Morgan? Oh, hell." She screamed as a wolfman leaped through the air, landing on the cat man.

"Karma, eyes on me."

"Be easier if I could see more of your face." She gasped, her eyes wide with panic as she stared into his pale green peridot eyes.

"No can do, lass, but I'll tell you my name. I'm Ryder. Eyes on me, lass. They have your hands bound so tight, it's going to hurt as soon as I cut the ties. We're getting you out of here. Morgan sent us."

"Oh, crap!" She screamed the moment Ryder cut her bindings.

"Bomb," someone shouted.

Ryder flung her over his shoulder in a fireman's carry and ran, causing pain to radiate through her. The second they exited the building, a blast deafened her as heat engulfed them.

Ryder leaped into the back of a black van. "Go—go—go," he shouted, lowering her onto a gurney. Faint sounds of sirens wailed in the background.

"Hey, Karma, I'm Cade." The cat man held a syringe in his clawed, fur-covered hand. "This will make you feel better."

"Dude, seriously? Change," Ryder ordered. "She's hyperventilating."

"Oops, sorry." Cade's furry paw turned human again, and the mask he wore slipped down, revealing eerie green eyes.

"Please. No more drugs," Karma begged. "I don't like hallucinating. Please."

"This will help your pain," Cade reassured her as he injected her.

Tears rolled down her cheeks. She hated crying, but she hated not having control of her body even more. "No, you turned into a kitty and ate the doggie," she slurred.

Karma rolled her head back and forth, fighting to stay conscious. Her eyelids slowly closed, and she snapped them open. Great, now the cat man was a vaguely familiar elderly black woman.

"Don't fight it. Relax." The woman dabbed something on Karma's eyelid. "I'm Doctor Mavis Crumpler."

~ ~ ~

Morgan drove through the electric gate then continued down the narrow dirt road leading to his cabin. It wasn't anywhere near sunset yet, but his house glowed like a friggin' Christmas tree with every light on, including the yard floodlights. What was Ryder thinking? He might as well have a blinking arrow pointing Lincoln Whitehall the way.

Morgan parked alongside the other vehicles in the yard, got out, and slammed his door. He made it three steps before Cade flung open the door and strode toward him.

"Why are all the lights on?" Morgan roared.

Cade recoiled and shook his head. "Sorry, I was checking to make sure they all worked—anyway, Morgan. You missed Ryder and his bunch, they ran a perimeter check before they left, but he didn't like the fact your place is easily accessed from the shoreline. I mean, it is stupid to have a fence around three sides of your property if anyone can simply walk up from the beach. Ryder also swept your place for bugs. Said you were clean for bugs, but your dust bunnies were procreating." The cat grinned and pushed his hand through his sandy blond hair. "I told him you thought dust was a furniture protectant."

Morgan didn't give two cents what Ryder thought or Cade's smart ass comments. "Where's Karma, and how is she?"

A crack of thunder rumbled in the air. It was going to be another rainy night.

"Oh, right. Assholes beat the crap out of her. Mavis is with her now, helping her get cleaned up a little. Lincoln tagged her. I guess he was planning on ransoming her. Anyway, I removed the tracker from her. And yes, it was an exploder. Just thought you should know."

Morgan reined in his wolf. The cat didn't need or deserve his anger. "Sorry. I was hoping to get here before y'all arrived, but things didn't go according to plan."

"We were expecting you an hour ago. What happened? Trouble?"

"If you consider Dani taking her sweet ass time in gathering things for Karma, then yes. I don't know how Magnus puts up with her crap." He hefted the heavy duffle onto his shoulder, wondering what the devil the woman packed.

"The same way my brother puts up with Stacey. It's called love." Cade chuckled.

"Well, if I'm ever so blessed with a mate, I'll be damned if I hand over my balls."

Tim Drummond loomed in the doorway. "You'll hand them over the second you get her scent." The man grinned, making the scar bisecting his face more prominent.

"I didn't expect to see you here, Captain." Morgan extended his hand to the man. In the few months he'd known the human, Morgan had developed a trust for him.

"I'm Mavis's bodyguard and driver for the time being. Once she's finished here, we'll head back to home base."

It looked like a few would be bunking on the floor. Morgan wasn't giving up his bed. His house wasn't big enough for so many people. He'd designed it so he wouldn't be overrun by family and friends who'd invite *themselves* to his place.

He trudged up the steps to his beach house. The moment Morgan stepped into his home, the scent nearly brought him to his knees and had his wolf clawing to break free. The loco beast started spinning in his head, urging him to follow the delicious smell.

Our den, his wolf growled.

Morgan gave a quick knock on his bedroom door. His wolf rode him hard, growling, and snarling in his head as he turned the knob and pushed open the door. "How is she?" He barely caught a glimpse of Karma's battered and bruised face before he sagged against the door, closing it. His legs no longer supported him, and his lungs couldn't draw breath.

A lightning flash lit the room.

He had a mate...a beautiful and battered mate. His wolf shoved against his mind, and fur pushed from his skin, wanting to kill the bastards who'd hurt her.

"You haven't healed her," he growled out.

"Out," Mavis shouted, snapping the covers over Karma's body as she whirled on him, baring her fangs. Slowly Mavis's eyes softened, and her fangs retracted. "Why didn't you tell me?"

"I didn't know." He'd been drawn to Karma's photo and her voice but hadn't put two and two together. Heck, he'd always been the pragmatic one. How could he not have the smallest suspicion she was his? "Why haven't you healed her?" He didn't want his mate in pain.

Mavis exhaled as she eyed him up and down. "Get a rein on your wolf, then roll up your sleeve."

You heard her, back it down, he told his wolf and pushed away from the door. Morgan dropped the duffle then struggled to get his wolf to heel as he eased closer to his bed, his sight falling to the battered woman lying in it. Her face was severely bruised, her eyes were swollen, and her nose looked broken. He also noticed she wore one of his flannel shirts.

A needle pricked his arm, and he snarled at Mavis.

"You want your mate to have your blood or Royce's?" Mavis glared at him as she pulled back on the plunger.

"You could have warned me."

"Most people suspect something when a tourniquet is tied around their arm. Except you, but then again, you were in la-la-land." She untied the tourniquet then removed the needle from his arm.

"Is that enough blood?"

Mavis glanced over her shoulder at him with a look that said he was dumber than dirt. "Yes. You should know, Karma woke up once we arrived, despite the pain meds Cade gave her. The second she recognized me from Dani's and Magnus's wedding, Karma relaxed and allowed me to help her clean up. I gave her one of your shirts to put on and a pair of your boxers. I also assured her she was safe." Mavis shook her head. "She fell back to sleep the second her head landed on the pillow."

Morgan drew in a breath and mentally gripped his wolf by the scruff. "When she was held, did they…"

"Beat the crap out of her yes, sexually assault—no." Mavis reached over and gripped his hand, giving it a firm squeeze. "There's something else you need to know. Karma saw things and thinks what she saw were hallucinations brought on by the drugs she was injected with. I'm running a full panel and should have the results back tomorrow. Your blood should counter react what they gave her."

"Should?"

"Yes, should. I'm a Healer, not a miracle worker. When I spoke with Dani, she informed me, Magnus and she will be here the day after tomorrow. Good luck with this one. She's a smart cookie." Mavis patted his cheek. "Now that you're here, I've gotta run. Until your brother decides to get back to work, the rest of us are running around like chickens with our heads cut off. Callie's handling what she can, Sam's dealing with West Grove. I'll give Quaid six months, then I'm going to jerk a knot in him."

"Whoa—wait. Where are you going? Karma isn't healed." Morgan pulled his attention from Karma and glared at Mavis. She couldn't leave his mate in this condition. "You can't leave her like this."

"I gave Karma enough of your blood to heal any broken bones, but she's still going to be stiff and sore for a few days, giving you time to explain things."

"I don't want her stiff and sore. I want her healed."

Mavis drew in a deep breath then exhaled. "I want a night of uninterrupted sleep, too." She patted his cheek again. "I'll be back as soon as I can to check on her. Call me if anything hinky occurs. That's hinky, not kinky. Don't want to know about your mating."

"But—"

"She'll be fine. You'll be fine." Mavis smiled and strode from the room. "Be happy, you're one of the lucky ones. You've found your mate."

He followed Mavis into the living room. Drummond hefted Mavis's bag then held the door for the woman. Morgan stood dumbfounded as she and Drummond left.

Cade strode into the room, naked. "If you don't mind, I think I'll run in my skin. I wish you'd reconsider putting in a pet door "

"In this weather?"

Cade stretched, then shifted into his cat. He pawed at the closed door.

"Have it your way." Morgan opened the door for the scarred mountain lion. The cat raced across the lawn toward the trees. Even with Morgan's night vision, the cat vanished into the shadows. Morgan closed the door and exhaled.

He had a mate. Morgan should be howling in celebration instead of feeling like an idiot. He had a mate—a beautiful, voluptuous, sexy mate, who'd been beaten.

Morgan pushed his hand through his hair, then bolted the door. First things first, he had to ensure Karma's safety. Not a problem. Morgan had security cameras around his property to alert him to any trespassers. He also had a deadly cat prowling the perimeter. What worried him was Karma's abduction was more than he'd first thought.

Pulling out his phone, he dreaded making the call, but Royce needed to know, and Morgan needed answers.

"Oh, goodie, another growling wolf. What do you want, Morgan?" Royce answered.

"From the manner you answered, I take it you've spoken to Quaid. So how is the all-powerful alpha?"

"The same. Why are *you* calling?"

From Royce's snappish tone, the man was in the mood, which was fine with Morgan. "I don't know how much you've been briefed."

"The woman has been retrieved, trackers removed, and Lincoln Whitehall was behind the hack. Anything else?"

Morgan resisted the urge to disconnect. Instead, he eased down onto the couch. His cousin and leader of the Dhampir could be an ass at times, but this wasn't like Royce. "There're a few more things you should know. First, my brother is an ass. I blame Mom. She spoiled him with the whole, my son the Healer thing."

"I'm so glad I was an only child." Royce barked out a laugh, and Morgan pulled the phone away from his ear. "I'm good, Morgan. Quaid hit a nerve. I shouldn't have taken my anger out on you. As for Lincoln, watch your back. He's gone rogue. I've asked Cade to stick around, just in case."

"He's running in his fur, and we have a storm on the way."

"You sound concerned for the cat."

"What can I say, Royce? As for Whitehall, what are the odds he's working with some of his father's friends?"

"Not a chance this time. His father's cronies are all trying to save their own skins. Some have even handed over emails. I think they're afraid Lincoln will come after them next for betraying his old man. While I have you on the phone, our new Liaison is Edgar O'Brien."

"Raven's brother? That's great, now they can still stay connected."

"As far as it being bloody excellent, time will tell. Anything else?"

"Karma's my mate."

Dead silence. No congratulations. Nothing. Hell, Morgan couldn't even hear Royce breathing, and the longer the silence continued, the angrier his wolf grew.

"Congratulations. You can stop growling, Morgan. But correct me if I'm wrong, haven't you known Karma for a while?"

"No. I've never met her face to face before. I wasn't at Magnus's wedding, remember, I flew out to Japan, then they decided on a quickie wedding."

"I remember. Negotiations were at a critical point."

"But they worked out. I've only seen Karma's photo and have recently spoken to her on the phone. Magnus and Dani have tried many times to introduce us, but something has always popped up, preventing it."

"Wow." Royce laughed. "Karma...ah, fate, I mean. Listen, Morgan, I'm serious, be careful."

"I will." Morgan ended the call and glanced around his place. A few cobwebs did hang from the exposed ceiling beams, and there was a layer of dust coating the barrel of his old Winchester 1873 rifle. "If Pop saw the condition of the gun, he'd slap a hen egg out of me." Hmm, when was the last time it been taken down and cleaned? For that matter, when was the last time this place had a good once over? Morgan wasn't a slob, and the place was relatively clean. There weren't any empty food containers or trash lying around. He kept the place picked up, but dusting wasn't his thing. His robotic vacuum kept his floors somewhat clean. Too bad they hadn't come up with a robotic duster.

Morgan shoved from the couch and made his way to his room. "Guess I know what I'll be doing tomorrow." He paused and turned, heading toward the kitchen. Karma had been held for nearly three days, and he doubted the assholes fed her. Morgan yanked open his fridge. Just as he'd feared. Empty. Unless he wanted to feed his mate condiments, there was nothing to eat. Well, damn, he'd not thought this out. Morgan glanced out the window. When was the last time he'd cleaned those? He could order online and stay here cleaning, but then his order wouldn't arrive until tomorrow morning, not like if he were in a large city where stores were open 24-7.

Sunset was still an hour off, and the local store was a few minutes away. If he headed out now, he could be back before nightfall and hopefully before the storm worsened. Stay or go? He should go, then he could cook Karma a good breakfast in the morning. Hmm, while he was at the store, he'd pick up some cleaning supplies. If he were lucky, he could get up in the morning and clean the house before she noticed what slob he was.

He strode toward the door, pulling out his phone and arming the alarm. Karma could still move around inside effortlessly without setting it off, but if a fly farted anywhere near the outside of the place, he'd know about it and be back before any harm came to his mate. This was the best option, especially with Cade patrolling. Nothing would go wrong.

Chapter Three

Her mind was so foggy she could hardly think. At least no one was punching her anymore. Where the heck was she and who had rescued her, or hadn't she been rescued? Maybe, 'cause someone had tapped her nose. Another good thing, she was lying on a soft mattress instead of strapped to a chair. She was definitely not in a hospital room, so where was she?

Lightning, then thunder rattled the windows, causing her to jump.

Trying to clear her mind and calm her racing heart, Karma smoothed her hand over the flannel sheets. She breathed in the delightful scent of citrus and spice, the fragrance reminiscent of the Christmas tea her grandmother used to make. Karma loved the aroma, but before she got too cozy, she'd best figure out where she was and with whom.

Lord, she prayed she was safe. She couldn't rely on her memories. People didn't vaporize into dust or turn into animals. If she didn't know better, she'd swear someone spiked her wine. One thing for sure was her in pain. She ached so bad, she felt like she'd been hit by a truck then backed over her to finish the job.

Groaning, Karma sat up and glanced around the room as best she could with her blurry vision. She sat in a massive room with a large stone fireplace. *Fancy.*

She spotted the open bathroom. Slowly fuzzy memories of someone helping her came to mind. Karma tried to focus, searching for any clues telling her where she was.

From what else she could tell with her crappy vision, the furniture appeared to be expensive cherry with the modern, clean lines she loved. So maybe she was at one of Dani's and Magnus's homes? Only nothing was familiar. Of course, she'd not been to all their properties, but she knew Dani's taste, and this wasn't it.

Karma slid from the bed and gripped the headboard, steadying herself until her head stopped spinning. For the first time, Karma noticed she wore a man's flannel shirt large enough to cover her curves and hung to her mid-thigh. It could belong to Magnus. The man was tall and muscle-bound. But why didn't Dani give her one of her nightshirts? They were the same size. Nothing was making any sense to Karma's rattled brain, pissing her off. There had to be a logical reason for everything.

The door to her room was ajar, and Karma peered out into the hall. Again being blind as a bat didn't help a bit. Keeping a hand out in front of her, she eased toward the door. She couldn't hear anyone else in the place, which meant they were either asleep, she was alone, or whoever had her wasn't in the vicinity. She could hope for any or all of the above. With her next step, she jammed her little toe against a duffle bag in the middle of the floor. "Ouch! Crap, that hurt!" What was in it, rocks, and who would drop it there? Well, one thing for sure, she was alone, or her captors were deaf.

She eased into the hall and peeked into the room across from her. Desk, bookshelves, okay, the room was an office. Unfortunately, she couldn't see a laptop or computer. She stepped into the room as thunder rattled the house.

She could take a hint. No prob, she'd come back and search for one later. Right now, she wanted to see more of the house. To her right were two more closed doors, possibly bedrooms. To her left was a lighted room. Karma inched her way cautiously down the hall toward the light.

She stepped into a spacious open living room, and from what she could tell, she was alone. The room was nicely furnished with two couches, two recliners with an end table between them, and a large stone fireplace like one she'd expect to see in a hunting cabin, complete with a rifle over the mantel. She ran her hand over the throw on the back of one of the recliners. She wasn't a fan of wool but to each his own.

The rain pelted the floor to ceiling windows. Karma crept across the room. Maybe she could tell where she was at.

The windows were coated with a thick mist, making it hard to see out. Karma cupped her hands, pressing her face against the glass. Each time lightning flashed, she caught glimpses of the rough ocean in the distance. She couldn't see any vehicles. Looking out the windows hadn't helped. She couldn't tell if she was in San Fran or Timbuktu.

Wherever she was, it was beautiful and expensive. At least she wasn't being held in an old shack or smelly basement. The kitchen had stainless steel, state of the art appliances, and the cabinets were high-end, farmhouse style with granite countertops. Too bad she didn't know how to cook.

Karma looked around, opened cabinets, and peeked into the pantry. They'd left her here to starve to death. The proof was the lack of food unless she wanted to eat ketchup. She could stay here tonight or risk running out into the dark to find help. The woman who helped her knew Dani and had been at the wedding, maybe…no she was, Karma was sure of it. So staying here would be her safest option.

God, her face hurt. She hadn't bothered to check out her injuries and…darn it. There wasn't a mirror anywhere, either. Maybe she could find some aspirin or something to help with the pain. But why would someone *rescue* her, bring her here, then leave her alone and without food? She was being a whiney bitch, but nothing made sense. Nothing with a capital N. She hurt so much she couldn't think clearly. Maybe there was something in the medicine cabinet.

Karma closed the pantry door and then jabbed the same little toe as before against the cabinet's corner. "Motherless goat, that hurt!"

Limping, she started back to the bedroom and paused at the fireplace. The rifle probably wasn't loaded, and she didn't know a thing about guns, but she'd feel a heck of a lot safer with it at her side. She reached up, lifting the rifle from its hooks.

The door banged opened, and she spun around, facing a blurry intruder.

"What the hell are you doing and put that thing down before you hurt yourself," a masculine voice shouted.

She knew that voice, but it couldn't be Morgan. Karma squinted to focus as much as possible. Well, the man wasn't short, fat, and unless he wore a black hat, he wasn't bald, either. She tried to get a better look at him. Curse her stupid vision. "Morgan?"

"Who taught you how to hold a rifle, beautiful?" He smiled, or at least she thought he did.

"No one." She leaned the rifle against the fireplace.

"That's obvious. Sorry I wasn't here when you woke up, but I thought it best to run to the store for some food. To be honest, I didn't think you'd be up until morning." He set several bags on the counter. "How are you feeling?"

"Confused, and my face hurts. Where am I?"

"Why are you confused?"

Mr. Sexy-Voice strolled toward her, and she tipped her head back to peer up at him. Jeez, the man was tall. She could use his arm to do chin-ups. If she did chin-ups. "Because I can't trust my memory. People don't turn to dust or into animals."

"Let me help you, beautiful. You look like you're about to pass out, and why are you limping." He slipped his arm around her waist and led her to one of the couches.

"I stumped my toe against a duffle bag full of rocks or something, then jabbed it again just now."

"Oh." He winced. "Sorry. I sorta dropped it on the floor. I wasn't thinking at the time. As far as what's in it, I don't know. Dani packed it for you. She also said you'd need these." Tall, dark, and blurry, reached inside his coat, then pulled out her neon yellow glasses case. "I'd meant to set these on the nightstand for you but forgot."

"Thanks." A wave of memories assaulted Karma, of being kidnapped, beaten, and…crap. Why did her luck suck when it came to men? She was standing before a man she'd dreamed about, and she looked like hell. "I'm beaten, bruised, and broken, Morgan. I'm not beautiful, so stop the bullcrap."

"It's not crap. You are beautiful. Here." Morgan took her glasses, then gently slid the black cat-eyed frames on her face.

"Well, I don't feel beautiful." Dang. If she thought Morgan was gorgeous when she couldn't see. Lord have mercy, the man was sex on a stick. Her imagination had not done the man justice. What she wouldn't do to run her hands through his ink-black hair and over the rest of him.

She watched him walk away. The way his jeans hugged his rear-end was a sin. "Is Dani here?" Since Karma was among the living, maybe her BFF could spring her from this…hum, wherever she was before she made a total ass of herself.

"No. She and Magnus are still in Dallas. When I left, Dani was threatening to kill the boys." Morgan winked at her then yanked open the freezer. "The only thing I have for pain is acetaminophen and an icepack. Which do you want?"

"Both, please." She couldn't remember seeing an ice pack in the freezer, but then again, she could have overlooked it.

Morgan flashed a panty-wetting smile as he brought her the ice pack, a glass of water with a straw in it, and a bottle of pills. Oh, hell, Karma was doomed. "Apparently, Danny and David informed their grandmother Lacrosse practice had been canceled, when it wasn't, then snuck out of the house and headed over to some friends to play video games."

That sounded like something the boys would do. Karma replied, trying to open the bottle of pills, "Let me guess, Megan and Maggie ratted out their older brothers."

"Beauty and brains."

Morgan took the bottle from her, opened it, then handed it back. Morgan then handed the glass of water to her and even turned the straw toward her.

Dang, he was racking up the brownie points. Even if the only reason he was nice was out of guilt for what happened to her. She might as well enjoy it while it lasted. "Thanks." The cold water quenched her parched throat as she finished undressing Mr. Sexy with her eyes. "Where am I? How long have I been out? Why don't you have a mirror?"

Morgan stared at her, and Karma stared right back into his amber eyes. His lips twitched, bringing the hint of dimples to his cheeks. Dang, she'd love to get a better look at his muscles. Karma sipped on her water until she made a gurgling sound, waiting for him to answer her questions.

"Mirror's in the bathroom. Would you like more water?" His smile grew until she got a good look at his perfectly straight white teeth.

The man was stalling. Great, simply great, and so not good. "No, I'm good. Thank you. So, where am I again?"

Thunder boomed, making her jump. "Storms don't frighten me, but wow, that was close."

Morgan took the glass from her, his fingers brushing against hers. Her heart pounded, partly due to fear and partly due to the sensation his touch created.

"Storms here can last a few minutes to a few days, but you're safe, Karma. Nothing and no one is going to harm you anymore. You're at my beach house. Here, I'm going to let you apply this." He handed her the ice pack wrapped in a dishcloth.

"Thanks." She took the cold compress, realizing it was a bag of frozen peas, and gently pressed it to her left eye. "Your beach house? Which is where?" The logical part of her brain screamed to run.

"Oregon." He sank down onto the recliner closest to her.

Okay, she hadn't expected that. "Why?"

Morgan quirked his left eyebrow and tilted his head, kinda reminding her of a dog. "Because I like the Oregon coast. It's beautiful, and most of it is untouched."

"No. I mean, why am I here?" Karma drew her legs up on the couch, keeping her bits covered.

"If you're cold, I can build a fire for you." Morgan gracefully unfolded himself from the chair. He snapped open a throw, draped it over her legs, then grabbed the other throw and wrapped it around her shoulders.

She pulled the wool throw tighter around herself. "No, I'm fine, honest. Why am I here and not a hospital? Level with me, Morgan, what's going on? Because, right now, part of me wants to bolt, and the other part wants to go home."

"You can't go home, Karma." Morgan eased down beside her, close but not crowding her. "The men who attacked you trashed your apartment. Percy scrubbed your computer before you even made it out the window, so the creeps didn't get anything personal. They just got you."

Weird. His eyes seemed to glow. "What about my stuff? What about…" She lost her grandparents years ago, and all she had left of them were memories and a few photographs.

"Magnus and Dani had a team go in, box everything up, then place it in storage for you. Dani wanted me to tell you your photos are safe, but according to her, they destroyed Mr. Cuddles."

"Mr. Cuddles…" She moved the ice pack to another part of her face. "No big. He was a stuffed…never mind. Childhood memories. So, again, why am I here?"

"Because the individuals who kidnaped you are still at large, and only a select few know about this place. With all the precautions Percy put into place, even your own mother shouldn't have been able to find you."

"Yeah, well, Melody had my address. Not that my mother could pull herself away from her organic gardening to visit or even spend time with me when I went to see her…sorry, didn't mean to vomit that bit of info." To add to her mortification, her stomach decided to rumble. Maybe the couch would swallow her up.

Morgan abruptly stood and stared down at her. "Let me fix you something to eat. As bruised as you are, I'm thinking something soft. I bought some canned soup, or if you'd like, I can make you scrambled eggs."

"Scrambled eggs would be fine." It'd been days since she'd eaten, and she was starved. Maybe with some protein in her, she'd be able to think.

"With or without cheese?"

"Whatever is the easiest."

Morgan drew in a deep breath. In the faint light, his light brown eyes appeared to glow again. *So weird.*

"Egg omelet with Canadian bacon, it is."

"You don't have to go through all that trouble for me." Karma pulled the scratchy throw tighter around her shoulders, wishing she could hide from him. Why was she with Morgan and not Dani? Right. Family and kids.

Karma wasn't delusional. She knew a man like Morgan Wolfe would never give her a second glance. As she always told people, she was nerdy, curvy, and southern fried with a vertically challenged side. Men like Morgan tended to chase after the tall, blond, supermodel types.

Morgan laughed. "Oh, I'm not doing this for you. I'm starving, too."

She watched him move around the kitchen with the grace of a dancer, putting away the food, then whisking together the eggs. Hell, the man cracked the eggs with one hand then tossed the shells in the trash with better grace and finesse than any television chef could do. He caught her watching him and smiled. "So, tell me, what did you plan on doing with that old rifle?"

"I have no idea. Why me, Morgan? Why did they come after me?"

The storm outside raged, and more than once, Morgan glanced out the window. She wondered if he was looking for something or someone.

"I don't know for sure, but I have my suspicions," he said, still staring out the window.

"Your suspicions?" She eyed him, wondering if he'd tell her.

He tore his attention from the windows. "One of the men we know has a vendetta against us. We assume he knew he couldn't get to Magnus or me, so he went after you." Morgan plated their food. He glanced out the window once more before he carried the plate over to her.

"Thank you." She took the dish from him. "This looks amazing and smells wonderful."

"Only because you're hungry and haven't tasted it yet?" Morgan sat in the recliner closest to her and watched as she took her first bite of food.

She closed her eyes, and a faint moan escaped her. Good looking and could cook, too. The man was a keeper. "Wow, this is amazing. If you ever decide not to be a billionaire businessman, you could always be a short-order cook. Where did you learn to cook like this?"

"Being a short-order cook." His eyes sparkled with mirth, and she couldn't tell if he was joking.

"Seriously?"

Morgan nodded as he swallowed his food. "Seriously. After a couple stints in the army, I did a few odd jobs here and there. Being a cook for a mining company was one."

"I don't remember reading that about you." She forked the last of her omelet into her mouth, not believing she'd admitted to googling the man.

"You googled me?" He grinned like a cocky bastard.

Heat crept in Karma's cheeks. "Maybe."

"Maybe, huh. Here I thought you'd ask Dani about me." He stood, taking her plate from her. "Would you like another omelet?"

"No, thank you. That was amazing, and I did ask her. Dani said you were short, fat, and bald."

He chuckled. "To think I offered her a job." He carried the plates back to the kitchen.

"I'm going to go and put on some of my pajamas. Not that I don't mind wearing your stuff, but, you know, my stuff."

"I figured you would want to change." Morgan set their plates in the sink. "If you feel like soaking in the tub, let me know."

Karma paused and stared at the rifle. She might as well put it back where she'd gotten it. She lifted the rifle to its hooks.

Another boom of thunder rumbled the house.

"What are you doing?"

Morgan's outburst startled her. She let go of the rifle, and it clamored to the stone hearth and discharged.

Morgan tumbled forward, crumpling to the ground.

"Morgan!" Fear and adrenaline catapulted her forward toward him. "My gosh, I shot him!"

Karma rounded the recliner and jerked to a stop. Where she'd expected to see Morgan, dead, was Hollywood's version of a werewolf. Morgan's clothes hung in tatters. Blood coated his tail and hip. The creature howled, looking up at her with glowing amber eyes. His lips pulled back in a snarl.

Her knees bent, and she slowly spiraled toward the end table.

The wolfman twisted, yipped, and lunged toward her. It caught her with his massive paws preventing her from smacking her already bruised face against the sharp corner.

She stared into the concern filled eyes of the creature that could not exist, should not exist, and yet there was no denying what she saw. Morgan was a werewolf.

Unable to look away, she watched as his animal maw shrank and returned to human. His long pointed ears shortened and rounded, and the black fur covering his face receded, leaving mostly naked Morgan staring down at her. Dear lord, his muscles had muscles.

"Karma, are you all right? Are you hurt?" He leaned over her, a low growl rumbling from him. "Answer me, beautiful."

Her heart pounded. "You're...you're..." She tried to draw breath but couldn't. For the first time since she was a teen, a panic attack assaulted her. *Oh, please, not now.*

"Breathe, Karma. In through your nose, that's it." She did as he said, trying to calm her racing heart. "Hold it, now exhale slowly." The less furry Morgan smiled, revealing far sharper and pointed than human teeth. Good grief, the man had fangs. "That's my girl. One more time, in through the nose—"

"I'm good." She tried to sit, but he tightened his hold, preventing her.

"Relax. I'm not going to hurt you."

"You're...you're..." For some stupid reason, her brain and month weren't communicating with each other.

Morgan arched his black eyebrow. "Sexy as hell?" His lips twitched with a smirk. "The love of your life?"

"What? No."

"So, you don't think I'm sexy?" He rolled out his lower lip.

"Yes. . . ?"

A slow grin spread across his face. "So, you do think I'm sexy?"

"You're a werewolf," she shouted.

Morgan shook his head. "Dhampir, but we'll get to that later. Did you hurt yourself when you fainted?'

"I didn't faint."

That sexy smirk was back on his face. "Okay, when you involuntarily sank to the floor unconscious?"

"No, you caught me—Oh, shit! I shot you. Well, I didn't shoot you, but you were shot. I need to call 911."

"You don't need to call 911. I'll be fine." He glanced at the door then back at her.

"Because you're whatever you said you were?"

A tight smile pulled at his lips. "Do you pass out at the sight of blood?"

"Only if it's mine."

"I can work with that. The wound feels like it was a through and through. Can you look at my ass and tell me how many holes?" He dropped his head forward. "That didn't come out right." Morgan lifted his head and frowned. She didn't think his expression was due to his verbal faux pas but more from the pain he suffered.

"I'm going to have to clean you up some to get a better look. Where's your first aid kit?"

"Don't have one, and before you ask, I don't have hydrogen peroxide or Band-Aids either. The acetaminophen I gave you was left here by my sister-in-law, Niki."

"You have to have some alcohol, at least."

"I have *Pappy Van Winkle Bourbon*, but it's too expensive to pour on my ass." He glanced at the door again.

"Fine." Karma pulled herself up, using the edge of the chair. "Let me get a washcloth and some soapy water."

~.~.~

Morgan stared at the door, knowing Cade had to have heard the gunshot. Then again, if he were at the far end of the property, he may not have, especially with the storm. Morgan hoped the stupid cat hadn't gotten into trouble. Then again, it was a good thing he wasn't here. Morgan rested his chin on his folded arms He did love the wiggle of Karma's butt as she hurried away from him. If his brothers heard his mate shot him in the ass, Morgan would never hear the end of it. It was a good thing Cade hadn't rushed back.

Morgan stifled his laugh. Karma had shot him in the ass. Lord help, he'd never be able to live this down if anyone found out.

He leaned up and twisted to get a look at his rear. Yep, the bullet went in right below his ass cheek. He wished he could see where it exited. Morgan turned back around and flopped back to his stomach when he heard her bare feet slapping against the floor as she hurried back to him.

Karma rushed past him, heading toward the kitchen. "Let me get a bowl of hot water, and I'll be with you." She knelt beside him, placing a small bowl down. He noticed she also had the roll of paper towels with her. "Let me know if I hurt you."

He tilted his head to see her better. "Ouch."

"I haven't even touched you." Karma glared at him.

Her face wasn't as bruised as it had been earlier, but he wished she was already healed. He didn't want her in pain.

"Says the woman who shot me in the ass." He wished he could immediately call back his words at seeing the crestfallen expression on Karma's beautiful face. He grabbed her wrist, ignoring her flinch. "Hey, I was teasing. I'm not mad. My wolf, well, he's sulking because you got the drop on us."

"Well, how many more loaded guns do you have hanging around?" Karma gently pulled back the tattered fabric of his jeans. "Are you sure you don't want me to call for an ambulance or at least drive you to a hospital? This looks like a lot of blood."

"I'm positive." He winced as she pressed the warm cloth to the wound. "That rifle shouldn't have been loaded. I kept it for decoration." He angled his head, trying to see her better. Karma's heart was beating regularly, and she didn't reek of fear anymore, but what a way for his mate to find out about his Dhampiric side.

"When was the last time you used it?" Karma wiped another area, and some water trickled down his crack. He tried not to wiggle too much. "I don't mean to hurt you."

"You're not." He cleared his throat. "The last time I fired that rifle was right before I boarded a ship to China."

"Wouldn't it been quicker to fly to China?" Karma patted his butt with a paper towel then sat back on her heels. "It looks like you've stopped bleeding. The bullet appears to have entered just below your butt cheek and exited above your crack. If you think you can stand, I'll help you."

"No, let me lie here for a while." There was no way he could roll over and let her see his raging hardon. No way in hell.

"What else can I do to make you feel better?"

He couldn't keep the grin off his face if his life depended on it. "You can always kiss it and make it better."

Laughing, she patted his arm. "Poor baby's suffering from a head injury, as well." Karma pushed to her feet, then carried the bowl and blood stained paper towels and washcloth toward the kitchen.

"You can kiss my head and make it better." He laughed. Damn, he was lucky. Now he had to make sure he didn't mess it up.

A not so lady-like laugh came from her. "And delusional."

He watched as she tossed the paper towels into the trash and stared briefly into the can. He knew what she was looking at.

"Date didn't go as you planned." She strode toward the couch.

"You could say that. They were for you. I'd planned to be at your apartment the night everything went down and take you out for dinner."

"You were going to surprise me with yellow roses and dinner?" The smile and surprised look in her eyes gave him hope. Maybe she felt the same connection he did.

"Dani said they were your favorite."

Karma strode toward him. She grabbed the throw and a pillow from the couch. "You didn't know me but took the time to find out what flowers I liked?"

"I know we hadn't met in person, but I really liked you and wanted to impress you."

"You did." Her smile lit up the room. "Since you won't let me help you to bed, I can at least make you a little more comfortable on the floor."

She covered him with the throw then handed him the pillow. He watched as she wrapped the other throw around her waist before sitting on the floor, not as close as he'd like, but he wouldn't complain. Karma leaned her back against the recliner. She smiled, but her eyes were way too serious for his liking. "Why do you keep looking at the door?"

Very observant, that was good. "A friend of mine is patrolling the perimeter. He should have heard the gunshot and rushed back, but he didn't."

"You're worried about him."

"I am, but if something serious had happened, I would have known. Right now, I'm curious as to what's kept him."

She nodded, and her gaze slowly roamed over him. "So, what exactly is a Dhampir?"

Chapter Four

Morgan swallowed hard. He knew he'd have to have *the talk* with Karma eventually, but he never thought he'd have it like this, lying on the floor with his rear exposed. Well, it wasn't anymore, but still not the way he'd expected to be doing this. "Do you want the abbreviated explanation?"

Karma smiled sweetly at him. "Start talking, and I'll ask questions."

He lay there, staring up into her eyes. *What do I tell her? How much?* The last thing he wanted was to frighten the ever-loving daylights out of her. This was his mate. His one and only mate. "You asked me why I didn't take a plane to China. I boarded a ship with 98 other men to become part of the First American Volunteer Group of the Chinese Air Force."

Karma's eyes widened. "You were a Flying Tiger? No way."

"You know your history. Are you going to panic?"

She shook her head.

"Good. After the war, I found and purchased my P-40."

"Just because I love numbers doesn't mean I can't be a history buff. So what did you do when they were disbanded?"

"Re-upped with the Marines. Pappy pulled strings, so I joined his squadron."

"You went from a tiger to a Black Sheep." She laughed. "A wolf as a sheep." Karma exhaled, sagging more against the recliner. "So, you're immortal. Okay, then."

"No. Long-lived but not immortal." He eyed her, drawing in the faint scent of fear again, but at least her heart wasn't pounding out of control. He smiled, hoping to put her at ease. "My siblings and I were born like you. My mother is Dhampir. My father is a human."

"I guess my next question is, when were you born followed by, why do you look like a vampire right now?"

Oh hell. "Sorry. I didn't realize they were extended. I guess I should have started from the beginning, but…" He glanced over his shoulder, then panned back to Karma's beautiful face, and shrugged. "I'm sorry."

"I get it. The fangs are because you're in pain and not because you want to suck me dry."

Oh, he wanted to suck her, alright. "Again, I apologize. This is why Magnus handles the board meetings. As my dad says, I tend to go around my thumb to get to my toenail." Laughing, Karma covered her mouth. At least he had her giggling. "My race, the Dhampir, landed on Earth when humans still lived in caves. It's believed we gave rise to the legends of the vampire, shapeshifter, and gargoyle. Some of us can fly, some can fade into mist, others like myself can shapeshift. Before you ask me to turn into a pink unicorn, forget it. I can only shift into animals with approximately the same mass as me and are real."

Karma eyed him, her lips twitched again, and she laughed. a full heartfelt laugh. "I promise no unicorns. They're not my thing."

"Thank you." He chuckled. "The Dhampir, like humans, have both good people and bad. My family, friends, and I try to do the right thing. Some governments know about us, some don't. Wolfmoon Corporation is one of many Dhampir owned companies." He eyed her, considering his next statement carefully, then forged ahead. "So is DuMond Enterprises. As you know, Magnus is the CEO, and I'm—"

"The CFO." A soft gasp escaped Karma. "This explains why Wolfmoon is a sister company to DuMond Enterprises and why you and Magnus control both companies and the subsidiaries worldwide. You guys have your paws in a lot of stuff. Wow, just wow! I take it Magnus is like you?"

He hadn't missed her little pun. Damn, the woman was yanking his tail, and he loved it. "Not exactly. He can fly. I want to assure you Magnus's and Dani's union is a true mating."

"I never suspected. So, Dani can fly?"

"No. When we find and claim our mate, they become long-lived like us. The mating will join the two as one, and the female will immediately conceive."

"What you're saying is when they did the horizontal tango Dani got pregnant. That's not right. The boys weren't born until almost a year later."

"Dhampir pregnancies last eleven months."

Karma drew in a deep breath. "Wow. Okay. Moving on. All those theories about ancient aliens landing on Earth are true, or at least partly true, and you're vampire-ish. Which explains why the only mirrors are in the bathroom."

A laugh tore from him as he shook his head. "No, that's not why. If you must know, it's because I've broken the one in here twice and don't need any more bad luck."

"Superstitious, much?" Karma giggled, and the sound eased him. She was handling this better than he expected, even if he sensed sadness from her. "From your fangs, I take it you drink blood?"

Morgan nodded. He wouldn't lie to her. "However, we do not kill for blood. We have humans we consider family, who willingly bleed for us, and in return, receive an exceptionally long and healthy life. Some families have been with us for generations. In fact, my hometown of Tumbleweed was founded by families who returned to America with my folks." He watched her expression and could nearly see the wheels turning in her head. He also could see her bruises fading. By morning, they'd be gone. "As for when I was born, my parents met and mated in the spring of 1778 in Georgia. I was born in England eleven months later."

"Your dad's human, and he's still alive?"

"Yep. When we find our one true mate, it's forever. They live as long as we do, so Dani will be around for a long time. You're taking this all pretty calmly." He eyed her, noticing flecks of gold in her eyes he hadn't seen before.

"Because what you're telling me sounds plausible. Otherwise, I have to believe I've lost my mind. Those creeps kidnapped me, ran me up with a bunch of drugs. Lord only knows what type. Then they beat the crap out of me all to get information. So, yeah. It's easier for me to believe what you're saying than to believe those motherless goats did something to make me crazy. I'm not crazy. Pissed. Upset, but not crazy. What I saw really did happen." She stared him in the eyes. "Right? It did. Didn't it?"

"I…What did you see?"

"Like I said before, people turned to dust and animals, then add in the ghostly people dropping in from the ceiling and walking through walls."

"When we die, we turn to dust. As for the animals…" Morgan motioned to himself. "The ghostly people are an example of the ones who can turn to mist. We call it fading. What else?"

"When they nabbed me on the street, they injected me with something. Once I regained consciousness, they took the smelly pillowcase from over my head. All I saw was Psycho's fists or Evil's sneering face. Evil Prick kept injecting me with something that kept my mind foggy." Karma exhaled, and a somber look clouded her face. "For all, I know he could have injected me with some virus."

This may be the biggest mistake in Morgan's life, but he couldn't let Karma worry she'd die any moment. "Hey." He reached over, gripping her hand. "Don't worry about whatever they injected you with. You won't die. I'm positive."

Her mouth gaped, then she briefly closed her eyes. "You know this how?"

"I couldn't bear knowing you were suffering. Doctor Crumpler gave you some of my blood." He held his breath, waiting for her reaction. When she didn't scream or say anything, he continued, "She gave you enough of my blood to heal you. I wish I could go back in time and stop them from getting their hands on you."

"Don't feel guilty," Karma whispered so softly he barely heard her. "You didn't know those guys would come after me." A sad smile curved her lush lips. "While I was being held captive, I blamed Dani. I even planned on killing her, but then I thought about how her kids would take it. So, not worth their drama."

He chuckled and pushed up on his elbows, resting his chin in his palms. "You planned on killing Dani?"

Karma shrugged. "Not the first time. She made a voodoo doll of me in college because I did better in math than her. Or are you feeling guilty because you gave me your blood?"

"I didn't give you my blood out of guilt. I did it because I like you, and I didn't want you in pain."

"You like me?" Karma rolled her eyes. "But you don't know me. How can you like me when we never met? I can understand about the flowers."

"Never met? We talked for hours every night for the past four months."

"About the case," she argued.

"True, but the first night, you called me on my bull. Few people other than my close friends and family will do that. Now I've met you face to face, I want to get to know you better. You already know more about me than most."

"Yeah, yeah. Oldest of six, parents own and run a profitable cattle ranch, nothing that I couldn't find out about on Google."

He smiled, allowing some of his Dhampiric side to show. His fangs lengthened, and he knew his eyes glowed. "Didn't find this out on Google. So, let's get to know each other better.'

"Like going out on a few dates? That type of getting to know me?"

He knew he was grinning like a fool. "Getting information out of Dani was like pulling hen's teeth, and Percy wasn't much better."

"Now you sound like a stalker." She yawned, covering her mouth. "Sorry. Trust me, it's not the company."

He couldn't help smiling. "Karma, go to bed. You're exhausted, and your body is still healing, even with my supersonic vampire blood."

"On that note." She pushed from the floor. "Sure you don't want me to help you get to bed?"

"I'm sure. I'll come to bed once I'm finished healing. Thank you."

"Alright, goodnight. Oh, crap. Your sweet peas have thawed."

"That's fine. Leave it, and I'll put them back in the freezer when I come to bed."

The look on Karma's beautiful face said he was stupid. "I may not be able to cook, but even I know refreezing them is not healthy."

"Love, those peas expired about 10 years ago. I hate sweet peas, but they make the perfect ice pack."

She rolled her eyes, snatched up the peas, then unceremoniously tossed them into the trash. "You're a billionaire. Buy an ice pack."

"Yes, ma'am." He saluted her.

His wolf yipped and wagged his tail. *Our curvy little mate isn't afraid of us and won't put up with our crap.* The sound of the shower running had the loco beast wagging his tail harder and begging for them to join her in the shower.

Slow your roll, fella. We do, and we'll end up in the dog house. However, seeing she's in our den and our bed...nothing says we can't join her.

~ ~ ~

Karma carefully pulled the medical tape from her nose. The reflection in the mirror wasn't as bad as she'd feared. Her eyes had a little greenish-yellow around them, but that was all. Of course, her nose was a bit crooked now, but still, it wasn't bad.

She pressed her face closer to the mirror. Her nose wasn't *that* bad. The miracle of Vampire blood. No. Dhampir blood.

The thought of Morgan giving her blood didn't gross her out. No, if she examined her feelings, she'd have to say she felt elated Morgan had cared enough to see to her injuries. Since her grandparents' deaths, Dani was the only one who seemed to give a hoot about Karma. Still...what did all this mean for her? Would she now be part of these so-called friends of the family? Did this mean Morgan expected her to work exclusively for Wolfmoon Corporations? So many questions, but they wouldn't get answered tonight.

After slipping into her own pajamas, she burrowed under the flannel sheets and nuzzled against the pillow. Maybe she should carry Morgan another blanket and pillow. No. He'd said he'd be fine. Still, perhaps she should get up and check on him. No. No. No.

Morgan was a grown man. A sexy, drool-worthy, grown man. The image of his bare muscles sent desire rushing through her. When Morgan had shifted back, his shirt lay in tatters, and his jeans were split at all the seams. Dang, the man had a fine looking body. Karma shivered and closed her eyes. Images of Morgan flooded her mind's eye as she drifted off to sleep.

The bed dipped, and she snapped her eyes open. "What?"

"Shh, go back to sleep, beautiful. It's me." Morgan tugged on the covers. "A little blanket, please."

"No—no—no—hell, no! I'm sleeping here." She yanked the covers from him.

Morgan raised up on his elbow and leaned over her. "In *my* bed?"

"I didn't know it was *your* bed, and besides, I was here first." She stared right back into his amber eyes for all of a second before her attention drifted southward to his bare muscular chest and the thin dark line of hair trailing south from his navel, surreptitiously, of course. She quickly shifted her focus back to his eyes and squeezed her thighs together. "As big as your house is, I'm sure there are other bedrooms."

"There are." A smirk curved his lips. "And you're welcome to either one of them." He yanked the blanket from her, pulling it over his shoulders as he flopped down on a pillow.

"Me? But I'm…" She hated women who played the damsel-in-distress, but dang it, she'd use it if it meant not having to get up and crawl into another bed.

"The woman who shot me in the ass?" he drawled.

"Okay, fine. You can sleep in the bed with me tonight, but no funny stuff, buddy." Karma snatched two of the many pillows on the bed and stuffed them between her and Morgan. "Good night." She flopped down, turning her back to him.

"Funny stuff? If you're talking hip action from me, beautiful, that isn't going to happen until I'm healed."

"Good night, Morgan."

He shifted behind her then suddenly kissed her temple. "Good night, Karma." He rolled over, giving her his back. "Can't sleep on that side." He turned toward her. "Much better. Good night."

Good night, indeed! There was no way she'd be able to sleep with him in the bed with her. None what so ever! After several long moments of lying there, she breathed in, drawing in the scent of something delicious. *Bacon?*

Karma cracked open an eye, then opened both and sat up in bed. Sunlight peeked in around the blinds, bathing the room in a warm glow. She also noted the covers had been smoothed out and pulled tight where Morgan slept.

She crawled out of bed, then pulled her side of the covers tight. Her huge travel duffle still sat in the middle of the floor. Last night when she opened it, her pajamas were on top, so she didn't dig through it to see what Dani had packed.

Karma gripped the handles and strained to lift the heavy bag. Her sore muscles complained as she struggled to lift it onto the bed. "Ah-ha! That's what I hit my toe on." She pulled out her hiking boots. From the looks of it, Dani packed everything she could, but she didn't see her purse or wallet. Crap. That meant Evil Prick and Psycho Asshole had to have it. Nothing she could do about it now.

Karma found her favorite jeans and cozy dark red cardigan. She pushed back her short, pixie cut hair with a matching dark red retro hairband. After glancing in the mirror one last time, she followed the mouthwatering aromas to the living room.

Bright sunlight bathed the room and kitchen. She bet Morgan had a cleaning crew in at least once a week. Even the windows glimmered without the thick coating of mist.

"This place really shines in the daylight. Last night the mist was so thick on the windows, I couldn't see a thing."

"Thank you." Morgan pulled a knife from the block. "Coffee will be ready in a moment. Sorry, I drained the first pot."

She strolled toward them, taking in the trees and view of the ocean in the distance. "Oh, my gosh! This view is gorgeous. I can see why you like it here, and whatever you're cooking smells fantastic."

"My variation of eggs in a basket. I use bagels and scrambled eggs with cream cheese, bacon, onions, and peppers." Morgan looked up from dicing an onion on the cutting board and smiled at her. Dang, the man kept getting better looking each time she saw him. He wore a cream sweater with the sleeves pushed to his elbows. "Enjoy the sunshine. October begins the rainy season. Sunny days will be few and far between. Speaking of sunny, you look fabulous." He grinned even bigger. "Red is definitely your color. How are you feeling?"

"A little stiff but a million times better than I did when I woke last night." She pulled out a barstool and sat. "Thanks to your supersonic blood." She motioned to him. "How's the tush?"

"It's good. Even if someone wouldn't kiss it to make it better. I mean, I did give you a few CCs of liquid me." He winked and placed a bell pepper on the cutting board. "Any allergies or food you don't like?"

"No allergies, and I'll eat anything. Except for sardines." She shivered. "Too salty, and I don't like my food looking at me."

"You don't have to worry about sardines." He glanced up from his slicing. "Since I told you my deep dark secrets last night, tell me about yourself."

"You already know Dani, and I have been friends since grade school. We were in Miss Miller's third-grade class." Karma watched Morgan slice the pepper faster than a food processor. How much should she tell the guy? There was such a thing as oversharing. "What do you want to know?"

He glanced up again. "For starters, what's your last name, and is Karma a nickname? I've gone as far as to bribe both Percy and Dani with babysitting for a weekend to find out, but neither will tell me anything except your last initial is P."

"Pick another question."

He placed two plates and flatware on the counter in front of her. "Come on. I mean, it's the least you can tell me after shooting me in the ass last night."

"Are you going to hold that over my head for the rest of my life? Seriously?"

The man batted his long black lashes at her. Batted them! "I will be telling our grandchildren about it."

"Learned that from Percy?" Karma rested her elbow on the counter, placing her chin in her palm and ignoring his comment about grandchildren. She would not let her heart or head lead her down that path. At least not before coffee.

"No, my sister Miranda."

"Don't do it again. It's not a good look for you."

"Are you going to tell me?" Morgan went back to slicing and dicing.

"Promise not to laugh?"

"Cross my heart." He raked his diced veggies into a mixing bowl then removed several bacon strips from the frying pan and handed her a piece. "I'm not above bribery."

"Being a businessman, I wouldn't admit that." She took the offering and popped it into her mouth. The bacon was perfectly cooked, not too crisp, and not too wiggly.

"In business, it's called *quid pro quo*."

"It's Peamoor." She watched Morgan's lips vanish inside his mouth just before he turned his back to her. His shoulders shook. He was laughing. "I learned in kindergarten after being teased unmercifully, never to raise my hand and ask to use the restroom. Do you know how embarrassing it was during school assemblies to listen to the deafening sound of snickering when my name was called? Then there was graduation when even the parents laughed. If Adele, Cher, and Madonna can use their first names, so can I. And yes, my given name is Karma because my mother, bless her heart, thought it would be cute to name a girl Karma. Sorry, didn't need to overshare." Karma lowered her head, unable to look at Morgan. One of these days, she'd learn to do as her grandma always told her, think before she spoke.

Morgan's calloused finger tipped her chin up, forcing her to look him in the eyes. "Yes, I snickered, and I'm sorry. As for your last name," A smile pulled at his lips. "It'll be Wolfe soon enough." His smile bloomed into a huge grin.

"Really?" She rolled her eyes. "You know something I don't?"

"Nope, just know what I want." A deep rich laugh came from him, and his eyes crinkled. "Come on, tell me about yourself. Was your mom in the service? Was that the reason your grandparents raised you?

Karma sighed and slid from the barstool. "Again, stalkerish, and no." Morgan was right. She did know some pretty dark stuff about him. She needed her morning caffeine fix before they played twenty questions anymore.

"Here, let me." Morgan set his knife down and poured her a cup of coffee. "Cream with two sugars, right?"

"Yes, thank you." She took the cup and cradled it in her hands as she tried to put her thoughts in order. "Please don't interrupt, because if you do, I don't know if I can start over." She stared into the cup, shutting down her emotions. "Melody got knocked up her freshmen year in college. When she came home, she was too far along to 'deal' with the problem. I've heard this story so many times now it doesn't hurt as much, knowing the people I loved and who raised me wanted my mom to abort me. Anyway, as I said, my grandparents raised me because Melody was and will always be flighty. Since my birth, she has followed her muse. She's been a glassblower, a painter, a Shakespearean actor who followed the Renaissance festivals. At one time, she even raised llamas. Now she's in San Fran working on an organic farm. All of her muses seem to be men capable of bankrolling her latest endeavor. Her current muse is named Mateo. I've never met him."

Karma needed to do something other than standing there, vomiting up her life story. She washed her hands then dried them before picking up a bagel and the bread knife. "My grandpa was diagnosed with Alzheimer's, and my grandma was his sole caretaker while I was in college. She died before him, I guess, due to the stress. Dani's parents helped me with the funeral arrangements and getting my grandpa into a memory care facility. They took care of selling my grandparents' home to pay the medical bills. They also helped find me affordable housing while I continued with school. I don't know what I would have done without them. They've always been there for me."

As Karma pulled the knife through the bread, Morgan grabbed her wrist.

"As much as I would love to taste your blood, I'd prefer you to keep all of your fingers." He took the knife from her.

She looked down, realizing she'd stuck her middle finger through the bagel hole, and couldn't believe the stupid move. Heat warmed her cheeks. She could be an idiot at times. "Told you, I didn't cook unless it's microwavable or could be heated up in the oven. Trust me, the few times I have attempted the art, I nearly killed people, and who buys bagels that aren't already pre-sliced?"

"Note to self, keep firearms and sharp implements away from you." Morgan took the bagel, sliced it, then placed it in the frying pan. "Go sit down. Breakfast will be ready soon."

She picked up her coffee cup and carried it over to the bar.

"Where was your mother during this time?" Morgan poured the egg mixture over the sliced bagels.

"I think Melody was saving the trees and living somewhere in Canada. Or it could have been when she was saving the whales. Melody did show up at my grandfather's funeral. She left the next day. I would have had to drop out of college if it wasn't for the scholarship I received from Wolfmoon."

Morgan jerked his head, staring at her.

"Don't tell Dani or Mr. and Mrs. Rossi. While going through the files, I stumbled upon some interesting items. During the time I *won* the scholarship, Mrs. Rossi had a portion of her paycheck transferred to a bogus account. The amount she had transferred was the same as the scholarship I received and never applied for. The Rossies are some of those particular humans who know about the Dhampir, aren't they?" She'd always thought of them as her family, but now she knew they'd kept her at a distance.

"They are." Morgan placed a trivet on the counter then set the frying pan on it. He came around the bar and sat next to her. "You okay?" he asked, serving her, giving her a little too much food, but she wouldn't complain.

"I'm fine-ish." She took a bite, savoring the taste. "This is really good."

"I'm glad you like it." Morgan piled more food on his plate than she thought possible for any one person to eat. "Did your mom have any other children?" He shoved a fork full of food into his mouth.

"No." Did Karma want to go down that road with Morgan? Dani was the only other person who knew what happened. Well, Dani and the two goons. Karma glanced at Morgan, watching him eat as if he hadn't a care in the world. Hell, he already knew everything else about her. Why not this?

"After my grandparents' deaths, I took one of those DNA tests. I received my results with the names of people I might be related to several months later. A couple of weeks after, a letter came from a law firm requesting a meeting with me. I didn't want to go at first, but Dani persuaded me. I agreed to a meeting on campus in the library. I figured it would be safer in case it was a scam. I allowed myself to get excited, thinking I would meet my biological father. Instead, dickhead and dickhead showed up. They sat across from me and politely informed me their client, while in college, donated his sperm to a fertility clinic, and apparently, my mother became pregnant that way."

"Bullshit." Fur rippled over Morgan's forearms.

Instinctively, Karma placed her hand on his arm, and the fur receded. "No need to be upset. It doesn't bother me."

"Sorry." Pink colored Morgan's cheeks. "I can't believe how callous some people can be. Did they say anything else?"

"I was informed I had no claims to his estate, and I wasn't to contact him or any of his family. If I did, legal action would be taken against me. They handed me a bunch of papers then left." Karma forced a smile. "That's my life in a nutshell. Still want to get to know me?"

"More than you know." Morgan covered her hand with his, giving it a firm squeeze before letting go. His simple touch sent warmth through her, grounding her. "What do you feel like doing today?"

"I guess I need to call Dani, and I should check in with Melody. I haven't spoken to her in over a week."

Morgan's cellphone rang, and Karma jumped. "Speak of the devil."

"My mother?"

"Dani." Morgan swiped his finger over the screen and placed the call on speaker.

Before Morgan could say anything, Dani's voice came through the speaker, "Has she woken yet? Magnus told me you gave her your blood. She should be awake by now, Morgan. Why haven't you called me?"

Karma snatched up the phone, strolling away from Morgan. As her grandma would say, the devil jumped in her. Maybe because she'd felt left out of a secret and finally knew, or perhaps it was because she wanted to tease Dani. "What do you mean, Morgan gave me his blood? What are you talking about, D?"

The line went dead.

Dread washed over Karma, and she stared at Morgan. What had she done? "Lord have mercy, Magnus isn't going to kill her, is he?"

Chapter Five

Morgan burst out laughing. Life with Karma would be fun. Hell, he bet she'd be able to put up with his brothers' crap, especially Paul. He loved his baby brother, but Paul had turned into an angry, antisocial ass since Peter's death. Morgan's laughter died as the color drained from Karma's face. "Hey, what's wrong?"

"You're sure Magnus isn't going to kill Dani?"

"He would rather die than to harm her."

"But…"

"But nothing, she's his true mate. Magnus worships the ground Dani walks on and the air she breathes. If anything, he might punish her by tossing her across his lap then paddling her butt." Morgan slipped his arms around Karma's waist, thrilled when she didn't pull away from him.

"I don't think that would be a punishment for Dani?" Amusement flickered in Karma's eyes.

"Probably not." The longer he stared at her lush lips, the more he wanted to taste their sweetness. He lightly brushed his lips to hers, and Karma slid her hand up his chest.

His phone rang, and she pulled away. Groaning, Morgan glanced at the ID, wanting to kill whoever it was. "It's Magnus. I'll put it on speaker if you want."

"Please."

"How bad?" Magnus snapped.

"Relax. Karma knows. She saw my wolf last night." Morgan smiled at her, allowing a bit of his beast to come forth. Fur pushed from his pores as his nose shifted into a snout.

Karma's lips twitched with laughter. She reached up, scratching him behind his ear. Instantly, he shifted back.

"She knows?" Dani squealed, nearly shattering Morgan's eardrum. Good thing he didn't have the phone to his ear. "He showed her his doggie?"

"I'm a wolf, Dani."

"Why'd you do that? Never mind. K, we're on our way," Dani shouted.

"No, babe," Magnus corrected. "We'll be there in the morning."

"We'll see you when we see you." Morgan ended the call, pocketing his phone. Knowing Dani like he did, they'd be here soon. He hoped Magnus would persuade her to wait until morning. Morgan would like a little more alone time with his mate.

A lot of alone time, his wolf growled.

Karma strolled to the windows. She pushed aside the curtain. "Magnus didn't sound happy."

For all her bravado, Morgan saw through his little mate's armor. She put others' feelings ahead of her own. In a way, they were the same.

He slid his arm around her, turning her to face him. "Don't worry about Magnus."

Despite her smile, worry filled her eyes. "You never said, but I have a feeling it's serious if humans find out about you. What happens to the people who find out but aren't supposed to know?"

"They're not killed if that's what you're worried about. Usually, we either bring them into the family or the memory of the incident is erased from their mind."

"Erased? You can do that? Wow. I see."

Her grief was a physical vice around his heart. "No, you don't see," he reassured her. "No one will erase your memory, I can guarantee." He could because he'd kill anyone who tried.

"Because I'm friends with Danielle."

"Because you're special," he corrected.

"Those who are brought into the family, what happens to them, and their relationships with their friends and families?"

"Want to go for a walk on the beach?" He could always think better outdoors.

"You're avoiding my question."

"No, I'm not. The sun's shining. This time of year, there's no guarantee how long it will last." He was hesitating, only because he was trying to figure out how to tell her. He'd learned a long time ago never to open his mouth unless he knew how to word things to get what he wanted.

A smile lit Karma's face. "Sure, but I don't have a coat."

A few moments later, they strolled outside. Karma wore one of his jackets that hung to her knees.

"This is wow." Karma stared out over the Oregon coastline. "Simply wow. This is nothing like the Gulf Coast or the Atlantic. I can see why you love it here. This view is stunning."

"I'm glad you like it. I fell in love with the view the first time I saw it."

"Which was when?' Grinning, Karma strolled toward the fire pit and Adirondack chairs he'd made.

Damn, he loved the way her hips swayed. "Right after the war...the Civil War."

"Figures." She ran her hand over the back of one of the chairs as she eyed him. "I didn't realize last night your house was on a cliff." He could get used to seeing her smiling face every day. "I also didn't realize how big the place is. How many bedrooms do you have?"

"I originally built a one-room cabin. The living room and fireplace are part of the original cabin. That's why the roof beams are exposed, the kitchen was the last thing I had upgraded, but to answer your question, it has three bedrooms plus my office. We can always add more rooms when needed."

"We?" Karma tipped her face up at him, shaking her head. "How do *we* get to the beach?"

"Come on, it's this way." He took her hand, leading her to the steps.

"Do you know any of the people who live around the cove?" Karma asked as she took the last step.

"I own all the land circling the cove. I like my privacy, especially when I want to run in my fur. It's a mile around if you go from point to point."

"It's so beautiful here. Have you ever seen any whales?"

"During certain times of the year, you'll see them. I've seen the green flash at sunset a few times, too."

"I thought that was a myth." Karma bent over to pick up something. "Look." She opened her hand. "Amber sea glass."

"That's a nice piece, too."

"Funny how trash can turn into something pretty." She pocketed her find then continued down the beach. "So what now, Morgan. I mean about me. What's going to happen to me?"

"Nothing will happen." He wanted to tell her she had nothing to worry about because she was his mate, but it was too soon for that tidbit of info. It would be best if she came to like him, desire him, maybe even love him before he revealed that.

"I'm not going to be forced to… I don't know, for some reason, I feel my life has changed."

"Hopefully, in a good way." His life had. "I'm not going to lie to you. Usually, human mates are forced to say good-bye to their friends and family after a few years." Karma gasped, but he pressed on. "That's because once humans mate with a Dhampir, they age in the same way as the Dhampir. In other words, you can toss out all your skin rejuvenating facial stuff. But with your relationship with your mother, I'm sure we can work around it. Besides, your BFF is Dani, so no worries there."

"If I hadn't found out about you, Dani would have one day vanished from my life?"

He didn't like the grief he heard in Karma's tone. "As much as your friendship means to Dani, I'm sure that's the reason she insisted we hire you. I think she was trying to figure out a way to bring you into the family."

"But you're not sure. So, what now? What about my life, my job?"

They continued along the shore until they came to a large log across the path. He climbed over then helped Karma, letting go as soon as she got her footing. "Do you like living in San Francisco?" If she did, he would relocate.

She shrugged. "Yes and no. I moved there to try to have a relationship with Melody. To be honest, that's not working out so well. With my job, I can live anywhere. Most of the time, I work online." She sighed, picked up a rock, then threw it into the water.

"After Dani married, I rarely saw her. Our once a week girls' night out turned into once a month then whenever." She kicked at a pebble. "I sound like a loser."

"No, you don't. I get it, trust me. You want to be around people. I know."

"Dani and I are still close. It's ...I miss her. Which," Karma said brightly, "reminds me, tell me about this whole mate thing. You said she and Magnus had a true mating."

"For us, it's like love at first sight. We only have one true mate. If we're lucky, we find that person created just for us. Magnus had given up on finding his mate when Barbra brought Dani in for Take-Your-Daughter-to-Work Day."

Karma gasped. "I remember that! Dani called me, crying because she thought her mom's boss was going to fire her. That was Magnus? Dani was a kid!"

"I know. Dani was a teen. Magnus stayed away from Dani until she started working for him, then he kept away from her as he tried to figure out how to win her heart."

"He acted like an ass, always flaunting his model girlfriends. Dani cried her eyes out so many nights over him."

"I can assure you, from the moment he sensed Dani as his mate, he was true to her, body and soul."

Karma rolled her eyes. "Seriously? Then why would he go out with those other women?"

Morgan picked up a stone, throwing it into the surf. It skipped once before a wave covered it. He could tell Karma the man had to eat, but. . . "Appearances."

"I guess. I can testify that the man does worship Dani and the kids." Karma picked up a stone, then tossed it. "So, you get one chance at finding your mate?"

"Pretty much. There are exceptions. My brother, Quade, found his mate when she was brought into the hospital he worked at. Sadly, she died before she even woke. Maybe that's why fate blessed him with a second chance at happiness. Quade had given up. In the past hundred years, he'd forgotten how to enjoy life."

"What if your mate is old or ugly or just plain mean? What if you don't like them? Don't you get a choice to say no?"

"I've never heard of a Dhampir who had denounced their mate willingly." He knew many Dorjan's had, but they were certifiably insane. "Like I said, for us, it's love at first sight."

"You mean lust. What happens if, say, I was your mate but already happily married, then what would you do? What happens then? Would you kill my husband?"

"I would walk away, leaving you to live out your life."

"And live miserably ever after?"

"Pretty much." Karma had a point, but he'd never given it much thought. He was thankful fate had blessed him with such a beautiful woman, both inside and out. Karma's heart was huge. The proof was her desire to have a relationship with her mother.

"Seems totally unfair to me." She threw another stone. "So what, you wait around for Miss Right to come along, or do you actively search for your mate? Or are you?" Karma glanced over her shoulder at him with raised eyebrows. Her eyes dipped to his crotch.

"A virgin? Hardly, but I've never led any of my lovers on. They all knew there would be no happy-ever-after with me. As for actively searching—no. I figured when it was time, I'd find her. Gotta have faith. What about you? Any boyfriends we need to notify?" He cringed at the growl of his wolf. The beast was already planning on removing any competition if she did have a boyfriend.

"Hardly, my dates tend to fall into two categories. The ones who find out I'm a forensic accountant and instantly want me to help them get a bigger return on their taxes. The others think they can help me lose weight simply by pointing out I should eat less and exercise more. I do exercise. I just don't jog or run, but I take spin classes, and I also swim laps. When I tell the jerks this, the look on their faces is often, liar, liar pants on fire. They can't look past my imperfections to see the real me."

"I see perfection, not imperfection."

Karma rolled her eyes again. "Will you stop that, please."

"Stop what, speaking the truth? Beautiful, you're hot. The more I get to know you, the more I'm attracted to you."

"I think when Dani and Magnus arrive, I should leave with them."

"Why?" What in the hell had he said wrong?

"Look, Morgan, I'm not desperate, okay. I'm fine in my own skin. Yes, I think you're hot, and you have one sexy as all-get-out voice. But you're not getting gratitude sex from me, so stop it. It ain't going to happen."

"Gratitude sex! Is that what you think I'm after?"

"Isn't it?" She planted her hands on her round hips, tipping her face up to his. "Then, from the looks of you, you're a shower instead of a grower."

His wolf went into a play bow. The loco beast was getting turned on by her feistiness. Plus, the fact she'd checked him out. Morgan wasn't about to point out that little fact to her. Nope, for once, watching his brothers put their feet in their mouths was going to be his saving grace. "I can't help I'm strongly attracted to you both physically and intellectually."

Karma rolled her eyes then continued down the shoreline. "You're a tease, Morgan Wolfe, you're nothing but a tease," she shouted over her shoulder.

~ ~ ~

He was attracted to her? What did that even mean? The man was a tease, nothing but a tease. He'd just explained to her about mates, then in the same breath told her he was attracted to her. Lord have mercy, men say women were fickle. Still, Karma couldn't think about Morgan waiting for a woman who might never show up, or worse, be a total bitch. If his mate was a bitch, she'd have to deal with Karma. No—no, she wouldn't.

Morgan was an idiot believing in love at first sight. But Karma wasn't one to talk. Hadn't she been waiting for Mr. Right? Curse Dani for her perfect marriage. Curse Melody for not settling down with one man. Curse Morgan, too, for being the one perfect guy. Too bad she wasn't his mate. If she was, he'd be like, let's get hitched now.

The silence grated on her.

They came to a place where she could see a fence in the distance. "Is that where your property ends?"

"On this side, but I'm considering purchasing more land when it comes up for sale. If I have kids, I think this is a nice place for them to run and play."

"More room to run, I can understand that. So you want kids?" She'd always dreamed of having a family. One thing for sure, she planned on being a far better mom than Melody had been."

"If my mate and I are blessed. What about you?"

"I love kids and would love a house full, guess because I was an only child." She couldn't help but notice the sad smile on Morgan's face. "Why wouldn't you be able to have any?"

"The only guaranteed time of conception is during the first mating. Many Dhampir couples have one child, some none." His smile brightened. "However, when the mate is human, there is a greater chance the couple will have more than one child."

"Let me get this straight. The first time you and your mate have unprotected sex, she gets pregnant?"

"If they're lucky."

"And these children, will they be human or Dhampir?" If she were his mate, would she have werepups or babies?

"They'd be Dhampir and would have my ability to shift."

"So, I'd be running after little werepups." *Motherless goat! Slip of the tongue.* "So, superpowers?" Karma pulled Morgan's jacket tighter. The sun was out, but the wind coming from the ocean was cold. "What else can you do?" Regretting she'd asked that, Karma focused her attention on the surf, knowing Morgan was smirking. *Open mouth. Insert foot.* She didn't want to know about his sexual abilities, even if she'd fantasized about them. She bent over and picked up a piece of sea glass, reflecting in the sun.

You drive me crazy when you bend over like that. Morgan's voice reverberated in her mind.

"What the…" Karma jerked around, losing her balance.

Morgan lunged forward, sliding his arm around her waist. He caught her, preventing her from face planting. "Sorry. I guess I should have warned you."

"That you can speak to my brain?" She looked up into his warm amber eyes and licked her dry lips. "That would have been nice."

"I can think of another nice thing." He lowered his lips to hers, brushing against them. The faint touch sent lightning bolts through her all the way to her core, making her girly parts quivered. Dang, she wanted to wrap her legs around him and climb him like a tree.

My Country, 'Tis of Thee, blared from Morgan's cellphone.

Karma pushed from his embrace. "I didn't take you for the patriotic type."

"Actually, it's *God Save the Queen.*" He caught her hand, lacing his fingers with hers as he answered. "What's up, Percy?"

Karma pulled her hand free. "I'll see you back at the house." With her back straight and head high, she strolled toward the steps. *I'm not my mother. I'm not my mother!* But what would it have felt like had Morgan taken his kiss deeper? For that brief second, when he held her in his arms, she felt like she'd found home.

She had to get out of here and as far away from Morgan as humanly possible before she had her heart broken. What was she talking about? Her heart was already broken.

She climbed the stone steps, noticing an SUV and a black truck parked near the side of the house. She didn't remember seeing either vehicle when they left on their walk. Then again, she'd been more interested in the ocean. Besides, where they were parked, she might not have noticed them.

Had it only been a few hours? It seemed like she'd been with Morgan longer. Karma ran her hand across the back of one of the chairs, imagining herself and Morgan sitting by the fire pit, enjoying the sunset. "Not going to happen."

The cabin door flew open, startling her.

"What the hell did you do to Morgan?" A naked man with a crazed look shouted.

Karma backed up, bumping into one of the Adirondack chairs as she eyed the man storming toward her. His green eyes were vaguely familiar. "I didn't do anything to Morgan."

The man's eyes blazed, and he hissed like a cat. "Then why does the place smell of his blood, gunpowder, and cleaner?"

"I—I." Her chest suddenly became too tight to draw breath. Her blood turned to ice, freezing her in place. "You smell blood because I accidentally shot him."

"You shot him!" Tawny fur rippled over the man's face, and his eyes turned feline as he lunged at her.

"I didn't mean to!" Karma gasped, wanting to flee, but her feet refused to move. This was it. She was going to be turned into cat litter.

A massive black wolf raced past her, shoving her against the wooden chair, causing her to lose her balance. She tumbled to the ground as growls and snarls filled the air. Karma pushed herself upright as she took in the horrific scene before her. Morgan's wolf had the cat man pinned, snapping at the cat's throat.

The cat didn't fight back. No, he only tried to keep Morgan from tearing out his throat. So, the cat wasn't a threat to Morgan.

"Morgan, stop!" Karma shoved to her feet, but before she took a step, she heard the sickening sound of bone snapping. Morgan was going to kill the man. Just because the cat man was a jerk didn't mean he should die. She strode toward the two. "Stop it."

Morgan snarled at her, keeping his jaws locked on the man's arm. As crazy as it was, she understood every growl and snarl Morgan made as if he spoke the words. Had to be because he'd given her his blood.

"Yes, he tried to kill me, but only because he thought I'd killed you. You can't kill a friend because he's stupid."

Morgan swung his glowing red eyes toward her and snarled.

"Morgan! That wasn't nice." Karma dug her fingers into the thick fur on the back of his neck, giving him a good yank. "I will not have the guilt of his death on my hands. Bad puppy!"

Despite his broken and bleeding arm, the cat laughed. Okay, the idiot had a death wish. Morgan swung his attention back to the cat, snapping at him but with less ferociousness.

"I said, stop it!" She yanked on Morgan's fur, knowing it had to hurt.

Morgan sat back on his haunches, his weight pressing against her leg.

The cat man scooted back, cradling his arm. He drew his tongue over the wound, eyeing her. "You understood Morgan. You knew what he was saying in his wolf." The man chuckled.

She kept her attention on Morgan because staring at a naked man that wasn't Morgan felt wrong. She ran her fingers through his soft fur, smoothing out the area she pulled.

"I guess," she answered, marveling at the size of Morgan's wolf. He was twice as large as a normal wolf. His eyes were the shade of amber as Morgan's and his fur the same ink-black as his hair. She scratched him behind the ears, noticing a few strands of silver.

"You guess? Naw, you understand Morgan because you're his mate."

"No, because he gave me his blood." Right, that had to be the reason. If she were his mate, he would have told her. Right?

"Not," he laughed.

She stared at the cat man, keeping her eyes on his face and his shimmering green eyes.

"Damn, bro, no wonder you were so adamant about rescuing her." The cat grinned even more.

Karma's heart pounded. "You're wrong, Cat man, and do me a favor. Put some clothes on, or at least hide that thing."

"It's Cade, and it's not a thing. It's a legend. But I'm right, you're Morgan's mate. Wait until I tell Chase."

"Cade? You were the one…You ripped the doggie's heart out to protect the other guy." Suddenly her lungs couldn't craw air. Her vision blurred. He *would have* killed her.

Morgan leaned against her. Instantly her panic vanished. She turned her attention to the massive wolf staring up at her. He wore a stupid grin on his muzzle. "If I were your mate, you would have told me. Wouldn't you, Morgan?"

Chapter Six

"Morgan?" Karma stared into his amber eyes. She held her breath as her heart pounded in her chest. Cade had to be wrong. "Am I your mate?"

Morgan barked, wagging his tail.

"Seriously, you want me to *fetch* your clothes instead of talking to me?" She couldn't believe the audacity of his request. "Fetch your own clothes."

"Dude!" Cade rolled to his feet. "Sorry, K, but you misunderstood Morgan. He wants *me* to fetch his clothes, not you. Morgan doesn't want to talk to you naked. He also doesn't want you comparing his junk to my magnificent staff." Cade strolled back inside the house, shaking his head.

She rolled her eyes, marching away from Morgan. She hadn't misunderstood. Nothing was lost in translation. Fetch his clothes, indeed. The man thought he was a comedian. "You know, even though you're a billionaire, you may want to consider wearing stripper clothes with Velcro seams. It would be a lot cheaper on your wallet."

She gathered up his tattered clothes as her mind and heart battled. Her emotions were so conflicted, excited a guy like Morgan wanted her at the same time, hurt because he'd kept his feelings a secret. "Speaking of wallet, I don't see it. I've found your cellphone. Which reminds me. I think Evil Prick and Psycho have mine."

Strong arms pulled her back against a firm bare chest. "My wallet's in the kitchen," Morgan whispered against her ear, sending shivers down her spine. Her body didn't care about her heartache. "As for yours, we'll let Percy know."

Karma shoved his tattered clothes against his chest as she stepped from his embrace. She noticed Morgan only wore a pair of sweatpants. The man had to be cold.

Her attention dipped down. Morgan's abdomen was ripped. Heck, he could've been the model for Michelangelo's David. Lord have mercy. Morgan even had those sexy lines that made her drool.

She snapped her attention to his face, seeing the smirk curving his lips. "Cade's a good friend. You should thank him. When he admits he doesn't understand wolf-speak, you should also tell him not to lie five seconds later, pretending he does to cover your furry butt. As for you, don't ever tell me to *fetch* again. You ask. Nicely." She turned on her heels only to have Morgan's arm wrap around her waist once more.

"When I'm in my wolf, my primitive brain is in control. I'm still me-ish, but the wolf is a wolf." Morgan sat in one of the chairs, pulling her down with him across his lap.

"I'm listening. Not buying it, but I'm listening." She'd learned over the years, the more you yell, the less people listen. As the old adage goes, it's the quiet ones you have to worry about.

A deep laugh erupted from him. "I know that look, beautiful. It says I'll get out of this hole faster if I put the shovel down."

"Pretty much."

"The beast thought he was funny. After all, you did call us a puppy."

A few moments ago, it was bright and sunny. Dark clouds now loomed on the horizon, both figuratively and literally, just like her life.

Karma crossed her arms as she stared out over the water. She would not succumb to Morgan's hard-muscular-bare-chested sexiness. Would not.

Who's the liar now?

Morgan Wolfe was tall, bronzed, and his frigging muscles had muscles. Oh, how she wanted to trace every line of him with her tongue. Yes, she was attracted to him. Any woman with a pulse would be. Lord have mercy, she thought the man was sexy as hell, but being sexy meant nothing if he wasn't honest with her. Did he not want her as his mate? She pulled his coat tighter around herself, trying to hide her more than generous curves.

Crimson Shores

He'd talked of knowing his mate would be perfect for him, but she wasn't. Not at all. His mate was short, round, and blind as a bat. How many men had told her she'd be cute if she lost a few pounds? Too many.

Morgan nuzzled her neck, sending chills through her Curse her traitorous body.

"Cold?" he asked.

The firepit flamed up, startling her. She jerked, smacking the back of her head against Morgan's face. "Sorry!" she blurted, glancing over her shoulder at him.

"Ooo, that hurt, but I deserved it." He rubbed his nose.

"You can start fires?"

"Little ones. I can't incinerate the world." Morgan leaned back, taking her with him. "I've hurt your feelings. I'm sorry. I shouldn't have tried to make a joke."

"Your joke wasn't what hurt my feelings. Why did you keep it from me that I was your mate?" She didn't want to sit here, listening to him come up with excuses. She wanted to go inside, borrow Cade's phone, then find a way to leave. She was done with people who didn't want her. Finished. Kaput. Over it.

Morgan exhaled, relaxing his hold, allowing her to shift on his lap to see him better. This wasn't the smirking man she'd come to know in the last twenty-four hours.

"Because I was afraid you'd reject me." He pushed her glasses up on her nose.

Wait. What? Okay, she'd not expected to hear that from him. Morgan wasn't blowing smoke, either. She heard the truth and conviction in his voice. "Excuse me. Why do you think I would have done that?"

"I don't know. Maybe because of the whole turning into a wolf thing." A faint smile tugged at his lips but didn't reach his eyes. "You could be a cat person."

Lightning flashed on the horizon, and a few moments later, thunder rumbled.

"Hardly. I mean, Mr. Cuddles was a plush cat, but deep down, I'm a dog person."

"Wolf." Morgan's smile spread.

Karma rolled her eyes, realizing she'd been doing that a lot with him. "Still a canine."

"Better than a dog. You should know I'm not the alpha of my pack." Unease filled his voice, and he lowered his gaze.

Motherless goat! She didn't care if he wasn't top dog. He was hers. Well, not hers—hers, but yeah. Hers. "So," she countered. "I'm not a size 2. Never have been, never will be. I also will not do taxes for friends or family. Ours, yes…friends and family—hell to the no."

"Ours?" His sexy smirk teased the corners of his lips. Not his full grin but almost. "I think my wolf knew you were our mate over a year ago."

"What? We hadn't even started talking then. Are you also psychic?"

"No. No, I'm not psychic. But I can predict a storm coming." He pointed out toward the water. "That's kinda obvious, but you being my mate, it wasn't. A little over a year ago, I noticed the wedding photo on Magnus's desk. I couldn't stop looking at your image. Every time I went into his office, I always ended up staring at you in the photo. One day when Magnus was out, I broke into his office and *borrowed* the picture."

"Stole."

"I returned it after I copied it. I keep it in my desk drawer so I can look at your beautiful face. I have a smaller one in my wallet."

"Sounding a little stalkerish again." As much as his words made her happy, that doubting part of her brain raised its ugly head. "I still don't understand why you didn't tell me. I know what you said earlier, but what's the real reason?"

"For me, it's love at first sight, but you're human. I know it's not the same for you. I mean, if the first thing I told you last night was you were mine, you'd have run screaming your head off, thinking I was nuts. Then after you saw what I am, I feared frightening you more."

Morgan had a point, and his sincerity eased her hurt. It probably wasn't easy telling people you could turn into a dog—correction,

wolf. Besides, had he blurted out she was his mate, she'd think him a few French fries and a small drink short of a Happy Meal. As for him being in love, she wouldn't argue with him, but she doubted it was love. Lust, yes. Love, no.

Google didn't really have that much on him, other than he was the CFO of one of the largest corporations in the world. His hometown was Tumbleweed, Texas. Dani wasn't much help, just telling Karma she wanted her to meet him. As for getting information from Magnus, well, he was Magnus.

She looked into Morgan's eyes, seeing his wolf peering back at her. "So, now what?"

"I'd like for us to date," He lightly stroked her cheek, and she leaned into his touch. "get to know each other better, have you meet my insane family, then, later on, get married."

"I'd like that. I'd like to meet your family." She wouldn't address the get married part. Not yet. Maybe not ever.

"You would?" Morgan's smile turned to a full grin that crinkled his eyes. She bet if he'd been in his wolf, his tail would be wagging.

It was the truth. Karma would like to get to know Morgan better, to see where their relationship would go. "Yes, I'd really like to date you. Maybe in a few months, even meet your family." Karma bet her timeline and Morgan's were totally different. "I felt that."

"Felt…what?"

"You stiffen when I said months." She hated talking about herself, but he needed to know why she tended to run away from relationships. "Morgan, I'm gun shy."

His huge grin dazzled against his bronze skin. "Could have fooled me."

"Not talking about shooting you in the ass."

"Better there than my nuts—and I know that look, so shutting up." Morgan traded his huge grin for his signature sexy smirk. Would the man ever take anything seriously?

Karma looked deep into Morgan's eyes wanting him to see the honesty of her words. "Your humor is your shield." He opened his mouth, and she firmly pressed her finger against it. "Hear me out. All those nights we talked on the phone, I couldn't understand how you could be the CFO of a corporation because at first, you were quiet, almost shy. The more we talked, the more talkative you become. You don't talk to hear your voice or to boast. You're constantly calculating. Plotting. Subconsciously looking for an angle. That's your shield. What makes you so darn good in business."

"You know me better than my family does." A sad laugh escaped him. "You're right. I don't like to waste my time arguing. I let my numbers speak for me. I don't get mad. What's your shield?"

"My shield? I guess I'm like you. I don't argue with people, either. I point out the facts then walk away."

"What's the rest of it? What aren't you telling me, Karma?"

It clicked. Morgan honestly wanted to know about her.

"For the most part, I grew up happy. I knew deep down my grandparents loved me. I think Melody even loves me in her own quirky way. Which is why I'm trying to build a relationship with her. However, it doesn't erase the fact, I was told I was a *mistake* all through my childhood. Like I said, I know they loved me, but... Their words scarred me, probably the reason why I went to the same college as Dani. It was far away from my grandparents. Things weren't much different there. I was the lard-ass-nerd."

"I love your curves." A growl rumbled deep within Morgan's chest.

"Stop that. I survived because of Dani. She was always there for me. The point of my story wasn't for sympathy. I like you, Morgan."

"Yeah?" He grinned.

"Yeah, I do. However, you may be a wolf, but I'm a hedgehog. Hurt my feelings, I will roll up into a ball. You not telling me I was your mate, then finding out the way I did, hurt."

"Sorry." He lightly stroked her back.

"Water under the bridge. But you're right. Before you run out and put a ring on it, our relationship needs to grow. If you think this will be a wham-bam-thank-you-ma'am relationship, think again."

"Wham-bam?" Morgan's lips twitched. "Beautiful, everything is on your timetable. However, right now, I'd very much like to kiss you."

She'd like that, too, and licked her dried lips. "You would, huh?"

"Uh-huh." Morgan brushed his lips lightly over hers, drawing a moan from her. He teased the seam of her mouth, and she opened to him.

She savored his flavors as their tongues danced. Morgan tasted of coffee and something dark and addicting. Wanting more, Karma turned more toward him and cupped the back of his head. She ran her fingers through his thick hair, enjoying the feel of the silky strands.

Morgan caressed her hip and outer thigh, nothing more. But his caress heated her body. Oh, how she wanted him to touch her there.

She slid her hand up his bare chest as the kiss grew more passionate, flaming as the fire crackled and popped in the pit. She wanted him, and judging from his hardness, pressing against her hip, he wanted her, too. The feel of his bare skin against her palms grew hotter. She wasn't a fool. She knew they needed to stop before things got a little out of hand.

A throat cleared. "Hey, Morgan."

Morgan slowly ended their kiss, then rested his forehead against hers. "So, going to kill that cat. What, Cade?"

Her brain was thankful for Cade's interruption, her girlie parts not so much. Trying to get her racing heart to calm, Karma rested her head against Morgan's shoulder. She breathed in then exhaled. She was thankful Cade had pulled on a pair of jeans and a sweatshirt. The blond was an Adonis, but she didn't want to see his junk.

Cade flopped down into the other chair, placing his phone on the arm. "I want to apologize again. I mean when I entered your place and smelled your blood and lemon-fresh cleaner. Then, when I looked around, I knew something was wrong. I mean, hell, man, your place has never been this clean. I mean, before your dust bunnies had bunnies. Lord love a duck, the dust on your things used to be so thick it had geological lines. So, seeing your place sparkling clean. I knew something bad went down."

"For the love of—the place wasn't that bad! Sure, there was dust, but it's always neat and tidy."

No one would make Morgan feel bad, even if she did like the cat's phrase, Lord love a duck. Karma snuggled against Morgan, wrapping her arm around his shoulder. "You cleaned it for me? That's so sweet," She pecked his cheek, "cause, yeah, I hate housework. I'm not a slob, everything has to be in its place, and there's a place for everything. If we do get married in a few years, we will have a housekeeper. I've always wanted one of those."

"*When* we get married, not if, beautiful."

"Sure of yourself, are you?" She patted his cheek. Who was she kidding? They'd be married within two years if her body had anything to say about it.

"Anyway." Cade chuckled. "Like I said, the place reeked of your blood and lemon fresh cleaner. When I saw the bullet hole in the doorframe, my first thought went to Lincoln getting the drop on you and kidnapping Karma again."

Morgan bristled, and fur rippled over his body. "Lincoln Whitehall couldn't get the drop on a flea. I may not be the pack's Alpha, but that doesn't mean I can't protect my mate. Besides, if you were so concerned, where were you last night when it happened. Why didn't you come running?"

"I thought it was thunder." Pink tinged Cade's face. "I did prowl around the house. It wasn't until I entered that I knew something was wrong."

Karma cupped Morgan's chin, turning his face so she could see his eyes. "Cade's making it sound like you could have died."

Morgan grunted. "Hardly."

"Lots of blood, dude. Just saying," Cade snorted. "So, how did it happen?"

Heat rushed to her face. She'd never live this down. Never. Karma dropped her head to Morgan's shoulder, stroking his chest. Touching his bare skin was causing her to cream her panties, dang it. "I was putting the rifle back over the fireplace when it slipped, hit the hearth, and discharged."

"Really?" Cade leaned forward, stroking his chin. He dropped his gaze to Morgan's leg. "From the angle of the bullet, it had to hit low."

"It doesn't matter where I was hit," Morgan growled, his fangs lengthened, and his eyes bled to red.

"Sorry, man." Cade recoiled, dropping his head to his chest. "I thought the bullet hit the femoral artery, especially with the amount of blood I scented. Thought you'd need blood."

Karma didn't know Cade's story, but the man definitely looked up to Morgan. She ran her fingers through Morgan's thick hair, gently tugging on it. "Stop growling. Cade's concerned about you. Besides, you did say you were going to tell the grandchildren the tale." She wanted to reassure Cade, Morgan's injury wasn't as bad as he'd thought. "The bullet hit Morgan in the tush, okay."

"Oh, bloody hell, that's rich!" a voice boomed from Cade's phone.

~ ~ ~

Morgan would kill the cat. Kill him, then use his fur as a rug. As soon as the thought formed, he cringed. Cade's family put the dis and fuck in dysfunctional. Nearly four years ago, Cade's f-ing father forced him to skin his brother Chase. Kill the cat—yes, skin him— no. "Glad you got your jollies, Royce. Cade, do cats have nine lives? Might have to test that theory."

Karma nuzzled him, easing his anger.

She was right.

Morgan couldn't kill Cade. The cat was like a stray barn cat looking for a home.

Morgan breathed in Karma's scent. It amazed him how merely being in her presence calmed him and his loco beast. He drew in another deep breath, filling his lungs with the musky hints of her arousal. His dick instantly responded.

His wolf growled, not wanting Karma near the unmated cat.

Easy, boy. He told his wolf. *She's attracted to us, not the cat.*

"Sorry, mate," Royce's laughter echoed from Cade's phone. "Stop growling. You have to admit Karma shooting you in the ass is hilarious. I've heard of her biting one, but shooting?" Another deep laugh echoed from the phone. "Bloody hell, I love it. Morgan, you can't kill the cat, he called me, freaking out that you'd been killed, and Karma nicked again. Bloody hell, Morgan, Percy, and Viktor were readying the plane. Which reminds me, I best tell Vaughn to stand down." The screen went black on Cade's phone.

Karma's lips tightened as she stared up at Morgan. "Royce, as in Magnus and your boss? That Royce? Great. Just…Great."

Morgan cringed, wondering how much Karma could handle before she bolted from him.

He'd be damned if that would happen. He'd sniff her out no matter where she went. However, there was a ton of crap he hadn't quite explained to her, like his desire to drink her blood. "Royce isn't actually our boss, more like the future leader of our people."

"So, in other words, *your* boss." Karma patted his chest. "Your boss knows I shot you in the tush because I vomited that bit of info." She exhaled. "Thank goodness Cade didn't tell your family."

"Oh, I called Momma Gwyn first." Cade grinned bigger, folding his arms behind his head.

Morgan wondered just how pissed Royce would be if the cat suddenly vanished.

Karma's entire body heated, and her face turned an unnatural red, a color Morgan had never seen a human turn in his whole life. A tomato, yes. A human, no.

"I ah.." She wiggled on his lap, pushing from him.

"Where are you going." Instead of letting her go, he held her tight until she rested her head once again on his shoulder.

"Away."

"Why?" He didn't keep the growl from his voice as he glared over her head at Cade, knowing full well it was the cat's fault Karma was upset. Yep, Cade and he would go for a walk in the woods, but only he would come back. Royce shouldn't mind…much.

"To save my life, 'cause your family hates me now." The smell of her fear stung his nose.

"What? No. What gave you the idea my family will hate you?"

"I may not understand a lot of stuff about the Dhampir, but I know if I had a kid and someone shot him, that person wouldn't survive until sunset." She fought again to escape him. "Let me go, please."

"After what you said?" Cade laughed, sounding more like a jack-ass than a cat. "You and Momma Gwyn have more in common than you think."

Morgan glared at the Cat, watching Cade's grin slip. "My mom won't hate you. She might give you some shooting lessons, may even teach you how to cook if you want to learn, but she won't hate you." He wasn't about to tell Karma his mom would have their wedding planned out before he finished telling her he'd found his mate.

"Ah," Cade stammered. "Momma Gwyn won't hate you, Karma. Hell, once she finds out you're Morgan's mate, she'll have the preacher lined up and John making another bassinet."

Karma paled slightly before an array of emotions flashed over her face.

Crap! Morgan recognized every one of them. Confusion, hurt, and a little anger. Yup, he was in the dog house, all thanks to that friggin cat.

The next second, a light mist started falling. His spoiled beast wanted them to get out of the weather. Their mate didn't need to be in the rain. Plus, the smell of wet wolf wasn't sexy.

True, he agreed with his wolf, but they needed to comfort their mate.

Can do that in our dry den. His wolf growled.

"Hey, beautiful." Morgan caressed her cheek with the back of his hand, enjoying the feel of her silken skin. "Our relationship is on your timeline. Not mine, not my mother's. Yours." He pressed a kiss to her forehead. "Understand? You're mine."

"Yeah, but..."

Morgan didn't want to hear her arguments so, he pressed his lips to hers. "But nothing. This is about us. No one else." He kissed her again.

The fire hissed as larger raindrops splattered it.

"It's raining." Karma scooted from his lap then ran toward the house. His coat was caught on her hips, giving him an unobstructed view of her heart-shaped derriere.

Morgan ran after her as the rain fell harder. Damn, he loved the way her butt wiggled. His dick was in full agreement.

As soon as he was inside, the rain poured. Morgan closed the door then helped Karma out of the coat. "I meant what I said. No one is going to rush us. Not my mom, not me." He hung the jacket on the coat rack.

"Why don't you two get some dry clothes on while I clean up the kitchen." Karma reached up, pushing his wet hair from his eyes. Her way of saying the conversation was over, he guessed. "Go on." She headed toward the kitchen.

"Leave it. I'll clean it." Morgan called as he headed toward their room. Yes, *their* bedroom. Morgan would not claim Karma, would not enjoy the pleasures of her lush, curvaceous body. However, if he had anything to do with it, she wouldn't be sleeping alone with the cat in the house. Morgan yanked a soft sweatshirt over his head then opened the door.

Cade stepped into the room. Morgan's wolf growled, not wanting the unmated male in their den.

"What?"

Cade tilted his head in submission. "I know I effed up. Sorry, man, but I...I freaked. Anyway, I pulled a phone and laptop from your office in case you wanted her to have them."

Morgan hadn't noticed the boxes Cade held. "Thanks. Karma should like them."

"Do you think she'll forgive me?"

He studied Cade looking every bit a lost stray. "Karma's right. You are a good friend. She also said not to lie to her again."

"Lie to her? I've never lied to her."

"You told her you didn't understand what the wolf said, then turned around and told her I wanted you to *fetch* my clothes."

Pink colored Cade's face. "Oh, I did. She caught that, huh? Oh, well. Anyways, Royce wants me to hang close, so I'm going to run in my fur."

The scent of blood filled the air.

"Morgan!" Karma shouted.

Chapter Seven

Any minute now, she'd wake up from this friggin' dream. It had to be a dream. 'Cause, how had her fairy godmother fixed her up with a man like Morgan, especially since she didn't have a fairy god-anything? Karma dried the cast iron frying pan then set it on the stove. She may not know how to cook, but she knew how to clean a prized skillet. She turned her attention to the dishes soaking in hot soapy water and searched for her next target. Finding it, she carefully washed the knife Morgan used to dice the veggies. The dang thing was sharp enough to cut through anything. She wasn't about to embarrass herself by slicing off a finger. She'd already tried it once today.

She set the knife in the drainer then picked up a plate. Her mind wandered with the many questions she had for Morgan. How did the Dhampir explain their life to those who weren't supposed to know about them? When she'd Googled him, it said Morgan took the company over from his father, but that wasn't so, which meant they…changed identities…they moved, or did someone else assume their identity? If she'd never found out about the Dhampir, would Dani have suddenly vanished from her life? Morgan thought Dani wanted to bring her into the family. Maybe…but.

She and Dani had been friends since they'd met in the third grade. However, since Dani mated, she and Karma had drifted apart. Slowly, Dani was separating herself from Karma. It was Dani who'd suggested Karma should travel the world. Because of her BFF, Karma moved to San Fran. Funny, they seem to talk more on the phone than they had when Karma still lived in Georgia.

She picked up a glass, running the dishrag inside it.

Karma's heart ached as her mind confirmed her deepest fear. Before she jumped to any conclusions, she'd confront Dani. Karma also needed to ask Morgan about Melody. What would happen to her if Karma married Morgan?

A faint pop and pain pierced her palm. The sudsy dishwater slowly turned pink. Oh, crap! "Morgan!"

He was at her side before his name died on her lips.

A furry arm wrapped around her waist. "Let me see your hand."

Karma clenched her fist tighter as embarrassment heated her face. It was bad enough she was a curvy geek, but now she'd demonstrated she was a super-sized klutz.

Morgan probably wondered what he'd done to get saddled with her as a mate.

"Beautiful, let me see your hand, please." His tone was soft, full of concern, not patronizing as her grandparents' had been whenever she screwed up.

Karma did as he asked, opening her hand. A dark crimson line flowed from her palm. Her knees turned to spaghetti as cold sweat beaded her forehead. She fisted her hand again.

Morgan pinned her against the sink, using his body to keep her upright. Gently, he unfolded her fingers.

Karma slammed her eyes shut, not wanting to see her blood on the outside of her body.

"It looks like there's still a piece of glass in your palm. Hold still while I remove it." Morgan's warm breath teased her cheek as he scraped something over her palm. Like a fool, she opened her eyes, seeing Morgan using his claw to slide the tiny bloody shard from beneath her skin.

The longer she watched, the more her vision blurred. Her knees buckled.

"I gotcha," his voice rumbled with a growl as he turned her facing him. "Let me stop the bleeding, then you'll be good as new." He lifted her hand then licked her palm.

"Gross!"

Morgan gripped her wrist tight, preventing her from pulling away. "I'm not finished healing you." He ran his tongue over her palm again. His expression reminded Karma of Dani's whenever she bit into a chocolate bar.

Each time Morgan lapped at Karma's wound, it had an odd effect on her.

Red eyes met hers. She swallowed. Her heart stuttered, and her breath hitched as desire flared through her. Since when were glowing eyes and fangs a turn on?

Morgan's nostrils flared as he ran his tongue over his bloody lips. "Delicious."

His sexy smirk teased his lips again as he eased his hold on her.

As she stepped from his embrace, she stumbled over her own feet.

Morgan caught her before she fell. "You okay?"

"I'm fine." Everything she did screamed klutz. She tipped her head back, realizing how tall Morgan stood. The man was a good foot taller than her. "A little embarrassed." Karma gently pushed from him. "Let me finish washing the dishes."

"We have a dishwasher. Cade, get in here."

Her temper flared. "I can finish washing the dishes. I broke a glass. I didn't slice off a digit. I'm not helpless."

Morgan's black eyebrow arched. "I never said you were, nor have I ever thought it. But, we have a dishwasher, so there was no need for you to hurt yourself. My granny's cast iron does not get put in there."

"Dude, you're about out of those little tablet thingies." Cade strolled past them again, heading toward the door. "I'm outta here." He pulled his shirt over his head, then dropped his pants, turning into a massive cougar.

Heat once again rushed to her face, and she turned away from Cade's bare butt. She wasn't a prude, but it felt wrong seeing a naked man other than Morgan.

"Cade!" Morgan glared at the cat. Karma swore the beast was laughing at Morgan. He flung open the door. "Don't get shot."

Cade snorted, or at least it sounded like he did to her anyway.

"Gonna kill him." Morgan snagged her hand, tugging her forward. "Come on, I have something for you." He led her to the couch then motioned for her to sit.

"If you're going to take a knee and put a ring on it, forget it. It's not even been a day yet."

"So tomorrow, huh? I can put a ring on it tomorrow?" Morgan's rich laugh rang in the air as he strode down the hall.

"No," she called after him, then instantly sat up straight, recognizing the two boxes Morgan carried. "They're for me, right?"

Morgan's eyes twinkled. "You know they are." He handed her the phone and computer. "Seeing yours are gone. We still need to get up with Percy about your wallet."

Decisions, decisions which should she open first? She couldn't wait to get online, but it would be quicker to set up the phone, then she could set up the computer. Phone first, then the laptop. Yep, she had a plan.

Karma opened the phone box, inhaling the new phone smell she so loved. Her hands trembled with excitement as she removed the top of the line phone she'd planned on buying. This was better than Christmas.

The pin of reality burst her happy little balloon of joy. "I need to activate it."

"Percy takes care of everything before he sends them out. For some reason, he only trusts us to insert the SD cards if they're still functional." Morgan motioned to the phone. "You have unlimited everything, by-the-way."

Her happy little balloon of joy re-inflated.

"If I'd known giving you a new phone was a form of foreplay, I'd done it sooner."

"You don't give up. Do you?"

"Mmm. No. No, I don't." Again with his sexy smirk.

Karma mentally rolled her eyes then called Melody. Like always, her call went to voicemail. "Hey, Melody. It's me. Just calling to see how you're doing. I have a new phone, so this is the new number. Talk to you later." Exhaling, she ended the call.

"You okay, beautiful?" Morgan whispered. His concerned tone warmed her.

"I'm good. Melody is probably weeding or something. She never answers but always calls back. I hope she listens to the voice mail, seeing this is a new number."

"What is it? I need to add it to mine." Morgan fished out his phone.

She tapped the screen, went into the settings, then rattled off the number. "Now, let me call my bank." She made the call, then listened to the recording, not believing what she heard. *Well, she-it.* She kept pressing numbers until she could actually speak to a human.

Morgan strode outside. She guessed he sensed her desire for privacy.

"I can understand my accounts being frozen. But what do you mean, I'm dead?"

Karma didn't know how long she'd gone around and around with the other person on the line, but by the time she finally hung up, she'd accomplished absolutely nothing. It wasn't even lunchtime, but already the day had been a rollercoaster. What else was going to happen? Lord have mercy! She knew better than to ask. "Curse Psycho to freakn' Hell! You slimy little bastard! You have messed with the wrong bitch! I will make your life and freakn' afterlife a monetary hell!"

Karma closed her eyes, leaning her head against the back of the couch. She was so going to kill Psycho. She knew it had to be him, especially since he wanted money so bad. She hated scammers, spammers, and assholes!

The seat beside her dipped. She opened her eyes, meeting Morgan's amber glowing orbs.

"Let me give Royce a call. Maybe he can get to the bottom of this." Morgan's voice was thick with his wolf, and his fingernails had turned to black claws.

"Even as good as Percy is, there's nothing to be done. The butts hacked into my accounts, added a note I was deceased, then transferred my money into the account of a beneficiary—an account they created, which they then closed. Funny thing, I never got around to setting up a beneficiary. Which made this all the easier for them." She closed her eyes and slammed her head against the back of the couch, wishing she'd wake up from this nightmare.

The door slammed a second later.

"Karma has contacted her bank. It looks like Whitehall has her wallet." The heavy thud of Morgan's booted feet echoed through the cabin as he paced across the porch. "How is it even possible?"

She pushed aside the curtain and peered out, searching for Morgan. She spotted him leaning against a porch post. His clothes were stretched to their limit. His wolf was about to tear from him once more.

Knowing Morgan needed her, she set the laptop down then went to him.

"What do you mean?" he shouted. "I thought you had everything under control. How could this happen?" He growled, and the phone shattered in his grip. Bits of glass, plastic, and metal rained down onto the worn wood porch.

The unmistakable sound of popping thread told her Morgan would be naked again. She wrapped her arms around his waist, pressing her cheek to the center of his back. "Morgan, breathe."

He shuddered, drawing in a deep breath, then exhaling. Bones popped, and his wolfish form slowly returned to human.

Morgan turned in her arms until she was pressed against his chest. He hugged her tight, resting his chin on her crown. "I can't. I won't lose you."

His words had her heart pounding. Karma clung to him as his words sank deep into her pores, her heart, infusing with her soul. As odd as it sounded, she couldn't lose him either.

~ ~ ~

Morgan clung to her, wishing he could take away her grief. "Don't worry. I will correct this problem one way or another. I promise, beautiful?"

"Just wondering. Why me? They must have drained my account sometime between kidnapping me and my rescue."

"Percy assured me he's on it. Come on, Royce wants to speak with us."

Faint amusement shimmered in Karma's eyes, and the sweet smile he loved so much curved her lips. "You killed your phone. Poor thing didn't deserve to die."

"No, it didn't." He laughed.

"Guess you want the phone you gave me back."

"Nope. I have extras. Come on." He led her back inside, kicking the door shut behind them.

"I hope Melody doesn't think I'm dead."

His wolf howled in his mind so loud the furry bastard gave him a headache. The beast wanted out to comfort their mate.

"I'm sure once she hears your voice, she'll think it was a clerical error."

"Hopefully, you're right."

Morgan lifted the computer lid then powered it on. "Royce wants to video chat."

Percy appeared on the screen. "Lady K, I am so sorry. We will get them, and they will pay for what they did." Percy shifted his attention to someone then back at them. "We'll talk soon," he said, moving out of view.

Royce appeared, occupying the seat Percy had vacated. "It's nice to see you again, Karma. You look good for a dead woman."

She sat ramrod straight, and her lips curved into the same smile Morgan saw his mother get when she thought someone was dumber than dirt. "Mr. Lucard."

"Not so formal, please. Morgan, I see you've gained control of your beast."

"Because of my mate." He didn't keep the wolf from his voice.

"Yes, well. If it is any consolation, Percy is trying to figure out how they got in…Again!" Royce's horns pushed from his forehead.

A soft gasp escaped Karma, but she kept all expression from her face.

"Sorry, but bloody hell, I want to know how this is happening." Royce pinched the bridge of his nose. "With that said, let me explain—"

"Before you start," Karma interrupted. "I need to know, was my kidnapping part of some elaborate plan?"

"Bloody hell! No! Most definitely not," Royce snapped.

Morgan knew Royce could be an ass, but he wouldn't use an innocent for any means. At least not without their full knowledge and willingness.

"Morgan explained to me about humans and Dhampirs and what happens to them when they find out about you." Moisture shimmered in Karma's eyes, but she blinked it away. "I mean, as big as your corporation is, why call me in the first place? Was it because of my friendship with Dani? Then add in the fact, I've been declared dead. You have to admit it is a little suspicious."

The screen split with Percy on one side and Royce on the other.

Percy cleared his throat, drawing their attention as well as Royce's. "Lady K, when Wolfmoon and DuMond Enterprises were initially hacked, I needed help. I needed an accountant I could trust. At first, I assumed the hack was an inside job. Dani assured me of your integrity and sent me your credentials. After working with you, I'd hoped we could bring you into the family when all was said and done.

"I knew how close you were with Danielle Rossi." Percy flicked his attention to Morgan. "I got my wish." He cleared his throat again then pulled on a stiff facade Morgan seldom saw. "*I* knew we would get you back, safe and sound. I wished we'd managed it before any harm came to you.

"As for your wallet when Dani informed me she couldn't find it. I froze all of your accounts, reported your wallet as stolen, but I did not have you declared dead. However, it appears our dear Mr. Copperhead somehow did. I'm going to attempt to undo the damage. Worst case scenario, I'll have you a new identity before morning. Has Morgan given you a new phone?"

"Yes." She grinned, holding up the phone. "He also gave me a new computer."

"Brilliant. I will be honored if you assist me in taking those bloody bastards down once and for all. Both devices have the latest in anti-viral and security software created. In addition, they have software to alert us if an outside source tries to track your whereabouts. However, as we've learned, no software is infallible."

Royce nodded. "This should have never happened with our precautions."

"Precautions, Royce?" Adrenaline driven rage filled Morgan's blood. "They got around our *precautions* once before and got her. They beat the holy hell out of her then planned on killing her."

Karma squeezed his leg, letting him know she was there, and his anger bled away.

"I know," Royce droned.

For the first time, Morgan noticed the dark circles under Royce's eyes. "You do realize Whitehall may not be working alone."

"I know. To be honest with you, Morgan, if it was up to me, I'd rip strips of flesh from each of the bloody Councilmen's hides then gut them while they still breathed, finally showing mercy by tearing out their still beating hearts."

"So, tell us how you really feel," Karma muttered.

Royce chortled, pointing at Karma. "I like her. Sadly, I can't kill them. I have to show the clans I will protect them, even from their worthless family members." Royce exhaled, his attention going to someone else in the room, and held up his hand. "Mummy said bad dreams woke you from your kip, son."

A small boy wearing an Iron Man sweatshirt scurried forward, climbing onto Royce's lap. With thumb in mouth, Michael wiggled until his head rested on Royce's shoulder. "Monsters were after me, Papa."

"Monsters won't get you, son. I won't let them." Royce raised his brows, staring at the screen. "I won't let them get to you either, Karma. Morgan, I have Ryder and his team on stand-by, along with Declan's group. I've also notified Edgar, though he's working on another project.

"Once I turn you over to Percy, I'll call Magnus and fill him in on this development. I'm sure Danielle Rossi will have something to say about Karma's death. Anything else before I turn you over to Percival?"

"Yes," Morgan replied. "When I deal with Whitehall, should I expect repercussions?"

Royce shook his head. "The cleaners are on standby. Just don't create an explosion seen from space. One was hard enough to explain."

Royce's side of the screen went black, then Percy's smiling face filled the entire screen.

"Lady K, before we get started, it seems it's easier to create you another identity than to resurrect you. I also went ahead, changing your last name to Wolfe. I hope I wasn't too presumptive."

"No. No, you weren't. I never liked my last name anyway," Karma replied. "By the way, why the dark green hair today?"

Morgan's wolf yipped with glee. Their mate shared their name.

"Too many irons in the fire," Percy replied. "I let the color stay on too long."

"Sorry, I asked."

"Don't be, love. On the plus side, it's Viktor's and Hope's favorite color. I've created you a new bank account, so you should be receiving your cards within a few days. They'll be delivered to Wolfmoon."

"Thanks, Percy, but what about my 401K, my business contacts, my social media. Do you know how many pictures of waterfalls I'd pinned on *Pinterest*? I know, lame, right?"

"Sorry to say, but I scrubbed your social media accounts. As for your 401K, don't worry about it. I'll take care of it. I downloaded your client list to an external before erasing your hard drive. Even if they manage to get into your computer, the virus I infected it with will destroy everything. Your information is safe."

"Good. I feel a little better."

"Are you ready to get to work?" The wicked grin on Percy's face shouldn't have frightened Morgan, but it did.

"Yes." Karma squared her shoulders. "Psycho Asshole is the first to pay, followed by Evil Prick."

"Brilliant. Let's see if we can track Lincoln through his human counterpart."

Morgan reached over, covering her hand. "I wish I knew which one was Lincoln Whitehall. From your description, either one could be. The Whitehalls were Southern plantation owners before the war."

"I take it you're talking the civil war," Karma teased.

"Let's see if I can't help," Percy replied.

Karma gasped the instant her screen changed to several photos of Lincoln Whitehall. "That's Evil Prick. He gave me the heebie-jeebies, not the broken bones and bruises."

"Excellent." Percy tapped a few keys, and the photos vanished. "Now, we know the human is more than likely one of Lincoln's underlings. Let's see. These are the humans we know of who work with Whitehall, fitting your description, and have computer knowledge." Percy tapped a few keys, then the monitor went into a split-screen. Photos populated the display to the left of Percy's image. "Tell me if you recognize any of these faces."

"None, so far." Karma's fingers flew across her keyboard. "Let me see what I can find."

The minutes ticked by as Morgan watched Karma. He could tell her concentration was so focused on the screen she wouldn't notice if elephants strolled through the cabin. He was the same way, too, when he went over investments.

An idea formed. Morgan wondered how much it would help. He knew he'd explained to Karma the small amount of blood he took from her, and the amount he'd given her allowed him to see into her mind. If she concentrated on the man, Morgan would know who he had to gut. The downside, if he didn't know the ass, they'd be back to square one.

The phone beeped, causing Karma to jump. "It's Melody."

"Go ahead and answer," Percy replied. "I'll continue searching."

The hair on the back of Morgan's neck rose as he handed her the phone. "Put it on speaker, if you don't mind, please." With his hearing, he could hear both sides of the conversation, but he wanted Percy to listen in also.

The phone rang again. Karma gave a quick nod, answering, "Hey."

"Oh, thank God! Even after hearing your voice, I thought this was a prank," a woman's excited voice filled the room.

"I wish it was. Someone's stolen my identity. So how are you?"

"I'm good. How are *you* Karm? You're not in any trouble, are you?"

Karma cringed, apparently not liking the nickname. "Like I said, Melody. Someone stole my identity and has upended things."

"Did you move because your identity was stolen? Where are you *now*?" Melody demanded in a voice so shrill it hurt his ears.

"Move? Who told you I moved?"

"The officers. They said you ran out on your rent payment."

"What? What officers?"

"I don't know. They were cops."

"My rent's been paid. As for moving, while I was working on this job, my apartment was broken into. Dani had movers go in and pack up my stuff. You know, with what I do, I could pretty much live in hotels."

"So, nothing bad has happened to you?"

"Other than being robbed, I'm good," Karma kept her tone light.

"Where are you right now," Melody insisted.

Karma's brown, wide-eyed gaze slammed into Morgan's. "This isn't like her," she mouthed. "I'm in Oregon."

"Where in Oregon are you?"

Morgan headed toward the kitchen bar, where he kept a pen and pad. He didn't want Karma revealing too much information since they didn't know if Melody was alone or if her phone was tapped. He strode back, scribbling Whaler Bay, Oregon, then turned the pad for her to see.

"I'm in Whaler Bay. Wolfmoon is putting me up."

Morgan fished Cade's phone from his discarded clothes then texted Ryder. From what Karma told Morgan about Melody, this conversation was entirely out of character. Once he finished his message, Morgan scribbled the name of the corporate hotel.

"Where are they putting you up? You're not very forthcoming with information. Don't you want Mateo and me to drive up and visit you? You know, you still haven't actually met him."

Karma scrunched up her face as she read his message then mouthed Japan? "I'm at the Tree Top but will be flying out soon, I don't know when. The company is sending me overseas. I'm either going to Japan or England, not sure yet where or for how long."

"Do you think we could visit before you fly out? Mateo and I could leave now."

Morgan quickly wrote his response. He didn't want to deny Karma a visit from her mother if she wished one, but on the other hand, he didn't want to lead Whitehall to his front door, either.

"It may be better for you to wait until I return. Don't get me wrong, Melody, but why the rush? When I visited you a few weeks ago, you didn't have time for lunch with me, and my visit had been planned. What's going on?"

"Nothing's going on." The woman sounded panicky to Morgan. "Can't a mother simply want to see her daughter before she flies off to who-knows-where? Especially after being told the police were searching for you."

"I'm sorry. Melody, is everything okay with you?"

"Everything is now that I know that you're safe. When can I see you?"

Tears freely ran down Karma's face, tearing at Morgan's heart. He reached for the phone, covering her hand.

"I don't know, Melody. I have to head back to a meeting. I'll call you soon and let you know when we can meet. Bye." Karma ended the call, setting the phone on the couch. "They got to her."

"We don't know that." Morgan drew Karma into his arms, knowing full well she was right. Lincoln somehow had gotten to Melody. Whether they held her against her will or simply tried to get information from her were the questions he needed answered.

"I do. Morgan, I'm scared." He hated the sadness marring Karma's pale and beautiful face.

"I know you are. I texted Ryder. He's on his way to reconnoiter and intervene if necessary. I told him we'd let him know about the human once we figure out who he is. Your mom will be okay. Trust us.

A choked sob escaped her. "Melody might be a hummingbird fluttering from feeder to feeder, but she's still my mother."

Morgan smoothed his hand over Karma's back, wanting to take away her fears. "It sounds to me like the story they told Melody was to rattle information from her. Don't worry until we hear back from Ryder."

"Okay, but why me?" Karma's eyes pleaded. "Why target me?"

"They had your wallet, making you an easy target."

"Sir, if I may," Percy spoke up, causing Karma to jump. "You've given Karma your blood, then perhaps you could see into her mind?"

Her brown eyes snapped up to Morgan's. "See into my mind? What's Percy talking about?"

"Didn't I tell you?" Her arched eyebrows and tight lips said no. Good grief, there should be a handbook for talking to human mates and a checklist to ensure you covered everything.

Morgan might as well pull his tail from between his legs and get it over with. He stroked Karma's cheek, then cupped her chin, encouraging her to look at him. The challenge in her eyes had his wolf howling in appreciation. Their mate was formidable and wouldn't put up with their crap.

"The sharing of blood binds us with the individual allowing us to speak to them telepathically as I did this morning with you. The sharing of blood allows us to access your memories."

Karma opened and closed her mouth. "I don't know what to say."

He rushed on, "Because you are my mate, and we've shared blood, you can also speak and see into my mind. Our mating binds us, heart and soul. I will never block you from my mind. You will always know what I'm thinking if you so choose."

"Morgan," Her soft whisper held so many questions. "explain."

He rested his forehead against hers, drawing in her unique scent. She was his, and he'd kill to keep her safe, but he needed to know who the hell to gut. "Because I gave you my blood, and I've tasted yours, we are tied together, not as strong as when we mate. You're mine, and I'm yours."

"So, Christmas and birthday gifts will suck because you'll know what I buy for you and vice versa."

He crossed his heart. "I solemnly swear never to do that."

"I trust you, but if I don't know who he is, how will we find out if you don't know him?"

Being so close to Karma, he needed to taste her sweetness, to absorb her flavors. He needed to calm his beast. Morgan pressed his lips lightly to Karma's, wanting her to decide whether to deepen the kiss.

She lapped at the seam of his mouth. Morgan eagerly opened for her, drawing from her what he craved.

Karma was his. There was no way he'd ever let her go. Okay, maybe he did sound a little stalkerish.

"Morgan," Percy's tenor resonated in the room. How was it Morgan forgot the man was there?

"What?" He didn't keep the growl from his voice.

"We don't have all day, sir."

When Karma peered up at him, her cheeks were tinged pink. "How do we do this?"

"You just have to think about what happened and imagine their faces. Are you ready?"

Chapter Eight

Was she ready? Was he kidding? The last thing Karma wanted to do was remember the pain she'd endured. While she wanted to erase those events from her mind forever, the men might never be caught if she didn't face her fears. If they were never caught, she'd always be looking over her shoulder and jumping at shadows. "Okay, let's do this."

She closed her eyes, allowing her mind to drift back. In her mind's eye, she was once again strapped to the metal chair and heard the five or six other men traipsing around inside the warehouse.

Psycho Asshole fisted her hair, yanking her head back while a wolf's snarl pulled her from her thoughts.

A rumbling growl vibrated from Morgan as he sat beside her more beast than man. She stared into his glowing amber eyes and dug her fingers into his fur. "I take it, you know Psycho."

Morgan's shirt hung in tatters about his chest, but at least his jeans were still intact. Bones snapped and reshaped as Morgan shifted back, rubbing the back of his head. "Woman, are you trying to snatch me bald?"

"If that's what it takes." The flicker of amusement in his eyes had her laughing. "From your furriness, you don't like Psycho Asshole any more than I do."

"His name's Derrick Canaday," Morgan growled, snatching up Cade's phone, then started texting someone. "But how did he hook up with Whitehall?"

"I might have the answer," Percy eagerly replied. "According to Cade, Zeno contacted Ruby Canaday after seeing an article with a photo of Tiberius. From what Cade said, Zeno paid Ruby for this information. As you know, she repaid him by setting up the appointment with Tristan. I assume Lincoln somehow discovered this and contacted the Canadays. Granted, this is my guess, but considering he's a desperate man."

"I don't see it," Morgan argued. "Zeno's dead. Royce and the Council are looking for Whitehall, so I can't see him having the money to pay the Canadays. Besides, Whitehall hates humans. We're missing something."

"Wait a minute." Something clicked in Karma's mind. "Whitehall was being hunted before my abduction? Okay, this shines a new light on things. If he's smart, he wouldn't be using credit cards. He'd have to use cash or a stolen identity."

Morgan glanced at her, his black eyebrow arched. "Go on."

"He's Dhampir. I assume, with your longevity, you guys have to create new identities, but how hard is it to do?"

"A lot easier than you think," Percy acknowledged, "but it's getting harder with technology. You think he's using a false identity?"

"Yes. If my hunch is right, I think I may know whose." The realization left her reeling. Why hadn't she thought of this before? Money. Psycho had screamed he wanted *his money. His!* "Oh, my gosh! Copperhead666 has to be Canaday!"

"Bloody hell! You're brilliant, Lady K. Simply brilliant!" Percy's praise did wonders for her spirits.

Morgan's left eyebrow rose a fraction. "Explain, please."

"The hacker, I recognized his code as someone who goes by the name Copperhead666. Right before the cavalry arrived to rescue me, Derrick screamed he wanted *his* money back. He has to be the hacker. I can't believe it's taken me until now to think of this. I had it all wrong. I'd thought Copperhead was located overseas somewhere. Oh, this will make it so much easier to get him." She fist-pumped. "Yes! If I'm right, then I bet Copperhead went after the identities of your new hires to get both a new ID and money for Whitehall. *And* I bet when my computer got the blue screen of death, saying I was dead, right before they kicked in my door, he was telling me he'd electronically killed me." The knot in Karma's stomach eased. "This would also explain why he's after me. I've been a slight pain in his ass for five years."

Karma wanted these men locked up where she didn't have to keep looking over her shoulder or checking her bank accounts every second. "Percy, let's cut the head of this snake off."

"Right with you, my dear."

This time Copperhead was going down. Karma pulled the sturdy coffee table closer to her then placed the laptop on it. She typed Derrick butthole Canaday's name into the search bar. Immediately an old news article popped up, with a photo of a younger version of Psycho. Even as a teen, the man had a crazy look in his eyes.

"While you two are doing your thing." A grin spread across Morgan's lips as he ran his thumb over the screen. "I have someone in mind who would be more than happy to deal with Canaday."

Whoever answered Morgan's call grunted.

"Tobias, Derrick Canaday is working with Lincoln Whitehall."

The evilest laugh Karma had ever heard came through the speaker. "Hot fuckin' hell, I'm gonna have some fun."

"Happy hunting." Morgan set the phone on the table then stood.

Percy shook his head. "You called Tobias? I could have sworn Royce said not to destroy the world."

"And I won't. Toby will." Morgan tore the remanence of his shirt off as he headed toward his room. "Give me a second, then we'll go into town for lunch."

Karma would not drool. Would not. She did anyway…just a little.

"Toby will," Percy muttered.

Curious, she asked, "Who's this guy Morgan called? A hitman for the Dhampir?" Karma searched through a few articles, mostly showing Canaday escorting his aunt to social events. She clicked on another link.

Percy chuckled. "Hitman? Funny you should say that. Tobias has a history with the Canadays. What have you discovered?"

"An article on Derrick Canaday. It says he was sent to prison for assault and battery of his cousin. Hmm, he also has a long history of arrest for drug possession. Oh, here's something. He was accused of identity theft, go figure. Hmm, looks like a case of *Affluenza*, seeing his aunt used her wealth and influence to keep bailing him out of trouble."

"I agree with you. The girl he beat up was Niki. She's like yourself, human. She's mated to Tristan, Morgan's middle brother."

"Niki and Tristan Wolfe? Wait a sec. I met them and their children at Megan's and Maggie's birthday party this past summer. Dang, I'm slow. All this time, I never connected Tristan as Morgan's brother."

"I guess it's true about what they say about it being a small world, huh?"

"I guess so." Karma went back to reading. If Niki's human, then her grandfather would be human, as well. "Do you think it's wise to send an old man after this guy?"

"You know the older the Dhampir, the stronger, right?"

"Ah, no." Something else Morgan *forgot* to tell her. She scanned more of the article, looking for anything to help them find this guy.

"Tobias is probably the oldest Dhampir living."

Karma tore her eyes from what she was reading and peered at Percy. "You said he was Niki's grandfather. Did he adopt her or something?"

"Or something."

"Getting information from you is like pulling hen's teeth."

"Let's say their relationship is unique."

Karma continued searching for anything on the Canadays. "Grandfather then, so he's what a few hundred years old?" Hmm, bingo. "Percy, I've found a photo of Evil Prick talking to Psycho."

"Are you sure?"

"Yup. Even with my crappy vision, I'd know those faces anywhere." She enlarged the photo, which didn't help much because of the grainy quality of the picture. As she studied the image, chills inched down her spine. "Dani and I were at this same event. We could have been standing a few feet away from the two."

"Let me sign off and speak with Royce. He's going to want to know about this. In the meantime, don't go off alone."

"Thanks, Percy, for making me feel much better."

"Sorry, love." He signed off. The article she'd been reading filled the screen.

Morgan strolled back into the room then dropped down beside her. His knee brushed against hers as he pulled the protective film from another new phone.

Being this close to him made it hard to concentrate. "You got a small phone store tucked away in one of your rooms somewhere?" Karma teased, pointing to the device.

"Maybe." Morgan chuckled. Still smiling, he set the phone down and faced her. "You don't want to go out, do you?"

"Not really. Even though Percy's signed off to talk to Royce, I'd like to stay here and find everything I can on Psycho. I may not be able to track Whitehall, but Derrick has a fascinating social media account."

"Okay, sandwiches for lunch. What would you like for dinner, seafood, home cooking, or Chinese take-out?"

She clicked on another link. "Whatever you want, I'm not picky."

Morgan reached across, closing the laptop and pissing her off. "I don't think you want raw venison. Do you? Because my wolf's craving fresh kill. Now, what would you like to eat?"

Karma merely stared tongue-tied as her anger ebbed. It hadn't occurred to her Morgan would eat fresh kill. "If you don't mind cooking, then how about we stay here?"

"Beautiful, I'll always cook for you." The smile on Morgan's face gave her a glimpse of what he'd looked like as a teen. Dang, he was hot. "Next question, buffalo, deer, or cow? I'll place an order with the local butcher."

"Since Wolfie is jonesing for some venison, let's have some deer."

"Wolfie?" He stared at her. Morgan's lips twitched before he burst out laughing. "Usually, I have a better stocked freezer, but I haven't been here for several months. It looks like the butcher has duck and turkey. Do you want me to place an order for foul?"

"I've never had duck, so sure." She leaned over, looking at the website with him. She couldn't believe the amount of meat Morgan had ordered. "Are you planning on an apocalypse or something?"

"It's not a lot." He laughed. "Okay, our order will be delivered in two hours."

She wasn't fooled by his innocent look and laughed along with him. "I get it. Hungry as a wolf. Let me show you what I found."

"What?" Morgan's warm breath teased her neck, sending a shiver through her.

She peered at him as he lowered his head. Karma couldn't help it. The second the soft touch of Morgan's lips met hers, she molded herself to his hard body. The man was as addicting as a drug.

Karma snuggled against Morgan. Alone, at last, she wondered if the delivery guy wouldn't mind taking the scenic route?

Morgan groaned, then nipped her bottom lip. "You can't think things like that, beautiful unless you want me to carry you to our room."

His words or at least the intensity of his gaze should have frightened her, but she wasn't scared. If anything, it turned her on. "Think things like what?" There was no way Morgan knew what she'd thought.

"You, wanting the delivery guy to take the scenic route. I can cancel the order if you'd like." His eyes glowed again, looking more red than amber.

"You were in my head again?"

"Well, in a way, yes. I heard your thoughts."

"Wait. What? You can *hear* my thoughts?" Surprisingly, she wasn't mad, nor did it make her feel violated. Hell, she'd already flung open her closet door, revealing all her skeletons.

"We're bound together. Not as tightly as we will be once we're mated."

"Bound together? Mind explaining?"

"If you concentrate, you should be able to hear my thoughts now and have a sixth sense of where I am. These abilities will be stronger after we mate. You'll also be able to sense my family and hear their thoughts. It'll be like the background noise of a radio turned down low. Once you get used to it, you won't even realize it."

"I take it your family will be able to hear mine as well?"

"Yup."

"Let's see, so far, I know you can turn into a wolf, you drink blood, can see into my mind, hear my thoughts, and start fires just like that." She snapped her fingers.

"You mean like this?" The fireplace roar to life.

Karma jumped. She should have expected it, but she jumped anyway. Maybe someday, she'd be used to Morgan's superpowers. "Yes, like that. Am I leaving anything out?"

"I'm an amazing cook and…" He lowered his head and lightly brushed his lips against hers. "I've been told I'm an amazing lover, guaranteed to make you come a million times."

Great, let's hear about all the previous conquests he'd banged. Was she jealous? You betcha. "Oh, yes, I did forget something. Conceited."

"Ouch." Pink tinged his bronzed face. "Sorry." Morgan's shoulders slumped slightly. He sat back against the couch, putting way too much space between them. "What did you and Percy find?"

She eyed Morgan, not liking the guarded apprehension she saw in his eyes. He'd said she could see into his mind. Karma concentrated.

She did it! She slipped into Morgan's head.

Her excitement died. A dark whirlwind of faces and events had her fleeing.

"I'm sorry." Morgan pushed his hand through his thick hair, causing a few strands to poke up. "I'm just…I'm…" Morgan rested his head on the back of the couch, staring up at the ceiling. "This is harder than I thought."

"What is?" Karma angled herself, so she could see him better. Gone was the confident, cocky businessman.

"Getting you to like me."

"Stop trying so hard, and be you."

He rolled his head toward her, meeting her eyes. "All my life, I knew my mate was out there somewhere. I never actively searched for her. I figured I'd find her someday. I didn't care what my mate looked like or who she was, I knew she'd be perfect, and you are.

"Four months ago, I started falling in love with a voice." A wistful smile curved his lips. She wanted to lean over and kiss him. "From the very beginning, Karma, you made me laugh. I looked forward to our phone calls every night. All the added accounts I'd asked you to go through were ploys, so I could keep you on the phone a bit longer."

She reached over, smoothing his hair back into place. "As crazy as it sounds, for the amount of time we've known each other, I like you more than a little, Morgan. I like you a heck of a lot. However, you're going to have to understand I'm still coming to terms with your superpower paranormal stuff."

"Superpowers, huh?" Amusement rang in Morgan's voice, and his cocky grin returned.

"Get the grin off your face. There's a lot I need to know and understand before we get horizontal."

"How about vertical?"

"That, too. There are also a few things you need to know about me, even though I think I've already spewed my life story."

"I—"

She waved her hand, cutting him off. "For starters, I'm self-conscious with a hell of a lot of insecurity. When you tell me you've been *told* how great a lover you are. I hear you've banged so many women while waiting around for your mate you're just shy of being a manwhore. It's like me telling you I give the best blowjobs in the entire Northern Hemisphere."

A growl rumbled from him.

"I've got the feeling you didn't like hearing me say that."

"Names," Morgan snarled.

"Yeah—no." She ignored the fur sprouting from his forearms and the fiery glow in his eyes. The fangs, however, fascinated her. How could things so long and sharp not hurt his mouth?

"Mine," he snapped. Morgan's upper lip quivered. "When we mate, we will know everything about each other, including who we've slept with."

She patted his chest. His possessiveness was creepy in a sexy way. "The point is, I've had lovers, you've had lovers, and as long as they don't cause trouble, we're good. Meaning you don't compare me to *Bunny*, and I don't bring up Mad Max."

"Mad Max?"

Karma rolled her eyes—twice for good measure.

"You roll your eyes at me a lot, or do you have a nervous twitch?"

"Only when it comes to bull. Look, I don't get to electronically destroy your exes," she poked him in the chest, "You don't get to kill mine."

Morgan grinned and not in a smirky-sexy way either.

"You can't send Cade or anyone else to do the deed either."

"Killjoy." Morgan rolled out his bottom lip.

"You'll get over it." She giggled, patting his less furry arm. "So, what else haven't you told me?"

"We have supersonic hearing."

"Wonderful. Then I don't have to strain my voice shouting like I do with Melody. I swear the woman has selective hearing." The thought of Melody had Karma glancing at her phone. Maybe she should call her mother back. After all, she'd been concerned.

"Don't worry, beautiful." Morgan hooked his pinky with hers. "As soon as Ryder puts eyes on her, he'll call."

"Back in my head again?"

"Nope. I see the worry in your eyes. Ryder's good. He'll message us when he knows something." Morgan motioned toward the laptop. "What did you find?"

"This photo of Psycho and Evil. It's a recent photograph taken several months ago."

Morgan clicked on the image, enlarging it. "I was supposed to attend this event but didn't. I can't remember if Magnus attended."

"He didn't, but Dani and I did. She persuaded me to go with her so she wouldn't have to do it alone. I agreed and flew in."

"Let's see if there are other photos." Morgan clicked through the article.

"On the way to the event, Dani hit me up about working with you on the embezzlement. Small world, huh? Knowing what I do about you, is it possible Whitehall overheard Dani and me talking? I know I told her about the apartment I had in San Francisco. Do you think that's how they knew where to find me?"

"I don't know. If I hadn't blown off the event, you and I would have met months ago."

"Wait a sec. You blew off the event?"

"Maybe." Morgan smirked, stretching out his arm for her to snuggle against him. "The main reason Magnus is the CEO is I hate crowds. I hate business and cocktail parties where I have to pretend to like brown-nosing idiots who think one plus one equals eleven."

"So, tell me how you really feel." She tipped her face up, noting the twitch in Morgan's jaw.

He exhaled, hugging her tighter. "I can explain pie charts and trends. I can tell our investors how much our companies have made. What products we should invest in, and the importance of checks and balances in spending. Numbers always follow an unwavering set of rules. But dealing with people...I feel like an idiot whenever I have to attend a cocktail party. I hate having to stand around, making small talk. It seems I always get tongue-tied."

The abacus of her heart perked up. "Did you say checks and balances in spending?"

He nodded.

"I think I'm in love."

"If I recite the federal tax codes to you, will it get me in your bed quicker?" Morgan jiggled his brows.

"I'm not telling. A girl has to have some secrets."

"Let's find out, U.S. Code 26 Subchapter A—"

Karma hushed him the only way she knew how. She kissed him, pressing her lips to his, then moaned when Morgan slanted his mouth and opened for her.

His tongue dueled with hers in a slow sensual dance as he gently reclined her.

His kiss turned challenging, demanding, arousing her.

The chiming of a phone broke through her foggy mind, and she pushed against Morgan.

"They'll call back." His lips brushed against hers as he spoke.

The phone dinged this time, and she stiffened.

"Why do I feel you're not into this?" Between each word, Morgan planted light kisses to her lips, cheek, then her forehead. He rolled to his side, grabbing the phone from the table.

"What if it's about Melody?" Karma sat up, noticing somehow while they were kissing, Morgan had unbuttoned her cardigan. Dang, she hadn't noticed his fast fingers.

He swiped his finger across the phone screen. "Ryder sent a text. No signs of either Whitehall or Canaday. Ryder encountered two of Whitehall's people. They've been dealt with. Melody doesn't seem to be in any distress. He also said he'll leave a few trusted men to keep her under surveillance."

Hearing the good news lifted a massive weight from Karma's shoulders. "Good, I'm glad she's safe and not in the clutches of Evil Prick or Psycho. What do you mean by dealt with?" She re-buttoned her top as she stared at Morgan. "Did Ryder question them? Did they tell him where to find Whitehall? How did Ryder have your new number?"

"When I powered up the phone, I put my SIM card in it, transferring my number to the new phone."

"You didn't answer my first question. I take it Whitehall's men aren't breathing anymore."

Chapter Nine

Morgan didn't move when Karma pushed from him. He sniffed the air, then relaxed some not scenting fear from her. However, if she ran, she wouldn't make it to the front door. His wolf would make sure of it.

"Keep in mind, we're the good guys," he informed her.

Karma brought her feet up on the seat, putting more space between them, but the action put him at ease. His wolf, however, stayed alert, ready to give chase.

She exhaled dramatically as she rested her chin on her knees. "You know when you start a conversation off like that, generally doesn't give someone a sense of security. Also, I know you're one of the good guys."

Morgan stared deep into Karma's vibrant chocolate eyes. "If you run, I will chase you."

She rolled her eyes, motioning to herself. "Does this body look like it belongs to a runner?"

He let his gaze slowly roam over her lush, curvy form. He'd love to strip her bare then savor every inch of her body as he paid tribute to each of her perfect curves. A low growl rumbled from him. "Every womanly inch of you makes me feel that much more a man. Beautiful, you have the body of a goddess."

"You say the cutest things, but drooling like you are, kinda ruins the sentiment." Her pink tongue slid across her bottom lip, causing him to groan. "Your eyes are glowing again, too. I hope this doesn't mean you're going to eat me."

"Such a loaded question." The woman was flirting with him. Morgan breathed deep, drawing in the scent of her musk. His wolf growled for them to claim her.

Karma snapped her fingers in front of his nose. "Focus. Did those men attack Ryder? Did they pose a threat to Melody? Stupid question. Forget I asked. If they worked with Evil or Psycho, they weren't at the farm to find out how Melody grew her tomatoes. Okay. Answer me this, before Ryder *dealt* with them, did he at least find out some useful information?"

Well, hell. Morgan had expected some reaction from her, just not this.

Karma stared at him. "Well?"

Morgan didn't have to be asked twice. With a sigh, he picked up his phone then called Ryder instead of texting the kid.

"What?" Ryder answered on the first ring.

"You're on speaker."

"Ooo-kay. What's up?"

"My mate wants to know if you got any information from Whitehall's men before you dealt with them?"

"I didn't have a chance. The second we apprehended them, the cowards committed suicide. I guess they never removed Zeno's lethal capsules implanted in them."

"Zeno's dead," Morgan reminded the kid.

"Cut the head off the hydra, and two more takes its place."

"True."

"You're sure Melody was fine," Karma asked.

"She was, and so was the man with her."

"You're sure the man's Mateo and not someone forcing her to behave? I have a photo of them. Crap. No, I don't. It was on my computer. Oh, wait a minute, Percy said he saved all my stuff."

"Not a problem, Karma. This is Karma, right?"

"Yes, sorry, I should have introduced myself."

"You're fine. Percy sent me a photo, but I also took one. Let me forward it to you, then you can verify the people are your mum and her friend."

Morgan's phone pinged, and Karma opened the photo. "That's Melody and Mateo. You're sure they were fine? You're sure?"

"You have my word. Anything else?"

"No. Thank you, and thank you for rescuing me."

"You'll have to thank Morgan. He's the one who sent us in. By the way, Morgan. You should know, the men were dressed as cops."

"I figured as much since Melody said cops visited her. Thanks for everything, Ryder." Morgan ended the call, setting the phone on the coffee table. He didn't like how this was playing out. Lincoln wanted Karma, probably for her knowledge as an accountant or her computer skills. Either way, it looked as if he would stop at nothing to get to her.

"Hey, you're growling again."

"I'm pissed." He laced his fingers with hers, needing the calming effect of her touch. "I will protect you and keep you from harm."

"I know you will." Karma's stomach rumbled. "Sorry."

"No need to apologize. I'm hungry, too." The all too familiar chill ran down Morgan's back, and he pushed from the couch. He knew they'd be here today. "We have company."

"Do your superpowers tell you who?" Amusement flickered in Karma's eyes as she met his gaze.

"Yep, something else I forgot to tell you. We can sense others of our kind." He opened the door, and the aroma of food made his mouth water.

"Cool, so no surprise drop-ins from family. So, who's here?"

"Magnus and Dani."

Karma bolted from the couch, rushing out the open door. She nearly slammed into Magnus as he strode in, carrying an arm full of take-out.

"Dani!" Karma shouted over Magnus's, "We brought lunch."

The two women squealed like little girls as they hugged. Hell, his wolf recoiled from the high pitched sound.

Dani leaned back, still holding onto Karma. "Oh, my gosh, let me look at you! No bruises, but your nose is a little crooked."

Karma instantly touched her nose. Her smile slipped.

No one made Karma feel bad. "There's nothing wrong with her nose. It's cute," Morgan growled, slipping his arm around her waist.

"Whoa, what big teeth you have?" Dani's eyes widened and she eased back.

Magnus stepped in front of her, ready to defend his mate. "Remember what we talked about?"

"Yeah, but," Anxiety filled Danielle's voice. "why's he snarling at me? He should be pissed at the bastards who used K as a freakn' punching bag."

"Karma's gorgeous," Morgan growled again. "As for Whitehall and Canaday, they're dead men walking. They don't know it yet."

"Stop it." Karma fisted Morgan's fur. "Dani didn't mean anything. She was stating a fact."

His growl grew louder with each passing second. "I felt your hurt."

Karma dug her fingers deeper into his fur, tugging a little harder. "Not from her words, but from the memory of being hit."

Dani cocked her hip, glaring at Morgan. "Maybe for a mating gift, we should get you a fido-shock."

"What? No." Karma went up on her tip-toes, pressing a kiss to Morgan's chin. The action immediately calmed his loco beast. "Besides, it's going to be a while before we marry."

Dani cackled. "Keep telling yourself that."

"I will!" Karma rolled her eyes, "You crazy witch, Morgan and I haven't even known each other a full day yet."

"I give y'all a week."

"Changing the subject. Do I smell Chinese?"

"We swung into Whaler Bay on the way here. Good thing you don't live that far out of town. Anyway, Magnus said we needed to bring a peace offering for coming on such short notice." Dani hooked her arm with Karma's, yanking her away from Morgan. "You know Magnus wouldn't even stop for coffee. I mean, seriously, the man knows I turn into a homicidal maniac when I'm not caffeinated. I hate flying without my coffee."

"You flew?"

Dani frowned. "Do you honestly think I could have survived a car trip without coffee? Girl, please."

Morgan snarled at having his mate snatched from him.

"I hope I wasn't this bad." Magnus chuckled.

"This bad about what?"

"You, snarling so much." Magnus laughed even harder. "When do you plan on mating her?"

Morgan blew out a sigh, answering, "If it were up to me, I'd throw all of you out." Hell, he couldn't wait to bind himself to Karma. Just being with her kept his loco wolf calm. Well, calmer than usual. But he and the beast were in agreement, the more people around Karma, the safer she'd be.

"Come on, let's have lunch. By the way, Ryder contacted me." Opening his mind, Morgan met Magnus's eyes, not wanting to verbally rehash everything.

"We'll talk." Magnus stole a shrimp from Dani's plate, earning him a smack on the hand. He kissed her cheek as he took another.

Morgan couldn't wait until Karma was his, not because of the mating urge, but because she was gorgeous. She was beautiful, intelligent, witty, everything he wanted in a mate. How had he gotten so lucky?

As he ate, he observed the interaction between Karma and Dani. The two were actually finishing each other's sentences.

Magnus stole the last sushi roll from Dani's plate. "Morgan, you're awful quiet. Cat got your tongue?"

Dani peered at her empty plate. "K, do you see what I have to put up with?" Dani huffed, waving her chopsticks around like a friggin wand.

"Lord have mercy, girl, you're gonna put someone's eye out."

"Better than shooting someone in the ass." Dani crowed, pointing her chopsticks at Karma. "Was this before or after he," She flicked her wrist, pointing her chopstick at Morgan. "turned into a doggie?"

"Wolf," Karma corrected, with a thin thread of warning in her voice, or had Morgan imagined it? "It was an accident. The rifle slipped, discharging when it hit the floor. I was so frightened I'd killed him."

"Naw, bullets just piss them off." Dani waved her chopsticks again. "You have to stake 'em and cut off their heads if you want to kill them. The best thing, you don't have to worry about getting rid of the body, vacuum 'em up, and you're done."

"Good! Too bad Copperhead is human." Karma held up her hand. "Sorry, I don't mean to sound like a homicidal maniac, but they kidnapped me, beat the crap out of me, tried to blow me up, and now they've electronically declared me dead. I really hate freakn' assholes."

The chopsticks fell to the floor as Dani grabbed Karma's hand. "Everything will be alright now. We know who they are, and they will be dealt with." Dani slipped from the barstool then pulled Karma into a hug. "Come on, the guys can clean up while we catch up."

"Go on, beautiful." Morgan bussed Karma's cheek. "We've got this."

"If you're sure?" She brushed his lips with hers then joined Dani on the couch.

"Only a day, and you're already playing kissy-face." Dani beamed. "Come on, K, and let me fill you in on how lucky you are."

Morgan carried the women their drinks. Seeing how close they were, he knew he'd be spending a lot more time with Dani and Magnus than he did with his own family.

"Thank you." Staring at Dani, Karma took her glass from him. "Lucky? Right now, I don't feel lucky."

"You're alive, aren't you?"

"True."

"And something you may not realize, you've scored in the I got my forever family. I mean, girlfriend, you now have a ton of brothers, a new cool sister. I know you're going to love Miranda. You got along fabulously with Tristan and Niki when you met them at the girls' birthday party, and to top it off, you got yourself a mother who no one in their right mind will ever mess with."

A sense of pride welled in Morgan the longer he listened to Dani brag about his family.

"You mean in-laws."

"Um, no." Dani flicked her wrist in the air. He swore if someone bound her hands, the woman wouldn't be able to speak. "Because of the blood tie, you'll have a connection to all of Morgan's family. Didn't he explain it to you?"

~ ~ ~

"He did." Karma set her drink down. She loved Dani like a sister, thus the reason for her heartache. "I'm still trying to process everything, including Melody. Whitehall and Canaday sent men dressed as police officers to talk to her. Can you believe it? Ryder contacted us shortly before you arrived to assure me Melody was okay."

"I wouldn't worry about Melody," Dani snorted, picking up her tea glass. "The woman is a dilettante, pretending to be whatever the man she's with is interested in. I'm surprised she's stayed with this guy for as long as she has."

"True, but how did they know where to find her?" That concerned Karma the most. "I didn't have her address written down. I didn't have her number or any number saved on my phone. As far as any of my social media accounts go, Melody never befriended me."

"K, how do you find things out about people? You Google them. There can't be that many Peamoors. Besides, nowadays, when you Google someone, you can find out possible relations to people. *I* can see how they found her."

"You're right, but still…Why go to Melody in the first place? Never mind. Stupid question. They were probably trying to see if she knew where I was."

"I know I'm right, Karma. I mean, even as careful as we are, things still get leaked. It's getting harder to keep the Dhampir's secret."

Karma drew in a deep breath, trying to silence the nagging voice in the back of her mind, the one demanding she question Dani about whether or not she planned to end their friendship.

Karma realized the Dhampir had to keep their secret. Humans had a tendency to hate anything they didn't understand. Look at the many wars waged over the differences in religion, never mind how some viewed different races or sexual orientations. She'd hate to think what would happen if the world found out about the Dhampir. But the idea Dani thought so little about their relationship she would have simply ended it was a physical vice around Karma's heart.

"You're awful quiet. What's up?" Dani smiled, eyeing her curiously. "I can tell somethings bothering you." Her friend knew her all too well.

"Just trying to process everything."

"Like?" Dani leaned forward, jerking her head toward Morgan. "I've known him all my life. He's a pretty good guy."

"I know he is." Karma glanced toward the kitchen, seeking out Morgan. It shouldn't take them this long to clean up. It appeared he and Magnus were involved in their own conversation, probably discussing business.

"Then what's the problem? Are you worried about Morgan drinking your blood during sex? 'Cause if you are, let me tell you, you'll have the best O of your life." Dani shuddered as if she'd had one thinking about it.

Remembering Morgan's red eyes and fangs, Karma crossed her legs, squeezing her thighs together at the thought of Morgan drinking her blood. "No, it doesn't bother me. I find his otherworldly side kinda sexy. I know, weird, huh?"

"No, not really. So, you don't have a problem drinking his blood?" Dani continued.

"Wait. What?" Karma flicked her attention to Morgan. He and Magnus were still engrossed in their conversation. "I can't remember if he mentioned it to me. Morgan may have, but Dani, I'm still trying to process everything. Give me time." Why couldn't Dani leave well enough alone? "I'm fine. Trust me." Now wasn't the time to get into it with her.

"Karma. I know you. You are not fine. We haven't ever kept secrets from each other, so tell me what's eating you."

"Excuse me," she snapped. Not kept secrets? That was a bald-faced lie, and Dani knew it. "So when were you going to tell me about the Dhampir, Dani? When? Or were you simply going to toss our friendship out the window? What were you going to do if I wasn't Morgan's mate, have someone erase my memory? Answer me that."

Dani flushed slightly but kept her features deceptively composed. "You're Morgan's mate, so it's a non-issue."

"Non-issue?" Karma didn't like the higher pitch to her voice. She would not get mad. That was a joke, she already had. This was her best friend. Karma drew in a calming breath. "You're right. I'm hurt you kept this from me along with the idea you and…your entire family would have cut me from your lives." She blinked against the burning in her eyes. It was the truth. Karma felt closer to Dani and her family than she did her own. Heck, since she and Dani first met, the Rossis never forgot Karma's birthday. Too bad she couldn't say the same about her own mother.

"It's not that I didn't want to tell you," Dani rushed out. "I couldn't. I couldn't risk my children or my mate."

"Couldn't risk—What?" Karma choked on the emotions assaulting her. "You thought I would blab it to TMZ or call the local paper? Seriously?" Karma stared down at Dani, daring her to deny the fact she hadn't trusted her.

Dani gasped. "You don't understand. You don't have a family needing protection."

Dani's words cut deep. "I can't even breathe the same air as you right now." It was true. Karma didn't have a family anymore. Maybe this was the reason she tried so hard to forge a relationship with Melody.

"Karma, wait." Morgan caught her by the arm.

She jerked free of him, flinging open the door. She had to escape before she said something she could never take back.

It'd stopped raining, leaving a dark gray sky. She hurried past the fire pit, nearly tripping over the huge cougar stretched out in her way.

Cade sprung to his feet, snarling at her.

"Leave me alone," she snarled back then continued toward the beach.

"Karma!" Morgan shouted behind her.

She reached the steps as a delivery van stopped in front of the cabin. Probably the butcher bringing Morgan's order. Good, at least he wouldn't be following her.

The rain had stopped, but a biting cold wind blew off the ocean. Karma shivered, continuing down the beach. She couldn't go back until she analyzed everything. No, not everything, just why Dani lied.

Karma exhaled. Dani hadn't lied. She hadn't shared her knowledge of the Dhampir. If Karma dwelled on the facts, not knowing about the Dhampir wasn't what bothered her. Nope. The fact someday Dani would have simply vanished from Karma's life was what hurt. Plus, the fact Dani hadn't trusted her best friends, or at least Karma had thought she'd been, and therein lay the crux of the problem. Had everything they shared been her pathetic need of wanting someone, anyone to like her? She was such a loser.

They'd shared everything, clothes, dorm room, food, secrets. Hell, Karma knew when Dani lost her virginity to Magnus, and Dani knew when Karma lost hers to Mad Max, asshole-extraordinaire. Karma picked up a stone, hurling it at the ocean as she pictured Max's sneering face. Life lesson, number quadrillion. *Wonder where the asshole is today?*

Dani had been there for Karma, patching up her battered self-esteem and getting her over her first heartache. Hell, Dani had always been there. She was Karma's personal cheerleader.

She tossed another stone. This time yesterday, Karma woke up in a strange man's bed. Strange was putting it mildly. The man was a friggin' vampire. Or was he a werewolf? More importantly, was she in a coma somewhere and this a crazy dream? She bet Alice's Wonderland adventure wasn't this crazy, even with the March Hare and Queen of Hearts. Karma sat on a log then pinched herself. "Ouch! Nope, not in a coma."

Movement in her periphery had her groaning. "I want to be alone."

Morgan plopped down beside her. "At one point in my life, I wanted to be a blue-eyed white man. Guess what, you don't always get what you want."

"Fine." She stood and took a step before he looped his arm around her waist. "Let me go."

He pulled her down on his lap. "Stop fidgeting." He tightened his hold. "I'll let you go after you answer my question."

She glared at him. "I don't feel like answering anything right now."

He grinned, and his white teeth contrasted nicely against his bronze skin. "I'm not letting you go until you do."

The darn man wasn't showing any signs of relenting. "Fine. What's your question?"

"At what point in your relationship with Dani would it had been appropriate for her to tell you about the Dhampir without you thinking she was making fun of you?"

Karma lifted her chin, meeting his shimmering amber gaze head-on. "To be honest, I don't know of any particular time." Morgan opened his mouth, but she forged on, "But it doesn't rectify Dani didn't trust me and would have simply vanished from my life," Karma's voice cracked, and she fought against her tears. "As if I didn't matter." Her anguish shattered the last threads of her control.

"Oh, beautiful." Morgan ran his thumb under her eye, catching a tear. "I know for a fact, you mean so much to Dani. The second you were taken, she went nuts."

"Then why didn't she trust me?"

"It's more about how she was raised."

Karma wasn't about to sit there listening to him any longer. "I've heard what you had to say. Let me go."

"No. Not until you've listened to everything I have to say. Dani grew up among us. Her family has served the Dhampir, mainly the DuMonds, for seven or eight generations."

"Eight," Dani whispered. "Don't tell was drilled into me for as long as I remembered." Tears shimmered in her eyes as she leaned heavily against Magnus. "I attended Peter's and Jean's funeral."

Karma looked at Morgan. The names were familiar.

"My brother and his mate," he explained. "They were murdered, not by humans, but by Dhampirs who wanted Shelby."

Dani sniffed. "It was the first Dhampir funeral my grandmother could remember. I kept thinking during the service, what if it happened to Magnus and me?

"You watch shows where the vampires are hunted, and mutant children are turned into lab rats. Everyone thinks it's okay because it's make-believe, but it's not. Can you imagine what would happen to the twins if some nutcase got ahold of them? K, I know it hurt finding out this way, but trust me. I was working on a way to tell you. Percy and I had broached the idea to Royce, so Magnus and I could tell you."

"Then, I got kidnapped."

Dani nodded. "Royce agreed you should be brought into the family immediately."

Magnus hugged Dani to him, kissing her crown. "Karma, I had my suspicions about you and Morgan being mates. Every time he came into my office, he stared at Dani's and my wedding photo. I found where he'd copied it and hid it in his desk. I would have been pissed, but you see, Karma, he'd cropped the photo, so it was only of you. Then when he couldn't keep control of his wolf .." Magnus shrugged. "I told Dani not to worry anymore about telling you. I knew everything would work out."

"K, are we good?" An almost imperceptible note of pleading shown on Dani's face.

Chapter Ten

Soft feminine whispers and giggles woke him. Morgan stretched, thankful Karma and Dani had resolved their issues last night. Magnus had been right. The women were closer than sisters.

Morgan scrubbed his hands over his face and stretched again, breathing in the wonderful aroma of freshly brewed coffee. He should get up, but he wanted another few hours of sleep. Preferably snuggling with his mate. That wasn't going to happen, so he tossed back the covers and trudged to the bathroom. After a quick shower and shave, he pulled on his favorite pair of jeans and a sweatshirt. Perhaps Magnus and Dani would leave today, taking Cade with them.

Morgan opened his door and found Magnus leaning against the wall.

He pressed his finger to his lips, then pointed toward the women. "They've been staring at the computer all morning," Magnus whispered.

"They're probably working with Percy. It was almost frightening watching the three of them working last night. But not as much as when Karma couldn't find her phone."

"True. By the way, did she ever locate it?"

"It'd slipped between the couch cushions. I turned it off last night and plugged it in for a good charge. Come on. I smell coffee."

"Cade made sure the ladies were fed. Are you going to tell him about the job offer?"

"Nope. I'm going to let the head of Daemon Security have the honor. Whoever it will be." The fresh smell of coffee had Morgan's mouth-watering, but not as much as seeing Karma in those red silk pajamas. They even had a black K monogrammed on them to match the piping. She looked hot. With her cat-eye glasses and hair tied with a scarf, Karma reminded him of a 1940s pinup he'd once had.

"I can't believe the women are up so early," Magnus said, trying to stifle a yawn.

"Tell me about it. I finally carried Karma to bed around three. Come on, let's see what they've found."

Karma grinned up at him. "Morning, you. Cade made coffee. There're also bagels and cream cheese."

"Morning, love." He brushed a gentle kiss across Karma's lips, leaving his body demanding more. "What have you found so interesting?"

"These!" Karma turned the computer for him to see. "Aren't they adorable! They're made from felt, and each pair is unique. Dani has a pair."

Morgan stared at the image on the screen, trying to figure out what was so fantastic about them. "They're cat slippers."

"Siamese," Dani corrected, wiggling her slipper clad foot at him."

"Still a cat."

She huffed. "You've clearly never had a Siamese "

"Not for breakfast," he teased.

Dani snorted. "I'd expect that coming from a *dog*."

"Wolf," he corrected.

"Fleabag."

Karma tossed a pillow at Dani. "Stop it."

"Fine." She crossed her arms, smiling at Karma. "Magnus ordered them online because he knows I love Siamese. Now the kids are older, I'm hoping for a kitten for my birthday. Hint. Hint."

"I used to date a Siamese once," Cade declared.

"TMI," Karma shouted.

The kid chuckled, handing Morgan a cup of coffee. "I may have a kink or two in me, but I don't swing that way. She was a performer in *Cats,* a *very* flexible performer."

"Why doesn't it surprise me?" Morgan didn't have to see Karma's beautiful face to know she'd rolled her eyes. Probably twice. As for Dani's birthday gift, Cade had it taken care of for Magnus. No way would Dani find out what she was getting this year.

"Well, at least you were allowed a pet." Karma twisted on the couch, grabbing her phone from the charger behind her. "The closest thing I had was Mr. Cuddles."

"I'm your Mr. Cuddles now, beautiful." Morgan laughed, knowing Karma had rolled her eyes.

A phone dinged.

"Gotta text from Ryder," Cade informed them. "Hopefully, good news."

"You're more like Mr. Cover Hog, Morgan. I thought werewolves ran hot." Karma winked at him and powered up her phone.

"Let me toss everyone out, and I'll show you hot."

Her lips thinned, and her face reddened. "Motherless goat!"

Fear sweetened the blood, but anger made it spicy. The rage rolling from Karma would have hers tasting like a vat of ghost peppers. Morgan was at her side, pulling her into his embrace.

"I'm...I'm fine." She jerked free of him, showing him the screen. "They've probably cloned Melody's number. Friggin butt wipes!"

His wolf howled as he read the text. A skull and crossbones with *You can't hide*, in chiller font glared at him. "Karma, we'll deal with them."

"Oh, we'll deal with them, alright," she snapped, pacing in front of the fireplace. "We'll deal with them. They've messed with me long enough."

"Ah, Morgan," Cade called to him, trying to get his attention.

"Not now. You're not fine, beautiful."

She spun on her heels, hands planted on her round hips, and her eyes blazing. "You're right, I'm not fine. I'm madder than a wet setting hen. It wasn't enough those a-holes kidnaped me, beat the crap out of me, stole my identity, but now they have to play friggin mind games. I'm done being nice." Grabbing her computer, she flopped down on the couch.

Morgan dropped down beside her, then tugged her until she sat across his lap. "Breathe."

"I get it. I understand why governments and agencies can't track down every hacker. They're rats hiding in dank, dark crevices. Well, it's time we go rat trap on their butts."

"Let's do it by bringing them to us." Morgan held Karma, ignoring the tears shimmering in her eyes. She was his, and he'd be damned if he'd allow Whitehall's little mind games to continue. It ended now. "Cade, get Ryder on the phone."

"Already on it." Cade's thumbs flew across his phone screen. "Sending a group text to him, Percy, and Royce. However," the kid's face pinked. "I missed an earlier text from him." Cade looked up from his phone. "It appears Melody is heading here. She tossed a suitcase in a car this morning and headed to the airport, where she purchased a one-way ticket. According to Ryder, her plane should be landing at three."

"What?" Karma groaned, closing her eyes. She leaned her head against Morgan's chest. "We're not at the resort. What will happen when she arrives, and we're not there?"

"It will be fine, beautiful. Trust me." He smoothed his hand up and down her back.

His wolf paced in his mind, wanting out to hunt and kill Whitehall and Canaday.

They'll pay, but our mate needs us now. Morgan assured his beast.

Dani slid from the couch then crawled onto Magnus's lap. "You know, Morgan, I can give you the name of my wax girl. She's excellent. Just ask Magnus. Of course, with the amount of fur you're sporting, she may charge you triple."

Morgan winced. More information than he wanted to know about Magnus's grooming habits.

"Stop picking on Morgan, Dani." Karma sniffed and wiped at her eyes. "I know what you're doing."

Don't ask, Magnus's voice echoed in Morgan's head.

Morgan chuckled. *Did you get a bikini or a full Brazilian?*

Asshole, Magnus's deep laugh resonated in Morgan's mind.

Dani grinned. "Got a smile out of you, K."

A small laugh escaped Karma, and she slid her arm around Morgan's neck. "Still, bad image."

"Sorry, but I don't like it when my K cries, even tears of anger. Hell, girl. You've cried more since I've been here than you did when your grandparents passed." Danielle glared at Morgan as if it were his fault.

"What?" He met the woman's dagger filled eyes head-on.

"Any idea how we're going to deal with these asses?" She arched her brows. "You plan on blowing them up?"

Karma snorted. "A little extreme, don't you think, Dani? Besides, Morgan's a businessman, not an explosives expert."

"I might know a thing or two about explosives." He pressed a kiss to Karma's crown as he held her close. Something else he'd neglected to mention to her.

"A thing or two, huh?" She toyed with his hair, twirling it around her finger. "We'll address that later. What do you have in mind for dealing with Evil and Psycho, once and for all?"

Morgan had an idea. He hated it. However, he'd run the numbers in his head, and this plan had the highest probability of working. "We call Melody, invite her up to Whaler Bay, and hope Whitehall takes the bait."

Dani stared at him as if he'd grown a second head. "Why should Karma call Melody? Didn't you hear Cade say she's already left?"

Killing the woman would greatly piss off Magnus, but more importantly, it would upset Karma. "I'm sure they've hacked Melody's phone, so they can listen in on her phone calls. I want to make sure they show up and when they do." Morgan smiled, allowing his fangs to descend. "We hunt them in *my* territory, then deal with them." He turned his attention to Karma. "I promise, Melody won't get hurt.

"Cade, tell Ryder to rendezvous with us this evening at the Tree Top. Contact us immediately if anything changes or if Whitehall intercepts."

"Roger that. Anything else."

"No. Hopefully, Whitehall is following her." This could work out better than he'd first thought. He and Cade could drive to the resort, leaving Karma with Magnus and Dani. But, if Whitehall doesn't see Karma, he might not reveal himself. Well, hell.

Karma tugged Morgan's hair. "I hope you don't plan on me sitting here while you and Cade go after them."

Morgan liked the determination showing in Karma's eyes better than the tears. However, if it were up to him, he'd lock her perky ass in the bedroom away from any danger. "I was, for all of a millisecond. But seeing you are an intricate part of the plan, you're coming with us. So, here's the plan. Go ahead and give Melody a call, inviting her up. Tell her we'll put her up at the Tree Top. Act surprised when she tells you she's already on her way."

"I'm ready for this to be over." Karma fished out her phone and made the call. "Morning, Melody. If you can swing it, I'd really like for you to come up. Morgan said he'd send a plane for you and don't worry about where to stay, we'll get you a room at the Tree Top. It's Whaler Bay's premier resort hotel. You can't miss it. Give me a call back as soon as you get this message." Karma ended the call then tried to scoot from his lap again. "Let's see if she calls back."

"Where are you going?" He liked having Karma on his lap.

"To get dressed so I can go with you. Or did you expect me to wear my jammies?"

"Beautiful, you look good in anything you wear."

~ ~ ~

It was nearly four, but Melody still hadn't returned her call. Ryder had already informed them Melody's plane had landed, and she'd taken a cab. Karma glanced from her phone for the millionth time to stare out at the gorgeous view. It was easy to see why Morgan loved Oregon so much. She stared at the large stone obelisk, standing as a monument to the numerous shipwrecks along the coast.

Warm hands rested on her shoulders, gently pulling her back against a hard chest.

She tipped her head back, looking up at him. "I'd like to get a photo of the monument in the daylight."

"We can. We can even have a picnic by the shore if you'd like."

"That sounds nice." Karma leaned back, giving Morgan more of her weight.

"I love the ocean. It's beautiful. Deadly but beautiful. The only time I've ever be afraid of it was when Mount St. Helens erupted. The force of the explosion rocked the Cessna I flew. "

"Wow." She turned in Morgan's arms, meeting his amber eyes. "I remember reading about it in school when we studied volcanoes in grade school."

"Wow, now I feel old." Morgan laughed, and the sound warmed her.

"Says the man who fought in the Civil War. What happened?"

"I was flying back from Vancouver, Canada. I've been in dogfights." He smiled and pointed upward. "Aerial dogfights," Morgan bobbed his head side to side. "And dog dogfights. "When St. Helens blew, the shockwave was so strong I lost control. I'll be honest with you, I've never feared for my life as much as I did then. I finally gained control of my plane just in time."

Her heart lurched at the thought of Morgan crashing his plane. She shouldn't have such strong feelings for him in the short amount of time she'd known him, but she did. "There's so much I want to learn about you, Morgan Wolfe. I know you've told me when we mate, I'll know everything, but I think I'd prefer you to tell me yourself."

"I'll warn you, my life's story is pretty boring." His boyish grin made her laugh.

"Says the man who just told me he was in the air at the time a volcano erupted, and why are you grinning?"

"You said *when* we mate instead of if."

"Oh, well, you'll have to thank Dani. She kept singing your praises while we drove here. She wore me down."

"Did she now?" Morgan lowered his head, pressing his lips to hers.

The touch of his lips sent a shock wave through her, and she clung to him, eagerly returning his kiss.

Someone pounded on the door shattering the moment.

"It's Ryder and Magnus. We should see what they want." Morgan's soft breath fanned her face as something dark replaced his once smoldering look. He didn't like them being interrupted any more than she did.

Karma wanted to ignore them and drag Morgan to bed. All his kissing had made her hornier than a cat in heat. "Let's see what they want."

"Enter," he barked, pulling her tight to his side.

Magnus strolled in, followed by a man in his late teens or early twenties. The guy pushed his hand through his thick auburn hair and smiled. "You look a lot better now, lass than you did when I first saw you."

"Thank you..." Karma levied an iron control to keep from laughing. It was one thing hearing the thick Scots brogue coming from a man dressed in black fatigues, but hearing it from someone wearing worn jeans, snakeskin cowboy boots, and sporting a belt buckle the size of a dinner plate when you would expect a thick Texas drawl was something else. "Ryder, right? At least now, I get to see your face."

Ryder held out his hand, ignoring Morgan's rumbling growl.

"Will you stop?" She elbowed Morgan then shook Ryder's hand. "I swear I'm going to take Dani up on her offer "

Magnus threw his head back, letting out a huge peal of laughter. "Karma, he's going to keep getting worse until you two mate. His primal side doesn't want *any* unmated men around you while you remain unclaimed."

Great, add a little more pressure, shall we? "I'll keep that in mind."

Chuckling, Ryder tilted his head slightly and offered his hand to Morgan. "Congratulations."

"Thank you. To you also. Momma informed me you and Rae have set the date."

"We have. I'm thankful Rae grew up with the Dhampir, seeing how close she and her family are."

Morgan motioned toward the sitting area. "Let's sit while you bring us up to date."

Magnus poured himself a glass of whiskey. "Can I get anyone else something?"

Both Morgan and Ryder shook their heads.

"Karma?"

"I'm fine, thank you. Where's Dani?"

"She's napping." Magnus leaned against the bar, eyeing Ryder. "So what's up?"

"A lot." Ryder leaned forward in his chair, resting his arms on his thighs. "Karma's mum is here. I've stationed two men on her floor. One's in the room next to hers, and the other is across the hall. This will leave Cade to watch this floor. We spotted three of Whitehall's puppets and apprehended one. Kim Chan, due to self-preservation, was more than willing to talk."

"The name isn't familiar." Morgan's brow furrowed.

"I didn't think it would be. He was with the Wu until he left." A faint smile fluttered across Ryder's face. "We gleaned a lot of info from him. First, they're here looking for you." He glanced at Karma.

Right on cue, Morgan turned furry.

She clutched his hand, lacing her fingers with his. Then placed her free hand on his forearm, digging her fingers into his fur. "Look at me." Karma waited, staring at Morgan's profile until he faced her, meeting her eyes.

"One, you don't have to worry about me running off with someone else," she ignored his rumbling growl. "I'm yours, and you're mine. Just because we haven't done the boom-chick-a-bow-wow doesn't mean I'm not yours." Keeping her eyes locked with Morgan's, she flipped both Ryder and Magnus off for laughing.

Assholes.

"Second, you have to get a grip on your wolf. Otherwise, someone who shouldn't find out about you will, then there will be no sexy times because you'll be in a lab somewhere, being experimented on." That earned her a snarl.

"Third, I don't care how rich you are. The way you've been going through shirts is insane. It needs to stop. Now. Shift back, so I don't have to translate."

Morgan's bones popped and fur receded. "I just found you, and I can't lose you." His voice more wolf than man.

"You won't lose me. But the sooner we catch these creeps, the sooner you and I can run away just the two of us." Was it too soon for her to be thinking about making this permanent? Maybe…Not.

She broke eye contact with Morgan and turned her attention to Ryder. Something told her there was more to this than simple hacking. "What else have you found out?"

"My intel confirmed the info we got from Chan. We're not dealing with the Council. Lincoln has decided to go into crime, think drugs, prostitution, cyber. According to Chan, it pays more. This is why he wants you, seeing you were able to thwart Copperhead a time or two. From what Chan said, Copperhead really hates you. Unfortunately, Chan didn't know his real identity."

Karma stroked Morgan's leg, hoping to keep him calm. "We believe Copperhead is Derrick Canaday."

A high pitched whistle escaped Ryder. "I'm surprised Tristan isn't here to take the bloke down."

"He's protecting Niki and the kids," Morgan replied, sounding more human. "But I notified Toby."

The whiskey glass slipped from Magnus's hand, shattering on the marble floor. "There have only been a few times I have questioned your actions. This is one of them." He squatted, wiping up the mess.

Morgan shrugged. "Why hit our company? Did Canaday come after us because of my brother, or were we simply an opportunity because some idiot opened a stupid email. As far as I know, Canaday doesn't know about us, but Lincoln does. He's Dhampir and hates humans. Then consider they set the warehouse to explode, which would have killed Karma. None of this makes any sense. So, yes, oh horned one, I called Tobias."

Horned one? Karma would have to ask Morgan what he meant.

Magnus tossed the broken shards into the trash along with the dishrag he used. "Ryder?"

"Toby is Toby. He could be here, but we'll never know unless he wants us to. If he is here, I welcome it. When Zeno was taken out, we rounded up most of his followers. Most. Not all. Just like after WWII, look how many Nazis we dealt with well into the 90s. If Lincoln is into organized crime, who knows how many are with him. Human and Dhampir. We don't know if Lincoln is in charge or if someone is pulling his strings. Chan wasn't much help, said the info was above his paygrade."

"I see your point." Magnus strolled to the windows with his hands clasped behind his back. "If they are going to make a move, I think it will be soon. This Friday is the shareholders' meeting and charity gala. By the way, Blythe is already here. She checked in yesterday with Avery and Frank."

"I take it Avery didn't have any issues flying." Morgan didn't care about Blythe, but he did worry about Avery.

"Not with her father with her. As for you, you've escaped the bachelor auction, again, Morgan seeing you're engaged. Perhaps we'll have Cade participate."

Karma tugged on Morgan's hand to get his attention. "Gala?"

"It's black tie, and I would be honored if you'd be on my arm."

"I'd love to, but I don't have anything to wear."

"That won't be an issue." Magnus held up his finger. "Dani can help you out."

"See, everything's taken care of." The warmth of Morgan's smile sent shivers through her body. "I can't wait to show you off."

"Okay, but question. If your company's home offices are in Atlanta and Dallas, why hold a charity event here? Curious."

"That was Dani's idea. You know we have offices and research facilities located throughout North and South America. Dani came up with the idea of us holding our annual charity event in one of the towns we're located. This way, those employees and municipalities feel they are a vital part of Wolfmoon and DuMond."

"Makes sense." Karma's phone chimed. "It's Melody's number. Hopefully, it's her."

Morgan nodded. "Go ahead and answer it."

Karma's stomach knotted as she lifted the phone to her ear. "Hey, Melody."

"Is this a joke or what?" Melody's high pitched voice came through the speaker and untied the knots in Karma's stomach. "I'm at the Tree Top, and they don't have a listing for you."

"I'm on my way down. Stay where you are." Knowing Morgan could hear both sides, Karma pressed a kiss to his cheek then left.

"Why can't I simply come up to your room. I can stay with you. I don't need my own room."

Karma raced to catch an elevator. "Because I'm sharing a room with someone. Why didn't you call me back sooner, Melody?" She punched the button for the lobby.

"I wanted to surprise you."

"Is Mateo with you?"

"No," Melody dramatically huffed. "He couldn't leave his garden for so long. I did bring my passport. I could come with you to England or wherever you're flying. We could make it a girls' trip. I bet Mateo doesn't even know I'm gone."

Lord have mercy, not again. "It wouldn't be much of a girls' trip with me working eight to ten hour days." The elevator's doors slid open, revealing her mother.

"There you are," Melody greeted with both hands waving. "You could always blow work off for a couple of days, maybe a week. I'm sure whoever you're working for, Wolfram whatever, wouldn't mind."

"It's Wolfmoon, and yes, they would mind." Karma pressed a kiss to her mother's cheek. "I already have your room key, come on, and I'll take you to your room. Where's your luggage?"

"It's right here." She pointed to a small duffel and an overnight case. "Let me get a look at you first."

Karma forced a smile as her mother's critical eye perused her. Over the years, Karma had grown immune to Melody's hurtful words. In her mind, she was being helpful. Karma's grandmother had been the same way, always complaining about Karma's weight. Her mother and grandmother were pencil-thin women who could eat sweets all day and never gain an ounce. But for all their boasting of how thin they were, neither woman could walk a mile without having to take a break, never mind swim the mile laps Karma did weekly.

"I don't know why you like dressing in vintage clothing. You should wear something more stylish, more up-to-date, or at least from this century, Karm."

No matter what her mother was into, she always dressed the part. "As opposed to your current style, Melody. Personally, I don't know how you can wear linen. I find it scratchy. I do like your hair pulled back into a braid. As for me, I like the 40s look." Karma smoothed her hands down the hunter green dress she wore with the sweetheart neckline. Her heart fluttered, remembering the heated look in Morgan's eyes when he first saw her wearing it.

Her mother's lips thinned, and she rolled her eyes. Probably where Karma learned it. "Linen is more environmentally friendly than whatever fabric you're wearing."

"It's cotton. But my bra and panties are silk."

Melody huffed. "I know I've stated this a hundred times, but if you'd only lose a couple of pounds, Karm, you might get a man."

"She has a man who loves every inch of her," a deep growling voice replied.

Oh, please, Lord, don't let him be furry.

Chapter Eleven

Her mother wasn't screaming. This was good. Karma peered out of the corner of her eye at Morgan's visage, noting his human appearance, and breathed a sigh of relief.

"Who are you?" Melody had a little bit more sultry tone to her voice than Karma liked.

"Melody, this is—"

"Morgan Wolfe." He slipped his arm around Karma's waist in a pure dominant move.

She should be pissed for several reasons. One, he'd interrupted her, and two, he was…standing up for her, so yeah—not pissed. "Melody, I'd like you to meet my fiancé, Morgan Wolfe."

Melody's eyes shifted from checking out Morgan's body to Karma's hand. "Can't afford a ring, I see. Oh well, at least he has a great body. The face isn't bad, either. A little too clean-cut for my liking. I prefer a little fur on the face."

"Melody, seriously?"

"What? You say he's your fiancé, yet you don't have a ring. I get it. He doesn't appear to have any money. But, hey, it's your business. And considering how those jeans hug him," Melody licked her lower lip as she eyed him up and down once more. "I say you go, girl."

Gross! Yeah, Morgan was hot but gross. Her *mother* was checking him out, mainly his crotch!

"I say we go." Morgan snatched up Melody's bags then herded her inside an elevator. "You're on the 2nd floor, Miss Peamoor."

"Call me Melody, Morton—"

"It's Morgan, Mother."

"Morgan." Melody rolled her eyes. "I've told you not to call me mother. I had you so young, we can pass as sisters. I refuse to accept the fact I have a daughter your age. Mateo, on the other hand, is happy to flaunt his *grandchildren*. I hope you don't ever make me a grandmother."

Karma risked a peek at Morgan. His smile was bleak and tight-lipped, and his usual warm eyes were cold orbs as he stared at Melody. At least he wasn't furry.

"Sorry to disappoint, but we are planning on having children. Don't worry, Melody, they won't call you granny. Changing the subject, have you eaten?"

"If you call the bag of chips and water I grabbed at the airport eating."

"Would you like to join us? Morgan and I were meeting Dani and her husband at a restaurant walking distance from here. It's a farm to table with great reviews. A lot of locals eat there." Deep down, she hoped Melody would say no.

The elevator finally stopped. Silently, she and Morgan escorted Melody to her room.

"Is it Dutch?" Melody's smile slipped.

"No, it's on me," Morgan replied, carrying her bags into the spacious room.

Melody perked up when she entered her room. "Wow! This is luxurious with a capital lux. The view isn't shabby."

"Melody, dinner?" Karma couldn't keep the exasperation from her voice if her life depended on it. She watched Melody inspect every inch of the spacious room as if she'd never been in a hotel suite before.

"Sure! What time. It'll only take me a second to get ready! I hope it isn't fancy. I only packed casual clothes."

"You don't have to change. It's casual."

"So, I guess you're wearing *that* dress. I guess Morton likes your cleavage."

"It's Morgan," he growled, "and Karma is gorgeous just as she is."

It took Melody an hour. Karma couldn't be mad at her mother. She was who she was and did whatever she wanted. Melody had told them to go on without her as she spoke to Mateo on the phone.

Dani and Magnus decided to order room service. There was only so much Melody either one could take. Karma had to agree. The woman was acting strange, even for Melody. She kept looking around the restaurant, mostly at the men, as if she were looking for someone in particular.

"The food here is wonderful. The lamb you and Morgan ordered looks delicious." Melody glanced around as she finished her brick pressed chicken.

"It was. The eggplant and grilled radicchio were divine. You've been looking around all night. Who are you looking for? Mateo?"

"The man won't waste money for a plane ticket." Melody stopped her perusal of the restaurant. "I can't believe the number of sexy men in this place. Who'd thought Oregon would have so many hunks? The cute blonde over at the bar, Karm, he keeps glancing at us." She tore her attention from Cade, sitting at the bar, and focused on Morgan. "So, you work for Danielle Rossi's husband, too?"

Morgan cleared his throat. His five o'clock shadow was thicker than it should be. Yeah, he was struggling with his wolf. "No, we're business partners." He forked a piece of lamb into his mouth.

His canines were a little too pointy for her liking. Karma placed her hand on his upper thigh, giving his leg a gentle squeeze. Maybe she could keep him from killing Melody.

Her mother quickly finished her meal then lifted her purse to her shoulder. "Karm, I have to powder my nose."

"Well, you know where." Karma covered Morgan's hand, lacing her fingers with his. He'd been quiet most of the evening, only contributing to the conversation when he needed to.

Melody huffed, giving Karma a wide-eyed stare. "Come with."

"Fine." She gave Morgan a peck on the cheek, then slid her chair back.

"Do you want dessert?" he asked, squeezing her hand.

"Maybe when we get back to the room." She didn't think she could sleep next to him another night without doing more than just sleeping. The heated look in his eyes had her wanting to snag his hand and drag him back to the hotel.

"Karm, are you coming?" Melody tugged on her arm.

"You know, I really despise Karm. Call me Karma, like you named me, *Mother*," Karma said with a smile, but her tone may have been harsh.

"Come on." Melody tugged again.

People were watching, so Karma obligingly followed. Once they entered the ladies' room, Melody pushed open every stall door.

"What are you doing?" Clearly, Melody had lost her last screw.

"Making sure no one's in here." Melody turned, meeting Karma's eyes. "I have to get you away from him. He's dangerous."

"Morgan? No, he's not. If this is why you wanted me to come with you, I'm out of here." Karma turned and reached for the door.

Melody grabbed her upper arm. "You don't know the monster he is."

Karma froze, looking over her shoulder at Melody. "What do you know about him?"

"He's dangerous. I have to get you out of here."

Karma jerked free. "He's not dangerous. Who told you?"

"Those officers when they came! They said he only wants you for your mind." Melody reached for Karma again, and she backed away. "Karm—Karma, you don't realize the danger you're in. I'm trying to rescue you even though you never did anything for me." Melody fished her phone from her purse. "Let me call them, and they'll come and take you to safety."

"No!" Karma snatched the phone from Melody. "Listen to me, Melody. They lied to you."

"No." Tears shimmered in the woman's eyes. "I may not have been a good mother to you, but I will not allow him," She shoved her finger at the door. "to lock you away." She grabbed for the phone, and Karma held it out of her reach.

"He rescued me. Those men were the ones who broke into my apartment. They kidnapped me and held me in a warehouse—"

"To protect you."

"No, Melody. They…" Karma didn't have bruises anymore, and it would be hard trying to explain why she didn't. "They did things to me."

Melody paled and ceased reaching for the phone. "They lied?"

"Yes, Melody," Karma jerked open the door. "They lied." She stormed from the restroom, only to be grabbed by her upper arm again. "For the last time, Mel—"

A large hand covered her mouth as a man dragged her toward the service exit. "Shut it, bitch," he hissed.

She rammed her elbow into his gut as she slammed the back of her head against his face.

"Don't fight him, Karm. It's for your own good," Melody pleaded, following.

The man shifted his hand from her mouth to the back of her neck and slammed her face into the metal door, pushing it open at the same time. Her glasses flew from her face, leaving her with her crappy vision. "Copperhead said he wanted you. He didn't say in what condition." She stumbled forward into the darkened alley.

Morgan! He'd said he could hear her thoughts.

"You didn't have to hurt her," Melody shrieked.

Her eyesight might suck, but she recognized the object in front of her with the motor running. If she got in the white panel delivery van, Morgan would never find her.

Morgan! God, she hoped he heard her thoughts. Anything was worth a try because she wasn't getting in the van. Karma dug in her heels, then went limp. She was a curvy girl, and her deadweight would be hard to drag.

Melody grabbed the man's arm. "You're hurting her!"

He kept his grip on Karma as he pushed Melody to the ground then pointed a gun at her. "Copperhead didn't say a fucking thing about you."

Melody paled. Her eyes widened, and she opened her mouth in a silent scream as she scrambled backward on her rear

This was it. Her mother would die before Karma's eyes, and she'd be a prisoner.

The gun slipped from the man's hand as he crumpled to the ground.

Karma's knees buckled. An arm slipped around her waist, catching her. She balled her fist, swinging, striking a rock hard jaw. "Morgan! Sorry."

"Are you alright?" He hugged her to him. "God, I was so afraid I'd lost you." His lips captured hers in a possessive kiss that spoke more of his feelings than mere words.

"You killed him," Melody shouted.

Karma peered over her shoulder at Melody, standing and pointing to the would-be kidnapper. For once, Karma was thankful for her crappy vision. She could tell the man's eyes were opened and imagine them staring blankly up at them.

Cade strolled toward them. "Naw, Morgan just subdued him." His shirt rode up, revealing a handgun tucked in his waistband as he squatted next to the body then touched the man's neck. "Yep, *subdued*." Cade picked up the kidnapper's gun, tucking it in his waistband. "Come on, fella, let's get you to the authorities."

Cade stood then hauled the dead man to his feet. The corpse's head rolled around unnaturally as Cade looped the man's arm around his shoulders. He slid the dead man into the back of the van.

Subdued, her foot. Morgan snapped the man's neck. Her stomach knotted. What if someone saw? Everyone had security cameras. "What about the cameras?"

"They took care of them for us." Cade pointed at a camera. "Paintball guns aren't for just fun. They also disabled the security lights back here. Morgan, you have an escort out front. I'll see you after I dropped these two off." Cade opened the van door and pushed a dark object from the driver's seat. He climbed in, giving a wave, he pulled away.

Karma opened and closed her throbbing fist. "You heard?"

Morgan nodded, slipping his arm around her waist. "Can you walk?" He gently brushed a kiss to her cheek. "We need to put ice on your noggin." His eyes glowed with his wolf.

"I'm good. I just want to get back to our room."

"Before we can do that, we have to meet with Ryder." Morgan led them back inside, pausing to pick up something from the floor. "Here, beautiful." He slipped her glasses on her face.

"Thank you." She held tight to Morgan's hand as he led them through the restaurant.

He nodded to their server as they left.

Melody silently followed.

While they waited for the light to change to cross the road. Karma took in the night lights. Whaler Bay was a beautiful resort town. Most of the people were like them, walking. Nothing appeared threatening, but the hair on the back of her neck stood. Maybe because of how vulnerable she felt. Perhaps because of her mother.

A flicker caught her attention to a man leaning against a building. The light of his e-cig glowed in the darkness.

"You're safe. He's one of ours." Despite Morgan's calm exterior, Karma sensed the battle raging inside of him. There'd be hell to pay if his wolf broke free.

The signal changed, and they crossed the street. She noticed the man with the e-cig also crossed, keeping abreast of Melody.

Once on the sidewalk, Melody darted in front of them and stopped. "I was only trying to help. Can I have my phone back?" She huffed, holding out her hand. "Mateo may call."

Morgan glared at Melody. At least he wasn't furry. Then again, his wolf would have been less frightening than the cold tight expression he wore. "You put your daughter's life in jeopardy. You'll get your phone back when I'm finished with it." Morgan yanked open the heavy glass door of the hotel and escorted them inside.

With so many people milling inside the lobby, it would be a perfect opportunity for Melody to be… well…Melody. Karma held her breath, waiting for her mother's performance.

None of the hotel staff stopped or questioned Morgan as he kept his determined stride. A few did scatter.

Holding firmly to Karma's hand, Morgan led her behind the reception desk and through a heavy door marked private and into an empty hall.

"It's my property, and I want my phone now." Melody stomped her foot.

There was the behavior Karma had expected.

Morgan drew in a deep breath. A few threads popped on his hunter green pull over as it strained against his chest. "Ms. Peamoor, had I not shown up when I had, you would be dead. Your body probably would have been discarded in one of the dumpsters." He jabbed his finger in the direction of the restaurant. "Karma would have been tortured and probably killed, thanks to you."

The door at the end of the hall opened, and two men strode toward them. One man was dressed in a suit and carried Melody's luggage. The other man had a striking resemblance to Morgan. Eyeing them, Morgan's look-a-like pocketed his e-cig then entered a room to his right.

"He has my things." Another octave higher and Melody's voice would shatter glass. "Why does he have my things?"

"Because you are going back to San Francisco with Flint. He will accompany you all the way to your front door. Now." Morgan's lips twisted into a cynical grin.

"But I just got here, and I've been traumatized."

"At your own making." There was no vestige of sympathy in Morgan's voice.

"I saw you *kill* a man. You snapped his neck."

Morgan stared at Melody, and for a brief moment, there was a blankness in her eyes. "You saw me disable a man holding a gun on you and Karma."

Flint held out his hand. "Ma'am, if you'll come with me. We have a plane waiting. Your husband will be picking you up once we land."

"Husband?" Karma jerked, meeting her mother's wide-eyed, innocent expression. "When did you two get married, and why didn't you tell me?"

Melody rolled her eyes and flicked her hand. "It's not important, Karm. Are you going to let them treat me like this? I'm your mother."

Not important? Her mother got married and didn't even bother to tell her. "Melody, please go. I'll contact you when I'm ready."

Melody's mouth gaped as she stared at Karma. "Fine. My phone," Melody snapped.

Morgan slipped his arm around Karma's waist. She leaned against him, needing his strength. Dealing with Melody could be emotionally draining on a good day.

"There'll be a new one for you on the plane." He guided Karma down the hall then paused. "Mrs. Cruz, one more thing. I hope you didn't receive payment for your actions tonight."

Karma's step faltered, and she looked over her shoulder. Her mother was self-serving, but surely she wouldn't have taken money. "Melody?"

"I was only trying to cooperate with the police and help you at the same time. They said," She pointed at Morgan. "He was evil."

Flint motioned toward the door at the end of the hall. "Lady, are you that naïve, or are you this dumb?"

"I'm not stupid." She rolled her eyes and planted her hands on her hips. "They had badges."

Shaking his head, Flint led Melody away.

"Karma, you okay?" Morgan brushed a kiss to her forehead.

"I think so." She lightly touched her forehead. "I can feel the goose egg growing, but I'm fine. You know, Melody really is naïve."

"I know. Come on, Ryder is waiting for us in the office."

"Before we meet with Ryder, how and when did you find out all this information?"

"Ryder investigated Melody when we sent him to check-up on her. I didn't tell him to bug her room."

"He did?" Karma should be furious, but...

Morgan nodded. "During dinner tonight, Ryder was constantly in my head."

"That explains why you weren't very talkative. So, what did he tell you?"

"Ryder didn't like what he heard from Melody's side of a conversation. It seems before meeting us in the lobby, she made a phone call informing whoever where we'd be. Ryder took it upon himself to notify Cade and my brother, Paul."

"The guy who flanked us from the restaurant?"

"Correct, and the one with an attitude lately."

"I see. Good to know I'm not the only one with a difficult family member."

"Come on, I want to introduce you to him. If he's still here." Morgan opened the door for her.

"He just walked in." Ryder held his phone out toward Morgan. "It's Cade."

Karma glanced around the office just big enough for a desk, two chairs, and a small sofa against a far wall. She smiled at Morgan's brother leaning against the desk, twirling an e-cig between his fingers.

Should she introduce herself to him or wait for Morgan? If she did, should she say, hi, I'm Morgan's mate, or simply hi, I'm Karma?

Paul tapped Ryder on the shoulder. "Who's the chubby," he whispered.

"Apologize," Morgan growled.

Karma slipped between Morgan and his brother. She wasn't going to have her future mother-in-law hate her because Morgan killed his little brother.

"Hi, guess I should introduce myself," Karma held out her hand and plastered her 'you're an asshole' smile on her face. "I'm Karma, and judging from the family resemblance, you're Morgan's younger brother. Correct?"

"Mine," Morgan snarled.

"Yes, babe, I'm yours." Still holding out her hand to Paul, Karma slipped her free arm around Morgan's waist.

"You're Morgan's mate?" Paul crossed his arms.

Guess he wasn't going to shake her hand. Not her problem. She smoothed her hand up Morgan's chest, trying to keep his wolf from breaking free.

Paul pushed by them then sat on the edge of the desk. "Don't understand why you needed help walking her across the street, bro."

~ ~ ~

Morgan mentally shoved his beast into his cage. He hated this time of year. Hated. It. He understood why Paul acted the way he did, but…enough was enough. "You will apologize and show respect to my mate."

Breathe, Karma's words brushed against his mind as she leaned into him. She laced her fingers with his. An hour ago, her life had been threatened, now she calmed *him*. "Demanded apologies only get you empty words." Karma pressed a kiss to his cheek as if his brother's actions hadn't bothered her. She sat in one of the chairs then patted the arm of the one beside her.

"I'll stand." His wolf paced, slamming against his mental cage.

"Fine." Karma smiled at Ryder. "I want to know what Cade said and what you found out. Then Morgan," She tilted her head back, looking up at him and blew him a kiss. "I want to retire to *our* room."

Morgan rested his hands on her shoulders, feeling the tension knotting her muscles. "I think a good soak in the Jacuzzi would do you good."

Over her head, Morgan noticed the brief wounded look in Paul's eyes. Without knowing it, Karma had stabbed him in his Achilles heel. Paul hated being ignored.

Ryder leaned back in the chair, propping his feet on the desk, promptly shoving Paul from his perch. "So far, no hit in any databases. Both assailants' fingerprints burned off. No help there. Cade collected DNA from both. If it's any consolation, I believe Melody thought she was dealing with the police."

"I feel a little better, knowing she didn't do this out of malice." Karma reached up, grasping Morgan's hand. "And you're sure she and Mateo are married?"

A sad smile pulled at Ryder's mouth as he nodded. "They had a Vegas wedding six months ago, about the same time you started working with Morgan."

"I see. Well, at least this relationship has lasted longer than any of her others. Maybe, she's finally grown up."

Paul coughed, drawing everyone's attention. "What? Can't a guy clear his throat?"

"Paul," Ryder slid a room key across the desk. "You and Cade are sharing a room. You'll be taking the first round of patrols. Once Cade wakes up, he'll relieve you. When Flint returns, he'll resume his duties here."

Paul opened his mouth then shut it, exhaling. "I guess this is my cue to leave." He took the key then strolled to the door. He paused, looking over his shoulder at Karma. "What's your real name, cupcake?"

She stood, facing him, and smiled. "My. Name. *Is.* Karma."

A choked laugh escaped Paul, and he nodded. "Congratulations, you two. If Pete were here, he'd be over the moon." Paul flung open the door and left.

"Morgan, I'm sorry." Ryder met his eyes. "I should have told you, but Paul showed up at the same time Cade asked for an escort. I sent Paul, then pulled Flint. Guy's been asking for fieldwork, said he's tired sitting behind this desk."

"I was wondering why you had Flint escort Melody instead of someone else."

Ryder chuckled. "All the newbies think fieldwork is glamorous."

Morgan slid his arm around Karma's waist. He wanted to get her back upstairs, but he needed to know something. "Did Paul volunteer? Last I heard, he stayed behind with Declan."

Ryder shook his head. "Long-story-short. When Paul heard Quaid was heading to the lodge, Paul *had* to go for a run. He didn't return until after Quaid and Simone had left. Declan and Paul had a throw-down. When the dust settled, Declan ordered Paul to pack his gear. He showed up with an attitude, wanting to work with us. My gut told me to send him packing, but I welcomed the extra body with it being Whitehall and all the Dhampir staying here. I apologize again, Morgan. I know how Paul gets this time of year."

"Don't worry about it, Ryder. Not your dog. Not your fight. I get it. Hell, we all suffer anniversary depression. For me, it's the day Pete and Jean were killed. For Paul, it's his birthday. For 90 days, he's a total pissant. The month leading up, the month of, and the month after. I get it. He and Peter were identical twins, but it's been over five friggin' years. When was Paul going to get over it?"

"When you stop taking his crap." Karma sighed. "It's one thing to be mourning. It's another to be disrespectful."

Morgan didn't miss the hurt in her voice. He should have pushed Karma out of the way and beat Paul senseless for his comment. Which proved he was as big an asshole as his brother.

"Come on, beautiful. Let's go on up to our room."

Ryder picked up his phone. "They're heading to the elevator now."

Morgan appreciated Ryder's diligence and couldn't wait to get Karma safely in their suite. From the tingle at the back of Morgan's neck, he figured there were about twelve Dhampir he didn't know staying at the hotel. He knew of three applying for employment within DuMond and Wolfmoon. The others were possibly tourists, but he wouldn't risk Karma's safety on assumptions.

His wolf pushed him to get Karma safely in their room. He swiped his keycard, then waited for the private elevator door to slide open. It shouldn't take this long. Magnus and Dani must be using it.

"What's on the agenda for tomorrow?" Karma covered a yawn. "Sorry."

"No need to apologize. You've had a chaotic day. As for tomorrow, nothing like today."

The door finally slid open.

"Oh, jeez. Thanks for jinxing us." Karma laughed, entering the car.

Chapter Twelve

Karma laughed and stifled another yawn as she trudged into the elevator. This evening's escapades would make the writers of a reality television series shake their heads. No one would believe her mother had tried to have her kidnapped. Okay, to be fair, Melody thought she was helping. But still…Then meeting Morgan's brother…Wow. Just wow. At least Tristan and Niki liked Karma, or did she just assume they did? It didn't matter. What was important, Morgan liked her.

Her heart pounded. He'd said he loved her. Did she love him back? Heck, it'd only been a handful of days, but yeah…she had a case of the serious likes going on. She turned around, smiling up at Morgan as a smokey apparition oozed through the ceiling.

Morgan's eyes turned red, his fangs descended. His clothes tore as he shifted into Hollywood's version of the werewolf.

As Morgan faced the smoky intruder, he shoved Karma into the corner so hard the force knocked the wind from her.

The apparition solidified into a lithe blond swinging a wicked blade.

Morgan ducked, barely missing having his head severed. A clump of his black silken hair drifted to the floor.

The bitch tried to swing her blade again, but the cramped quarters prevented her.

Morgan lunged, clamping their attacker's neck in his maw. A quick shake snapped her neck, then he thrust his hand into the blonde's chest and ripped out her heart. Morgan tossed his head back and howled as the body crumbled in a cloud of ash.

Crouching over the body, Morgan looked at Karma. The intensity of his glowing amber eyes should have concerned her, but it didn't. She perused him as intently as he did her. Blood coated Morgan's mouth and chest.

He stood, and the remainder of his clothes fell away, stirring up the ash. He growled.

Amazing, she understood him. "I'm good. Are you okay? There's a lot of blood coating your chest." The gore should have sickened her. It didn't. Tentatively Karma reached her hand out, needing to know if the blood was his or their attacker's.

Before she could check Morgan for injuries, the elevator door slid open. Karma gasped. Two men aimed guns at them. Her heart calmed when she recognized Cade and Ryder. "I thought you said bullets only pissed you off?" She took a step forward, staggering on shaky legs.

Morgan growled, reaching for her, then stopped as he glanced down at himself.

"I'm covered in bitch-ash anyway." Karma slipped her arm around his waist and leaned into him, needing his strength.

A rumbling growl vibrated from Morgan as they exited the car. Good thing she knew he laughed at her choice of words, considering his menacing grin filled with sharp teeth.

"Well, what else would you call it?" She rolled her eyes, and he growled, hugging her to him.

Ryder poked his head into the elevator. "As soon as we lost the security feed, we tried to stop the elevator. They must have overridden the controls."

"You know who he was?" Cade asked, squatting and poking at the pile of ash.

A growl and bark comprised Morgan's reply.

"Dude." Ryder strode toward them. "Shift, so we know what you're saying."

"Ah, no," Karma snapped. She'd be all for Morgan shifting if Dani wasn't standing off to the side, grinning and wiggling her fingers. Karma didn't want any female to see her man naked. Her man? *Not going down that rabbit hole.* "Morgan said he didn't know the bitch, never met her, but she had to be about his age from how long it took her to crumble." Karma jerked her attention to Morgan. "What do you mean there's an *open* contract on me?"

"Female?" Ryder sounded shocked to know a woman could kill. "Karma, you understand him?"

"She does." Cade dropped Morgan's phone and wallet into his pawed hand then slid a keycard, unlocking their door. As Cade stepped into their room, he pointed at Morgan's chest. "That's a lot of blood. Good thing you got the bitch before she dusted you."

"What's he talking about, Morgan?" Karma eyed him, noting blood matted his fur.

"Clear," Cade shouted.

Morgan shrugged.

"Fine. Don't tell me. Just get some clothes on." She wasn't stupid. Morgan not answering her question meant some of the blood was his.

Morgan sighed and headed toward the bedroom, swishing his tail back and forth.

If Morgan wouldn't tell her. She tapped Cade on the shoulder. "What did you mean?"

"The cleaners are here." Cade *ran* from the room.

"Coward," she shouted after him.

A man dressed as a janitor vacuumed out the elevator.

"You okay?" Concern showed in Dani's eyes. "I mean. I know you're not hurt, but how are you holding up?"

How was she? Barely standing. If Karma voiced her honest emotional state to Dani, she'd go all mother hen. "I need a bath, and I want answers." Karma shifted her attention between Ryder and Magnus. Getting info from Magnus would be impossible.

"What did Cade mean, and what's this about a contract on me?" She poked Ryder's chest. "Speak."

"Ah, Morgan."

She turned around in time to see Morgan strolling toward her, pulling a t-shirt down over his head.

"Whitehall and Canaday put it on the dark web. They'll pay a million to anyone who delivered you to them, alive. Percy and Viktor are working on taking care of the post."

Karma yanked his shirt up, then ran her fingers over the marred flesh above his heart.

Morgan covered her hand. "Hey, beautiful, if you want me naked, just say so."

"Her fingers were in your chest." Morgan could have died.

"And I had mine in her." Morgan lifted Karma's hand, pressing a kiss to her palm.

"She could have killed you." The thought of losing Morgan caused physical pain.

"But she didn't, love."

The intensity of Morgan's gaze had her leaning into him. Why did there have to be so many people in their room?

"Damn, y'all having a party in here," Paul's voice boomed in the room, startling her. "and ya didn't invite me."

"Not now, Paul," Morgan growled.

"Fine." Paul turned toward the door.

"Stop," Ryder shouted. "You were supposed to have secured the elevator and this floor. What happened? You allowed a fader to get through."

Paul's eyes widened slightly. "We're in a resort hotel with over twenty Dhampir who aren't familiar. I didn't sense any malice from them. Besides," He grinned. "Morg's fine, so no harm, no foul."

"No harm?" Karma repeated softly. "No foul, Paul? Look. At. Me."

"You know, this suite does have a shower." He smirked.

Her temper got the best of her, and she jerked from Morgan's hold, stepping in front of Paul. "This," She wiped her hands on his shirt, "could have been your brother."

"Maybe you should have a little more faith in your mate."

Karma would not let the pin dick see that he got to her. Turning her back, she headed for the bedroom.

"I don't envy you that one, bro."

The sound of flesh striking flesh and possibly bone crunching echoed in the room.

Dani's wicked laugh filled the air. "Paul, you have heard the adage, Karma can be a bitch, right? Just asking."

Karma shut the bedroom door then leaned against it. The last thing she needed was to hear Paul's sarcastic comeback. Anniversary depression explained much about his behavior. She got a little melancholy each year around the time of her grandparents' deaths but was never mean-spirited. At least she didn't think so. Nope. If she had been, Dani would have called her on it.

Paul was right about one thing, Karma should've had more faith in Morgan. She did. She had all the confidence in the world in Morgan, up until she saw the wounds in his chest and realized how close she'd come to losing him. Still didn't excuse Paul from being an ass. His comeuppance would happen sooner than he thought.

She needed to put that jerk out of her mind and wash this day from her body. A hot shower could do wonders for her right now.

Karma pushed from the door and trudged toward the bathroom. Catching her reflection in the mirror, she groaned. The bathroom's bright iridescent light was not her friend. She looked worse than she'd imagined. Gray ash covered her from head to toe—gray ash of a dead woman sent to kidnap her and kill Morgan.

The thought of something happening to him was gut-wrenching. Karma needed to stop lying to herself. She'd fallen in love with the man on the phone all those months they'd worked together. Her heart told her she was in love, her mind still wanted facts. Well, it was time her heart and mind were on the same page.

"Hey, beautiful, you okay?" Morgan strolled into the bathroom.

She wasn't, and she was. "I'm good. Let me wash this crap from my face, then I'll be right out." Karma smiled at him in the mirror as she turned on the faucet. They needed to figure out what to do, probably call Percy.

"I've sent everyone packing. Dani protested, but she and Magnus are back in their room. Cade is camping out in the hall. You're safe."

"Safe?" She rinsed the soap from her face then stared at him in the mirror. "Morgan. I know I'm safe." She turned and leaned against the vanity. "I'm worried about *you*! Some sword-wielding bitch wanted to take your head. What's going to stop someone else from oozing through the ceiling?"

"Ryder and Paul have stepped up security. They've stationed several faders on the roof. No one will get to you tonight."

Karma's eyes stung. Didn't Morgan understand? She didn't care about herself. She worried about him. "I'm sorry. I shouldn't have let your brother get to me."

"No, stop right there, love. I'm the one who should apologize. Not you."

"But—"

"No, buts." Morgan lifted his hand, then dropped it. Blood coated his knuckles. "Let me wash before I touch you."

"You're hurt."

"Nope."

"You punched your brother." A tiny part of her did cartwheels.

Morgan shrugged as he dried his hands. "Broke his nose. Now, let me take care of you like I should have. How about a nice hot bath?" He cupped her face. His thumb caressed her cheek. "Bubbles up to your chin as you soak in lavender oil."

"That sounds amazing, but no. I'm not crawling in a tub while I'm covered in gunk. Sorry, my girly bits, and I have no desire to soak them in ash water."

"Then, a shower it is."

The twelve dual jets and overhead shower head reminded her of a human carwash. The marble stall was big enough for a car, too. Or two people. The thought of Morgan all wet had her girly parts quivering and dampening her panties.

"Turn around, love." He unzipped her dress then slid it over her head, trying not to stir up a cloud of ash. Then Morgan carefully placed her dress in a laundry bag. "I'll make sure laundry services take special care of this."

She loved everything about the dress, from its vibrant hunter green color to the fitted flare style, which perfectly suited her curvy body. "Thanks, it's one of my favorite dresses."

Karma faced him, standing before Morgan in only her bra and panties. She didn't bother sucking in her stomach. He might as well get a good look at her body before they went any further. She forced herself to look him in the eyes, praying she wouldn't see disgust.

Her heart pounded. Then relief. In all of her life, she'd never had a man look at her with such heated desire. There was no way he could fake it, especially by the evidence straining his jeans.

"Damn, you're gorgeous." His face pinked, and his eyes glowed. "I...ah..." Morgan stepped back, motioning toward the doorway. "I'll let you have some privacy."

Heat rushed to Karma's face, and she grinned. It was now or never. "What if I don't want privacy?"

~ ~ ~

Morgan locked his knees to keep from sinking to the floor. His wolf yipped, *yes, please*, and did friggin backflips in his mind. He closed his eyes and drew in a deep breath. "Beautiful—"

She cupped him, and he snapped open his eyes. "Oh, my, what big...*fangs* you have."

"Karma," his voice cracked, and he covered her hand, bringing it to his lips. "Beautiful, you're playing with fire." Carefully he scraped his fangs across her palm. Morgan held onto his self-control by a thread—a frayed thread.

"Are you saying I'll get burnt?" She drew her finger across his bottom lip.

He captured Karma's hand, placing it over his heart. Morgan would never do anything to harm her. If she said stop, he would. Lord help, he hoped she didn't. "I know things between us are moving very quickly. However, I will never mistreat you. I *will* always protect you, even from myself. I'm saying I won't be able to just make love to you. I will mate you, tying us together for eternity. I love you, Karma. You'll be mine forever, beautiful." He grinned as she rolled her eyes. "I know, caveman."

"Well, caveman, I think one of us has on too many clothes." Karma gripped the bottom of his shirt, tugging it up.

He wasn't about to tell her they had on the same number of items, two. He'd let her find out for herself. Morgan lifted his arms up over his head, knowing full well she wasn't tall enough to pull his shirt off over his head.

"You know, you could help." His curvy little mate stood on her tiptoes then flicked his nipple with her tongue.

"That tickles." He laughed and pulled his shirt off. "Better?"

"Some." Mischief shimmered in her eyes. "So, you're ticklish."

"A little." He drank in her curvy form, wanting to see more of her and less of her lingerie. "I think one of us is a little overdressed now." Damn, he wanted to see her full breasts.

Karma licked her lower lip and slipped an arm behind her back. She pressed her other arm against her bra then slipped her bra strap down. Keeping her bra in place, she slipped the other strap off.

Her shy moves were making him harder than he'd ever been in his life. He wanted to push her hands aside and snatch the garment from her.

Grinning, his minx spread her arms wide, allowing her bra to drop to the floor.

His knees buckled as he drank in her firm round breasts with berry red nipples he couldn't wait to taste.

"This is me, stretch marks and all—" Karma squealed when he gripped her waist, lifting her up on the vanity.

Morgan captured a nipple in his mouth, sucking and lapping at it as if he were a starving man. His action wasn't romantic, but he wouldn't let Karma think she wasn't desirable.

"Morgan." She shoved at his head. "I'm nasty."

She wasn't yet, but give him a moment, and his little mate would be.

Karma yanked his hair. "Morgan." His name sounded more like a moan than a warning. At least she wasn't telling him to stop. "I'm covered in dead skank ash. Stop."

Well, crap. Morgan let her nipple pop from his lips. "I can't wait to taste your honey." He didn't miss her shiver or the increase in her heart rate. "Before I do, this luscious breast needs attention." He brushed his thumb over the perk hard nipple, enjoying the shiver wracking Karma's body. His little mate was so responsive. He couldn't wait to see her come, screaming his name.

Morgan slid his hands down to her hips, hooking his thumb in the waistband of her panties.

Karma jerked, grabbing his wrist. "Nope. You still have on more clothes." She hopped from the vanity, wagging her finger at him. "Off with those jeans, mister."

"Yes, ma'am." Keeping his eyes locked on Karma's, he slid his zipper down one tooth at a time.

Karma squinted, then her eyes widened. "Um, you're commando," she gasped. "And huge."

He slid his jeans down, then kicked them aside, resisting the urge to stroke his dick, pointing to high noon. "You noticed."

"Wolfie, I'd have to be completely blind not to notice."

"Wolfie?"

"Yes, I've seen you furry more often than not." His curvy mate laughed then turned her back to him. She shimmied out of her panties, then stuck her arm under the water.

The sight of the round globes of her pale ass, weakened his knees. He groaned and fell to his knees when she faced him. He didn't want to come off as an ass, staring at her like he was, but good grief, Karma was a curvy goddess.

Morgan let his gaze roam from her lush, firm breasts down over her rounded stomach to her neatly trimmed dark brown curls at the junction of her thighs.

"Silly, are you going to stay on the floor, gaping? Or are you going to join me?" Karma stepped into the shower. Her soft moans nearly had him coming.

Morgan scrambled to his feet, nearly diving into the shower after her. He didn't have to be asked twice.

He watched as shampoo bubbles ran down her body as she rinsed her hair.

"You're beautiful."

"You're not bad, yourself." Karma perused him, pouring more than enough body wash onto the washcloth.

Steam filled the bathroom along with the clean fragrance of the soap. Once Karma got all clean, Morgan planned to get her all *dirty*.

"Let me." He took the cloth from her. Tears spilled from her eyes. His wolf whimpered in his mind, and his dick went from high noon to six. Soap must have gotten in her eyes.

Sadness, not soap, filled her eyes. Morgan washed the ash from her arms, trying to figure out what he'd done wrong. Her radiant smile contradicted the tears in her eyes. Morgan glanced at her breasts. Maybe he'd hurt her. Nope, the one he tasted didn't look abused to him. He paused in his care of her. "Beautiful, what's wrong?"

"Nothing, except you're taking forever." Karma took the washcloth from him, giving him her back. She scrubbed herself, then squirted more body wash onto the cloth. "Here, get my back, please." She held the cloth out for him, dripping with soap. As he washed her back, Karma wiped at her eyes.

What the hell had he done? He turned Karma in his arms then ran his thumb under her eye, capturing a tear. "Have I hurt you?"

"What? No."

"Then why the tears?"

Her bottom lip quivered. She flung herself at him. "I could have lost you."

Chapter Thirteen

He was a dick, an ass, and a prick! It was a good thing Karma couldn't see the grin splitting his face. He shouldn't take satisfaction in her tears, but hell! Her tears meant she more than liked him. Karma might even love him.

She sniffed again, wrenching Morgan's gut. It'd only been a few days. Did he really expect Karma to throw herself at him and beg to be mated?

Patience. She had feelings for him, it was evident in her worry, and here he was relishing her tears. Paul wasn't the only ass in the family.

"Hey, beautiful, don't cry." Morgan smoothed his hand up and down her bare back, enjoying the feel of her silken skin.

His dick twitched.

Now wasn't the time.

Later.

If he was lucky.

Karma angled her head, peering up at him through thick lashes. "Sorry, not how I expected the night to go."

"You have nothing to apologize for." Damn, if it wasn't the truth. His little mate had been through enough tonight. She deserved to shed some tears.

Morgan knew the direction he'd wanted the night to end. Unfortunately, his hopes were slowly circling the drain. "It's late, and today has been a rollercoaster of emotions for you. Let's dry-off then get a good night's sleep."

"Oh," Karma whispered. "You're right. It is late. Let me just rinse off."

"Talk to me." Morgan kept his arms around her. He was missing something.

"I could have lost you."

"I could have lost you, too." Hell, he'd nearly lost her twice. When Whitehall kidnapped her, then when Karma's batshit-crazy mother fell for Whitehall's lies.

Karma drew her finger over the faded, faint pink scar on his chest. "I have a confession to make."

His heart sank, and his wolf whimpered. Those five words were as deadly as *it's not you. It's me.* "I love you. You're my mate, Karma. I will always love you. I'll always put you first in my life."

"That's just it, you love me and well…"

Here we go. This is where she tells me she only wants to be friends.

"All those months we talked on the phone, I kinda fell for you, too—"

"Whoa—wait—what?" He hoped he'd heard her right.

"I want to be your mate, even if you do prefer Star Wars over Star Trek. Nobody's perfect."

"Minx!" Overcome with joy, he pulled her into his arms and lifted her. "Are you sure?"

Karma wrapped her legs around his waist and her arms around his neck. "Yes! I don't want to wait, Morgan. Call me selfish, but I don't want to live a life without you." Her bright smile had his wolf howling.

"Once I claim you as mine, once we share blood, there will be no going back. You'll be mine forever." He didn't want to remind Karma of his brother…but. "You'll be tied to my family, as well."

She rolled her eyes. "Lord have mercy, I'll see your Paul and raise you a Melody."

Morgan captured her mouth and delved into its sweetness. This wasn't a gentle kiss, but the possessive kiss of a man claiming his mate. His dick brushed against her sweet sex. It would be so easy for him to claim Karma, but she deserved soft, silk sheets and so much more.

Karma pushed her hand through his hair then leaned back, breaking off their kiss. "What is in your hair?" She glanced at the muddy ash coating her fingers, and he cringed. "Yuck!" Karma shimmied out of his arms, sliding down his body. She held her hand under the running water. "Didn't you grab a shower when you put on clothes?"

Told you. His wolf moaned, slapping his paws over his eyes. *Just don't tell her what we did.* Morgan didn't care what his mangy beast thought at the moment. However, he'd keep his mouth shut. Telling Karma he'd only shaken off wouldn't go over well.

She eyed him, then grabbed the bottle of complimentary shampoo. She squirted a glob into her hand. "Before we can have sexy times, someone needs to get clean."

"Sexy times? As in tonight?" His cheeks hurt from his grin.

"Unless you don't want to." Karma stretched, reaching her hands toward his head. The action lifted her full round breasts, not quite high enough for his liking.

"Let me make this easier for you." He sank down onto the teak bench. "Better?" It was for him. Each time she leaned forward, her nipples brushed against his lips.

"Much, thank you. So….What type of father can I expect you to be? Hands-on or what?"

"I plan to be very hands-on. You and me, beautiful, will be a team and the best parents ever. There won't be any playing one of us against the other like I've seen kids do with their folks."

"Best parents ever, huh?" Karma leaned forward again, and this time he knew she'd rubbed her breast against him on purpose. "I like the sound of that."

A wolf could only take so much teasing. He snaked his arm around her waist then captured her taut nipple in his mouth, sucking it.

"Morgan?" Karma moaned out his name and leaned forward, digging her fingers into his scalp. Morgan spread his legs wider, gathering Karma closer to him as he worshiped her beautiful berry tipped breast.

He was a lucky man to have such a gorgeous, sexy, intelligent mate.

The musky aroma of her desire had him dragging his mouth from her breast. He wasn't a cat, but this wolf craved him some cream.

He stood and switched positions with Karma in a quick, fluid motion, drawing a surprised and plaintive cry from her. Morgan dropped to his knees.

She moaned as he pressed his lips to the valley between her breasts. Planting fairy light kisses, he traveled downward over the soft swell of her belly.

"Morgan," she giggled his name when he dipped his tongue inside her navel. He teased her again, drawing another giggle from her. He could stay and play longer, but he was a wolf on a mission.

Hot water pelted his back as he knelt before Karma. The steam intensified the scent of her arousal. He wanted to see if she tasted as sweet as she smelled.

He nuzzled her soft curl covered mound. The choice was hers if she wanted him to taste her. Karma parted her thighs, and he nestled between them. He closed his eyes and drew in a lung full of her sweet scent.

The first lick, the first taste, and he thought he'd died and gone to Heaven. He knew he had each time he heard her blissful cries of his name as his tongue stroked her swollen nub. He knew he'd achieved sainthood when her channel clenched and spasmed around his fingers.

Karma bucked her hips and thrashed as she dug her fingers into his shoulders. When she finally found her release, Karma tugged at his scalp, squeezed his head between her thighs, and screamed his name.

Mine! His wolf howled. The cocky beast then strutted around in his mind.

Morgan stroked and licked until his glasses-wearing sexy mate enjoyed her last tremor.

Karma eased her hold on his head and shoulder. With a sated smile curving her lips, she slumped against the shower wall. "Wow. That was…Wow."

"My pleasure." He knew he was grinning, but damn, he couldn't wait to continue this in bed. He stood and held out his hand to her.

"Cocky." Karma's laughter echoed in the shower as she stared up at him. "However, after that, Wolfie, you have a right to be cocky." Her smoldering gaze slipped down him. "Speaking of cock." Karma gripped his shaft, sliding her hand down to his root. "Time for me to pleasure you."

He caught her hands, bringing them to his chest. "As much as I would enjoy that, tonight's about you, love."

"What if I want to pleasure you? Do you know how hot it makes me, knowing I excite you? You make me feel desirable."

"You are desirable." Morgan squatted so she wouldn't have to strain her neck looking up. "I call you beautiful because you are. You are the most beautiful woman in the world to me, and you make me feel like the luckiest man alive."

"Then let me pleasure you."

The thought of Karma taking him into her mouth, sent shivers through him. "When I come inside you for the first time, I want it to be when we create our child."

"In that case." Karma stood and slipped her arms around his neck, pressing her lips to his cheek. "I think we should continue this elsewhere."

Morgan shut off the water then snagged a towel from the heated rack. It took all of his control not to throw Karma over his shoulder as he dried her. She needed romancing and tenderness. He should have ordered her some flowers when they arrived. He also needed to get her a ring.

"Whatcha thinking about?" She took the towel from him.

"That I haven't done anything to romance you."

"Hmm, let's see." She took the other towel then patted his chest. "You took the time to find out my favorite flowers are yellow roses."

"Not enough—"

Karma reached up and lightly touched the tip of his fangs, sending a jolt of pleasure through him. "Dani said your fangs were erogenous zones."

He swallowed, locking his knees. "They are."

"Yours are pretty sharp."

He hated not knowing what to say or how to answer. Was she afraid of him? No, he didn't scent fear. On the contrary, her arousal still sweetened the air.

"She also told me I'll actually grow to crave your bite." Karma squatted, drying his legs. She ran her finger down the deep groove on his hip. "Such a beautiful Adonis belt." Her warm breath teased him, causing his dick to twitch.

"My what?" *Oh, shit!*

She pressed her lips to his shaft. His little minx looked up with a coy guise. "Your Adonis belt. These deep lines on your hips, pointing to um…Mr. Happy. Are you sure you don't want me to…" Her tongue darted out, lapping at his tip.

"Woman!" He scooped her up in his arms and carried her, laughing toward the bed. It took all his willpower to get her in bed and not take her against the shower wall.

His mangy wolf didn't see an issue with it.

"Morgan," Karma giggled. "put me down." She pressed kisses to his face, then nipped the skin where his shoulder met his neck.

"As you wish." He dropped her in the center of the bed.

~ ~ ~

Karma rolled to her side and looked up at Morgan, bathed in the soft room light. He was hot, sexy, and gorgeous. His proud cock was surrounded by a thick black nest of curls. Her gaze followed the thin black line of hair up to his navel and rock hard stomach. In the dim light and with her sucky vision, Morgan's well-sculptured body was blurry. "Would you move a little closer to the bed, please?"

"You want me closer?"

"Yes, please. So I can see your sexy bod better."

"Would you like your glasses?"

She had to think about that. "No, I'd have to take them off."

Morgan eased closer, his movements reminding her of a predator stalking his prey. "What if I like the sexy nerd look." He slid onto the bed next to her and stretched out, folding his arms behind his head.

Karma rolled her eyes. "We can roleplay tomorrow." She pulled herself up, taking in Morgan's powerful body. He wasn't bulky like some gym rat. Morgan had a swimmer's body, tall, lithe, pulsing with power and strength. She trailed her fingers over his muscular, smooth chest, then up and across his broad shoulder. His body amazed her.

His eyes followed her motions. Even with his fangs peeking from his full lips and his glowing red eyes, the man was handsome beyond words. How could this amazing man fall in love with *her*-curvy-nerdy-southern fried-self? She wouldn't question it anymore, not when she saw the truth shining in Morgan's eyes.

Karma focused on his sharp fangs and drew in a calming breath. She could do this. She could endure a few moments of pain for a lifetime of love. If Morgan's kisses and other oral skills were indications, she'd have a lifetime of fantastic sex, too. Her body was still aroused from the shower, and her pink bits quivered with anticipation. She trailed her finger back down his chest, circling his navel. His stomach quivered. Morgan inhaled when she ran her finger down his length.

She was ready and met his eyes. "Okay, let's get to the biting, so we can get to the mating."

Morgan's lips twitched. His eyes faded from red to amber and shimmered with mirth. A second later, the room filled with his deep, robust laughter. "Beautiful, you weren't paying attention when I'd explained it to you. Were you?"

"At the time, I didn't know I was your mate and didn't want to hear you explain what you'd do to the woman who would be. So—nope. I wasn't."

"Morgan," Karma exclaimed when he pulled her down on top of him. Her legs fell to either side of him, and his erection brushed against her opening.

He brushed his hand through her hair as a faint smile curved his lips. "I don't want to keep anything from you, yet I'm afraid what I'm about to say maybe a deal-breaker for you. At least for tonight."

Karma and Dani had talked on the short flight here. She'd explained about the biting and the fact Morgan would drink Karma's blood. Despite Dani's assurance, the bite wouldn't hurt—much, Karma had her doubts. Not about mating Morgan, just about the amount of pain involved. "Hmm, let me be the judge. Spill."

"During our lovemaking, when you are on the verge of peaking, I will bite you here." He brushed the area where her shoulder and neck met. His hand then smoothed down her back.

"And," she prompted, resting her chin on her folded arms and staring into his eyes.

"I will drink your blood. Then I will encourage you to bite me and take my blood."

"Bite you!" She shook her head. "Nope, I don't want to hurt you."

Morgan's smile slipped slightly. "That's okay, beautiful. There are other ways for you to take my blood."

Karma didn't have Morgan's mind-reading abilities yet, but she knew this was important to him. "Talk to me. Why is it significant I bite you?"

He rubbed his knuckles across her cheek and smiled. Not the typical smirk she'd come to love. No, Morgan's smile seemed sad, distant. "As you know, Dhampir heal quickly. In fact, the only time our bodies scar is from a near-fatal wound or a mating mark."

Maybe it was the blood he'd already given her, or she was so attuned to him. Whatever the reason, she knew the answer. Morgan wanted the world to see she accepted him as her mate. "I see. So, you want everyone to think I nearly killed you when we made love," Karma teased.

"Yes," Morgan laughed out. "That's precisely the reason. I want everyone to know I've mated a wild woman." He bussed her lips then fell back against the pillow, grinning. "You should also know, when you take my blood, you'll experience my life and know everything about me. There will be no secrets between us. Because of our bond, I'll always know where you are and what you feel, just as you will know where I am and my emotions."

"So the next time I get kidnapped—"

"Won't happen again. I'll make sure of it."

She felt the growl rumbling in his chest and rolled her eyes. "Yeah, just saying if it did, you'd know where I was and come to my rescue in minutes instead of days."

"I will *always* come after you." Morgan's eyes flashed a dark red, and his fangs lengthened. "Mine."

"I'm not yet, Wolfie."

"Wolfie? I'll show you wolfie." Morgan peppered her with playful kisses.

She laughed and nipped his chest above his right nipple. Morgan flipped them, and Karma found herself beneath him. The action had them laughing more. Their mirth quickly heated as Morgan's playful kisses turned passionate. He palmed her mound, then his fingers stroked her.

She arched below him. "Morgan, make me yours."

Morgan raised up on his arms. Love glowed in his eyes, silently asking once more if she were sure. His hard shaft pressed against her.

Karma spread her legs wide and took Morgan into her. He entered her slowly, stretching her, filling her completely.

Morgan kissed her as he moved in her, their rhythm in sync. Karma locked her legs around his. She clawed his shoulders and back, pulling him closer to her. Needing him closer.

Her body hummed the closer she came to her release. She needed something to push her over the edge.

Morgan broke off his kisses then nuzzled her neck, where her shoulder met her throat. He sank his fangs into her.

Karma arched her back as her body spasmed, and she shouted his name. The longer and harder Morgan drew on her neck, the more intense her orgasm. Wave after wave of pleasure surged through her, along with the overwhelming desire to bite him.

She struck.

Morgan yelled her name with his release as the sweet taste of his blood filled her mouth and trickled down her throat. Warmth rushed through Karma, and she clung to him as another wave of pleasure washed over her.

Historical events she'd only read about flash through her mind. No, they were more than bursts of time. She was living the events.

Her lungs burned from the smell of gunpowder. Bombs exploded around her as planes flew overhead. The scene changed, and Karma sat in a classroom studying Finance. The scene changed again. Karma found herself standing by a grave as her brother and sister-in-law's remains were lowered. Karma was in Morgan's mind, experiencing his lifetime, his memories. The love he had for his family wrapped her in warmth.

The images changed once more. Karma found herself in Magnus's office, stealthily returning his wedding photo. Then she stood over a bed, staring down at her beaten body.

Tears spilled from her eyes at the love Morgan had for her. Did she love him just as much? They'd only known each other for a few days. Somehow the amount of time didn't matter.

She loved him.

The moment she eased her teeth from Morgan's neck, his skin knitted together, leaving a nasty looking scar. She cringed at what she caused, then pressed a kiss to the area.

Morgan moaned, then lifted up on his arms, taking his weight from her. "Just so you know," he kissed her neck, causing her to clench around him again. "Our mate marks are erogenous zones."

"They are?" She nipped his shoulder again.

~ ~ ~

Karma woke and wiped the sleep from her eyes. Her girly parts were sore and tingling, not in a good way, either. She'd lost count of how many times they made love. At least twice in the shower, once on the couch, and too many times to count in the bed. She bet she'd be bowlegged for a year. At least she'd have a thigh-gap for the first time in her life.

As much as she'd like to remain snuggled against Morgan's warm body, her body reminded her again why she was awake. Karma shifted in Morgan's hold, ignoring his low rumbling growl. She had to pee.

From the moment they'd mated, he'd been in her mind, knowing what she needed and liked before she'd even realized it. But this? The man was clueless.

She tried rolling from Morgan only to have him tighten his hold. For someone who changed into a wolf, he had a penchant for impersonating a boa constrictor.

"Morgan." She bumped him with her rear.

He grunted.

"I have to get up." Heck, he'd gotten up sometime early this morning and gone into the other room to make a few calls. She was too tired to eavesdrop. "Morgan, please."

"Five more minutes, beautiful."

"My bladder won't wait five more minutes."

"Sorry." He eased his hold from her then kissed her neck, making her pink bits quiver.

Karma's inner muscles protested as she slipped from the bed. She wouldn't be taking a spin class anytime soon.

She glanced at Morgan, looking smug. Shaking her head, Karma plodded toward the bathroom. He was up to something. She didn't know what it was, but he was. He didn't *hide* it from her. Nope, not at all. Morgan shoved it in the back of his mind, where he hoped she wouldn't go. Whatever he had planned, she wouldn't spoil his surprise.

A sigh of relief from Morgan brushed against her mind.

"There'd better be coffee," she called as she shut the bathroom door. Karma spent a little more time in the bathroom than she'd initially planned, taking time to wash her face, brush her teeth, then run a brush through her hair.

Karma also examined her mating mark. The scars on her throat were so tiny she could barely see them, even with her glasses and leaning as close to the mirror as possible. A small part of her was disappointed the marks weren't bigger.

She opened the door. The bedroom was empty, and the sounds of faint voices in the other room had her pulling on her satin pajamas.

Morgan cracked open the bedroom door, slipping in so she couldn't see out into the living room area. "You're gorgeous, and I'm the luckiest man alive." He took her in his arms and kissed her.

He tasted of… "Coffee."

"Come on, beautiful. Breakfast is ready." There was a smugness about him.

Whatever Morgan had up his sleeve, figuratively since he'd only pulled on sleep pants, she'd find out soon enough. He opened the door for her, and her breath caught.

"Morgan?" She couldn't believe her eyes. Bouquets of yellow roses were placed around the room. The dining table was set with a white linen cloth and several covered dishes.

"I wanted to do something nice for you." Red tinged Morgan's handsome face. "I haven't really romanced you." He pulled a chair out for her. Once she sat, Morgan lifted a sterling cloche, revealing a small red velvet ring box. He trembled as he took the box and knelt. "Last night, I may have snuck a peek at what type of ring you'd like." He opened the box, and her jaw dropped.

"Morgan, it's…" If she'd ever designed herself a diamond ring, this would be it. The filigree rose gold band supported the largest diamond she'd ever seen.

"Do you like it?" He held the ring between his thumb and forefinger.

"I love it!" She flung herself at him, knocking him backward. The ring flew from his hand and slid across the marble floor.

"So, you like it. Huh?" His smile curved his lips, and his eyes shimmered.

"You know I do."

"Then let's get it on your finger." Morgan stretched, shifting his nails to claws, and hooked the ring. He sat up, keeping her on his lap. Morgan took her hand and slipped the ring onto her finger. The fit was perfect.

"I love you." Morgan lowered his head, his lips pressed against hers, then gently covered her mouth.

Coffee could wait. Her fingers threaded through his thick hair as she parted her lips for him.

Morgan angled his head, his tongue plunging into her mouth, and she returned his kiss with equal passion.

A cold shiver ran through her.

Their room door flew open, and she flinched.

In a quick, smooth motion, Morgan set her from him. He crouched between her and the intruder. Black fur rippled over him as he snarled. "I broke your nose a few hours ago."

"Whatever." Paul shrugged and held out his phone. "Mom's on the phone. She wants to speak to your mate."

"Our door was locked."

"Master key." Paul grinned.

Anger and fear knotted inside of Karma. Anger 'cause she'd been cocked-blocked by Paul. And fear, 'cause yeah, she stared at the pissed-off face of her mother-in-law.

Chapter Fourteen

Karma swallowed hard. This wasn't the way she'd wanted to meet Morgan's mother. Smiling, Morgan took her hand, helping her to her feet, then brushed a kiss to her temple. He slipped his arm around her waist then snatched the phone from Paul.

"Good morning, Mrs. Wolfe," Karma greeted. Lord have mercy, it was a good thing she decided to put on pajamas and drag a brush through her hair. "It's a pleasure to meet you."

Liar. The word echoed in Karma's mind. Why did she hear Paul's voice in her head?

"I should have known this was one of Paul's cruel jokes." The anger faded from the woman's eyes, and a warm smile lit her face. "Please call me Gwyn, Karma. *It is Karma?*"

"Yes, ma'am. That's my given name."

Because her mother was too drunk to come up with something else. The foreign thought fluttered through Karma's mind, and her knees buckled.

Morgan stiffened and slipped his arm around her waist. He pulled her to him. "Where are my manners? Mom, I'd like you to meet Karma, my mate." She noticed Morgan tilt his head to one side, showing his mating mark. "Before you ask, I've given her a ring. We haven't discussed wedding plans." He glared over his shoulder at Paul and flashed his fangs.

Gwyn's smile grew broader. "I am so happy for you both. Karma, I apologize for the intrusion. Paul, one of these days, I'm gonna knock a hen egg out of you."

"Dream on, Mom." Paul laughed and plopped down into a chair. "Breakfast! Great! I'm starved."

Morgan reached behind him, sliding the cloche covered plate out of Paul's reach. "There's a nice restaurant in the lobby if you're hungry. I suggest you leave while mom can protect you."

Gwyn sighed. "I'll let you two get back to your celebration. Paul, you should leave. Before I go, Karma. Please call me whenever. I'd love to talk to you more and perhaps start making wedding plans."

"I'll call you, Gwyn. As far as wedding plans go..." Karma shrugged. "Perhaps Dani and I can do a video chat with you."

"Danielle Rossi?"

"Yes, ma'am. We've been best friends since we were kids. In fact, I'm closer to her family than I am my own."

"Oh, that's wonderful. I'll give Gina Rossi a call right now." The screen went black.

"That was rich." Paul laughed. "Karma, you should have seen your face. Damn, I haven't had this much fun since I punked Niki. Hell, I got you and Mom. It's a good thing you still had your clothes on when I came in. I wouldn't want Mom seeing you getting it on." *Hell, I would've hated to see your naked ass.*

Karma gripped Morgan's arm to keep her balance. Paul's hateful words echoed in her head.

"Beautiful?" The concern flowing from Morgan warmed her.

"I'm fine. Nothing that a little coffee can't fix." She drew in a cleansing breath and poured herself a cup.

"Here, sit." Morgan slid a chair out for her. "I think our breakfast is cold now." He glared at his brother. "But I can put in another order."

Karma started into Paul's dark eyes. She wanted him to know he didn't frighten her. If anything, he should fear her. "You lied to your mother about me, Paul."

He leaned back in the chair, grinning. "I wouldn't say I lied." *Told her how I saw you.*

"What did you tell Mom," Morgan growled.

"It's fine." Karma tasted her eggs. "The food's still warm. Let's eat, Morgan. Today's gonna be a doozy. We need to get hold of Percy, find out if he was successful in taking down the bounty. Did Cade get back safe, and have you heard anything about Melody?"

"Cade?" Paul pointed the remote at the TV. "He made the news."

The television flicked on. A young female reporter stood in front of a burned-out van. "According to the police, they believe this was a drug deal gone bad. Witnesses say the van exploded into flames. No one noticed anyone near the van prior to the explosion. We'll have more information at noon, back to you, Fred."

"Turn it off, Paul. Then close the door behind you on the way out." The vein in Morgan's forehead throbbed as he dug into his breakfast.

Karma reached over, covering his hand with hers. "I'll be glad when this nightmare is over." For some reason, the food didn't taste good anymore.

"Beautiful, it will be over soon. Viktor and Percy are working on the bounty. They've posted their own ads and warnings against harming you on the web. Royce has called in favors. Trust me, nothing is going to happen to you again." Morgan leaned over, bussing her cheek. "As for Cade, he's fine, and Melody arrived home safe and sound. Flint, however, said to tell you, bless your heart for putting up with that woman."

"You need to give him a raise." Karma bit into a slice of bacon.

"Are y'all seriously gonna sit there and eat in front of me?"

It seems my little brother doesn't like being ignored. Morgan's voice echoed in Karma's mind. He lifted his cup, hiding his smirk. *I'm sorry, beautiful. I'd planned something special for you, and he... Damn him.*

"The roses, my ring, breakfast, everything is wonderful. I'm proud to be your mate." Karma would tell Morgan what she thought of his brother but didn't want to harp on the negative.

Morgan winked. "You know, my mom may turn into a wolf, but she's a bulldog when it comes to planning weddings."

"I gathered that bit of info from you last night." She squeezed her thighs at the memory. "I don't think your mother will go for my dream wedding. Small, as in under twenty people. On *our* beach at sunset."

"I'd like the idea much better than what my mother would come up with ."

"Hey, didn't you hear me?" Paul raised his voice.

"Are you still here, Paul?" Karma flashed him her, you're an ass smile. Again. Second time in less than twenty-four hours. Some people are just thick.

"You're a real bit—"

Morgan's chair fell back, and before it hit the floor, he held Paul by the throat, feet dangling above the ground. "Since you walked through the door, you've done nothing but insult my mate. Tell me why I shouldn't rip your head from your shoulders."

Morgan had heard his brother's thoughts, too. As much as she'd like to see Paul get his comeuppance, she couldn't let Morgan kill Paul. "Wolfie, he needs oxygen. He's turning blue."

"We can't die from asphyxia."

"True, but when y'all die, you turn to dust, so yeah. Lack of oxygen kills brain cells, and I don't think your brother has any to spare. Just saying."

A faint grin ghosted across Morgan's lips. "You're right, beautiful." He tossed Paul toward the door. "Get out."

Paul's eyes glowed with his wolf, and gray fur pushed from his pores as he sprang to his feet. "You want to challenge me, bro? Bring it."

Anger was evident in every one of Morgan's muscles. If he went after Paul, it wouldn't bode well. Karma held her breath, knowing she wouldn't be able to stop the fight.

"You don't want to do this," Morgan's voice was way too calm.

"Coward," Paul taunted.

Cold chills ran down Karma's back again.

"You shouldn't talk about yourself that way, Paul. It's unhealthy," Ryder stated as he strolled into the room. He positioned himself between Morgan and Paul.

Cade, Magnus, and Dani entered, with her hurrying to Karma's side.

"K, are you all right?"

"I'm fine." She pushed her glasses up on her nose, thankful for the arrival of the others.

"Holy mackerel, look at the size of that rock. Dang, girl, Morgan's got good taste." Dani's eyes grew wide. "You have fang marks. You're mated. Yes! Cade pay up. I've gotta text Mom the news." She fished her phone from her pocket.

"You bet on Morgan and me?" Why wasn't Karma surprised?

"Just a teensy wager. Mom's going to be so pumped when she reads this."

Cade chuckled. "You call five Gs a teensy wager?"

Magnus patted Cade's back. "She did suggest babysitting if you lost, but you wanted to wager for cash."

"What are you all doing here?" Morgan growled.

Magnus was dressed in a suit and tie, nothing unusual here. Karma doubted the man owned a pair of jeans, but why the entourage? Something was up.

Tension filled Magnus's body as he maneuvered abreast of Morgan and patted his back. "If you two are going to have a meeting of the minds, I suggest you take it somewhere else. The last time, Morgan, the damage you caused to this suite set us back a hundred K."

Morgan kept his sight on Paul. So, not good. "You haven't answered my question, Magnus. What's going on?"

"Just a small altercation. Nothing as exciting as what's going on here."

Ryder gripped Paul's shoulder. "We're here ensuring you're alive and Karma not gone."

"Ha, even they know I can kick your ass, Morg." Paul jerked free, glaring at Ryder. "I wouldn't have killed him, and I sure as hell wouldn't have laid a hand on his mate."

"You may not," Ryder snapped, "but the three faders who slipped in when you left your post would have. Considering they mistook Magnus and Dani for Morgan and Karma."

"What?" Karma gasped. No, no, no. This couldn't be happening. "Dani, are you okay? What happened? How did this happen?" She couldn't lose Dani, but she'd die if she lost Morgan.

"Beautiful." Morgan drew Karma to his side. "No one's going to harm you."

"It's not me I'm worried about. Magnus, what happened?"

"They attacked as we were leaving our suite." Magnus's eyes glowed. He advanced, shoving his finger against Paul's chest. "Had my mate been injured in any way because of your carelessness, I would have killed you. Then I'd have swept your worthless ashes into an envelope and mailed them back to your parents with a note expressing my sincere apologies for your birth."

The color and smirk faded from Paul's face. "I secured my post. I made the rounds before I left. No one was there, and I didn't sense anyone."

"You also didn't wait for me to relieve you." Cade's pupils elongated, and tawny fur rippled over his face. "I called you, but your line was busy. Then I tried to mentally contact you, but you blocked me."

"Paul," Morgan snarled. "What were you doing?"

"I was busy."

"Really," the word spewed from Karma, and all eyes turned to her. "You were busy trying to put your little childish prank into action. This is twice your bull almost cost your brother his life. Lord have mercy, how old are you? Two?"

Paul just gaped at her.

Karma turned, heading to the bedroom. "It's too early in the morning and not enough coffee to deal with your crap."

Something weighed in her pajama pocket. Dang it, she still had Paul's phone. The last thing she wanted was to go back and return it to him. Never in her life had she wanted to shake some sense into someone.

"I guess your mate's a little hormonal, bro."

Hormonal? Smiling, Karma pulled the phone from her pocket. She'd show Paul hormonal.

~ ~ ~

This wasn't how Morgan imagined the morning after his mating. He didn't give a damn anymore about Paul's feelings. All morning Paul had made hateful comments. Not out loud, but Morgan knew Karma had heard them. He was as big an ass because he hadn't done a friggin' thing to stop it. Good grief, he should have sent his brother away last night. "Beautiful."

Magnus caught Morgan by the arm. "Nope. Not this time, we have issues to discuss. Dani." Magnus nodded toward the bedroom door.

"I'll make sure she's okay." Dani disappeared into the bedroom.

Morgan's stomach churned. Of all the people in the world, he should trust any of his brothers with Karma's life. "Paul, I can't trust you to protect my mate."

"What? I'm your brother."

"And her brother by our mating, but you've only shown Karma disrespect. In fact, you've been disrespectful to all the women. Nichole won't speak to you Simone won't look you in the eye. That ought to make you feel proud."

"Not my fault, y'all can't take a joke."

Morgan blamed himself as well as his family. For over five years, they'd treated him with kid gloves, allowing Paul to get away with his shit. He was well overdue for an ass-whooping. Paul didn't want to see the consequences of his actions. The night Peter was killed, Paul changed, becoming uncaring and reckless. "A joke? You think putting people's lives in danger is a joke? You're an ass."

"Better an ass than Royce's lapdog."

"Speaking of Royce," Ryder interrupted. "He and Declan have decided until you grow up and pull your head out of your ass, Paul. You're not on any team. We can't trust you to have our six."

"You're blackballing me because my stuck-up brothers can't take a joke."

"You're not being blackballed. You're being put on suspension until we can trust you to have our backs." Ryder's eyes glowed, and the kid's horns pushed from his forehead. "Your actions nearly made four other children orphaned like Shelby."

At the mention of Shelby's name Paul jerked. His eyes shimmered, and he stormed toward the door then stopped. "Morgan, my phone, please."

Dani strolled toward them, holding Paul's phone. "Karma accidentally slipped it in her pocket."

"Thanks." Paul snatched the device from her.

"Glad I still have all my fingers," Dani shouted at the slammed door. "K will be out shortly. She's getting dressed." She eyed Morgan up and down. "Something you might consider doing unless you want to go to the research lab wearing your PJs. I can't wait to see the progress Doctor Needham has made on the prosthetic eye."

"In a minute." Morgan met Ryder's cold eyes. "Tell me what happened with the faders. Do we know who they were?"

"They attacked Magnus and Dani as they were coming to meet with Cade and me." Ryder smiled. "Wasn't much of a fight. As for who they were…" He shrugged.

"I didn't know them," Cade replied. "Then again, I didn't know all of Zeno's loyalists."

"One thing we haven't mentioned," Ryder added. "It was three faders and a human. From the shock on the human's face when one of his comrades turned to dust, he didn't know about us."

Fur pushed from Morgan's arms. They had unknown groups after his mate. "What about the security cameras?" The Dhampir could only claim so many horror movies being filmed to explain what was captured on cameras.

"Flint's taken care of it," Cade replied. "As for the human, no prints, no facial recognition, so far. I've sent Viktor a photo. But does it really matter who he was? You're not planning on sending his next of kin a sympathy card."

"True. However, I'd still like to know who we're dealing with. I'm wondering if Whitehall and Canaday are working with or against each other?"

Magnus stroked his chin. "I don't think Canaday knows about us. I do believe they are working together, but with different resources."

Morgan had to hand it to Magnus. His hypothesis made sense. It also meant Karma was in even more danger. "I've decided until this is over, I'm sending Karma to the ranch."

"Think again, Wolfie." Karma strolled toward him, holding her cellphone. His eyes dipped to the gentle sway of her hips. He didn't know if he liked her better in a dress or the fitted, vintage, herringbone, brown slacks, and cream, fitted, button-down she wore. Her outfit accented her lush figure nicely. The only thing he didn't like was the cheap costume pearls around her neck. He'd have to get her a set of matching pearls.

"Wolfie? Bloody hell, I love it," Percy's amusement resonated through the room, pulling Morgan from his perusal.

"Yes, well," Magnus cleared his throat. "Percy, since you're on speaker, fill *Wolfie* in on the recent development."

I'm so sorry for not putting a stop to Paul. Morgan looped his arm around Karma's waist. "Remind me again, Magnus, why we're still partners."

Karma licked her lower lip and winked. *You can make it up to me tonight.* The sensation of her words echoing through his mind had him semi-hard.

Magnus patted him on the back. "Because we're the only ones who can work with each other. We'd kill anyone else."

"If you're ready, sirs." Percy was all business. "I've informed Lady K of our success. Viktor and I were able to remove the post. However, we do not know how many have already seen it. Royce has alerted Declan if you need a quick response team, they're ready."

"Thank you."

"Right, now to the bad news," Percy replied. "It's bothered me how someone made it past our firewalls and security. We've back-traced the breach to one particular computer at Wolfmoon Corporation. I've forwarded the information to Karma."

"Name! Whoever it is will be terminated if I don't kill them first."

"It's Avery, sir. Shall I have security question her?"

"I'll cancel our appointment with Doctor Needham." Dani sighed, pulling out her phone. "I'll talk to him tomorrow night about his advancements."

Every ounce of anger drained from Morgan. His wolf snarled, knowing there was more to this than they knew. Avery would never betray them. "No. I'll question her."

"I thought you'd say that, sir. I've taken the liberty of notifying her father. Avery and Frank will be waiting for you at ten in the conference room. Flint has already been made aware."

"Thank you, Percy." Morgan ended the call, knowing he was about to rip the heart out of an innocent.

Chapter Fifteen

Morgan didn't know why Magnus insisted they waited in their suite to go down and speak with Avery. Ever since Morgan had given Karma her ring, they hadn't had a moment alone. Well, after he dealt with Avery, he'd take Karma for a romantic picnic by the sea, just the two of them.

To help pass the time, he'd ordered scones and danish. Morgan glanced at the clock, wanting to get this meeting over with. He wasn't looking forward to the coming confrontation. "Magnus, let me question Avery."

"Right, because you won't frighten the girl. You go in there growling at the child, and her father will gut you."

"I don't know how my mother put up with you two," Dani huffed. " You've already convicted Avery without knowing all the facts."

Morgan sighed. "Danielle—"

"Don't Danielle me, Morgan Octavius Wolfe." She turned her attention to Karma holding up the coffee pot, wiggling it back and forth. "You know about Avery, right?"

Karma nodded and held out her cup. "I know she's on the Autism spectrum. Do you think she would let me have a look at her computer?"

"Probably. She's very trusting. What are you thinking, K?"

"The file Percy sent me was malware containing a keylogger, but it wasn't embedded in an email or attached to a file. I'm wondering if someone gained access to her computer. What are Avery's duties again?"

Morgan squeezed Karma's hand. "Basically, she's the assistant to my assistant, and despite her disability, Avery does a far better job than Blythe."

Karma laughed. "Well, you do have a tendency to go through PAs. As for Blythe, from what I saw in your mind, she's as useful as tits on a bull. Not to mention rude as hell. What business was it of hers as to why we were sharing a room?"

"Sorry, beautiful. I shouldn't have asked you to answer the call."

Karma rolled her eyes. "Kinda ironic, her ringtone is a funeral drudge."

"Tits on a bull are more useful," Dani chimed in. "I'm sorry I ever hired the twit."

"Tell us how you really feel, Dani." Karma laughed. "If Blythe isn't cutting it, why are you keeping her around?"

Why indeed? Morgan mused. "Hmm, maybe the Director of Human resources can answer that."

"Blythe hasn't done anything that's warranted counseling or termination. Granted, she's a certifiable bitch, but you can't fire someone for that. If you could..." Dani smiled and pointed to herself. "I would. As for Avery, I've been trying to get her to transfer from Dallas to Atlanta. She'd be perfect working with DuMond Enterprises, but she won't leave her family. Avery's a good worker. An excellent worker. Give her a task, and she'll put two hundred percent into it. I'm still shocked she even flew out here to help with the event."

"I'm curious. How did you come about hiring Avery?" Karma asked.

"You see, K. Avery's family has served the Dhampir for generations. As a matter of fact, her grandmother was my nana's secretary. Avery doesn't know about us, though. Her parents don't think she can be trusted with the secret simply because she's is too honest."

"What will you tell her in twenty years when you haven't aged?"

"Plastic surgery, dah." Dani reached for another scone then slathered it with clotted cream. "Besides, Avery doesn't like change. At. All. So, us never changing will be a plus."

"Danielle," Magnus groaned and shook his head.

Karma peered up at Morgan. "From what you've all said, I can't see Avery intentionally installing this on her computer. I saw in your memories last night of your amusement over persuading her to change her password. Do you honestly think, Morgan, Avery would have willingly downloaded this file or has the knowledge to do it?"

He knew she wouldn't. Avery hated any changes and was the last one to her take her laptop to tech support. "No, I don't. Avery is resistant to any change, including updating her laptop."

"Then we shouldn't rush to judgment until we have all the facts. Something doesn't smell right."

"If someone convinced her to do it…"

Karma smiled sweetly at him. "Even if it was someone she trusted?"

Well, hell. He hadn't thought about that. "Updates and patches were handled by IT. I'd hate to think someone in that department was responsible, but it makes more sense than Avery."

Dani drained her coffee cup then set it on the bar. "Who's idea was it to put this off until ten?"

Karma batted her lashes and blew Dani a kiss. "Yours, buttercup. You said it would give us plenty of time to develop a game plan before Avery and her father arrive. Considering we may have to investigate the IT department, I best make sure Percy's on standby."

"I've already texted him. He and Viktor are ready for us." He bussed her cheek.

"Why are you growling?" Karma patted his chest. "Stop it."

"Sorry."

"I know how much Avery means to you. Trust me, you're worrying for nothing." She snuggled against him, resting her head against his arm.

He wished he had Karma's faith. Morgan had watched Avery grow up and overcome so many challenges. Terminating her would be detrimental, as would moving her to another department, but what choice did he have if he couldn't trust her anymore? Morgan had to think about the Dhampir. Since Royce put an end to Zeno, over half of the Dhampir's wealth was tied up in Wolfmoon and DuMond Enterprises. When you live as long as the Dhampir, you had to have a means of securing your wealth without drawing attention.

"I can't sit here any longer." He stood, holding his hand out to Karma.

She took his hand. "Let's go. This way, we can set up anything we need to link in with Percy."

Ryder led their small group from the suite, with Cade bringing up the rear. After the last two attacks, Morgan wouldn't ever stop worrying about Karma.

She stopped and peered up at him. "Guys, give us a moment, please."

"Sure," Dani replied, "but they can still hear ya."

Karma rolled her eyes and cupped his face. *Morgan, I'm worried about you. These assholes want you dead, not me. I know I can't stop you from worrying, but I want the laughing, smirking man I fell in love with back.*

Morgan swept Karm up in his arms and kissed her. He knew Karma loved him. He'd felt her love for him when they mated, but she'd never actually said she did until now. She kissed back with a fury, matching his.

Magnus thumbed Morgan's back. "Save it for later, you two. The sooner we put this to bed, the sooner..." Magnus's taunting laugh echoed in the hall.

Morgan broke off his kiss and flipped Magnus a bird. "I love you, beautiful. Until I know Whitehall and Canaday are taken care of, I'm going to worry." He slipped his arm around her waist. Touching Karma kept his wolf at bay.

"I know." She followed him into the elevator. "I'm going to worry about you just as much."

As the doors slid open, Morgan didn't miss the subtle looks from the few employees who'd flown up for the event. They all wanted answers to the same question. Who was the woman on his arm?

"Who's the woman?"

"I don't know. Did you see her ring?"

"Girl, if I knew Hunk-master liked curvy, I'd have ditched the diet years ago."

"I'd pay anything to see Blythe's face."

Morgan didn't need to tell his employees Karma was special. His hand around her waist did it for him.

Karma glanced at him. "Why are you so smug all of a sudden?"

"You love me."

"Yes, I do."

He was giddy as a schoolboy. "How would you feel if I announce our engagement at the charity event?"

"You see those two over there? I'm sure they'll have us married and our kids off to college by the time we finished with our meeting."

"Office gossip. Gotta love it." He led her behind the reception desk.

"No, I don't. That's why I like working from home."

"So, I can't convince you to become my assistant?"

"Corporations forensic accountant, independent of the CFO. Plus, I want six weeks of paid vacation, onsite childcare, and a corner office." Heads jerked around at Karma's statement.

"Deal." Getting Karma to work with him was easier than he'd thought.

"Your grin is turning a little creepy." He pushed opened the door, and Karma gasped.

Sobbing, Avery leaned against her father. The two were flanked by security officers.

Morgan met the eyes of one officer. "What's going on here?"

"We're escorting them from the property per your instructions."

"My instructions?" Karma was right again. There was more going on than he knew. "Who relayed this to you?" He captured Karma's hand as they stepped into the hall, followed by Magnus, Dani, and Cade, who closed the metal door.

Their group forced Avery and her father, Frank, to move back. The hallway wasn't an ideal place, but at least with the heavy door closed, their conversation wouldn't be overheard by those lingering around reception and in the atrium.

"Blythe, sir."

"First we were told to be down here at ten, then we get a call demanding we show up at eight. Why in the hell did you terminate us?" Frank glared over Avery's head at Morgan. "Never mind. I ought to punch you in the face."

"I don't blame you, Frank. I'd be pissed too, but you're not terminated." Morgan glanced over his shoulder. "Ryder."

"On it." He pointed to the security guards. "You two with me now."

"Yes, sir." They followed Ryder down the corridor towards Flint's office.

Morgan wouldn't fault them for following orders, but what was Blythe doing?

"Mr. Wolfe." Avery lifted her face from Frank's chest. The hurt on her tear-stained face was a knife to Morgan's heart. "What did I do wrong?" Her words just twisted the knife deeper.

Morgan met Avery's blue eyes and pressed into her mind. Sifting through her cluttered mind, he tried to find anything that would prove her guilt. He discovered a wealth of information, showing her devotion to him and the company, but nothing indicating her guilt.

"Morgan." Karma squeezed his hand, drawing him from Avery's mind.

"You didn't do anything wrong, Avery," he assured the girl.

Frank squared his shoulders. "If she didn't do anything wrong, then why put her through this hell? You know the effect it could have on her? Good grief, the flight here was stressful enough."

Anything Morgan said would sound like an excuse.

"Hi, I'm Karma." She glanced up at Frank then smiled at Avery. "I'm the forensic accountant, and I wanted to meet with Avery to go through her laptop. I didn't want to alert anyone within the company. That's why Percy Westmoreland contacted you. I don't know why Blythe terminated you—"

"Especially since she doesn't have the authority," Dani snapped. "That's *my* job, and I can assure you, neither of you is terminated."

"You can't see my computer." Avery sniffed, dragging her arm across her nose. "Blythe took it. Why did you want to see it?"

"Morgan, we need Avery's computer."

"Already on it," Cade reassured Karma.

Morgan peered down the empty corridor then opened the door to one of the conference rooms. "Let's continue this in here."

Cade tapped Morgan's shoulder. "Ryder has secured Avery's laptop and is bringing it. Our tech guy was about to scrub the hard drive. Blythe delivered it to him, stating you ordered the scrub. Do you want Ryder to detain her?"

"No." *Keep an eye on her. I want to gather as much info as possible before we confront her. I hate to say it, but she may be innocent, too, though I doubt it.*

Blythe? Innocent? Cade's laughter resonated in Morgan's mind. *Maybe when she was born.*

Morgan flipped on the lights, gagging on the foul odor. Blythe's perfume lingered on the air, raising a question as to what she was doing here.

"Someone really likes the fragrance, Blood Rose." Karma waved her hand in front of her face then sneezed.

"*Gesundheit*," Avery whispered.

"Thank you."

"We just left this room." Avery sniffed and hung her head.

That answered his question.

Dani hooked her arm with Avery's, leading her to the adjoining bathroom. "Let's freshen up, then we'll tackle all this. Coming, Karma?"

"Right behind you."

~ ~ ~

Karma's heart ached for the young woman as she followed Dani and Avery. It was easy to see why someone would use Avery as a scapegoat, but to do so would be like kicking a puppy.

Karma's curiosity got the best of her. "Avery, do you know what a keylogger is?"

She gave a faint nod and pushed against a door. "It's a program that allows others to see what you are typing."

"That's correct." Karma was taken aback at the lavish bathroom. "Dang, this bathroom is as nice as the one in our room."

Only the best. Morgan replied. The sensation of his voice in her mind had her sighing.

"I knew I shouldn't have come on this trip." Avery twined her hands, staring at the floor.

"Nonsense." Dani handed Avery a paper towel. "Wash your face, then fix your makeup."

"Yes, ma'am." The red blotches on Avery's face slowly faded with the cold water.

After reapplying a pale shade of lipstick, Avery stared at herself in the mirror. A forced smile curved her lips. "Why did Blythe lie?"

Dani slipped her arm around Avery's shoulders. "We're going to get to the bottom of this, but we're going to need your help. Are you ready?"

"I'm ready." With a determined gleam in her eyes, Avery squared her shoulders.

Hey, beautiful. Cade just dropped off Avery's laptop. How's she doing? Morgan's voice resonated in Karma's mind.

She's good. We're coming out. Karma focused on Avery and smiled. "Morgan and Magnus have your computer."

"Good." Avery flung open the restroom door. "I'll need it to do my job."

"Ladies, let's get started." Morgan handed Karma the laptop then smiled at Avery.

The cherry conference table wasn't massive, but it dominated the small room.

"Where's Cade?" Not that it mattered, but Karma figured he'd be lurking.

"And Father," worry tinged Avery's voice.

"They're working with Ryder and Flint." Morgan pulled out a chair for Karma, then he motioned for Avery to take the seat beside her.

"Magnus and I thought it best they oversaw security." Morgan took the seat at the head while Magnus and Dani sat across from Karma and Avery.

"Father likes working. So do I."

"Okay, let's get started. Avery." Karma slid the computer over.

"Blythe won't be happy I'm not fired anymore." Avery lifted the lid and powered on the laptop.

The facial recognition didn't work. Well, poop. "Try your password, Avery." Karma watched each keystroke, trying not to laugh when she figured out Avery's password was cats rock 15.

"My password isn't working, either."

"Hmm, let me see." Karma slid the computer in front of her. Morgan's password was a master…Her fingers hovered above the keys. "Question. Magnus, how many times did you log into Avery's laptop?"

"Once…No twice. Twice, I'm sure of it. Why?"

"And you didn't change your password afterward? What about you, Morgan. How many times did you have to log Avery in on her computer?"

Morgan leaned back in his chair and steepled his fingers. His left eyebrow inched toward his thick black hair. "Since we were hacked, it's protocol for every employee to change their password every ten to twelve days. Why do you ask?" He cringed. "Magnus, we're idiots."

"Speak for yourself. I only did it twice."

"Yes, but you were the one who embezzled the money and sent it to an offshore bank."

"What am I missing?" Dani looked from Morgan to Karma. "Dang it, K. You know I don't like to be kept in the dark."

"I have a theory, but to confirm it, I'll need to get into Avery's computer. We know a keylogger was installed on this device. This means, every time someone logged in, their passwords were captured. Even after everyone changed their passwords."

"*Oy vey.*" Dani wagged her finger between Morgan and Magnus. "You could change your passwords a hundred times, and they'd still had access to it. I bet Avery had problems logging in shortly after you two updated your passwords."

A low growl came from Morgan, and Karma covered his hand with hers.

He pulled his hand from her and stood. Tension filled every line of his body. "This explains why it looked like Magnus embezzled the money. He was here while I was at the ranch taking care of family business. Is there any way to find out who installed the keylogger?"

"Blythe did," Avery replied. "She wanted to make sure I didn't go anyplace on the company website I wasn't supposed to. She also insisted I brought my laptop on this trip to work."

"Of course, she did." Dani's tight-lipped expression meant the hat was going on, and monkeys would fly. "Avery, each employee has a certain clearance level depending on their job title. There was no way you could have gone anyplace you weren't allowed. So, K, can you hack into it?"

"Should be a piece of cake."

Magnus pushed from his seat and headed toward the coffee pot. "Karma, you're starting to sound like Percy, not an accountant." She watched as he made a fresh pot.

"That's forensic accountant," she teased, fishing out her phone and cable. "I've learned a thing or two over the years. I had to in order to follow the money trail. You'd be surprised at the obscure files I had to dig through to find where people hid money."

"Kinda like you did, babe." Dani batted her lashes at her mate. "And you didn't even give me access to the accounts."

"That wasn't me, and you know it. Karma, would you like a cup of coffee?"

Dani huffed. "Karma? What about me?"

Avery was out of her seat and heading toward the coffee pot. "I can get the coffee, Mr. DuMond. That's my job."

Excuse me? Karma stared at Morgan. *Her job? Really?*

It's not like you think, beautiful. Morgan slid his chair back, standing. "I'll get the coffee. Avery, as of this moment, your *job* is to assist Karma." He winked. "Would you like a cup, too?"

"Yes, please." She eased back into her seat. "What would you like me to do?"

"Let's see. What are your normal duties other than getting Morgan coffee?"

Excitement lit Avery's face. "When I can log on, the first thing I do is gather all the financial reports. Mr. Wolfe showed me where to go and how to download the files. Then I send them to him and Mr. DuMond. While the files are downloading, I update Mr. Wolfe's calendar. After I do that, if he's in his office, I carry him his coffee and collect any intracompany messages he wants me to deliver. If he's not in the office, I check with Blythe, order her lunch, and run any errands she has for me. I don't understand why my password doesn't work. It worked fine yesterday."

Karma met Avery's worried face. "I think someone changed it."

"Why?"

"So you would have to ask Morgan or someone with higher clearance to log in for you."

Dani tugged on the cord. "How's this going to help, K?"

"It allows me to connect my phone to the computer and use Percy's password breaker to override the computer."

"Is that legal?" Dani asked. "I mean…"

Karma activated the program then watched the screen. "Percy's version is a little more advanced than the ones you can download off the net."

Morgan handed her a cup of coffee then one to Avery. "Will you be able to see who changed Avery's password?"

"Once I'm in, I'll be able to see a lot more, included when the keylogger software was installed."

After staring at the screen for several minutes, Karma huffed. This was taking longer than she'd thought. "If this doesn't work soon, I'll call Percy." She drained the last of her coffee, setting the cup down a little too hard.

Avery snatched it up. "Would you like another cup…Miss Karma?"

"No, thank you. And it's Karma, just Karma."

Morgan chuckled and leaned over Karma, resting his hands on her shoulders. "Not for long it won't be," he whispered. "Once we're married, you'll be Mrs. Wolfe."

Avery's smile could light up the darkest room.

Morgan laughed. "Avery, you are the first Wolfmoon employee to know I've asked Karma to be my wife."

"Did you say yes?" Avery's smile grew brighter and her eyes wider.

"I did." Karma held up her hand, wiggling her fingers. Her ring sparkled under the fluorescent office light.

Avery grabbed her hand. "Oh, that's beautiful, Mr. Wolfe."

"Thank you, Avery. I'm glad you approve." Humor rang in Morgan's voice, and his eyes shimmered.

Dani held up her cellphone, wiggling it back and forth. "You know, while we're waiting, I can always call mom."

Karma groaned. If it were up to her, she and Morgan would elope. "Oh good, I'm in. Let's see when this program was installed."

Dani laughed. "Chicken."

The conference room door flew opened, and a woman gasped. "I'm sorry, Mr. Wolfe. I didn't know you were having a meeting."

"Why don't you join us, Blythe?" Morgan's voice dripped with sarcasm, and a frightening sneer curved his lips. "You can have a seat at the end of the table."

"I...um."

"Whatever you were doing can wait." Morgan pointed to the chair. "Sit."

Karma glanced at him, making sure fur hadn't sprouted. She'd seen Morgan mad, but this...This was intense. His face was void of all expression, and his eyes were cold dark orbs.

Chapter Sixteen

The atmosphere in the room changed from lightheartedness to overwhelming oppression. Karma glanced at the woman long enough to see the vibe Blythe emanated. She didn't care who she stepped on her way to the top. Everything was about her.

Clicking on a file, Karma turned her attention back to the screen. She shouldn't prejudge the woman simply from the way she dressed or the attitude she projected. Karma had seen and worked with enough women like Blithe to understand her insecurities. Women like her always viewed other women as adversaries in both work and life. She doubted Blythe had any real friends.

Tearing her attention from Blythe, Karma focused on Morgan. "The keylogger was installed at the end of April. There's also evidence of large amounts of deleted data. Avery, did you delete a bunch of files yesterday?"

"No. I only changed my password. I don't like deleting anything. You never know when you may need it."

"Well then, let's see if I can figure out what was deleted."

Blythe shifted in her seat, angling her head. Obviously, she wanted to see the computer screen. "Too bad, you can't undelete the information."

Karma cut her eyes at the woman and smiled. She clicked through the files, finding a wealth of information. "Here's a little known fact, when you delete information from a computer, it's not gone. The computer marks the files as able to be used, and as long as the files aren't overwritten with new data, the deleted info can be retrieved. Bingo!"

Movement caught Karma's attention. Morgan pointed a remote at the flatscreen behind him. "Karma, you said April?"

"Correct."

The images of Whitehall and Canaday appeared on the screen. "Do either of you know these men?" he asked, punctuating each word.

Still not furry, but snarly.

Karma glanced at Blythe. Clear recognition showed on her face, but the idiot shook her head. Lying to Morgan was so not a good idea.

"That's Royce and Glen," Avery answered with excitement. "They took Blyth and me to lunch once."

Karma looked up and bit her tongue. She'd never met Glen McPhee but knew him through the connection she shared with Morgan. As for Royce, Karma had video chatted with him. Yeah …Someone was catfished.

Dani shot Morgan a glance while Magnus sat stone-faced.

What she would give to know what they were thinking, but wasn't going to peek in Morgan's mind. She went back to work, clicking through the deleted files and going further down the rabbit hole. Holy cannoli! She'd hit the motherload. "Ah, Morgan."

"I only met Royce that one time," Avery continued, "but Glen's picked Blythe up at work for lunch several times." She pointed to the image of Canaday. "They haven't asked me to go to lunch with them again."

"Avery," Blythe hissed.

Dani's eyebrows rose to her hairline. Oh, Karma had seen that look before. Yep, monkeys would fly, but what she'd found was more critical than Dani getting her bitch on.

"Morgan," Karma tried to get his attention again. He really needed to see this.

Not now, beautiful. His dark eyes bore down on Blythe. "How do you know them?"

Blythe shrugged. "I met them at the Two Dog. It's not against company policy to go out. Is it?"

"No, it's not," Morgan's voice grew even colder. "Avery, your father is waiting for you out in the hall to take you sightseeing."

"But I'm not finished helping you."

The muscles in Morgan's jaw twitched, but he smiled warmly at her. "You've done everything we've needed you to do. Go have some fun with your parents."

Avery opened and closed her mouth before standing. "Karma, it was nice to meet you. I look forward to working with you."

"Likewise." There was something about Avery, something special. Karma knew no matter what the future held, the Dhampir would always take care of Avery.

The girl wiggled her fingers at Morgan, apparently not noticing his ire. She strolled from the room, closing the door behind her.

Morgan. Karma tried once more to get his attention.

In a minute, beautiful.

Well, if Morgan wouldn't answer her question. "Dani," she glanced across the table. "employee number 1948502?"

"That's *my* ID," Blythe replied, critically eying Karma. "Excuse me. We haven't been introduced. You are?"

A growl rumbled from Morgan. "Blythe—"

Dani smiled. "I got this, Morgan. Blythe, I'd like you to meet Karma. She's the forensic accountant working with DuMond and Wolfmoon. You spoke to her this morning when she answered Morgan's phone. Karma is the HBIC. You know what that means, right? Head Bitch in Charge. Karma answers to no one." Lord have mercy, Dani batted her lashes. "Not even Magnus or Morgan."

The smirk and condescending look on Blythe's face faded.

"Why did you install the keylogger on Avery's laptop," Morgan snarled.

Blythe flicked her attention to him and paled. "I was tired of always having to reset her password. I figured this way, I would know what it was and wouldn't have to reset it when she forgot it."

Lies. Karma bit her tongue. As simple as Avery made her password, she wouldn't have forgotten it. Besides, there was no evidence of her password being reset prior to the keylogger installation. Afterward was another story. Karma glanced at Blythe.

She lowered her lashes, giving Morgan a demur smile. "I'm sorry. I shouldn't have done it, but you must understand my frustrations. I understand we have to hire individuals with disabilities—"

"Stop," Morgan bellowed.

His tone, more than the outburst, had Karma pausing. She glanced at him. Morgan wasn't furry, not even a slight darkening of stubble. But his eyes...Oh, so not good. *Morgan.* Karma laid her hand on his forearm.

I'm okay, beautiful.

She's lying, Morgan.

I know.

I've found something you need to see.

In a moment. I want to find out how Blythe was involved with the embezzlement if she was. Morgan exhaled. "No, Miss Wendell, you shouldn't have. In fact, there's a lot you shouldn't have done, like firing Avery and her father."

"I was following your instructions." Blythe gasped. "You sent me an email yesterday, ordering me to terminate them." She shifted her attention to Dani. "Mrs. DuMond, I haven't done anything wrong. I was only following Mr. Wolfe's instructions."

"I never sent you an email. Let me see it." Morgan held out his hand.

Blythe pulled her phone from a pocket then swiped a finger over the screen. "See for yourself." She slid the device down the long table.

Keeping his eyes on Blythe, Morgan handed the phone to Karma. "Can you tell where this email was sent from?"

"I already know. It came from this computer." Karma pointed to the laptop in front of her. "There was no way you sent the email. You didn't have access to the computer, for starters, and when the email was sent, you were busy driving us here. According to the system's GPS, the computer did leave Avery's room yesterday, which means someone visited her and did the deed. Also, the majority of the deleted files have to do with stock options. The rest of the files concern Love Match dating site." You also need to know there's a lot of other interesting information on here. I need Percy to see this." She sent off a text, hoping he'd respond.

Morgan leaned back in his seat, folding his hands behind his head. "The stock information wouldn't do them a lot of good as *we* are the major Shareholders. As for the dating site..." He shrugged.

We, she knew, meant the Dhampir.

Karma's phone dinged, causing all eyes to turn to her. She read the message, "Percy is taking over the system. The amount of information leaked from here is phenomenal." Karma glanced from Morgan to Magnus then back to Morgan. "Percy and Viktor should take over the investigation from here. They're experts in this. My skill level is nowhere near theirs."

Morgan exhaled. "How bad?"

"It looks like the breach even went into the research and development departments. This could cost both Wolfmoon and DuMond Enterprises millions if not billions in trademark and patents."

"I wasn't anywhere near Avery's room. Just ask her. Someone has set *me* up." Blythe shifted in her chair. "See, Mr. Wolfe. I didn't do anything wrong."

"Except downloading unapproved software," Dani pointed out, glaring at Blythe. "That alone is grounds to terminate your employment."

"I already explained why I did that. Yes, it was wrong of me, but it was exasperating, always having to reset Avery's password. I get it. She doesn't like change."

A low rumbling growl had Karma reaching over and touching Morgan's arm again.

Before he or Dani killed the woman, Karma had a few questions. "Blythe, where did you go to download this program?"

She cast her eyes up and smiled benignly. "The internet." At least Blythe didn't utter the implied *stupid.*

"Bull." Lord have mercy, Karma was tired of the woman's lies.

"Excuse me," Blythe sneered.

"Oops, said that out loud." Karma adjusted her glasses. "Your little download gave anyone access to both Wolfmoon Corporation and DuMond Enterprises. Mainly the passwords and user IDs of anyone who logged onto this computer. Within a few days of *your* download, both companies were hacked, causing a considerable sum of money to be routed to offshore bank accounts. Now, considering the quality of the program, I know you didn't download it for free. Let's try again. Who gave you the program?"

The color drained from Blythe's face. "I vented to Glen about Avery, and he gave me a flash drive with the program on it. He said it would allow me to see what she typed. It's not like we did anything wrong."

"Nothing wrong?" Morgan laughed. "Miss Wendell, because of what you did, thieves gained access to our company secrets. Good God, woman, what else have you done to jeopardize our businesses?"

"But Glen—"

Morgan jumped from his seat, sending it flying behind him. He slammed his fist so hard down on the cherry table, it was a miracle he didn't splinter it. "How dumb are you?" He flung his other hand at the screen behind him. "They are not Glen McPhee and Royce Lucard."

"But...but," Blythe stuttered. "They said... How do you know their last names? I didn't tell you."

"Royce Lucard and Glen McPhee are my cousins. Trust me. I know why you were given those names. But you should have known something was amiss, seeing the number of times both men have video conferenced with me." Morgan placed both palms on the table and leaned forward. Dark fur peppered his knuckles. "Did you not think it peculiar two sets of men had the same friggin' names?"

"Morgan." Karma covered his hand with hers. She peered at Blythe and didn't think the woman could lose any more coloring. Blythe would be transparent if she did.

~ ~ ~

Blythe dared to call Avery incompetent. Morgan's wolf wanted to tear from him and terminate the woman.

Permanently.

His nails darkened at the cuticles, and his fangs pricked his lower lip. Even Karma's calming touch hadn't soothed his beast. Morgan grabbed the animal by the scruff, tossed him to the back of his mind, and then drew in a breath. The action brought with it the sweet smell of fear. Good. Blythe should be afraid.

He ran his tongue across his fangs and willed them to retract. "Those men," He pointed behind him. "are Lincoln Whitehall and Derrick Canaday, the very ones responsible for hacking into our systems. Of course, with your assistance it was easy for them. Miss Wendell, your actions are inexcusable. You're fired."

"You can't fire me," Blythe screeched in a pitch that had his wolf snarling. She closed her mouth in a smirk, and her eyes narrowed. "I'll sue. You're only trying to get rid of me so you can give your girlfriend my job. I know my rights."

"Your rights?" Morgan reached behind him, retrieving his chair, then sitting. "You have no rights. You do have a choice. Termination or me bringing charges against you for your involvement in the breach. As far as Karma taking your job…that goes to Avery, seeing she's been doing it for the last year."

Cade? Damn it, Morgan couldn't sense him. He really needed to share more blood with the cat. Morgan fished his phone from his pocket. He needed the woman as far from him as possible. His wolf clawed at his mind, demanding they put an end to her. If she were Dhampir, it wouldn't be an issue. Instead of lunging over the table and tearing out Blythe's throat, Morgan sent a text. A second later, the conference room door opened.

"Cade, get her out of my sight."

"But…but," Blythe stammered as Cade lifted her to her feet. She jerked her arm from him. "Get your hands off of me!"

"I'll come with." Dani pushed from her seat. "We wouldn't want her to accuse you of sexual assault. Besides, I need to make her flight arrangements back to Dallas."

Morgan snagged Karma's hand. His wolf needed her touch. "Can you tell how bad the damage?"

"I'm not sure." She scooted her seat closer to his then angled the laptop for him to see. Code cascaded on the screen. "What I could tell before Percy and Viktor took over was apparently Canaday and Whitehall couldn't get through your firewalls and security. Viktor surmises they stalked a few of your female employees to find a target."

"They found one in Blythe," Magnus replied.

Karma shook her head. "Actually, they targeted Avery first, from her dating profile."

"It was Avery's?" Morgan couldn't see it, but hey...to each their own.

"From what Percy could tell, Avery didn't set it up."

Now he understood. "Blythe did."

Karma leaned over, kissing his cheek. "You get a gold star. After Blythe downloaded the keylogger, they struck. You were alerted because of the amount of money they stole."

The implication slapped him in the face. Had Whitehall siphoned off small amounts of money at a time, the theft could have gone on for years before anyone realized it. Before *he* realized it. "Anything else?"

"This isn't anyone's fault except Blythe for being so gullible..." Karma tsked.

"I know. This still doesn't explain why they were after stock information."

"Maybe to frame you for insider trading. It would be a perfect time with your shareholders' meeting and the charity gala tomorrow, right? Which reminds me, I still need to get a dress."

"As I said, there wasn't any information anyone could use, especially Whitehall and Canaday. Magnus, what do you think? Think we should cancel?"

"You already got out of the bachelor auction. You're not getting out of the gala. It won't kill you to put on a tux. Besides, the money we help raise is for children's hospitals."

"We can always cut them a check."

Magnus slid his gaze to Karma. "In case you haven't figured it out, your mate is more comfortable in jeans and pullover."

"Nothing wrong with that." Karma ran her hand up Morgan's chest. "But I would like to see you in a tux."

He knew when he was beaten. Morgan stood then held his hand out to Karma. "Let's go. Magnus can hold down the fort."

"Where are we going?" She took his hand, standing.

"You said you needed something to wear."

Magnus glanced up. "I've already told you Dani has it covered."

"Oh, good. Percy is still downloading Avery's computer, and…" Karma's beautiful eyes turned somber. "I really want to work on this with him. I didn't realize the extent of the damage at first."

"Then I guess Magnus and I should get some work done as well." Morgan turned on the big screen television. Stocks flashed across the screen. "If that bothers you, I can angle it away from you."

"No, it's fine."

Dani returned and worked effortlessly with Karma. Minutes turned to hours as the two women answered every question Percy had for them.

Morgan ordered them all lunch. Then at Dani's urging, made arrangements for Charlie to bring several dresses to their suite for Karma to try on. After he spoke with the man to confirm the time, Morgan placed a call to a jeweler. Everything was coming together perfectly. He even called down and ordered a picnic basket for him and Karma to enjoy tonight as they watched the sunset.

After a few hours, they knew the full extent of the breach. It was more significant than Morgan first thought, but not as bad as it could have been.

Karma closed the lid on the laptop then pushed her glasses up on her head. She dropped her shoulders and rubbed her eyes.

Morgan strode across the room. "You okay, beautiful?"

"I'm good. I know you said your blood wouldn't give me 20/20 vision, but I still wished your super-duper vamp blood would've at least made it, so I'd only need readers."

"Sorry. On a positive note, your vision won't get any worse."

She tipped her face up and blew him a raspberry.

"Don't stick that out unless you plan on using it." He leaned down and captured her sweet mouth.

"Sorry to interrupt," Cade's voice came through the intercom. "We have a situation."

Morgan broke off their kiss, nipping her lower lip. *"What's* the situation?"

"Paul discovered something on the beach. Ryder's on his way to investigate."

"My brother? Why doesn't this surprise me? We're on our way, Cade." Morgan glanced at his watch. Maybe this wouldn't take long, and he and Karma could enjoy the little romantic evening he planned. Fingers crossed.

Dani shot Morgan a twisted smile as she followed Magnus. "I swear, Morgan. If this is one of Paul's practical jokes," she hissed. "I'm staking his furry ass."

"I'll sharpen the stake for you."

She chuckled. "Deal. Oh, and Charlie rang me back. I gave him K's sizes." Dani rolled her eyes, shaking her head.

He may have forgotten that tad-bit of information. Possibly.

They trudged out of the hotel and toward the shore as a string of police cars with sirens blaring sped into the parking lot.

A gentle breeze had Morgan stopping in his tracks. "I smell death." So much for a romantic picnic by the shore.

"Well," Magnus groaned. "Let's find out who's dead."

"Hey, beautiful," Morgan turned Karma in his arms. "If you'd rather—"

"I'm good. A month ago, I'd be like—yeah—no. But hey, after being kidnapped. I think I can handle it."

The second they stepped onto the rocks, three things struck him—first, the pungent smell of blood mixed with Blythe's perfume. The second thing was where she'd lain face down as the waves inched closer to her lifeless body. This far from the hotel, he doubted the security cameras captured much of the event. The third and most noticeable was a large amount of blood spatter coating the rocks. That much blood didn't come from a simple slip and fall.

Chapter Seventeen

She couldn't handle it! Karma swallowed the bile rising in her throat as Morgan blocked her view of the body. It didn't matter. Uniformed officers had secured the area, collecting as much evidence as possible before the tide washed it away. The longer Karma stood there, the woozier she became. They'd been asked not to leave until their statements were taken. She understood, but still, the scene nauseated her.

The deaths of the creeps who'd kidnapped and beat her didn't bother her. It didn't even bother her when Morgan killed the psycho witch attempting to take his head…but Blythe. Karma didn't think she'd ever get the image of blood out of her mind, or the nauseating mixture of Blythe's perfume, the metallic odor of blood, and ocean spray. Heck, even Paul was visibly upset. The man looked as if he would face plant at any moment.

She should talk, the way her head felt. "Morgan." Karma gripped his forearm tight and closed her eyes, fighting off the dizziness assaulting her. "I have to get out of here."

"Lean on me, beautiful." He slid his arm around her waist. "I've got you. Ryder, Karma's not feeling well. I'm taking her back inside to our suite."

"Just a moment, sir." A man strolled toward them. Karma couldn't see a badge, and he was wearing a coat and tie instead of a uniform. However, the man exuded authority. It could have been his military-style buzz cut, the way he carried himself, or the fact the uniform officers all stepped from his path.

"I'm Morgan Wolfe. My fiancé isn't feeling well. If you need to ask us any questions, we'll be in our suite."

"Very well." The newcomer's lips turned into a thin white slash, but he had the intelligence not to argue. He gave a curt nod and continued toward the crime scene.

Looking at the area again had Karma's head spinning. She swayed, gripping Morgan's arm for support.

"You need me to carry you?"

"I can walk. I'm not going to be tonight's dinner topic."

"Karma," Morgan growled. "We already are."

"Don't remind me." She patted his chest. "I need to get away from here."

"We're coming with." Dani tugged Magnus with her, pulling him toward them. "I gave the detective our names and your room number."

Silently they made their way back to the building. Employees and guests stared out the large windows, drawn by the sirens and flashing lights. They huddled in small groups, whispering and craning their necks for a better view of the events. As soon as Morgan's group reentered the building, the staff scrambled, but the hotel guests remained trying to get a better glimpse.

The moment they returned to their room, Karma fell onto a chair. "I hope the detective doesn't see us leaving as a sign of guilt."

Morgan handed her a glass of cold water. "He doesn't."

The cold liquid was what Karma needed. For the past week, her life had been filled with total chaos. To be honest, the week wasn't totally awful. She'd ended up with a wonderful man. "Good to know."

Morgan took her empty glass. "The detective is leaning towards accidental death, considering the broken wine bottle they found. Once I tell him we terminated Blythe, I'm sure he'll conclude she went out on the rocks, not paying attention, slipped and fell."

Lord have mercy, Karma loved Morgan. She did. She also understood why Magnus did all the talking. "Those may not be the best words to use, Wolfie. Besides, it wasn't an accident. I'm not a cop, but that was way too much blood unless Blythe's skull was as thin as an eggshell. Accident—Nope."

Magnus nodded. "I agree with you, Karma. Blythe appeared to have slipped on the rocks, landing face down. However, with the waves washing in, it seems to me there was too much blood, even if it was a head wound, and she had alcohol in her system."

"The cliff isn't high," Karma argued. "Maybe six at the most. I can't understand how she died from a fall that high. I can't see it."

Morgan nodded. "Whoever murdered her thought when the tide rolled in the waves would wash away the body. Whitehall's tying up loose ends. We already know he's here somewhere. Knowing Blythe, I can assure you she called him or Canaday, letting them know we were on to her." Morgan sighed and dropped down in the chair beside Karma, facing her. "She'd probably called them last night. The main issue I have, is why didn't I scent either of them in the area?"

"I know you have a super sniffer." Dani pointed at him. "But let's be honest. All anyone could smell was Blythe's cheap perfume. I mean, even out in the open, the odor was still overpowering."

"Dani, Blood Rose isn't cheap."

"It is when you bathe in it. Geeze, it was making me gag."

A thought wafted across Karma's mind. "Has Blythe always worn so much perfume?"

"No." Morgan shook his head. "She started bathing in it in—"

"April?" Karma rolled her eyes. "Hmm, if I had to guess, I'd say someone encouraged her to do so. Which brings about another question. Why didn't she fight whoever attacked her? Her head wound was on her forehead, so she had to see them. Could Whitehall have taken her blood and made her, I don't know, like a puppet?"

"It's possible but doubtful. We can control some minds and erase some memories or events. But you would still maintain your sense of self-preservation."

"I guess. It makes sense." *Not.* Karma still didn't understand it. Then again, maybe she did. When she was held captive, she wanted a quick, painless death for all of three seconds. "Why try to blow me up at the warehouse then do all the other stuff later?"

"Hmm." Magnus steepled his fingers, bouncing them against his forehead. He finally pointed at her. "Because your worth was not evident at the time of your kidnapping. Then they only wanted to locate the money they stole. Now, they want you to steal money for them."

"I agree with you," Morgan's words ended on a growl. "Which is why they don't get handed over to Royce."

"What will you do with them?" As if Karma needed to ask.

Morgan opened his mouth then shut it, turning toward the door as it opened.

"Thank you again for your assistance." The detective shook Ryder's hand.

"You're more than welcome. We'll download all the footage we have and give it to Officer Tidwell." Ryder stepped from the room, closing the door.

"I hope you're feeling better, ma'am. I'm Detective Williams." He scanned the room as if he were taking a mental photograph.

"Thank you, I am."

"Morgan Wolfe." Morgan shook hands with the man. "My business partner Magnus DuMond, his wife and our director of HR, Danielle Rossi DuMond, and my fiancé, Karma Wolfe."

"What can you tell me about Blythe Windell," Williams asked, pulling out a notepad. "I understand she was an employee of yours."

Dani stepped forward. "Ms. Wendell's employment was terminated because she violated company policy concerning the downloading of spyware. As you know, Wolfmoon Corporation, DuMond Enterprises, and their subsidiaries all suffered a cyber-attack earlier this year. It was discovered this was facilitated by the software Blythe Wendell installed on a company computer. We thought termination of employment was a far better choice than having her arrested."

"Why?"

"Being naive isn't a crime," Magnus replied. "We probably wouldn't have fired her had she owned up to what she'd done. Instead, Blythe attempted to blame another employee."

The detective's eyebrow rose a fraction of an inch. "Yet she was still booked into the resort."

"Her flight wasn't scheduled to leave until in the morning," Dani replied. "I informed her we would pay for her room tonight, but that was all. Any room service or meals would come out of her pocket."

"I see. Was she known to drink a lot?" Williams looked directly at Karma.

"I didn't know her, so I can't answer your question." She glanced at Dani then over at Morgan. "Do either of you know?"

Morgan shook his head. "All I know is she would go out with a few other employees to Two Dog in Dallas. Other than that, I can't say."

"One more question. The man who discovered the body, Paul Wolfe. He's?"

"My brother," Morgan answered.

"Okay." Williams pocketed his notepad. "If I have any more questions for you, I'll be in touch."

As soon as the door clicked closed, Karma melted into the chair and released the breath she'd been holding. "What was behind his line of questions?"

Morgan poured himself a drink then tossed back the burgundy liquid. "Our detective is good. The crime scene screamed an accident, but he has his doubts. Which is bad."

Okay, now Karma was really confused. "It was murder."

"It was, beautiful. If we were dealing with Canaday, then I would ensure we did everything in our power to serve him up on a silver platter for Detective Williams. As it is, if he goes after Whitehall, it will mean the end of the good detective."

"I hadn't thought about it like that. So, what do we do?"

"Right now, we go to the Wine Cellar Restaurant, downstairs." Morgan helped her from her seat. "I've ordered us dinner."

Dani gathered up her things then smiled weakly. "Don't forget, Charlie will be arriving with dresses for us to try on." She sighed and leaned against Magnus. "Maybe some retail therapy will cheer me up."

Morgan looked intently at Karma before escorting her from the room. "If tomorrow night's event wasn't to help children, I'd insist we cancel."

Magnus slammed his palm against the down button. "And I'd second that notion."

~ ~ ~

Morgan nursed his whiskey, waiting for Karma to emerge from the bedroom. Their suite had more dress racks than he'd ever seen at one time. Hell, he didn't think there were this many during Fashion Week in New York. "Thank you again, Charlie, for doing this for us."

"The pleasure was all mine." He zipped up the last rack then motioned to his assistant. "I love dressing full-figured women. When I dress them, I feel I'm dressing the late, great Jane Russell." This from a man who bore a striking resemblance to Morticia Addams. "I knew the fitted-flare number with the off the shoulder sweetheart neckline would be perfect for her." Charlie returned Morgan's card along with two business cards. "If you ever need anything else, please don't hesitate."

"Thank you, and I'm sure we'll be getting in touch with you."

Giving a quick nod, Charlie opened the door, then left.

Morgan glared at the other man, standing in the hall until the door closed behind Charlie. The last thing Morgan wanted to do was deal with Paul.

A sharp rap had Morgan growling. "Go away."

Karma snuggled closer, resting her head on Morgan's shoulder. "You didn't have to buy me two dresses."

"I couldn't make up my mind which I liked best. I loved you in the dark red, but the blue was gorgeous on you."

"I'll have to repay you," she nipped his earlobe. "Later."

His wolf was all for making later now.

"After you deal with your brother." Karma ran her hand down his chest until it rested on his thigh. "You know he isn't going to leave until you do."

"You know she's right," Magnus added. "Besides, I, for one, would like to know what the detective had to say to your brother."

"I have questions for him, myself. We've stared at the surveillance footage from the time Danie and Cade left with Blythe until we're seen walking out toward the shore. There are several people seen walking along the shore. Blythe is seen carrying the bottle of wine, and there was an old woman near her. I wish there was a better picture of the older woman because something about her looked familiar."

"You think the person was the murderer in disguise? Of course, you do, seeing she kept her face down." Karma shifted, bringing her feet up on the cushion and hugging her knees to her. "When will this nightmare be over?"

Dani glanced up from her phone. "Counselors will be available for staff tomorrow and all of next week."

"Thank you. Make sure we do everything possible to assist her family with funeral arrangements."

"I've already taken care of it." Dani met Morgan's eyes and sighed. "You should know, gossip says Blythe got shitfaced because you introduced Karma as your fiancé. Sorry, K."

"No need to apologize. Office gossip is just that. It bothers the hell out of me Blythe was murdered. I didn't know her, but I feel in my heart she was a pawn in Psycho's game. Lord have mercy, I want this over with."

Morgan's gut twisted. Karma's misery was so acute it was a palpable pain, flowing across their blood bond. "Damn it. Come here, beautiful."

"I'm not upset with you." She leaned against him. "Blythe didn't deserve to be murdered."

The door rattled again.

Morgan was pissed off enough. He did *not* need to deal with Paul's bullshit.

"Paul isn't going away." Karma sat up, tucking her feet under her. "Let's see what he wants."

Morgan exhaled and sought out Cade with his gaze. The second their eyes met, the cat unfolded himself from the chair.

"Let him in, Cade."

"Do we have time to make popcorn?" Dani grinned and winked at Karma.

The cat stretched then trudged toward the door. Cade stretched again before finally opening it. "For me? You shouldn't have."

Paul strode into the room, carrying a slightly wilted bouquet of flowers. He tilted his head, baring his throat to Karma as he thrust the flowers at her. "I'm sorry for how I acted."

"Thank you, they're beautiful." She reached for the flowers. "Oh, Paul, what happened to your face?"

Morgan stood and took the flowers before Karma could touch them. "I'll put these in some water for you, beautiful." Knowing his brother, Paul probably wove poison ivy within the greenery. Surprisingly, Morgan didn't see any. He did notice the deep scratches across Paul's face. "What happened?"

"Bar fight."

Morgan glanced at the cat then placed the flowers in a vase. *Cade, I can fight my own battles.*

The cat picked at his nails. *I know you can, but the fight didn't concern you.*

He wouldn't call Cade a liar, but Morgan had worked on the ranch long enough to know bullshit when he smelled it. "I'm curious, Paul. What are you still doing here?"

Paul tilted his head in submission. Something he never did. "I needed to apologize to Karma and ask her something in private."

"You've apologized, but you're not speaking with her in private."

"Oh, come on, bro," Paul whined. "It's not like I have desires for your mate. I just need her help." His ears pinked, stirring Morgan's curiosity.

"I'm yours, and you're mine." Karma snagged his paw, calming his wolf. She tugged until he sat beside her. "Paul, help you with what?"

Something was up. Dani looked like she was about to pee herself, and Karma's voice was way too syrupy. What in the hell had she done? Morgan could peek into Karma's mind, but watching this play out might be fun.

"It's personal," Paul mumbled.

"Karma's an accountant, not a doctor. But I'm sure Penicillin will cure whatever is wrong with you. Oh wait, we're Dhampir. STD's don't affect us."

"Wolfie," Karma squeezed his hand. "be nice. Paul apologized and brought me flowers." His diabolical mate smiled ever so sweetly. "Paul, seeing your brother is on the furry side—"

"I don't want to have to pay a pet deposit," Magnus tossed out.

Karma pushed her glasses up on her nose, using her middle finger. "Stop it. You own the damn place. *Anyway,* as I was saying before, I was interrupted. Seeing these guys probably know what's going on, why don't you fill me in on what you want me to do."

Paul's face turned even redder as he shot a glare at Cade. "Fuck."

Morgan's wolf wagged his tail. This was getting good. He couldn't wait to find out what Karma had done.

Paul pulled out his phone. "It's a technical issue. I called Percy, and he said he couldn't help me. For me to ask Karma. After the dead woman incident, I asked Ryder. He handed my phone back to me and laughed."

Whoa. Wait. What? Morgan looked from Dani to Karma then at his brother. "Percy Westmoreland couldn't help you, or *wouldn't* help you?"

"It doesn't matter if he couldn't or wouldn't. He didn't."

"If Percy couldn't help you, I don't know if I'll be much help." Karma held out her hand. "I'll have a look, but Percy could rule the world with a click of his mouse."

Paul unlocked his phone, then dropped it in her hand. "*Someone* set up a dating profile with my photos. I don't even know how that happened."

"Probably from your cloud account." Karma swiped her finger across the screen. "Ouch. I can see why you want this gone."

"Let me see." Morgan snatched the phone from her. "Oh, hell, bro. The profile name is Pin-dick? I'm an ass with a micro-penis, but I'll look good on any woman's arm. Just superglue my mouth shut, and we'll get along fine."

Karma grabbed the phone back. "Your brother is embarrassed enough. No need to humiliate him even further." She tapped the screen.

Beautiful, it's incredible you know the password to remove this profile.

Karma's lips twitched at the coroners as she handed Paul his phone. "Here you go. All taken care of."

"Thanks. When I find out who did this. I'm going to gut them."

"I'm sure you'll find out who it was. How many people have you pissed off recently?"

Dani snorted. "Let's see, the barista downstairs, Ryder and his crew, Royce, all the women at DuMond Enterprises—"

"Okay, I get it. I've been an ass lately, but that didn't give whoever did this the right."

"Maybe not, but it's my experience, people who are bullied usually reach a point where they fight back." Karma snuggled against Morgan, resting her head on his shoulder. "I know from when I was picked on as a kid. One day I reached my breaking point. It wasn't pretty. Just saying."

"Thanks again, Karm."

Morgan bristled. Paul was back to his old self. "Her name is Karma. Before you go, I have some questions."

"What?" Paul's eyes blazed with amber fire.

"Now that I know *why* you're still here instead of on your way back to the ranch. Did you see or scent anyone on the shore, other than Blythe?"

"Who?"

"The victim." One of these days, Morgan was gonna gut Paul.

"Oh, the dead chick who took a swan dive. Nope. Couldn't scent anything, either, because of the blood and the cheap perfume she wore. Can I go?"

"Blythe was murdered." Karma narrowed her eyes.

Morgan rolled his shoulders, shoving his beast from the edges of his mind. "You're sure you didn't see anyone acting strange?"

"For the last time, I didn't see—wait. A Lincoln Continental sped away from the hotel just as I caught the scent of the blood."

"Did you see the driver? Young, old, male, female?"

"Sorry, bro. I didn't. Can I go? Unlike you, I have to drive back to Texas."

"One more question. What did you tell the police?"

"I was walking along the shore and looked down at the surf. That's when I saw her. Then I called 911. Now, can I go?"

"Don't catch your tail in the door on your way out." The second the door slammed behind Paul, Morgan turned to Karma and held up two fingers. "When and how?"

"The when was this morning when I had his phone. The how is a little more detailed. I called Percy. He gave me the pics then I created the profile. Percy uploaded it to Paul's phone, so he'd think it was real, but it never went live." Karma shrugged. "I know, I lowered myself to his level, but he pissed me off."

"My devious mate." Morgan kissed her crown. "Paul deserved it, but as you saw, he thinks himself the victim. I just hope he never finds out you're the one who did it."

"Oh, he knows." Cade peered at him. "Paul knows it was Karma. He knows when she did it, just not how she did it. Paul rang Percy, *demanding* he fix it." A Cheshire cat smile curved Cade's lips. "That went over like a fart in church. Knowing Paul, he's planning something."

Morgan had too much on his plate to worry about his brother. His first priority was Karma. "Magnus, Karma, and I aren't attending the gala."

"Oh, yes, we are!" Her eyes darkened to angry thunderclouds. "If you're worried about Paul, don't be."

"He's a distraction. I can't risk you, beautiful." Fur rippled over Morgan's forearms. "I can't let Whitehall take advantage and steal you from me."

"I can't live my life in fear, always looking over my shoulder. The gala will happen. It's too important for the hospital, and don't say you can write a check. I'll just be extra cautious."

"Beautiful."

"Look, Wolfie." Karma placed her hand on his forearm. "You're always going to be at my side. Ryder and his men will be there along with Cade. This could be our only chance of putting an end to all this. Then you and I are going back to our beach house." Desire flamed in her eyes. "Alone."

Cupping her chin, Morgan stared into Karma's determined face. "Fine, but you're getting microchipped."

"Excuse me!" She leaned away and crossed her arms. "I don't think so."

"With our blood bond, I can find you anywhere in this building, but the further away from me…Beautiful, if they manage to kidnap you and fly you to San Francisco, Mozambique, or anywhere in the world, it will take time to find you. I'll know you're alive, and I'll feel your pain, but I won't know where you are. With the microchip, Percy can locate you all the way to the 7th level of Hell, within seconds."

"Hey, K." Dani held up her left hand. "The kids and I are chipped. It doesn't hurt much. It stings a little, but so worth it. I have a sense of security, knowing if something happens, we'll be rescued in moments instead of days."

"Evil Prick scanned me. Several times, in fact. What's to say he won't do it again?"

"We can insert the tracker in the sole of your foot," Cade replied. "It'll sting more, but chances of Whitehall scanning your foot are slim. Morgan, I've got a trace on the Lincoln." Cade glanced up from his phone. His expression grew serious. "Umm, you're not going to like this. Then again, you might. The Lincoln was rented to Ruby Canaday." He held up his phone, showing a photo of the license of the woman who had tormented Tristan's mate, Niki, all her life.

Morgan stared at the face. "Damn, is it wrong of me to wish that old bitch would just die?"

"Nope. And your wish has been granted. She was found dead of an apparent heart attack, slumped over in her car."

"Was it a heart attack, or was Whitehall cleaning up loose threads?"

"Does it matter? Ryder is checking security cameras in the area, but I don't think it will do us any good."

"How do you know this?" When Morgan looked to the cat for clarification, stark and vivid fear shown in Cade's eyes.

"Ryder and I watched the security feed. Once Blythe dropped off Avery's computer, Blythe made a call. From her expression, whoever was on the other end wasn't happy. Before you ask, her phone was with her belongings, but the number she called went to a burner."

"You got this information from the detective?" Karma asked. "I thought cops were tightlipped about investigations."

"They are."

"In other words, someone slipped into her room and stole a peek at her phone."

Ryder shrugged, and Karma rolled her eyes.

Morgan grabbed her. She gasped and pushed against him as he sat her across his lap. "Stop struggling and listen to me." He buried his face in her hair. Morgan didn't give a shit they had an audience.

"Tomorrow night, I need you to stick to my side or Cade's if I have to leave you. I feel it in my bones something bad will happen, that Whitehall will make his move."

"Morgan," she sighed, relaxing against him. "I know you'll keep me safe."

"I can't let anything happen to you. I know you are a strong, capable woman, but you're my life."

"Morgan, I love you, too."

He smiled against her neck. "I'll drive you crazy by the time we're old and gray with a dozen pups and a few dozen grandkids."

Karma's heart raced, and a radiant smile lit her face. "Dozen? You plan on carrying a few?"

He leaned back and met her gaze. "Anyone who hurts you will die. Anyone, including Paul."

A single tear slid down her cheek.

"Aw, beautiful, don't cry."

Karma swiped at her tears. Behind her, Cade, Magnus, and Dani slipped from the room.

"We're going to have a future together, Morgan, crazy relatives, and all."

"Damn straight."

Chapter Eighteen

"Shareholder's meeting went well." Morgan knew it would, considering the major holders were Dhampir. Now, all he wanted was to get through tonight without an incident. He pushed back the curtain, staring out at the turbulent ocean. Whitehall was out there somewhere.

"For the love of *Yeva*, would you stop?" Magnus held out a glass of brandy mixed with blood. "Here, this will calm your nerves. One would think you're going to the gallows instead of a gala."

Morgan took the offered glass and tossed back its contents, savoring the burn. "This is a bad idea. We should have canceled the event."

"For the love of life, man. It's only for a few hours, four at the most. If we'd canceled, we'd be saying we value the life of one person over the health and well-being of the hundreds of ill children tonight's event is to benefit."

"If you're so worried, we could always write a check."

"True, but how would it look to all the people who have spent a year planning the event? This is even more of a morale booster than it is a fundraiser."

Damn it. He didn't give a rat's ass what people thought. This was about keeping Karma safe. "They're after my mate."

"Your mate will be on your arm." Karma strolled toward him. The hypnotic sway of her full hips had his wolf howling. "We go down, raise some money, have a few hors d'oeuvres, a glass of champagne, then come back here," She licked her lower lip, "for dessert. Besides, I didn't allow Cade to stab my foot for nothing. The dang thing still itches."

Cade stood and pulled on his jacket. "Well, if you hadn't jerked your foot, it wouldn't have hurt."

Karma narrowed her eyes, glaring at him. "Excuse me. You did stab my foot with a needle large enough to suck a milkshake throw. Don't tell me it didn't hurt. It hurt like hell."

"Aw, I'm sorry I hurt your dainty little tootsie."

Dani thumped Cade on the back of the head. "I swear you two argue more than siblings."

Morgan didn't miss the longing and hurt that flashed across Cade's face. The kid was searching for a place to call home. Cade hadn't realized he had it amongst a pack of wolves.

"I'm shutting up." The cat rubbed the back of his head. "You sure I can't get out of this meat sale?"

"Positive," Magnus replied.

"Dani," Karma huffed. "Stop beating up on my little brother."

"Little brother?" The cat grinned. "You do realize I'm older than you?"

Karma rolled her eyes. "Not mentally."

Ryder slid two fingers in his mouth and whistled. The ear-splitting sound had Morgan's wolf howling. "Before we go down, there are a few things I want to go over—"

"Oh, good grief," Magnus mumbled.

"We know Lincoln is here," Ryder continued. "We haven't been able to track him because he's in the wraith zone. You should be aware Lincoln can stay in there for days. We surmise he can drag humans in with him, and that's how he could murder Blythe. According to the witnesses, Blythe wasn't there, then she appeared on the rocks."

This was why Morgan wanted to cancel the friggin' *party*.

"Morgan, get a grip." Karma cupped his cheeks, forcing him to meet her fiery eyes. "We've been over this plan. It will work. I trust you to keep me safe. I trust Ryder and his team to keep me safe. I trust Cade and Magnus to keep me safe. But I don't trust myself if I'm worried about you going wolfie."

Morgan loved Karma more than anything in the world. "You're right." He bussed her forehead. "Damn, you're beautiful when you're mad. No, I take that back. You're always gorgeous, luscious, and pure perfection." Karma's midnight blue dress would be in tatters once they returned to their room tonight.

"You're not bad yourself, Wolfie." Karma titled her head back, met his gaze, and licked her lips.

"Are we ready?" Ryder touched the com in his ear. "Or did I put this monkey suit on for nothing?"

"Right." Magnus clapped his hands. "We're running late."

"In a minute." Morgan pulled the velvet box from inside his jacket. "I have something for you." Keeping his eyes on Karma's expression, he opened the box. "I know you like pearls."

"Morgan, it's beautiful." Her hands trembled as she fingered the four-strand pearl necklace. "Would you put it on me?"

"My pleasure." He fastened the necklace then leaned down and nipped her earlobe. "I meant what I said. You're gorgeous."

She turned, pressing a kiss to his cheek. "You take my breath away in your black tux." Karma's golden-flecked eyes darkened, and a faint whiff of her desire teased the air.

Morgan slipped his arm around her waist. If they didn't leave now, he'd sweep his mate up in his arms and carry her back to their room. "I guess we should get this show started."

"About time." Magnus flung open the door.

Morgan shook his head and pressed the down button. Magnus was so damn anal. "We're going down to the ballroom, not across town."

"Some of us are going to our deaths," Cade groused, slapping the number for the auction on his lapel. "13 used to be my lucky number."

"For Pete's sake, Cade." Dani tsked. "It's not like we're asking you to marry the woman."

"Maybe someone will toss a grenade I can throw myself on."

The tinkling sound of Karma's laughter filled the small compartment. "Overdramatic, much? Besides, *little brother*, the bad guys have already tampered with the cable suspending us. It's going snap, plunging us to our deaths just as a meteor crashes into the planet, killing all life forms."

Everyone focused on his little mate, even him. Where the hell had Karma come up with that crap? "Beautiful?"

"What?" An easy smile played at the corners of her lush red lips as humor shimmered in her eyes. "When an actor goes on stage, no one wishes them good luck. Nope, everyone tells them to break a leg." She shrugged. "Same thing."

"No, beautiful. It's not. Break a leg is one thing. What you said was dark. Really, really dark."

The door slid open, and he allowed Cade and Ryder to exit the car first. Holding Karma's hand, Morgan stepped from the elevator. Searching for any threat to Karma, he scented the air and opened his mind. The emotions from the other Dhampirs brushed his mind. Happiness, boredom, emotions he expected. Then hate assaulted him, digging into his mind. Morgan's wolf growled, ready to tear from him and hunt the one who threatened their mate. Wolf wanted to bathe in Whitehall's blood.

"Morgan?" Karma squeezed his hand. "What's wrong?"

"Whitehall." Morgan scanned the crowd, searching for his quarry.

"Don't bother," Cade whispered. "You won't *see* him. He's in the zone."

Lincoln's evil laugh brushed against Morgan's mind, leaving an oily residue.

Ryder tapped his com. "It's showtime." He eased away, speaking to his team through the tactical radio in his ear.

Music floated in the air from the ensemble. Morgan surveyed the crowd, the cream of Oregon society with a few Wolfmoon and DuMond employees scattered throughout. The men seemed to occupy the bar area while a few women surveyed the items up for the silent auction. Others appeared engrossed in conversation.

Morgan didn't miss the glances he and Karma received. By all accounts, tonight's turnout was a huge success. He just hoped it didn't turn out to be a huge mistake.

There were too many humans. Whitehall could turn this into a blood bath if he wanted. "Change of plans." Morgan snatched the number from Cade's lapel. "You don't let Karma or Dani out of your sight. If tonight goes south…"

"Don't worry," Cade gripped Morgan's arm, "I'll protect them with my life."

"With luck, it won't come to that." Magnus nodded toward Avery. "Why does she look so anxious?"

Avery clutched a clipboard and bit her lower lip as she stood next to Frank.

"Let's find out." Karma pulled her hand free and sashayed across the marble floor, heading directly for Avery.

Morgan caught up and slipped his arm around Karma's waist. "Beautiful, stay close to me," he whispered near her ear.

"Why?"

"Didn't you understand what Ryder said?" From her expression, Morgan's assumption was right. *Lincoln can walk through walls and has the power to pull you into the wraith zone with him.*

I heard. Karma batted her lashes and blew a kiss.

I don't have that ability to go after you there. Nor do I know the effects it would have on you. Ryder described the wraith zone as a space between dimensions. Morgan didn't know if Karma would be able to breathe in there.

Despite Karma's smile, her fear and her memories of the warehouse seeped into him. "Well, poop."

"Karma, Mr. Wolfe," Avery's voice hitched.

"What is it, Avery?" Whoever the bastard was who'd upset her, Morgan would find it exquisitely satisfying to kill.

His wolf agreed. They hadn't killed anyone in twenty-four hours.

Bloodthirsty bastard.

His wolf agreed.

"Umm." Avery fidgeted with the clipboard she held tight. "We're fifteen minutes behind schedule."

Well, that sucked, seeing he was the bastard. "Let's see what we can do to make up the lost time." Morgan took the clipboard, assessing it. If it were up to him, he'd do away with everything on the list. "Leave it to us, Avery."

"Cade, where's your number?" She worried her lip. "I don't think we have extras, and the pamphlets have been distributed."

"Avery, breathe. You're doing a wonderful job." Her eyes lit up, and a huge smile replaced her frown. "We've got this. You and your dad enjoy the evening." Morgan placed Karma's hand on his arm then wove their way through the sea of people.

The closer they drew to the stage, the heavier his feet felt. There was nothing he hated worse than public speaking. The three steps up to the stage might as well have been a thousand steps.

"Don't worry, love." Karma squeezed his arm. "Dani's got this."

Dani winked and strode toward the podium. She tapped the mic. "Good evening, ladies and gentlemen. I'm Danielle DuMond. With me are Magnus DuMond of DuMond Enterprises and Morgan and Karma Wolfe of Wolfmoon Corporation."

Muffled whispers hummed through the ballroom upon hearing Karma's name. He straightened his posture and slipped his arm around Karma's waist. He was proud to have her on his arm. And friggin' lucky, too.

"Each year, DuMond Enterprises, along with Wolfmoon Corporation, select a charity in one of our corporate locations. This year we choose the building fund for the Orthopedic wing of Children's Hospital. On behalf of DuMond Enterprises and Wolfmoon Corporation, we would like to thank you for coming out this evening and supporting both the silent auction and the bachelor auction. The money raised tonight will go toward the building of the new wing. DuMond Enterprises and Wolfmoon Corporation have both pledged to match the money raised this evening." She motioned toward the wall in front of her. "Behind you is a portrayal of how the hospital will look like once completed."

A round of applause went up. After a few seconds, Dani lifted her hand, silencing the crowd.

"At this time, I would like to thank the Tree Top Resort for hosting this year's charity. Ladies and gentlemen, we hope you enjoy your evening." Clapping, Dani stepped from the mic and nodded toward Flint. The man had gone over and beyond to make this a success.

"Dani, you made that look so easy." Morgan wished he knew her secret.

"I look over the audience's heads," she whispered. "Shall we mingle? Oh, wait a sec. I forgot something." Dani scurried back to the mic, tapping it several times. "I have one more thing, Ladies. I'm sorry to announce, but bachelor thirteen will not be available tonight due to a family emergency."

A few groans filled the air. Morgan guessed more than one lady liked Cade's bio. Ex MMA fighter. Lover of cats. Good thing the catalog didn't include photos of the eligible men, or they'd have a hard time explaining why he was here.

Karma peered up at Morgan and licked her lower lip. The action pulled his concentration to her lush mouth. "Would it be tacky if we bid on an item?"

"Depends on which item." He helped her down the steps then followed her toward the items.

He had an idea of what had caught Karma's eye.

"Well, you know I love waterfalls." She grinned up at him.

"Do I?" He slipped his arm around her waist. He didn't give a damn about the few raised eyebrows. He wanted everyone to know Karma was his. Caveman-ish? Damn-straight, but it kept his wolf happy.

"Morgan, I was hoping to see you tonight."

Morgan froze then turned, facing one of the people he'd hoped to avoid tonight. Morgan liked the man. He honestly did, but Mitch could talk the ears off a brass mule. "Doctor Weissman." In that second, two things became clear. The human knew about them, and two, he was mated to a statuesque blond Dhampir with a significant baby bump. Guess it's true. There was someone out there for everyone. "Congratulations. My fiancé, Karma."

"It's nice to meet you." Karma nodded to both.

"Thank you, and to you as well." Mitch motioned to the woman on his arm. "My wife, Abella Castello Weissman. Bella, Morgan Wolfe, and his ah…"

"A pleasure." Abella sniffed the air. "There are *others* here," she gasped. "Faders." Stark, vivid fear flashed in her eyes.

"We know," Morgan whispered. No need to panic anyone. "Our security team will deal with them."

Abella's eyes widened, and red ringed her irises. "Is that Cade Dorjan? I feel we should leave."

Morgan's wolf snarled. Cade and Chase had proven themselves time and time again. "If it were not for Cade and his brother, my niece would have suffered a fate worse than death."

The woman flushed but remained silent.

"Now, Precious," Weissman cooed. "I'm sure Morgan has everything under control. However, let me talk to a few more people, then we'll leave." He shifted his attention back to Morgan. "I just wanted to let you know I spoke with Quaid. We re getting a blade out to him along with another prosthetic I feel will serve him when he's…bulked up. His mate was really helpful."

"Mate? You mean Simone?" *Well, I'll be damned. I'm happy for him. Dang, maybe I should call Quaid and congratulate him. Naw.*

"You didn't know?" Mitch frowned. "Perhaps I shouldn't have said anything."

Morgan held up his hand. "No, you're fine, Mitch."

"Darling," Abella tugged on Mitch's arm. "there's Magnus. You should make your rounds so we can leave." She smiled at Karma. "It's been a pleasure to meet you. Perhaps when it is…less crowded, we can get together."

"I'd like that." Karma returned Abella's smile. As soon as the couple's backs were turned, Karma hooked her arm with his. "I want a closer look at that painting."

The nearer they drew, the wider Karma's eyes grew. Her breath hitched. "Oh, Morgan, it's beautiful. The artist captured both of Multnomah Falls' tiers and the bridge. You know I love waterfalls."

"I do. You know it's the tallest waterfall in Oregon." He should've kept the painting. "If our bid wins, where would you hang it?"

"Over the bed. The colors, the frame, everything about it would go perfect there."

Just where it had hung for the past fifty years. "We can go see the falls anytime you'd like."

"Soon, please." She eased closer to the painting.

He flagged one of the auctioneers. "Double whatever the top bid is on the oil."

"Isn't that the painting you donated?"

"And I'm buying it back."

"Yes, sir. I'll have it packed and made ready for shipping, or would you prefer to take it with you?"

"Ship it." Fear gripped Morgan, and he turned toward Karma.

Whitehall reached for her from inside the painting.

Chapter Nineteen

Karma leaned as close as she could, examining the oil. The artist's detail created such depth she could almost feel the mist rising from the pool as the bright orange and gold autumn leaves fluttered in the breeze.

Her eyes scrutinized every inch of the painting, freezing at the signature at the bottom left corner.—M. Wolfe with a paw print. Surely not.

Karma crossed her arms, thinking back to their mating. Morgan had opened his mind and his heart to her. She'd seen this waterfall in his thoughts several times that night and knew it was one of his favorite places. Yet, not once had she seen him painting it. Heck, she had no idea he could paint.

She stepped back, studying the entire canvas. Her heart pounded, and she broke out in a cold sweat.

Evil Prick stared at her from the painting. A demonic grin curved his lips as he reached for her. Suddenly he faded back into the picture, leaving her gasping.

No one around her screamed or fainted. So, he only wanted her to see his ghost act. If he wanted to scare her, it didn't work—much Who was she kidding? He'd frightened the daylights out of her.

"Beautiful?" Morgan slipped his arm around her waist, tugging her back against him. "Are you okay?" Unease tinged his words along with too much of his wolf for her liking.

"I'm good." She glanced up, noting Morgan's glowing eyes. At least he wasn't furry. So, everything was good-ish. "This doesn't change anything. I still really want that painting, and if we don't win it, then you can paint me another."

"Beautiful?" His canines were long, and his upper lip quivered in a snarl. "He could have grabbed you."

"I'm fine, Morgan." She pecked his cheek. "Breathe. Whitehall wanted to rattle me, and it worked. But just a little. I'm not going to allow him or anyone else to bully me again. I've been down that road once and didn't like the trip. Besides, I'm Karma. Remember?" She grabbed a flute of champagne from the tray of a passing server.

"Did I see what I thought I saw?" Dani snatched the flute from Karma's fingers.

"Probably. And get your own." She reached for her glass.

"Um…" Dani shifted her gaze to Karma's stomach. "No. You can't have this."

"Why?" They'd been friends forever, and Karma knew Dani wasn't telling her to lose weight.

"Because." She glanced at Karma's stomach, then at her eyes, then back to her stomach.

Whatever D was trying to relay, Karma's slightly fried brain couldn't interpret. Whitehall had rattled her more than she'd thought. "Will you just spill?"

"Um…baby."

"Oh, biscuits."

"Actually, the term is bun, but whatever floats your boat. Just an FYI, K. It'll be eleven months before you can have this." Dani tipped the flute back, taking a sip. "Don't worry, I'll be your personal taster."

"Gee, thanks, D."

Pregnant…Wow. Indescribable panic filled her. She was going to be a mom, and her only example of mothering was Melody. Karma rested her hand over her stomach. Morgan had said when they mated she'd become pregnant.

She peered up at him. "Are you happy?" Silly question, seeing the joy shimmering in his eyes.

"You've made me the happiest man alive. You're going to make a wonderful mom." Morgan captured her mouth, leaving her breathless. He ended their kiss too quickly for her liking, but they were in public. "I just hope I'll be a good father."

"You'll be a great daddy." Cade clapped Morgan on the back. "If you're half the friend to your pup as you are to me, you'll do good. But I think your mate could use something to drink, bro." Cade winked at her. "She looks a little peckish to me."

"I'll be right back, beautiful. Cade." Morgan glanced at the painting, then strode toward the bar.

"With my life." Cade glared at the painting. His pupils elongated then returned to normal.

"Don't pop a whisker," Karma warned. She'd already had enough excitement and didn't need to deal with a cat on the loose. Lord have mercy, what else would happen tonight?

"Oh, good grief," Dani gasped.

"Karma Peamoor."

A voice from her past made her cringe. It was terrible enough Evil Prick pulled a scene from a B horror movie, but now Mad Max haunted her. What the devil was going on? A Christmas Carol in October?

"Jonas Maxwell." Karma plastered on her I don't give a crap smile as she turned to look upon the creep, who all those years ago had used her and destroyed her self-confidence. They were both geeks, but Max was the only guy who'd paid any attention to her. Little had she'd known at the time, he needed her to help him through accounting and to put a notch in his belt.

"I never thought I'd see you on the west coast," he greeted. "I thought you'd never leave Georgia."

Slowly Karma looked at him. Mad Max was shorter than she remembered and looked a lot older than his thirty years

Standing beside him was Megan Atwood, cheerleader, homecoming queen, and all-around mean-girl. Megan and her group thrived on tormenting anyone they deemed beneath them.

Karma forced a smile. "Jonas, nice to see you again, and you, also, Megan."

Dani coughed, covering up her laugh. "Sorry, champagne went down the wrong way."

Karma smiled. "I didn't know you two were together."

Megan eased in front of Mad Max. "We do travel in different *social* circles. *My* husband's company just merged with Wolfmoon Corporation. Are you two," She motioned between Dani and Karma. "married?"

"Yes," Karma replied. "But not to each other. Actually, Dani's married. I'm engaged." She held up her hand, wiggling her ring finger.

Dani smiled sweetly at Megan. "You missed the welcoming speech?"

Jonas slipped his arm around his wife's waist. "We were running late. I was hoping to meet Mr. Wolfe. Though our companies merged, I've never personally met him."

Megan pushed Max's arm from her. "I told you, he's probably already left. Men with his and DuMond's power rarely stick around at these events. I must confess, I, too, prefer to arrive late and leave early to miss all the trivial speeches."

"I see." Dani tipped her glass at Megan. "Personally, I prefer such speeches. They inform you of what's going on, as well as who's who."

Jonas shot his wife a glance then turned his attention back to Karma and Dani. "So, do you both work for DuMond or Wolfmoon?"

"Please, regale us with what you two do?" As always, Megan's voice dripped with sarcasm. She shifted her focus to Cade then back to them. "Is he with either of you?"

"Karma," Dani motioned to her. "Is the forensic accountant for both DuMond Enterprises and Wolfmoon Corporation. As for myself, I oversee HR for both as well as all their subsidiaries. The gentleman behind Karma is her personal body-guard."

Triumph flooded through Karma when Megan winced at Dani's words or possibly at Cade's grunt.

"Wow, a forensic accountant. That's not surprising, Karma." Jonas smiled, nodding. "You were always great with numbers. If it wasn't for you, I would have never made it out of Dr. Schlemmer's accounting class."

"She is amazing." Morgan's deep sensual voice sent ripples of awareness through Karma. Morgan handed her a flute filled with a sparkling liquid as he slipped his other hand around her waist. "Try this, beautiful. I think you'll like it." He then eyed Jonas. "Have we met?"

"Oh, where are my manners, darling?" Karma motioned to Jonas. "Morgan, this is Jonas Maxwell and his wife, Megan. We met each other in college. Jonas, my fiancé, Morgan Wolfe."

"Maxwell. Yes, I thought you looked familiar. We've just acquired your company, Maxwell Technology. I can't remember. Are you coming aboard?"

Jonas paled, and he swallowed, causing his Adam's apple to bob. "Yes, I'm going to oversee my team."

Any animosity Karma had toward Jonas was gone, replaced by pity. Jonas got what he'd wanted and now would live miserably ever after.

Karma gently pinched Morgan's side. *Be nice. I have you. He has her.*

True. As long as Maxwell is with the company, his wife will know how happy we are. Fitting. "That's right." Morgan extended his hand to Jonas. "Welcome aboard."

"My husband." Dani smiled. "Magnus DuMond, of DuMond Enterprises."

Karma took a sip of her drink, watching the varying degrees of shock play across Megan's face. "This is wonderful."

The drink, or watching your old nemesis squirm? Morgan's deep masculine laugh reverberated in her mind.

Both. Karma smiled.

Megan's expression shifted from hoity-bitch to Miss Congeniality. "So, Danielle," her words were so syrupy-sweet Karma thought she might die of sugar overload. "Do you and Magnus have any children? Jonas and I have talked about it, but the time has never seemed right."

Dani's benign smile was the same one she used when dealing with her kids. "We have four. You do know Wolfmoon and DuMond offices offer free state-of-the-art childcare, correct?"

"Four? So, you've been married for a while. I didn't know."

An all too familiar mask of cold dignity fell over Dani's face. "Bless your heart, Megan. As you stated earlier, we *do* travel in different circles. If you'll excuse us, we have an auction to get underway." She hooked her arm with Magnus's then strolled toward the podium.

"Beautiful, I'm being summoned. Maxwell, if you'll excuse us." Morgan didn't wait for a reply as he led her away.

Two men eased the canvas from the wall.

"Our bid won?" Karma smiled up at Morgan.

"Did you have any...doubt?" His brow furrowed.

Fear inched up her back. "Who do you see? Is it Whitehall?"

"No, it's Weissman." Morgan nodded toward a crowd. "He's waving his arms around like a chicken attempting to fly. I thought his mate made him leave."

"Apparently, not. You should go see what the man wants while I head to the ladies' room."

"No."

No? She peered up at him. "No, you don't want to find out what he wants, or no, I can't go to the bathroom? Choose carefully."

"Take Cade with you," Morgan growled.

"To the ladies' room?" Morgan's eyes glowed with his wolf, and his five o'clock shadow was furrier than it should be. "Fine! Cade, come on." Karma nodded her head towards the bathrooms.

The few women inside the restroom rushed out when Cade entered. He leaned against the sink, crossing his arms.

Karma locked the stall door, then hiked-up her dress and screamed.

Whitehall appeared from nowhere and grabbed her. He knocked off her glasses as he wrapped his arms around her from behind, covering her with his body like a blanket.

She screamed again, her voice sounding hollow as Cade kicked in the stall door. From the shock in his eyes, she knew something was wrong.

"Karma!" he shouted.

The air around her grew thick and hazy. Her vision was terrible, but not like this. Karma gasped as her heart grew cold and empty. *Morgan!*

She couldn't feel him. *Dear God, don't let him be dead!*

"Cade!" She was right in front of him. Why couldn't he see her?

Whitehall laughed. "Scream all you want. The traitor can't hear you. You're in the zone." He dragged her from the stall as Cade pushed through them.

Through. Them.

What the hell? Cade had rushed through them as if they weren't there.

"Let go of me, you piece of shit!" Karma rammed her elbow back, missing him. She stomped down on his foot and went through his boot.

She could barely draw breath and her stomach clenched. Her bearings were in total chaos. Her head spun as she cut the faint thread of hysteria threatening to take over. Now wasn't the time to panic.

"Fight all you want. I control what happens here."

Karma dug in her heels, struggled to free herself, but no matter what she did, Whitehall was too strong. "Why are you doing this?" Her voice echoed.

"Because I can." He yanked her toward the sinks, then through them and the wall into the banquet hall.

She spotted Morgan talking to Ryder as Whitehall dragged her towards the opened patio doors. "Morgan!" She could have sworn he looked directly at her. His eyes glowed a darker red than she'd ever seen.

"Your dog can't hear you." Whitehall yanked her arm so hard, her shoulder popped as he pulled her further away from Morgan. "Or sense you when you're in the zone."

Karma had to do something to stall. Around the room, people moved about, not seeing her abduction. Flint stood on stage, speaking to the crowd. His voice was so stifled she couldn't understand him. People clapped, the sound muffled.

She searched out Dani or Magnus, not seeing them. Now, Morgan had vanished, too.

Panic rose its ugly head. Karma's brain was in tumult. She struggled to think. This couldn't be happening to her again. "Can't breathe."

"Then, I suggest you move your fat ass." He pulled her along behind him, through the open door into the moonless night, then down the steps.

Karma stumbled on the steps, losing a shoe, falling hard to her knees. Karma remained absolutely motionless for a moment, allowing the pain to ease.

Evil Prick dragged her backward on her buttocks down the remaining steps to the landing. "Get up."

Karma pulled herself to her feet, looking behind her into total darkness. She'd hoped to see Morgan or anyone coming to rescue her.

The moonless night and dark fog made her surroundings eerier. Everything in this in-between state was unearthly. Her senses were deadened. She couldn't feel the breeze from the ocean or hear the crash of the waves on the shore. The only semi-clear thing was Evil Prick.

"Why me? Percy will undo anything I try." Her heart pounded faster as Whitehall dragged her closer to the water.

"You underestimate me. I'm not going to have you hack into the company. I'm going to have Morgan pay to get you back." Whitehall paused and looked at her. His eyes were red, and his fangs showed. "Once I realized you were the dog's mate, I thought about packing up and leaving." He chuckled. "Then everything changed when I witnessed what his family thought about you. I knew I could grab you and not have to worry about a pack of dogs hunting me down. Morgan's on his own. Since you're breeding, he'll pay whatever I ask."

"I haven't met his parents, so how do you know what they think about me?" Karma had her ideas but wanted Prick to confirm them.

His smirk was answer enough for her. "I saw what Paul thought of you. Saw how he treated you." Whitehall's grin turned perverted. "I also saw the dog claim you. I would've been afraid your fat thighs would suffocate me when you came in the shower."

Despite nausea rising in her throat, she smiled. "I'm glad you enjoyed the show. I guess Morgan's more of a man than you."

"Bitch!" Prick backhanded her.

Falling on the steps had hurt, but the smack…that's going to leave a bruise.

A heaviness centered in Karma's chest, and she gasped. It made sense. Whitehall controlled what happened in here. She understood how he'd killed Blythe without any witnesses.

Blood tinged Karma's tongue, and she clenched her jaw to kill the sob in her throat. If she was to survive this, she had to be strong. "Oh, I'm not a bitch. I'm Karma."

Whitehall swung his fist connected with her jaw, jerking her head to one side.

Karma fell to the rock. Despite the pain radiating through her body, she would not relent. "Kill me, and you won't get a fuckin' penny." She curled her lip, snarling. "The pack may not come for me, but hurt their grandbaby, and they'll tear you to shreds."

An unearthly sound tore from Whitehall. He grabbed her by her upper arm, lifting her to her feet. "Move it." He shoved her forward. "Here's a little tidbit for you. Killing you would avenge my brother's murder."

"How? Morgan told me Dirk took Quaid's leg."

"Shut the fuck-up!" He fisted her hair, yanking her back against his chest. "I should leave your fat ass in here to die."

Karma's knees buckled as she stumbled forward. Cold, damp air, along with the smell of the ocean, surrounded her. The sound of the crashing waves was sweet music to her. She was free from the void.

"Where the hell did you come from?" Psycho Asshole stood just above the surf next to an inflatable boat. He grabbed her upper arm, digging his fingers deep into her flesh. "Let's get her in the boat before someone sees us."

Karma dug in her heels, struggling with all her strength. If she got in that boat, Morgan might not find her in time. No way would these two allow her to live. She needed to get her bearings. Far down, the beach lights of the resort illuminated the night. Too far. If she tried to run, she'd be captured again, but she had to make an attempt.

"She's not going anywhere with you."

"Morgan," a cry of relief escaped her. "Let go of me!" She rammed her elbow into Canaday's gut then ran all of four steps.

"Going somewhere?" Whitehall caught her around the waist, then pushed her at Psycho. "Get her in the boat. This won't take long." Whitehall charged Morgan.

Canaday looped his arm around her throat, yanking her backward toward the inflatable boat.

Karma dug in her heels. She wasn't about to make it easy on him.

A howl shattered the night. Morgan shifted from man to his massive wolfman. He charged, not waiting for Whitehall to bring the fight.

Morgan caught Whitehall around the waist, body-slamming him to the ground.

"Holy fuck," Canaday gasped. His arm tightened on her throat, nearly cutting off her breath.

Karma struggled for oxygen as Canaday forcibly dragged her backward. Being short gave her an advantage. Karma reached behind her, grabbed Psycho's balls, and twisted.

"Bitch," Psycho screamed, shoving her.

Karma stumbled, throwing out her hands to catch herself. Her wrist popped when she landed with full force on her palms and knees. Every inch of her body hurt.

A hand grasped her elbow and firmly lifted her to her feet.

"Thank you—" Karma sucked in her breath, staring at the Devil himself. Horns, wings, burning red eyes. Her heart pounded in her throat, cutting off her scream.

"You okay?"

She relaxed, recognizing Magnus's deep baritone coming from the devil standing before her. "I'm good." Karma exhaled. "Where's Dani?"

Karma looked over her shoulder, seeking out Morgan, but Magnus's wings blocked her view. A battle raged on the other side. Snarls, grunts, and the sounds of fists striking flesh drowned out the ocean.

"I ordered her to stay put."

Karma tried to peer around the massive dark wing. "So in other words, she's on—"

"Fucking monsters!" Canaday's shout was followed by gunfire, a familiar high-pitched scream, and Morgan's yip.

Karma ducked under Magnus's wing. She could make out Morgan's outline in the dark, holding someone by the throat. Karma exhaled. Morgan didn't appear to be hurt.

She screamed at another flash of light and crack of gunfire.

Magnus roared, snatching Karma by the upper arm. He spun her in the direction of Dani's scream. Bullets continued to ricochet off rocks. Sand flew up near her foot.

"I'm okay. Get over here, K." Dani huddled behind a rock, waving for Karma to join her.

Magnus pushed her forward as a boat motor roared. "Get over there with Dani."

Part of Karma wanted to argue, but she trusted Magnus to help Morgan. Karma hurried across the sand to where Dani hid. The moment Karma crouched safely behind the rock, a gust of wind stirred up the sand.

She squinted, trying to see Morgan. Damn her sucky vision. He wasn't where she'd seen him before. "Morgan!"

Dani pointed toward the ocean. "He's down by the surf, probably washing the blood from his hands."

"Blood? He's hurt." Her feet engaged before her brain.

Morgan stood as she reached him. Even as a creature from a horror film, she found him desirable. "Beautiful? Are you okay?" He held her at arm's length, his gaze roaming over her from head to foot. "Your knees and palms are bleeding." He growled, and his eyes glowed. "You have a black eye, and your cheek is swollen. I killed him too quickly."

"I'm good, Morgan." She didn't care about her scrapes, not when he'd been shot. Karma tried to see the wound but couldn't find his injury. "I heard you yip. Where were you shot? She ran her hands up his chest as tears ran down her face.

"He just nicked me. The blood I washed off wasn't mine." Morgan drew her into his arms, hugging her to him. His hand smoothed up and down her back as she rested her cheek against his chest and dug her fingers deep into his fur. "Hush. It's over."

She peered up at him. "Are you sure it's over?" She'd lost count of the number of times she'd almost lost him.

"I'm sure—Whitehall's dead. Magnus is taking care of Canaday. I'm fine, love. No one is going to take me away from you, or you from me. I'm fine."

Karma hugged Morgan as tight as she could, breathing in the woodsy scent of his wolf. In the short span she'd been with Morgan, he'd become as essential to her as air. She loved him, plain and simple. She was mad, not because she'd been kidnapped, but because she loved Morgan. He'd been shot! Where was his security team? What happened to all the precautions put in place to keep them safe? Where the hell was Cade? "You're not hurt?"

Morgan rested his cheek on top of her head. "My pride's a little bruised, but I'm fine, beautiful."

"Damn, K. You do understand Morgan's bark, snap and growl." Dani stood off to the side, staring up at the sky. "Mind asking him if he knows where my guy flew off?"

The sound of pounding feet growing closer had a flicker of apprehension coursing through Karma. The fact Morgan didn't flinch eased her rattled nerves somewhat.

"It's Cade and Ryder," Morgan snarled.

So now the calvary shows up. Karma swallowed hard, trying to get a grip on her anger. Where were they when Morgan was shot? Yeah, she'd been kidnapped, but it was Morgan everyone was trying to kill.

She would not take her frustrations out on them. She would not. If she repeated the mantra over and over again, maybe she wouldn't kill anyone.

Ryder continued to where Morgan had fought with Whitehall, while a grinning Cade dropped a duffle in front of them.

He squatted then unzipped the bag. "Figured you'd need some pants. Grabbed a pair of sweats for you and Mag. Where is he, anyway?" He held out a pair of sweats to Morgan.

"I don't know where sexy is," Dani huffed. "He flew off, and he's blocking me." She stomped her foot, crossing her arms as she still looked toward the sky. "I don't understand dog, so I don't know if Morgan knows?"

Understand dog? The last thread of Karma's control snapped. "Morgan was shot, but he says he's okay. Thank y'all for asking?" She turned her anger toward Dani. "You're mated with the devil himself so, don't ever refer to Morgan as a dog. He. Is. A. Wolf. How would you feel if Magnus was shot?"

Dani stared blankly as she opened and closed her mouth before forcing a weary smile.

"Beautiful." Morgan pulled her back against his bare chest. "I can't die from a bullet wound. Yeah, they hurt like a wasp sting but not fatal." He kissed her crown. "What Canaday had was the equivalent of a peashooter." He wiped her tears.

"As for Cade and Ryder," Morgan continued. "I told them to ensure the safety of everyone at the auction. Knowing Whitehall, I didn't put it past him to harm the humans."

That made sense. Karma sniffed. It didn't make her feel any better.

"Are we good, K?" Dani smoothed her hand up Karma's back.

She glanced over her shoulder and nodded. Dani was tucked under Magnus's arm. Guess he returned from wherever he'd flown off to.

"Where's Canaday?" Morgan asked.

Magnus smirked. "In the middle of the Pacific. If he survived the fall, it'd be closer for him to swim to Hawaii than back here, but not by much."

Morgan chuckled. "How high?"

"About 4,000 feet, give or take a few inches."

"Hitting the water from that high—we shouldn't have to worry about him anymore." Morgan brushed a kiss to her temple. "See, beautiful, it's over."

Ryder looked back in the direction of the resort, then back at Morgan and Magnus. "The only thing we didn't plan on was how to get you two back inside without raising questions."

"Easy." Magnus shrugged. "I'll fly Morgan to the roof, you and Cade escort our mates inside, and we'll meet you in our suites."

"Sounds like a plan." Cade offered his arm. "Karma?"

Just like that, it was over. Everything she'd endured these last few days had been taken care of, swept under the rug. Kaput. Finished. Done. Over with. "No. I'm done. I'm going home."

Chapter Twenty

The click of the door thundered through his brain. Morgan shivered and rolled to his side, pulling the covers up around his shoulders. The empty place beside him where Karma should have been confirmed he'd screwed up royally. All night Morgan racked his brain, trying to figure out how everything had gone wrong.

For starters, Whitehall had gotten the drop on them and managed to kidnap Karma. For over forty-five agonizing minutes, Whitehall had Karma in his clutches. During that time, he'd used her for a fuckin' punching bag. Morgan should have shoved Whitehall's head up his ass, then ripped his heart out. Instead of immediately seeking Karma, he decided to wash Whitehall's blood from his hand. No matter how you did it, ripping a heart out was messy. Karma didn't need to see blood dripping from his hands.

Last night he should have realized the extent of Karma's stress when she snapped at Dani. That was the first sign of danger. The second was when she threatened to *walk* home if someone didn't drive her.

Morgan tossed back the covers then snatched the sweatpants he'd discarded last night. He had a mate to hunt, and he knew just the bait to lure her into his trap, or at least get her to speak to him. She'd only uttered two words last night to him. Good and night, punctuated by a slammed door.

With coffee and his secret weapon in hand, Morgan drew in a deep breath and swallowed his pride. He opened the door, allowing in a gust of the Pacific Northwest wind and the scent of burning pine. Today would be a perfect day to lounge in front of the fire.

His wolf snarled. Unless they wanted to be lounging alone, Morgan had better move his tail and appease their mate.

Karma sat curled up in one of the Adirondack chairs. She was wrapped up in one of the wool blankets. Her eyes were closed, her left hand dangled down, fingers barely brushing Cade's fur.

The cat curled its lip, exposing a fang.

Yeah, whatever. "How do you know that's Cade, beautiful?"

She inhaled, and her nose twitched, but her eyes remained closed. "Natural cougars have blue eyes. Cade's cat has green." She inhaled again. "Do I smell coffee and bacon?"

"Maybe. Are you going to talk to me?" He lowered the coffee cup closer to her nose.

Her eyes opened to slits as she opened and closed her hand. "Give—me."

He pulled the cup back. "Are you going to talk to me?"

"Coffee and breakfast first, then talk."

"I made you an egg, cheese, and bacon sandwich on a bagel." He handed her the cup and sandwich.

"Thank you. Have you eaten?" She bit into her sandwich then moaned. The sound had him half hard.

"While I was cooking." Morgan wanted to speak with Karma without an audience. He glanced at the cat. "There's more inside if you're hungry, Cade." The cat took the hint, rose to all fours, stretched, then padded toward the house.

Karma finished her sandwich, then wiped her mouth. "Sorry. I kinda inhaled that."

"Don't apologize. Since we didn't return to our room, we didn't have dinner last night, nor did I see you eat any of the hors d'oeuvre at the auction."

Karma curled in on herself, wrapping the blanket tighter around her, creating a protective barrier, shutting him out. Her hands trembled. She gripped the cup so tight her knuckles turned white.

What the hell had he said to cause that reaction? Morgan pressed into Karma's mind, entering a void. No thoughts or emotions. Total darkness.

"Why are your hands shaking?"

She shrugged, lifting the cup to her lips.

"Beautiful, talk to me."

Karma inhaled then released it on a sigh. "There's nothing to talk about."

"Bullshit." He took the cup from her, setting it on the table.

"Morgan!"

He lifted her from her seat, then flopped down, pulling Karma to his lap. "Quit struggling, or you'll make me spill your coffee." He handed it back to her. "Now, talk to me since you've blocked me from your mind."

"I haven't blocked you. I've just cleared my thoughts, wanting to forget everything. But, *fine*. You want me to talk? I'll talk. Last night you got pissed because I didn't want to go back to the hotel."

"I—"

"I'm not finished," she snapped.

Dang, he could almost see fur ruffling. "Sorry," he muttered, knowing damn-good and well, if he said anything else, he'd be in the doghouse.

She arched her dark eyebrow, staring at him. "From the moment we stepped foot in that hotel, it was chaos. We had to deal with Melody and your brother. Add in Evil Prick and Psycho Asshole, plus a phantom killer dropped through the elevator ceiling. If that wasn't bad enough, I was kidnapped twice—no three times if you count the restaurant incident."

She sniffed and snuggled closer. "I know you told me bullets can't kill you...but..." her bottom lip quivered. "When I was in that place...I couldn't feel you, leaving my heart empty. Then everything on the beach...and everyone acted like it was no big deal. But it was a big deal *for me*. Now, I can't see a damn thing because my last pair of glasses got broke!"

Morgan's wolf snarled. They'd neglected their mate.

Tears spilled over her lower lashes, stabbing him in the heart. "I'm Karma, for Pete's sake, not chaos! But for nearly two weeks, that's precisely what my life has been. You ask why my hands shake? You're the best thing that's happened to me. Yet every time I close my eyes, I see you turning to a pile of dust. It's the only damn thing I can see clearly. Stupid, sucky vision!" More tears spilled from her eyes. "In that place, I didn't know what would happen to our baby." She gulped then fell against his shoulder, sobbing. Hot tears rolled down his back. "I can't lose either of you."

How could he have been so blind? He smoothed his hand up and down Karma's back until her sobs stopped. "What do you need me to do?"

Karma sniffed, sitting up. She wiped her swollen red eyes, then drew in a deep breath. "That's just it. I don't know. I need to call my optometrist and order another pair of glasses. Though I really don't want to go back there, I guess we should return to the resort and collect our belongings. I should call Dani to apologize. . .but all I want to do is sit here and enjoy the sound of the waves. Maybe I'll find my Zen."

Morgan held her, resting his cheek on her crown. "I've already placed a call to Percy. He's having another pair of glasses expedited to you. He assured me they will be here no later than tomorrow. However, we may have to go into town and have them adjusted."

"Thank you." She relaxed against him.

"As for our stuff, Flint is sending it over."

"Still need to call.....Dani," Karma's words slurred.

"I'm sure she understands you were upset."

"Mmm-hmmm." Karma snuggled in his arms, resting her head on his shoulder.

Cade slid into the other chair, dangling his legs over the arm. "Dude, I think she's asleep. I found her shivering when I came back from my run, so I started the fire."

"Thank you." Morgan didn't miss Cade's accusing tone. He didn't need the cat telling him he'd screwed up. He knew it. Now, he had to fix his debacle.

As carefully as he could, Morgan stood then carried Karma back inside. He didn't stop until he'd gently placed her on the bed.

Her eyes twitched, and she jerked.

Morgan eased into Karma's mind, instantly seeing the nightmare Whitehall put her through. Morgan materialized behind Whitehall, looped his arm around his throat, then shoved his free hand through the asshole's back. Morgan tore out the bastard's heart for the second time.

Karma jerked awake, screaming.

He gathered her in his arms, holding her against his chest. "I've gotcha, beautiful. I've gotcha. Whitehall's dead, and so is Canaday. They can't hurt you ever again." He could feel her heart pounding.

"Did you…Is that what you did to him last night?" Karma leaned back, staring up at him.

Morgan would never lie to her, even if it meant losing her love. "I tore his heart out of his chest, then held it up so he could see it in my hand. I might have laughed as he crumbled to dust."

Morgan inhaled, drawing in Karma's sweet scent, then forged ahead. "I knew the second you were taken. Magnus barely kept the wolf from tearing from me. I couldn't feel you, I couldn't sense you. The wolf wanted to kill everyone in sight until he found you. At the same time, my logical brain feared Whitehall would use your kidnapping as a distraction to attack the resort. Ryder had informed us earlier of a raft they'd spotted on the shore. I decided to leave Ryder and his men behind while Magnus and I headed for the boat. Had the boat been left as a ruse, we would have searched for you from the air with Magnus's ability to fly. Nothing would stand in my way of getting you back."

"You made the right decision. Whitehall said he would make you pay to get me back, but he wasn't after money. He was after revenge." Karma leaned against him, her finger drawing circles on his leg. Morgan could feel the tension draining from her body.

Karma peered up at him, the corner of her lips twitching with the beginnings of a smile. "So now, what do you want to do now for excitement?"

"I figured I'd let you get some sleep, then we'd go into town and get our marriage license. What do you say?" Or he could join her for a nap and maybe a little lovemaking.

Karma arched her eyebrows and laughed. "Seriously? Ya think that's gonna happen?"

"Did you hear my thoughts?"

"Yup. You're delusional, Wolfie. I'm wide awake now. Couldn't sleep if I wanted to." Karma threw her arms around his neck, knocking him backward on the bed. A smile curved her lush lips, but tears still clung to her lashes.

He held her in his arms for several minutes, listening to her heartbeat, waiting for her to speak. With everything they'd been through, they still didn't know each other very well. He did know now wasn't a good time to seduce her.

His wolf disagreed. Now would be a perfect time.

After several moments Karma drew in a deep breath then exhaled. "Up until a few days ago, vampires, werewolves, and whatever the heck Magnus is were all make-believe to me. They were stories told by kids around campfires or under the covers at sleepovers. They didn't exist."

"The DuMond clan probably gave rise to the legends of gargoyles and demons," he added, wishing he hadn't said a word.

"Makes sense." Karma rested her head on his chest. "The point, no matter how many times you tell me bullets won't hurt you, I'm still going to freak out." She shrugged. "I'm human, and it's going to take time for my human brain to accept all this hocus-pocus."

"Beautiful, it's not magic. It's real."

"I know it's not hocus-pocus. However, my human brain says it is."

"I never thought about how my world would appear to you. I mean, this is normal for me, but for you…yeah. I see your point."

"I know for the Dhampir it's special when you find your true mate, so I understand why your mom wants a huge wedding. You've never said what you wanted—and *don't* say whatever I want."

"I don't like crowds. But I would like my folks there." Karma stiffened in his arms. Morgan didn't have to read her mind to know her thoughts. "You're afraid Paul will find out and pull something. Like, I don't know…call Melody."

"Yeah…something like that."

"If you're serious about a small wedding, how's this for an option? There's a three day waiting period here. Once we have our license and everything planned, I can fly my folks up here under the pretense of meeting you. Just my folks. No one else."

"You think that will work, that they won't suspect something?"

"Good question." His mom always knew when he was up to something. Heck, even last night, she knew something was wrong.

"Mom wouldn't stop texting me until I called her back last night, reassuring her you were safe and okay. By the time I called her, she was rallying the troops to come after you."

"You took the time to call your mother," Karma's tone was way too calm. "Before you came after me?"

"No," Morgan reassured her. "I didn't call her until after you went to bed."

Karma sat up, staring down at him. Her brow furrowed as she twirled her finger at her temple. "Human brain, remember? So, if you didn't call her, how'd she know?"

"Remember, I told you that you'd be able to hear my family's thoughts?"

"Yeah. I clearly heard what Paul thought of me."

Thank you, little brother. Life would have been so much easier if his folks had stopped at one kid.

Karma shook her head. "I'm confused. I thought you had to be nearby. I mean, you said you wouldn't be able to sense me if I was far away from you. I don't understand how your mom knew. Did someone call her?"

"She sensed my distress." Morgan pressed into Karma's mind. He thought she'd understood about the blood bond they shared, but seeing the turmoil and questions swirling around in her mind, she didn't.

"Again, I thought she had to be close." She leaned back, looking up at him.

He palmed Karma's stomach. "Just as you are giving life to our child, Mom gave life to me. The blood bond between a mother and child is strong. Mom can't hear my thoughts this far, but she can sense if something bad has happened."

"Mother-child bond." Karma covered his hand with hers. "I hope I have the same connection. I mean, with Melody as a role model…"

"You will." A shiver inched up Morgan's back, telling him they had company. Great. Perfect timing as always. "You'll make a fantastic mom."

"Hey? Anyone home?" Dani's voice resonated in the room.

Morgan stretched out his senses. *Nothing. Whoever is with Dani, they're blocking me.* Cade hadn't alerted them…so not an enemy.

"I need to speak to her." Karma pecked his cheek then scooted from the bed. "Lord have mercy. I was such a witch last night."

He caught Karma's hand, bringing it to his lips. "But you're my witch."

She rolled her eyes. "Come on, Wolfie." Karma laced her fingers with his and tugged.

He couldn't shake the feeling people other than Dani and Magnus were here. Morgan opened the bedroom door and picked up the high pitch squeal of little girls. "Sounds like the twins are here."

Karma's face lit up. "The twins? Then Mr. and Mrs. Rossi must be here. Are you sure?" She let go of his hand and hurried down the hall only to stop. "Um, Morgan."

He stepped up behind Karma. Looping his arms around her waist, he pulled her back against him. "Hi, Mom. Where's Pop?"

Chapter Twenty-One

His mother! Karma drew in a calming breath and pasted on a smile. Calm. She wanted Calm. Why hadn't Morgan warned her? "Mrs. Wolfe, it's a pleasure to meet you in person."

Gwyn glared at Morgan then smiled warmly at Karma. "I'm sorry for the intrusion, Karma. I had to see for myself that you were okay."

"I didn't know," Cade whispered as he carried their luggage down the hall.

Someone strolled in, carrying a large flat shipping box. "Do you want your painting in your room, son?"

"Thanks, Pop. Just set it down, and I'll carry it back later."

The man set the painting down. He was shorter than Morgan, not by much, and slimmer. Other than that, Karma stared at an older version of Morgan. When his eyes met Karma's, he grinned. "Son, you have yourself a beautiful mate."

"Thanks, Pop. This is Karma. Karma, my father. And yes, that's her real name."

The man held his hand out to her. "You can call me John or Pop. Not Mr. Wolfe, and I'd prefer Pop."

Not knowing what to say, Karma shook his hand and smiled.

"Why are y'all here?" Morgan eyed his mom. "Where are Dani and Magnus?"

"Oh, they're down at the shore with the twins and the Rossis." Cade picked up the painting and carried it down the hall. "They're all staying at the resort," he shouted over his shoulder.

"Can we sit?" Gwyn sat on the couch facing the window. She patted the cushion beside her. "John."

Morgan took Karma's hand, leading her to the other couch. The knot in her stomach tightened with the ticking of each millisecond ticked they sat in silence.

Gwyn's lips curved into a placid smile as she pulled out her cellphone. "I'm going to start by saying we're here because of your lack of communication skills."

"My communication skills?" Morgan frowned. "What are you talking about, Mom?"

The saccharine-sweet smile on Gwyn's face sent chills down Karma's back. She'd seen Dani get that same smile right before she laid down the law to one of the twins.

"How many times did I text you last night?" Gwyn held up her hand, cutting off anything Morgan was about to say. "Forty-eight times. Four. Eight. Forty-eight. Let me read you a few of my texts. Are you okay? Is Karma alright? What's going on? Do you need us? Call me!" She scrolled down. "For the love of *Yeva,* what's going on? Morgan, is Karma okay?"

Gwyn dropped her phone back into her purse. Her eyes glowed amber. The tip of her nose blackened. Her ears grew pointy with a dusting of white fur. "And *what* was your reply? *K. K,* the eleventh letter of the alphabet. K! How in the hell did that answer any of my questions?"

Karma shifted her attention from Gwyn to Morgan. His mouth hung slack, and his cheeks were pink. Karma didn't know everything about Morgan, but she understood why Magnus did the talking at the business meetings. Still, Morgan could have been a little more forthcoming with information for his mom. "Morgan?"

He reached for her hand and awkwardly cleared his throat. "I left a voice message."

"At four this morning, and the only thing you said was we're fine." More fur covered Gwyn's arms. "Fine? That doesn't tell me crap!"

Gwyn was distraught. Her angry outburst wasn't like one of Melody's temper tantrums thrown for attention. Not at all. Gwyn's fury was a result of her worry for Morgan, and maybe just a bit for Karma.

"Gwenny." John slipped his arm around her shoulder. "Breathe."

"Don't Gwynne, me, John," Morgan's mother snarled. "Morgan, fine doesn't tell me what happened to my new daughter. I knew something bad had happened. I felt your fear over 1600 miles away as strongly as if you were in the same room as me. And I get we're fine!" Her fingernails were black claws. "Seriously?"

Her daughter? If only that were true. Karma's heart stuttered. Melody may have given birth to Karma, but she was no mother. The only time Melody wanted to be called mother was when she thought she'd get something out of it. Karma shifted her attention from Morgan to Gwyn, meeting the eyes of Gwyn's wolf, rimmed with red, not the red of her Dhampir, but the red of tears.

Gwyn's bottom lip quivered slightly. "I didn't know," her voice broke. "I didn't know in what condition *that bastard,*" she spat the words, "left her." A crimson tear slid down Gwyn's cheek. "After losing Peter and Jean, I couldn't bear the thought of losing another child."

Morgan deflated. His shoulders slumped as he hung his head. "I'm sorry, Mom."

This wasn't Morgan's making. It was Karma's. Guilt stabbed her. She covered Morgan's hand with hers, lowering her gaze to the floor. "It's my fault, not Morgan's. I couldn't go back inside that building. I'm a coward. I had to come back to where I felt safe." Tears blurred her vision even more. She sniffed. "Please, don't blame him." The last thing in the world Karma wanted was for Morgan to be blamed for her selfishness. She swallowed the lump in her throat. "It's just," her voice cracked.

A hand gently touched her. Karma turned with a start, meeting Gwyn's tear-filled eyes.

"It's just your human mind can't accept what it has perceived as unreal all of your life." The warmth of Gwyn's smile echoed in her voice.

Images from last night once again flashed through Karma's mind, the popping sound of bullets and of Morgan washing away blood. Karma wrapped her arms around her middle, giving up on fighting her tears. "Morgan was shot," Karma forced the words past the lump in her throat. "They may have been trying to kidnap me, but they wanted to kill him."

"You're safe now." Gwyn hugged Karma in a warm embrace, which had her crying harder. Neither her mother nor grandmother had ever comforted Karma with a hug. "Hush, now," Gwyn cooed, rubbing her hand up and down Karma's back.

The door opened, letting in a gust of wind before it closed.

Karma stayed cocooned in Gwyn's warm embrace. The door opened then closed once more. Karma still clung to Gwyn, basking in the love flowing from her. Each time Karma's tears slowed, another image of her screwed up childhood flashed in her mind, starting the waterworks again.

The seat behind her rose then dipped again, accompanied by the sweet scent of gardenias—Mrs. Rossi's signature fragrance.

"Oh, K, you're breaking my heart." Dani hugged Karma from behind. "Go make her a cup of tea, furball. Ginger—"

Morgan growled. "Ginger peach when she's upset, yes, I know."

Karma glared over her shoulder at Dani. "Don't call him that."

Morgan snorted. "Beautiful, she's been calling me a furball since she was two. I think it was her first word." He bent down, lightly kissing Karma's forehead. When he leaned back, he drew his thumbs under her eyes, wiping away her tears.

"Kettle's on," Mrs. Rossi said. She smiled at Morgan, nudging him aside as she maneuvered around him, then sat in the chair closest to Gwyn. "I regret not bringing you into the family after your grandparents passed." She dug around in her purse, pulling out a tissue. "Here, Karma, dry your eyes."

Gwyn nodded. "Gina, we can't worry about the past. We can only learn from it."

Karma dried her eyes, realizing Morgan's father wasn't in the room. "Where'd your dad go?"

Morgan poured hot water into a mug. "Pop and Cade went outside." He handed her the cup. When his fingers touched hers, instantly a sense of peace swept through her. The scent of ginger and peach teased her nose. "Let it steep, love."

"Thanks." Karma stared into the cup. "I'm sorry for losing it."

"Oh, nonsense," Gwyn groused. "You've been through more than enough to shake anyone of us. My asshole of a son certainly didn't help matters."

Morgan jerked his head toward his mom. "Excuse me."

"Not you." Gwyn cast her eyes upward. "Paul." She shook her head. "I'm sorry, Karma. When he called that morning…" Gwyn sighed and shook her head again. "I should have called him home, but a mother has hopes her children would rise to any occasion. Unfortunately, after what he did to Shelby—"

"What did he do to Shelby?" Morgan snarled. Fur pushed from his pores, rippling over his face and arms.

Karma set her cup down and took his hand in hers Morgan's fur receded from her touch, an action that didn't escape Gwyn's notice.

Gwyn waved her hand dismissingly. "Doesn't matter. Shelby stood her own. She informed your brother he may look like her daddy, but he wasn't nothing like her father." Gwyn wiped at her eye. "Shelby said her father wasn't mean like Paul."

"So, you killed Paul."

"Don't be ridiculous, son. I would never harm any of my children. After Toby handed Paul his ass, I packed your brother's things and sent him to Mishenka."

"For *him* to kill." Morgan grinned and winked at Karma.

"Oh, for heaven's sake, Morgan. No one is going to kill your brother. Adjust his attitude, oh yes."

Karma didn't ask who Morgan and Gwyn were talking about. At the mention of Mishenka's name, the face of a kindly elderly man with a striking resemblance to the old Hollywood actor Vincent Price entered her mind. She also felt he loved to play *games,* but not board games.

Welcome to the family, my child, echoed in her mind. Chills ran down her back as the man winked.

Before she could react, the door flew opened.

"Momma!" Megan and Maggie rushed into the house.

Their older brothers, Dany, and David chased after them, shaking strands of seaweed.

"Make them stop!" Megan cried.

David giggled, flicking the seaweed at his sisters. A piece flew across the room, hitting Maggie in the face. Her eyes turned red, horns pushed from her forehead. She hissed, revealing sharp fangs.

"Hey," Dani shouted and pushed from the couch. She glared down at her four kids. "What have I told you about picking on your sisters."

Four sets of eyes slowly panned to Dani.

Karma wiggled her fingers at the kids. Four small mouths gaped, eyes grew wide, as four tiny faces paled.

What the heck caused *those* reactions? Usually, they were ecstatic to see their Auntie K.

Morgan slid beside her. "You saw Maggie shift," he whispered.

Maggie's bottom lip quivered. Her horns and fangs retracted as she stared at Karma.

Megan growled and punched David in the gut. "It's your fault. Daddy's going to kill Aunt K."

"Why am I killing Karma?" Magnus strolled into the room, followed by Dani's father, Cade, then Morgan's dad. "Why is there seaweed on the floor?"

Dani tapped her foot, pointing at the green glob. "The boys were chasing their sisters with it, and a piece hit Maggie. David, pick it up and put it in the trash."

"Ah, no." Morgan interrupted. "Take it outside. That stuff stinks."

"I shifted, Daddy. Aunt K saw." Maggie sniffed, drawing her arm across her nose. "Don't kill her."

"Oh, sweet baby Jesus." Mrs. Rossi turned in her seat, facing the kids. "Maggie, where did you get that idea from?"

The two girls pointed at their brothers, who, in turn, pointed at Magnus.

"In my defense, the boys wanted to use their other-selves for show and tell." Magnus shrugged.

Dani planted her hands on her hips. "And you thought telling them anyone who sees their other self would have to die was appropriate? Seriously?"

"At the time, it sounded like a good idea."

"So, we can show our other selves to our friends?" David asked with too much enthusiasm.

Dani rolled her eyes. "No. If you do, you will be grounded for life and lose all screen time."

"Mom!" All four whined.

"Forever. Your tablets will be locked away, and all of your games will be given to less fortunate children. So no showing your other self to anyone, unless your father or I tell you it's okay."

Morgan threw his head back, laughing. He brought Karma's hand to his lips. "See what we have to look forward to."

"But what about Auntie K?" Megan was the quietest of the two girls, but her keen eyes didn't miss a thing.

"I think it's okay." Karma winked at her, wiggling her ring finger. "Morgan and I are getting married."

Maggie's tears instantly ceased. Grinning, she turned to Megan. Megan's lips curled up in, her eyes grew wide, then both girls squealed, jumping up and down. "We're gonna be flower girls," they shouted in unison.

Oh, crud. Karma breathed in then exhaled. She wanted a small wedding. Small, as in Morgan, her, the officiant, and a couple of witnesses. Now she had two flower girls. Okay, they could still have a small wedding. "Morgan and I had talked about going into town today to get our license, then hopefully have a small ceremony in three days on the beach at sunset."

Gwyn broke into a wide smile. "When you say small, how many people are we talking? A hundred?"

Karma had already broken down in front of Morgan's mother once. Lord have mercy. It was time for Karma to stiffen her spine. She took a deep breath then forced her voice to be respectful but firm. "Small as in the people in this room, and the officiant. Possible Ryder and his men if they want to come." There, she got it out.

"I see." Gwyn nodded. "So, you don't want your mother here?"

"Oh, hell no!"

"Oh, thank goodness." Gwyn exhaled. "I can't stand *that* woman."

"Mom," Morgan furrowed his brows. "When did you meet Melody? Or have you?"

John flung the door open. "Come on, kids, the tides going out. Let's look for starfish."

The boys rushed out the door with Mr. Rossi right behind them. Magnus helped Maggie with her coat while Cade helped Megan. The girls each took one of Magnus's hands, pulling him out the door.

"I don't know why we have to go back to the beach. We just came in," Cade grumbled.

John smacked Cade on the back of the head. "Get out that door."

"You hit me." Cade rubbed his head.

"I smack sense into all my sons. Move your tail."

A grin split Cade's face. "Right behind you, Pop." He closed the door.

"Mom?" Morgan slipped his arm around Karma's shoulders. "Spill."

"She showed up at the ranch. I didn't kill her. Wanted to, but I figured that wouldn't start my relationship off right with Karma. I mean, she already had to put up with Paul."

"Melody?" Karma said, surprised. "How did she know where you lived?"

"I'd like to know," Gwyn replied. "Anyway, she said she *knew things*. Knew we had money, but that was it." Gwyn flicked her wrist. "I didn't have time for her. I had too much to do that day. Weak minds are easy to read. After what Gina told me about the woman," Gwyn flicked her attention to Mrs. Rossi, then back to Morgan and Karma. "I...well. I pressed into Melody's mind and persuaded her to be a respectful person and stay away from you until she is invited." Gwyn smiled wider. "Now, about this wedding.

Chapter Twenty-two

Her name was Karma, not chaos. If she kept telling herself that, she might start believing it. Of course, she was getting married on Halloween. That alone created chaos. Karma ran her hands over the autumn gold, antique, shirred silk dress she wore. Charlie had come through big time, though she doubted he'd imagined her wearing the dress for her wedding. The dress even had hidden pockets in the skirt. Granted, autumn gold wasn't the typical color for a wedding dress. However, there was no way Karma would wear white. She'd look like a giant marshmallow walking toward Morgan.

She checked herself in the mirror one last time. "Something new is my dress. Something blue, my garter, borrowed, the canary diamond broach from Gwyn. My something old is—"

"That would be Morgan," Dani teased. "You have to admit three hundred plus is old."

"Funny. The vintage shoe clips your mom gave me are my something old." Karma exhaled. "I think I have it all. Nothing but good luck from now on."

"You don't have flowers."

"Yeah, I kinda forgot them, but I don't need flowers to get married."

"You don't have a cake, either," Megan groused.

"Young lady, you were there when Auntie K and Auntie Gwyn talked about this. They are having a celebration later, with cake and everything."

"But it isn't a wedding without a cake." Megan rolled out her bottom lip and crossed her arms over her chest.

Karma rolled her eyes. She and Morgan should have gone to the Justice of the Peace. Why had she let Gwyn talk her into a wedding?

"Do you want to eat wedding cake or go trick or treat?" Karma could almost see the wheels turning in Megan's head.

"Trick or treats," Megan muttered.

"Okay, then." Karma winked at Dani. "You will babysit for us? Right?"

"Pfft. You and Morgan moving to Atlanta?" Dani grinned and took Karma's hand. "You are beautiful. Are you ready?"

Karma drew in a deep breath. "Yes."

A quick knock on the bedroom drew Karma's attention. "That's Morgan. Would you let him in?"

"It's bad luck for the groom to see the bride in her dress before she walks down the aisle."

"Lord have mercy. He was there when Charlie showed the dress to me."

"But Morgan hasn't seen you in it, so no. What do you want, furball?" Dani glared at the door as if Morgan could see her.

"I have something for Karma."

"Set it on the floor, then step away from the door," Dani ordered. "Matter of fact, leave."

"I'm not just putting it on the floor. You step out, then I'll hand it to you."

"Fine." Dani eased the door open wide enough for her to slip out. A few seconds later, she stepped back in, carrying a floral box. "Morgan said all brides need a bouquet." She lifted the lid, revealing three black calla lilies arranged with green ferns and tied with a ribbon matched to Karma's dress.

Karma's heart pounded as she lifted the card from the box. "They're so beautiful. I think I have a new favorite flower." She opened the envelope and blinked against the tears that threatened as she read his note.

To my beautiful bride,

I love you with all my heart and soul. Three lilies, one for you, one for me, and baby makes three.

Forever,

Your "Wolfie."

Karma slipped the note back into its envelope. "Let's not keep my mate waiting." She tucked the envelope into her pocket.

Dani peered out into the hall then met Karma's eyes. "Are you sure you want to walk alone? I can ask Dad to escort you."

"I'm sure." Karma smiled, staring into Dani's emerald green eyes. "You are my dearest friend, the sister of my heart. If it wasn't for you, I'd never have met Morgan. Thank you."

"Okay, you're going to have me crying." She glanced over her shoulder. "It's showtime. Let's go, girls."

Megan and Maggie scooted from the bed.

"If we're flower girls," Maggie asked, "Then why don't we have flowers, too?"

Dani smiled indulgently. "Because your Auntie K is getting married on the beach, and *you* wanted to be mermaid girls. Now, grab your basket of shells, and no throwing them at your brothers. If you do, you won't go trick or treating."

"But we want flowers too." Megan pouted, rolling out her bottom lip.

Oh, Lord, help!

Don't worry, K. I've got this. Dani's voice echoed in Karma's head, startling her. She shouldn't be shocked—still, something else to get used to. Dani had taught Karma how to enter others' minds last night after explaining since Morgan and Magnus had shared blood over the years, then Dani and Karma would have a connection since they were Morgan's and Magnus's mates. A weak connection, but still a connection. It had worked, but Karma shouldn't have been surprised. She and Dani have been reading each other's minds for years.

"Okay, we can run to the store and get you flowers, making Auntie K wait to marry Uncle Morgan, but you'll miss trick or treating because by the time we get the flowers, then have the wedding trick or treats will be over."

Megan looked at Maggie, then they both nodded.

"We'll do the shells," Megan said with a huff.

"We don't want to miss trick and treats," Maggie added.

"See, not a problem." Dani followed the girls from the room

Karma grabbed her bouquet then hurried after Dani "I feel like I've got a herd of butterflies in my stomach."

"Shouldn't that be a murder of crows since it's Halloween?" Dani laughed as she followed her daughters down the stone steps.

"You're so funny." Karma's breath caught as she stood on the steps. The sky was stunning. The setting sun had painted the wisps of clouds in orange, violet, and navy with pink and gold highlights. Even the ocean had hints of orange. It was perfect.

She scanned the shore. Torches lit a path to where Morgan stood, waiting for her. Only about a dozen guests, but more than twenty people with Ryder and his men. Bless Ryder's heart. The man was set on ensuring everyone's safety, even if Whitehall's threats had been eliminated. Still, nothing said simple, stress-free wedding like a squad of men carrying assault rifles.

"You ready, K?" Dani glanced over her shoulder.

"More than ever." Karma followed Dani down the steps.

The girls dropped shells once they were on the sand. Maggie examined each seashell before she dropped it. More than one ended up back in her basket.

Karma's heart pounded the moment her eyes met Morgan's. Damn, he was handsome in his jeans and a white button-down. She couldn't imagine loving anyone but Morgan. How had she been so lucky?

Beautiful, Morgan's voice caressed her mind. *Damn, you're gorgeous. I'm the luckiest man alive.*

She kept her eyes lock with his as she crossed the sand. Morgan offered her his arm, leaning down to kiss her cheek. Karma handed Dani her flowers, then smiled at Flint.

Flint cleared his throat. "We are here to celebrate the mating of Karma and Morgan. May your hearts be bound in love. May the fates bless you. May the blood that binds you join your souls for eternity. Blessed be."

"Blessed be," everyone repeated."

"Who stands with this woman?"

"The Clan DuMond stands with this woman," Magnus declared.

What? Oh, yeah, last night Dani and Gwyn explained the families took an active part in Dhampir weddings. They also said

Magnus was claiming Karma to his clan, making her and Dani sisters through and through.

"Does the DuMond clan accept this man?" Flint asked.

"We do," Magnus replied.

Flint nodded. "Who stands with this man?"

"The Clan Lucard," Gwyn replied.

"Does the Lucard clan accept this woman as mate to Morgan Wolfe?"

"With all of our hearts," John and Gwyn spoke in unison.

"Then shall it be."

Morgan took her hands, staring into her eyes. "Karma, for centuries, I've waited for you. I knew you were out there, but I had to be patient. You own my heart and soul. For now and for eternity, I will love, honor, and cherish you."

"Morgan, I must confess. I slowly fell in love with you over the months we spoke on the phone. When we finally met, you stole my heart. I love you now, for eternity, and will forever be by your side."

"May we have the rings, please," Flint asked.

Dani and Magnus handed Flint the simple gold rings she and Morgan had chosen.

Flint held the rings between his thumb and forefinger between Morgan and her. "The circle is never-ending as your love for each other shall be. May these rings remind you of your everlasting love during troubled times." Flint handed Morgan's rings to Magnus and Dani. Then he passed John and Gwyn the ring Karma would wear. "Blood binds families. May these two families be joined as one."

Magnus slid the ring onto Morgan's finger then pulled him into a bro-hug, pounding Morgan on the back.

Gwyn slid the ring onto Karma's finger then pulled her into a hug. "Welcome, daughter." She kissed her cheek.

John hugged her. "You've made this old man happy."

Maggie tugged on Flint's trouser leg. "You didn't say kiss the bride. You gotta say it so we can go tricks or treats."

He laughed. "I wouldn't want you to miss Halloween. Morgan, you may kiss your bride."

Morgan took her in his arms. His wolf peered through his eyes as he lowered his lips. Morgan captured her mouth, kissing her gently and nowhere as thoroughly as she'd expected. "I love you, beautiful. Can we forgo the cake?" He jiggled his eyebrows.

"Okay," Maggie shouted. "We can go trick or treats. They kissed."

"Let's go!" Megan upended her basket then took off running toward the steps.

"Wait a second, young lady," Dani bellowed. "K, I'm sorry."

"There's nothing to apologize for. They're kids. Go, have fun. I will."

"Mom, did you pack our costumes?" David asked.

"Your grandmother has them in her room."

"Okay, come on," He tugged on Dani's hand. "Bye, Aunt K."

"We've got the kids if you and Magnus want to stay." Mrs. Rossi took David's hand.

Magnus smirked. "That's a wonderful idea, Gina. Dani and I would love to stay behind."

A lower rumble vibrated from Morgan. "But you would be missing an important event with your children."

Karma rolled her eyes. "Morgan, stop growling."

Dani elbowed Magnus. "Stop teasing." She hugged Karma. "We're heading back tomorrow." She kissed Karma's cheek. "I love you, sis. We'll see you in a few weeks."

Gwyn clapped her hands. "Before everyone leaves. Tonight, John and I are hosting a dinner at the hotel." She winked at the kids. "After trick or treating. We'd like *everyone* to attend." Gwyn smiled at Karma.

"Mother," Morgan growled. "We discussed this."

"It's your wedding day. You both deserve a nice dinner. What are you going to do? Pop a frozen pizza in the oven?"

"Gwenny." John slipped his arm around her waist. "You promised. Besides, I saw Flint stocking their fridge with pre-prepared gourmet meals, and he included some delicious looking desserts."

"Fine. You can't blame a mother for trying. Anyways, once we have a date, I'll let you all know so we can celebrate Karma and Morgan's mating in style. I want you all to please come." She peered around John. "Ryder, this includes you and your men."

"Momma Gwyn, we can't promise. You know how things are with us." There were a few groans and grumbles from his men. "But I'll see what we can do. I know how much these guys love John's grilling."

Magnus chuckled. "More for us." He scooped Megan up in his arms. "Morgan, Karma, congratulations. We'll see you when we see you." He looped his free arm around Dani's waist as they headed toward the steps.

Morgan strode toward Ryder. "I'll make sure to inform Royce your services will be needed to provide security." They shook hands. "Thank you for all you have done to protect my mate."

"Not a problem. As for the rest of your time here, Cade will be staying behind to run in his fur."

That caught Karma's attention, evaporating her happy euphoria, replacing it with dread. "Why? I thought all the bad guys were taken care of. Are we still in danger?" Was that why his men were so heavily armed?

Morgan slipped his arm around her shoulders, then pressed his lips to her temple. "There's no need to worry. I will keep you safe. I swear it on my life. No one will steal you from me again."

"The thought of losing you, terrifies me."

"Nothing will happen to you or Morgan. You have my word," Cade reassured her. "I'll make certain of it. You won't know I'm around.

Karma's spirits sank even lower. "Okay." What else could she say? Nothing. There was nothing to say. This nightmare would never end. She and Morgan would forever be looking over their shoulders.

"But if you think of it, maybe toss some pancakes outside for me?" Cade winked at her.

"Hey." Morgan placed his finger under her chin and tipped her face up. "Cade is staying behind because even though Whitehall and

Canaday are dead, we don't know if anyone is still responding to their post. I'd rather spend the next few weeks making love to you than burying bodies."

"When will this nightmare be over?" Her voice quivered as she looked up into Morgan's eyes.

"Karma," Gwyn's gentle voice drew Karma's attention. "There is no need for you to worry. I'm certain of it." She pressed a kiss to Karma's forehead. "Let's head back to the house, then we'll say our good-byes. I've enjoyed these few days together."

For some strange reason, Gwyn's reassurance put Karma at ease. She was worrying about nothing.

Ryder's men extinguished the torches and gathered them up. Despite the bright moonlight, Cade stood at the top of the steps, shining a flashlight so they could see as they made their way.

"I've enjoyed these past few days, too." Karma reached the top of the steps. Dani and the Rossis had already left, as had Flint. The only vehicles left were John's and Gwyn's and Ryder's.

"Congratulations, you two." Cade shook Morgan's hand, then blew Karma a kiss. "Don't forget to leave me breakfast and maybe a cup of coffee." He walked away, pulling his shirt over his head, then dropping his jeans.

"Cade," Morgan growled.

The cat flicked his tail then darted off into the night.

Her fingers brushed the wolf head broach from Gwyn. "Let me give this back before I forget." Karma fiddled with the clasp.

"I want you to have it." Gwyn smiled.

"It's beautiful. Thank you."

"You're more than welcome. We will see you for Thanksgiving? Right?"

"We'll be there," Morgan confirmed. "But you do know Karma does not cook."

"We know." Gwyn laughed. She kissed Morgan's cheek then waved as she climbed into the passenger side of their SUV.

Morgan scooped Karma up in his arms and carried her into the house. He kicked the door shut behind them, then secured the deadbolt. He looked down at her. Passion glowed in his eyes. "Are you hungry?"

Karma shook her head. They had slept together, but they hadn't made love since Whitehall abducted her. "Make love to me."

~ ~ ~

Morgan smiled at his mate, his beautiful mate, then carried her to their den and set her down. Karma slipped her arms around his neck, lifting up on her tiptoes, she kissed him. The fire burning in her eyes nearly brought him to his knees. He lowered his mouth to hers, lightly kissing her and guiding her back toward the bed. He wanted her so desperately if he took their kiss deeper, he'd end up ravishing her.

Karma kept her eyes locked with his as she slid her hands up his chest, unbuttoning his white shirt. She pushed the shirt down his arms, letting it fall to the floor. She licked her lower lip as she traced his chest muscles.

A man could only take so much. He covered her hands, stilling them. "Wait. I know you're fond of your dress." He turned her, then slid the zipper down. He pushed the silky fabric from her, letting it join his shirt. He unhooked her black crinoline, allowing it to join the other clothing on the floor, then turned her to face him. He sucked in a breath as his gaze roamed over her. Damn, he was a lucky man. Karma wore only her black bra, panties, and a sexy as hell garter high up on her left thigh. He made quick work of her bra and panties, leaving her with only the garter around her thigh.

Tenderly, Morgan lifted her onto the bed.

Keeping his eyes locked on hers, he toed off his boots. Making quick work of his jeans and socks, he joined Karma on their bed. Morgan rolled to his side, raising up on one arm. He looked down at her, drinking in her beauty. His wolf pushed to the forefront of his mind. "You're beautiful."

Her eyes turned stormy. "And you're all *mine*." She slipped her arm around his neck, pulling him toward her. The moment his lips touched Karma's, he lost control. She kissed him back with a passion, matching his.

Morgan pulled away. "I love you, beautiful. I'm sorry. I shouldn't be this out of control. My wolf knows you truly belong to us."

"Don't apologize. I want you now."

He moved over her and lowered his mouth to hers as he pushed into her, claiming her.

Karma wrapped her legs around his waist, her nails clawed at his back as her body tensed. He'd be damned if he'd come before he gave her pleasure. Karma gasped, then cried out as her muscles fisted him. Then...Then *she* bit him.

Morgan howled his release then bit down, savoring the sweetness of her blood. As he drank, he was swept away in a crimson sea filled with love—Karma's love for him.

Her suckling from him slowed, then stopped and her legs relaxed. Karma caressed him in a slow rhythm up and down his back. "I think you melted my bones."

He started to pull away, but Karma wrapped her arms around him. "Not yet."

"I'm heavy."

"Not complaining. I like the feel of you."

"I like the feel of you, too." He rose up, kissing her softly, then rolled to his side, taking Karma with him. "Rest your head on my shoulder."

She relaxed into his arms, surrendering to sleep.

"I will love you forever," he whispered, pressing a kiss to her lips. "Sleep, my beautiful mate." Carefully he eased from Karma's warmth, then made his way to the bathroom for a washcloth. He cared for his lady then tossed the cloth in the direction of the bathroom.

Karma snuggled against his pillow with a satisfied smile on her gorgeous face. He'd loved his lady well, which had his wolf prancing around in his mind like the cocky beast he was. Morgan slipped under the covers and pulled her into his arms. His palm rested over the gentle swell of her stomach.

Faint growls and snarls teased the corner of his mind. Gunfire had him fully awake.

Morgan eased from the bed. He pushed aside the curtain and peered out into the night. He couldn't see a thing, so he made his way to the living room. Through the massive windows, he saw a fire in the fire pit.

An amber glow lit Cade's face. The cat looked up, smiled, and held up a beer can. *Go back to your mate.*

What's going on?

Just taking care of a few party crashers. Nothing to worry about.

I heard gunfire!

That was one of Ryder's men making the world a safer place. We're good—no need for you to worry. Besides, Percy has posted a warning that's nonnegotiable.

Which is? Morgan wished the cat would quit fucking off and spill it.

Anyone coming after you or Karma will be dealt with. I'm sure some interesting photos are being uploaded on the dark web as we speak. The Feds and Interpol will be tickled. Cade popped another beer can. *Good-night, Morgan. Don't forget breakfast*

Warm arms slid around Morgan's waist. "Is something wrong?"

He turned in Karma's arms then kissed her before sweeping her up and carrying her back to their room. "I was just checking on Cade."

"I feel bad, him sleeping outside."

"You want him in the room across from us?"

"Didn't I see a tent somewhere?" Karma nipped his mate mark.

"Are you trying to seduce me?"

"Oh Wolfie, there's no trying about it. I intend to."

He had every intention of allowing her.

Chapter Twenty-three

Karma stifled a yawn as she peered out the windshield at the beautiful landscape. This part of Texas was nothing like she'd imagined. Guess she'd watched too many old westerns.

The car chimed for the billionth time, warning Morgan to keep his eyes on the road instead of her. "Do you want me to drive?"

"I can't help you're so beautiful, I can't keep my eyes off of you."

She rolled her eyes. "How much longer before we get to your parents' ranch?" Karma mentally patted herself on the back for not calling it a farm.

"We've been on the ranch for the last thirty minutes," Cade replied from the back seat. He poked his arm over the seat, pointing out the window. "Over there is the new wind farm John put in last year. He has another on the lower quarter. The cows don't seem to mind them. Oh! Look!" He pointed again, this time nearly smacking Morgan in the head. "There's a longhorn."

"Wow. Those horns could do some damage." She turned her head and gasped as a beautiful spotted horse ran along the fence. "One of these days, I want to learn to ride."

"Only after Mavis says it's safe." Morgan turned down a dirt road, passing under a large metal sign with two wolves on either side of a full moon. Crimson Moon Ranch.

"You worry too much. Mavis said the peanut and I are doing fine." Karma craned her neck, trying to find the house. All she could see were massive trees lining the long drive. "These oaks are beautiful."

"They're pecans," Morgan replied. "Mom brought them from Georgia. Some of these trees are over a hundred years old."

"Oh, wow. I love pecan pie."

"That's good. Mom usually bakes enough. Heck, she even puts pecans in the stuffing and makes these cookies."

"Pecan Sandies," Cade replied. "They're so good, especially dunked in coffee."

"I'll have to try them with my *decaf* coffee." Karma laughed.

Morgan cut his eyes at her. "Be thankful, Mavis said decaf was okay." The car chimed.

"Keep your eyes on the road."

"You know," Cade popped up between them. "I could have driven."

An enormous stone farmhouse with a wraparound porch came into view. Karma's laughter died in her throat. They were almost there. Her palms were sweaty, her heart pounded. She wasn't ready for the crowd.

"Beautiful, you've talked to all of my brothers on the phone, and you've spoken with Niki. There is no reason for you to be nervous."

She rubbed her palms on the vintage corduroy pants she brought in Whaler Bay. "You're right." Karma drew in a deep breath. It wouldn't be that bad. These folks were Morgan's family, her family now. He was right. She'd spoken to his brothers and sister. Karma loved talking with Niki. Being human, Niki gave her advice on what to expect during pregnancy, plus she sent a bag of delicious decaf coffee.

"You look beautiful, and Mom will love that you're wearing the broach she gave you."

The closer they drew, the more her spine tingled. "Oh, Lord, help. Please tell me your father owns a used car lot." She could not believe the number of vehicles scattered in front of the house.

Morgan stopped the car, still a long way from the house. "Nope." He exhaled. "I hate crowds. A crowd of family members is even worse. Mom said she was feeding the hands, but she didn't say my grandparents would be here. They must have flown over from Europe. Peachy. Just Peachy."

"You just told me there was no reason for me to be nervous, and yet you're freaking out over your grandparents?"

"No, you'll be fine. They'll spoil you rotten."

"Then what are you worried about?"

Morgan laughed. "You remember how Mishenka popped into your head?"

"Yeah, that was a little disconcerting. I still don't understand how he did it from England."

"Because he's an ancient and has mad skills that I'm not even sure Royce understands. Anyway, my grandfather is Mishenka's little brother. And just as meddling."

"No, man." Cade was back, leaning over the seat. "No one is as meddling as Mishenka. Except maybe Mimi."

"Is it too late to throw this thing in reverse?" Karma joked. Yes, she was nervous but also excited about finally meeting the rest of Morgan's family in person. She'd spoken to them enough on the phone, and through the blood bond she and Morgan shared, she already knew them. Sort of. Knowing someone through the blood bond and actually meeting them face to face was two totally different things. She just hoped his grandparents liked her.

Morgan laughed. "You know that tingling sensation you've been feeling?"

"Yeah."

"That's them sensing you."

"And me sensing them."

"Yep. So, unless you want a pack of wolves chasing us, snapping at the tires, it's too late to turn back now."

"Well, poop."

Cade popped up between the seats. "Told you we should have flown the helo in instead of driving."

"Cade," Morgan snarled, putting the car in drive.

"I'm shutting up and sitting back. It's just...I've never had Thanksgiving. Never celebrated any holiday."

Karma turned in her seat. Cade reminded her of a lost little boy. "If it's any consolation, my family never really did much celebrating either. For Thanksgiving, my grandparents went out to eat. Melody was never around. Christmas and birthdays were about the same."

"Really? Wow." Cade grinned. "Don't worry, we'll go with the flow."

Morgan stopped the car again. He turned in the seat, glancing from Cade to Karma. "This is what's going to happen today. Mom has the parade on a loop, so no one misses any of it—even if none of us like watching the thing. We humor her. We will eat more food than ever, then Pop will goad us into a game of football with the hands. He calls it furs against skins. As for Christmas—yeah, it's even more chaotic. One more thing—make that two. Tomorrow, after she drags us all off into town, Mom starts decorating for Christmas and playing Christmas music."

With each thing Morgan listed, Cade's eyes widened. His excitement was contagious and had her looking forward to the chaos. Karma's hand rested on her stomach. Next year they'd have their little one. Of course, he or she would be too young to understand what was going on, but she and Morgan would have their own little family.

"You know, Wolfie, no matter how many children we have—"

"We'll add one more. I know." Morgan winked at her as he parked alongside a truck.

"Is that *the* truck?"

"Yup. For all my brother's intelligence, Quaid never figured out I had it customized for him."

"You are going to tell him, right?" The last few weeks of refereeing between Morgan and his brothers, or Cade had more than prepared her for children. Men. Can't live with them, can't live without them.

She looked back at the massive stone farmhouse and noticed the more than two dozen picnic tables set up draped with orange plaid tablecloths. "I'm glad the weather is nice."

Morgan shrugged. "If it wasn't, we'd be eating in the barn. Looks like Mom outdid herself this year with the decorations. I wonder if Pop planted the pumpkins or if Mom purchased them from another farm?"

"The kitchen curtains are moving." Cade leaned over the seat, pointing toward the house. "Can we get out now?"

Karma rolled her eyes and opened the car door. "Lord have mercy! I can't believe you threatened your momma not to come out until I got out of the car."

"I didn't want you to get overwhelmed."

"Seriously? How bad can it be?" Famous last words. Karma barely had her door open when people spilled from the house, reminiscent of clowns spilling from a tiny car.

A slender woman with pink highlights hauled her from the vehicle. The extremely thin woman hugged Karma so tightly she knew a few ribs cracked.

"I'm so happy to finally meet you, my sister. I have a list of names for you to bite on the butt."

"Simone." Morgan gently pried the woman from Karma then slipped his arm around his wife. "Her name is Karma, but she isn't karma. So, she won't be biting anyone on the butt. That's what you have Quaid's for."

Simone's smile slipped, and she worried her lower lip as she tucked against Quaid. He kissed her crown, whispering something to her.

Karma elbowed Morgan, remembering their conversation. She couldn't imagine the hell Simone had lived.

Morgan grunted. "Beautiful, meet Simone, our resident hugger."

"There's nothing wrong with hugging. I like it." Karma winked at Simone and received a radiant smile.

Then it was Quaid's turn to squeeze the daylights out of Karma.

"How's the morning sickness been?" Quaid kissed her cheek then perused her from head to toe.

"So far, so good."

"Good. Good." Quaid dug in his pocket, pulled out a key, and held it out to Morgan. "Thanks for the loan."

"You put a bumper sticker on it. I don't want it back now." Morgan pulled Quaid into a hug.

"You sure?"

"Positive. Considering I ordered it for you."

"Well, if you're buying people trucks." A huge black man strolled toward them. The man was a good head taller than Morgan

and had muscles on top of muscles. "I wouldn't mind a red one—
Go Dogs!" He shook Morgan's hand then nodded at Karma.
"Welcome to the family." His voice was so familiar.

"Thank you." She couldn't stop staring at his black eyes ringed
in red. Being so tall and muscular, he reminded her of a giant teddy
bear. She dug through her connection with Morgan, trying to figure
out who the man was. Why couldn't she place him?

"Because I'm keeping it a secret." A deep warm laugh bubbled
up from him. "I'm Toby."

"Niki's grandfather. I knew your voice sounded familiar. It's so
good to meet you."

"Out of my way, handbag." An older woman with snow-white
hair elbowed Toby and bulldozed her way to Karma "Welcome,
Granddaughter." The woman was shorter than Karma but just as
curvy. Her warm silver-gray eyes glowed with love. "I'm Nana, and
this old goat behind me," She waved her hand at a tall man with salt
and pepper hair and the eeriest shade of blue eyes. "The boys refer
to him as Grands." The woman hugged her. "You've made my old
heart sing." She squeezed Karma tighter.

"Nana? I thought you and Grands were in Europe?"

"Pfft. Do you think I'd miss meeting my new granddaughter?"

Morgan kissed the woman's cheek then shook hands with the
man. "Karma, my grandparents, Vladisláv, and Prudence Lucard."

"It's a pleasure to meet you."

Prudence fingered Karma's broach. "Gwyn said she'd given
you the Bolkov crest. Oh, it looks beautiful on you."

"Thank you. I love it. I didn't realize it was a family crest."

"Oh, yes. My grandfather designed it." She cast her eyes
heavenward. "If he were still with us, he would be pleased you wear
it." She hugged Karma again.

"Prudence, you're squeezing the life out of the girl." Morgan's
grandfather pulled Prudence from Karma. "Please, call me Grands.
If it is comfortable for you."

"Thank you, Grands."

The old man smiled. "My brother sends his love. I am so happy
you have opened your heart to Octavius."

"Morgan is my heart," Karma told him. Morgan was her heart and soul.

Grads nodded, his gaze falling to her stomach. "Perhaps your babe will be like me." He gave Karma a hug and kissed the center of her forehead. "It'd be nice to have at least one flyer in the family."

"Flyer?" Karma glanced at Morgan then back at his grandfather. "You can *fly*?" Why hadn't she known that?

"Oh, yes." Grands' eyes shimmered. "The Lucards are known for their power of flight. Well, most of us, anyway."

Prudence elbowed her mate. "Hush, you. Whoever heard of a flying wolf?" Prudence placed her hand on Karma's stomach and smiled. "The *Bolkov* blood is strong with this one. He will be a fine wolf. Like his pappa and uncles."

"Maybe it will be a cat that can fly," Cade suggested. "Then Morgan and Karma can name him Griffin."

Prudence patted Cade's cheek. "Bless your heart. You keep thinking that."

Something tugged on Karma's pant leg. She looked down, smiling at the reddish-brown wolf pup growling, pulling on her pants.

"Aren't you a cutie?" Karma picked up the squirming pup, who shifted into a naked little boy. She propped him on her hip. "What's your name."

"I'm Wafe," he said around his thumb.

"Hey, Rafe." Morgan held out his hands. "You want to come to me, little man?"

The little rascal shook his head, pressing tighter against Karma's chest. "She's cuddly."

Toby laughed and smacked his thigh. "Your mamma's on her way."

"There you are!" A red-haired woman stomped toward them. She shook her head then smiled at Karma. "Hi, Karma. I see you caught my little nudist."

"Hi! Niki. It's so nice to finally meet you." Karma felt like they were good friends from the many times they'd talked.

"She is Karma, but not *the* karma," Simone clarified.

"Oh, I don't know about that."

Karma jerked at the sound of Paul's voice. He stood on the porch with Gwyn and John behind him. She'd wondered why Morgan's parents hadn't come out to greet them.

"Paul," Morgan growled. "thought you were in Europe."

Paul kept his eyes on Morgan as he approached. "I was. I'd forgotten what happened when one sassed Uncle Mishenka."

"Had your ass handed to you."

"Language," Niki whispered.

"Pretty much." Paul stopped a few feet in front of Karma and tilted his head, baring his throat. "I'm so sorry for how I acted and how I treated you. I do not expect you to accept my apology, but I beg you to give me a second chance."

"Fourth chance," Morgan snarled. Fur rippled over his face.

"Wolfie," Karma warned. Morgan might be mad at Paul, but he did love his brother. All of his brothers. Besides, it was the holidays. If need be, Morgan could gut his brother after the first of the year.

"Paul hasn't been much of a nincompoop since he's been here," Simone said to no one in particular, then gave a quick nod. "But Morgan can gut him after the first of the year."

Heat warmed Karma's face. She'd have to watch what she thought. "Sorry."

"Don't apologize, Karma." Miranda, Morgan's sister, hugged her. "About time y'all got here. Lunch is ready. By the way, I love your pants suit. I had a similar one in the…forties, I think, or was it the fifties?" She scrunched up her face. "Nope, the forties."

"I love vintage clothes. And this looks fall-ish." Karma shrugged, eyeing Miranda. For being over a hundred, the woman didn't appear older than twenty.

"We'll have to take you into town to the Rusted Rose. They have all types of wonderful clothes." Niki reached for her son. "Come on, Rafe, let's get you dressed."

He shook his head, clinging to Karma.

"Okay." His mother shrugged. "You know the rules. No naked bodies at the table. I guess you don't get any turkey for Thanksgiving."

"Fine." Rafe reached for Niki.

"Auntie Karma," a girl about ten shouted and ran toward her. "You know a lot about computers, right? Uncle Paul said you did."

"This is Shelby," Niki introduced the girl, then she glared down at the child. "What did I say?"

Shelby hung her head. "To wait until she at least made it onto the porch." Shelby turned woeful brown eyes up at Karma. "But this is important! You gotta help me. My whole education depends on it."

Karma bit the inside of her cheeks to keep from laughing. "Your entire education? Let me guess, you *accidentally* downloaded something on your school tablet you weren't supposed to. Am I right?"

Shelby's head bobbed up and down.

"Shelby got an eye full of sex education," Niki laughed. "Tristan and I spent most of the morning trying to get the info off the tablet, but we can't, and Tristan doesn't want to call Percy again."

"I'll see what I can do, but no promises."

Shelby hugged Karma tightly. "You're my favorite Aunt!"

"Hey, what am I? Chopped liver?" Miranda frowned, her lips twitching in a smile.

"Yeah." Simone planted her hands on her hips. "I was your favorite this morning."

Shelby peered up under her lashes at Miranda and Simone. "You're my favorite aunt that can draw." She pointed at Simone. "And you're my favorite aunt who knows how to ride." She pointed to Miranda. "You're my favorite who knows about math and computers." She hugged Karma again."

"On that note." Morgan slipped his arm around Karma's waist. "Let's get in line before Yak-yak has us standing hip-deep in manure."

An hour later, Karma couldn't eat another bite, possibly for the next year. She'd celebrated Thanksgiving with Dani and her family several times and always thought there'd been a lot of food. Boy, had she been mistaken. Karma had never seen so much food in her life. Or eaten so much. She'd taken small portions wanting to taste a little of everything, but that was just impossible.

There were salads of all kinds, three types of potatoes—enough vegetables to satisfy any vegetarian. Karma couldn't resist extras of the pecan stuffing. Then there were vast amounts of meats to satisfy the carnivores, turkey, an entire hog, and enough steaks to reassemble at least three steers.

Morgan had been right about the pecan pies. However, he didn't mention the countless other desserts, including a chocolate cake Tristan informed everyone was his and his alone. That had his three sons and Shelby glaring at him. Just looking at all the desserts gave Karma a sugar rush.

Morgan returned from the dessert table with a fourth of a chocolate cake. She knew Morgan had a high metabolism and a huge appetite, but Lord have mercy, she didn't know where he was putting all that food.

"Mom makes the best Devil's Food Cake, so I cut you a sliver."

"Humm, a sliver? Huh?"

"Hey, does anyone want this last piece of cake?" Cade asked, looking at a table of ranch hands. They all shook their heads.

"Good." Tristan snatched the piece of chocolate cake with his hand and shoved it into his mouth.

"Boy!" John smacked Tristan on the back of the head. "Your momma raised you better."

Cade sighed. "Thought chocolate was bad for *dogs*."

"Bad for cats, too." Tristan shoved the rest of the cake into his mouth. "Mmm, so good."

Karma glanced at the cake on her plate. There was no way she could even eat a crumb. "Cade, if you want, you can have mine."

"Are you sure?" He stood over her, practically drooling.

"I can't eat another bite. I wouldn't want it to go to waste." Her plate vanished before she finished her sentence. At least, Cade used a fork.

John stood and whistled. "Alright, boys. Y'all know the drill. The women cooked, we clean. Then we can have our traditional football game."

"Oh, come on, Pop," Morgan groaned. "We just finished eating a steer."

"Yeah, well, mated life has put a spare tire around your middle. You're on garbage duty."

"What can I do to help," she asked.

Morgan stood then helped Karma stand. "Go sit on the porch with the rest of the ladies." He bent down and bussed her cheek.

Within minutes the tables were cleared, stacked, then carried to the barn by Quaid and Tristan. Karma knew the Dhampir had superhuman strength, but… yeah, she was amazed.

"Aunt Karma." Shelby stood clutching a tablet to her chest and worrying her lower lip.

"Let's see the damage." Karma took the tablet. It didn't take long to find the corrupted file. "It looks like someone was able to download Percy's anti-virus software. This makes my job so much easier. A few more clicks and done." She handed the tablet back to Shelby. "Let it reboot, then everything should be good. Oh, and by the way, I reactivated the parental controls."

"Thank you." Shelby disappeared back into the house.

"Thank you." Niki sat in the rocker beside Karma. "You know she'll deactivate them. Again."

"Nope. Not without the password." Karma smiled. "If you need to remove the parental controls, text me, and I'll give you the password."

"You know she can ease into your mind."

"Yep. I feel someone tugging at my brain. I don't think Shelby likes tax codes." Karma laughed at the subtle huff in her mind.

"Oh, *you're* good." Niki laughed.

Gwyn sat on the other side of Karma. "So, what time do we want to go into town tomorrow?" She glanced at Karma's feet. "We'll take you first to Miguel's and have him fit you for some boots."

Karma exhaled. She hated to wear boots because they never fit her wide calf comfortably. She'd tried to explain this to Morgan, and he'd just waved her off. Even Cade couldn't or wouldn't understand. "My calves are too wide. I guess I could find some booties."

"My legs are too skinny, but Miguel made me a pair, so I don't look like I have bird legs. See?" Simone held up her foot, showing off a gorgeous pair of blush-colored boots. "You shouldn't worry about what people think. You're beautiful."

Any protest Karma had died in her throat. From the moment she stepped from the car, it felt like she was wrapped in a warm blanket of love.

Simone sat on the porch in front of Gwyn. "Are we going to find me a not white wedding dress? I am not a virgin. Karma wore a pretty gold. I want pink. Or red, maybe blue. I want a pretty color."

Lord have mercy. The more Karma was around Simone, the more she loved the woman. You always knew where you stood with her.

Gwyn just blinked and smiled.

Niki's middle son, Mason, came over, dragging a ragged toy cat. He had a Mr. Cuddles.

"Hey, Mason." Karma smiled at the sleepy-looking little boy. "I used to have a kitty just like yours."

"Hey, sweetie." Niki smiled at her son. "Are you looking for your brothers?"

He shook his head, then proceeded to crawl up on Karma's lap. "I sleepy." Clutching his stuffed cat, he snuggled against Karma and sighed, closing his eyes. "You soft."

His brothers appeared with bottom lips rolled out. They huffed. Peter crawled up in Niki's lap as Rafe sought out Gwyn's.

Gwyn rubbed Rafe's back. "They won't stay like this for long. Now, about your wedding dress, Simone."

"I wore black." Nana dragged a rocker over to their circle. "I don't see anything wrong with red. It's festive." She winked at Simone.

Simone grinned.

"Not helping, Mother," Gwyn said through clenched teeth.

"Oh, I have it!" Miranda flopped down beside Simone. "If Simone wears red, then we bridesmaids can wear pretty forest green or even gold. It'll be Christmassy." Miranda pulled out her phone. Her thumbs moved in a blur over the screen. "Found them."

"Let me see." Niki leaned forward.

Miranda held the phone up.

"I have that dress in navy." Karma stared at a hunter green version of the dress she wore to the charity event. "I also have it in burgundy."

Miranda's face lit up. "Did you get it from Charlie?"

"Yes." Karma eyed her.

"Cool, then he has your measurements."

"My measurements?"

"Oh, yes." Simone gave a quick nod. "You will be my madam of honor, won't you?" She leaned over and hugged Karma's leg. "From the first time we talked on the phone, I felt we are sisters of the heart."

"It's matron of honor," Miranda corrected.

How could Karma say no to Simone? There was no way she would. "I'd be honored."

Simone grinned wider than Karma thought possible for a person's lips to spread. "I'm so happy!" She hugged Karma's legs again.

Quaid came out of the house, followed by Morgan, Tristan, and Paul, then Cade. They only wore cut off sweat pants. And Lord have mercy, there wasn't a male review in the world that had anything on these guys. Karma drank in Morgan's carved abs and licked her lower lip. Pregnancy hormones had her horney as a cat in heat.

"What has you so giddy?" Quaid tipped up Simone's chin, giving her a heated kiss.

When their kiss ended, Simone sighed. "Orgasms when your football game is over."

"Thank you for sharing, Simone." Miranda rolled her eyes.

"You're welcome. I'm happy because Karma will be my madam and Miranda, my maid."

Quaid chuckled and kissed Simone again.

Not to be outdone, Morgan bent down, capturing Karma's mouth. One hand cupped her cheek, tilting her head as he wished. She surrendered to him, allowing him to direct their kiss. Their tongues moved in a sensual dance.

"Y'all need to get a room," Paul groused, spoiling the moment.

"Have to agree with you on this one," Miranda added.

Morgan ended their kiss then glanced over his shoulder at Paul. "Jealous much."

Simone had an even more giant grin. Niki's face was red, and her lips swollen from kissing Tristan. Karma didn't doubt her own lips were just as bee-stung.

She exhaled, staring deep into Morgan's wolf eyes. "So, why the cutoff sweats?"

"Football game." He turned, looking down the long drive.

"Ryder's here!" Cade leaped over the porch rail. "Let's go!"

"Break my rose bushes," Gwyn snarled, "and you'll be planted under them."

"Gwyn," Prudence whispered. "Go easy on the boy."

"Why? I treat him the same as the rest of my sons."

Cade glanced over his shoulder with a grin to rival Simone's. "Sorry, Momma Gwyn."

An old purple VW Bug rolled to a stop. Ryder unfolded himself from the driver's side, then hurried to open the passenger side door. He helped a young woman out then slid his arm around her waist. Like the guys, he also only wore a pair of cut off sweat pants.

The woman came up on the porch, and Simone was up and hugging her. "Rae! My dress will be red, and they," Simone pointed to Karma and Miranda, "will wear green, or gold or maybe green and gold. Oh, sorry. Karma, this is my friend, Rae. She runs Rollers, Ribbons, and Rouge in town."

"Hi." Rae waved. She eyed Simone. "If you want to keep your pink highlights, have you considered wearing silver? Your attendants could still wear green or even midnight blue."

"Humm. I have to think about this. I like my pink." Simone sat beside Karma's rocker again and pulled out a phone.

Rae's attention shifted to the sleeping boys. "Looks like the food coma hit hard."

Peter stirred and yawned. "I want to play football."

"Next year, little man." Niki kissed his crown.

He nodded and fell back to sleep.

"Karma." Miranda reached toward her. "Do you want me to take Mas?"

"No. He's fine. I enjoy holding him. But I have to ask." Karma pointed at the guys, lining up across from the ranch hands. It seemed the guys were outnumbered ten to one. "Why the cutoff sweats?"

Niki shifted her sleeping son. "So when they take on their Alpha forms, they're not playing au naturel."

"Okay, but what about their tails?"

"Watch." Niki giggled.

The guys all shifted. Tristan's wolf was solid black, whereas Morgan's gray with a hint of brown mixed in his fur. Quaid's wolf was a massive gray wolf. Paul's reminded Karma more of a coyote than a wolf, with him mostly brown. Then there was Cade's cat, and finally, Ryder's horned whatever the hell. He reminded her of a wingless gargoyle. They all reached behind them, wiggling like they were digging out a wedgy.

"That's wrong on so many levels," Miranda shouted.

Paul snarled and flipped her off.

The screen door slammed behind Shelby. "Hey, Uncle Paul's giving a unicorn fist."

Tristan snarled and slapped Paul on the back of the head.

The screen door bang again, and Toby rushed out. "Wait for me."

A chorus of no came from the ranch hands.

The old man stopped on the steps, his expression heartrending. "But—"

"No!" They shouted again.

John strode toward to porch, shaking his head. "Come on, you can help me referee."

Karma felt terrible for the old man. "Toby, they're probably afraid you might get hurt."

He stared at her, his lips twitching.

Gwyn gasped. Prudence snickered, Miranda laughed, sounding like a mule, and slapped the porch floor.

Niki touched Karma's hand, drawing her attention. "Toby put half of Pop's hands out of commission for six weeks last year."

Karma slowly panned to the old man. "What do you turn into? A bull?"

"Gator!" He tossed his head back, laughing. The outburst woke the boys.

She just stared after him, as he took the football from John. "Play ball," Toby shouted.

For some reason, Karma's human brain could see him as a gator. Maybe she was finally coming to grips with it all.

Mason scooted from her lap then turned and hugged her before joining his brothers on the porch steps with Shelby.

Karma swallowed the lump in her throat then sat back, watching the guys play ball. Lord have mercy. She didn't know what she'd expected, but it wasn't this. Sean, the Wolfe's foreman, punted the ball. Paul jumped and caught the thing in his mouth. He didn't make it too far before he was tackled by everyone.

"Ouch!" Karma cringed. "I didn't see that coming."

"Dogpile," the triplets shouted, running and jumping on top of the pile of men.

Rafe shifted. Snarling, he bit and tugged at someone's pant leg.

Laughing, one by one, the men stood from the pile. Morgan extended his paw, helping Paul to his feet. Every time Paul had the ball for the rest of the game, he quickly passed it to one of the boys.

"Hey," Nicki shouted. "Stop using my kids as a life preserver."

Karma laughed so hard tears trailed down her cheeks.

Simone rested her head against Karma's leg. "I feel happy, loved, and—"

"Cherished," Karma finished.

"Yes. And wanted."

Gwyn smiled. "Oh, you, girls are more than wanted. I prayed every night my children would find their true mates." She sighed. "I love you with all my heart."

Karma sighed. After always wanting a normal family to love her, the universe finally smiled on her. Karma had her loving family. Normal, well, that was seriously overrated.

Epilogue

One year later:

Morgan gently lowered himself to the porch next to Karma then placed his baby daughter, Skye, on the spread-out quilt. All fresh and clean. Lord help, he didn't know what Karma had fed her, but man, his little angel had been rank. How in the world something so tiny could stink so bad was beyond him.

He bussed Karma's cheek. "What did you feed her?"

Karma rolled her eyes and pointed to her chest. "I decided to give her turkey, stuffing, and pecan pie."

Ask a stupid question.

Quaid laughed and set his daughter, April, on the quilt. "You do realize, Morgan, when Skye takes blood from you, she eats what you eat. I tried to warn you about those jalapeno poppers last night. But no. You wouldn't listen to me."

"Hey," Paul shouted. "Y'all going to play this year?"

"Nope." Morgan would rather watch his daughter scoot around on her belly than participate in this year's annual football game.

In his whole life, Morgan had never been so happy or so frightened as he was the morning Mavis placed Skye in his arms. She was so tiny he feared he'd break her. Tiny but beautiful, just like her momma, with big brown eyes and dark brown hair. Skye also had her momma's lungs.

"Wait for me." Cade leaped over the porch railing.

"What have I said about my roses?" Gwyn half yelled, half laughed.

April rolled to her stomach and shifted, shaking off her diaper, then darting after Cade.

"Where do you think you're going?" Quaid grabbed his daughter, then nuzzled her fur before placing her back on the quilt.

Skye cooed, bobbing her head as she tried to scoot on her belly. She was a few weeks younger than April and showed no signs of shifting. Even when she was red-faced and fussing—nothing. Not even the slightest hint of fur anywhere.

"Stop it." Karma bumped his shoulder. "She'll shift when she shifts."

Morgan slipped his arm around Karma's shoulder and pulled her against him as they watched Skye and April play. When Skye tugged on April's fur, April barked then licked Skye's face. After a while, April yawned and curled up. Thumb in mouth, Skye buried her face in April's fur and sneezed.

"Oh, look!" Karma picked up Skye. "She has a wolfie nose. Look!"

Sure enough, his little angel had the black nose of a pup. Nothing else, but it was a start.

"See," Quaid said. "Told you. Don't fret now because she only has her nose. April went around for a day with only an ear. Skye will shift completely in time."

~ ~ ~

Coos and giggles woke him. Morgan rolled to his side and peered at the monitor. Skye made it to four this morning. Woo-hoo. He'd better get her before she woke April and the rest of the house. Morgan eased from the bed, trying not to wake Karma. He'd kept her up late making love. Damn, he was a lucky wolf. He had a beautiful mate and a perfect little girl.

Quietly he eased open the nursery door. "How's Daddy's girl?" He tip-toed to her crib, and his heart fell.

"Skye?" She wasn't in the crib. Immediately Morgan sniffed the air. No one other than family had been in the room. The window was locked, and the alarm hadn't sounded.

His wolf demanded to be set free to hunt their pup.

Morgan stretched out his senses. Skye was still in the room. He dropped to the floor, but she wasn't under her crib. She wasn't under the boys' bed or April's crib. "Skye, where are you hiding?"

He opened the closet, even though he doubted she'd managed to hide in there. She wasn't in the toy box. She wasn't sleeping with the triplets either.

"Morgan?"

He met Karma's concerned eyes. "She isn't in her crib."

Karma's eyes widened, her mouth gaped, and she pointed up. "Morgan!"

He tilted his head back, staring up at his furry little girl levitating above his head. "Skye, come to Daddy." He reached for her, but she floated out of his reach.

Giggling!

"Skye." Morgan jumped for her, but she dodged him. "This isn't a game."

Giggling, Skye floated around the room. Her laughter woke April and the triplets.

Rafe, Peter, and Mason jumped after her, as high as their little legs would allow.

"What in the blue blazes." Pop stormed into the room. "The one day I try to sleep in."

"Poppie." Rafe pointed up. "Skye fly!"

"Oh, Lord help. Gwynne!"

Karma held her arms out. "Skye Marie Wolfe."

Still laughing, Skye floated to Karma and wrapped her arms around her neck.

"You were having fun, weren't you?" Karma kissed her daughter then looked over her head at him. "Long-handled butterfly nets and ankle weights?"

"I was thinking a harness with a long leash and netting to go over her crib." Morgan hugged his girls, turning them to the door.

The rest of the family filled the doorway, all with shocked expressions. All but one. His grandfather grinned and reached for Skye.

"Come to Grand-grand, you little flyer."

Morgan groaned. Lord help. His daughter could fly.

Books in the Crimson Series:

Crimson Dreams
Crimson Hearts
Crimson Moon
Crimson Dawn
Crimson Haze
Crimson Shores
A Chaotic Crimson Christmas

Coming in the fall of 2021

Crimson Night

About the Author:

2019 winner of the Georgia Independent Author of the Year for Romance Georgiana Fields was born in coastal North Carolina. She grew up in a military family near Camp Lejeune.

As a child, Georgiana loved listening to her aunts tell and retell stories and legends surrounding New Bern, N.C., and other coastal towns.

Currently, Georgiana resides in a suburb north of Atlanta with her husband, two dogs, and two cats.

While she loves nature, horseback riding, and scary movies, she currently spends most of her time writing paranormal romance/suspense. She creates strong women and men who will fight to protect the ones they love.

Connect with Georgiana here:

https://www.facebook.com/AuthorGeorgianaFields

https://www.instagram.com/fieldsgeorgiana/

https://twitter.com/georgianafields

http://georgianafields.com/

http://amazon.com/author/georgianafields/

https://www.goodreads.com/AuthorGeorgianaFields